THE

BARCLAYS OF BOSTON.

BY

Mrs. Eliza Henderson (Bordman) Otis

"MRS. HARRISON GRAY OTIS."

'And thus 'tis ever; what's within our ken
Owl-like, we blink at, and direct our search
To farthest Inde in quest of novelties;
Whilst here at home, upon our very thresholds,
Ten thousand objects hurtle into view,
Of interest wonderful.'

FOURTH THOUSAND.

BOSTON:
TICKNOR, REED, AND FIELDS.
MDCCCLIV.

THURSTON, TORRY, AND EMERSON, PRINTERS.

To the Memory

OF

WILLIAM HENDERSON BORDMAN,

A BOSTON MERCHANT,

IS THIS BOOK

RESPECTFULLY AND AFFECTIONATELY DEDICATED,

BY

HIS DAUGHTER.

THE BARCLAYS OF BOSTON.

CHAPTER I.

> 'I was a child, and she was a child,
> In that kingdom by the sea.'
>
> POE.

In the cloak-room of a brilliantly illuminated house in Chestnut street in Boston, the capital of Massachusetts, stood a laughter-loving, gay, and particularly handsome youth, over whose bright and sunny curls some seventeen years had passed, holding in his hand a bunch of English violets, and eagerly awaiting the arrival of his 'ladye-love.'

Start not, gentle reader, at this announcement; such things occur even in the over-educated and overstrained city of the Puritan fathers.

Young love! what a sad pity that the only obstacle arising, in after years, when the tender passion exists and overwhelms its deluded victims so early in life, is the manifest difficulty of remembering and ascertaining the idolized object of the 'first dream,' and that the scent of the roses instead of embalming the fair vision, should be lost in oblivion.

But who thinks of after days at seventeen? So our boy-lover, if you will, was, in time, rewarded for his patient watch by the entrance of a pair of beauties and incipient belles, so extraordinarily alike, that even the youthful swain himself, enamoured as he was, and seeing them as often as he possibly could, now and then mistook one for the other, and was, much to his heartfelt mortification, frequently puzzled to distinguish the fascinating Miss Georgina Barclay from her no less attractive sister, Miss Grace. In point of fact, there is every reason to believe that, if Charley Sanderson, the young gentleman with the violets, had been cited to positively affirm at which of these lovely shrines he absolutely bowed and sighed, he could have hardly so promptly answered as the exigencies of his apparently desperate love passage would seem to demand.

At any rate, Mr. Charley made his very best dancing-school bow, offered the flowers, which were graciously accepted, and requested the honour of Miss Georgiana Barclay's hand in the first dance, and was not denied the boon he so earnestly craved. Just then he suddenly recollected a very important message with which he had been charged, and addressing the fair young creature before him, he exclaimed, 'Oh! Miss Barclay, the extreme pleasure of beholding you has nearly caused me to forget that my very shy brother Gerald is awaiting my return to him in the hall, I've no doubt with immense impatience. I have literally dragged him here to-night under a solemn promise that I would use all the very small influence I possess in your quarter, to persuade you to dance with him; you well know he goes nowhere, and never speaks to any young ladies. Now I have told him such pleasant tales of your engaging and agreeable ways, frank and charming manners, that, having lured him here, I am bound, even if I must renounce my own coveted dance, to entreat you to smile upon him. Gerald declares he will not enter this room unless you promise to patronize him, so please be kind, as you always are.'

Now, it must be confessed, that the youthful school-girl to whom this speech was addressed, had begun to half comprehend the power of her superlative charms, and in some degree to take state upon herself in consequence; so she listened and smiled, and replied that, if Mr. Gerald Sanderson did not think her of sufficient consequence to prefer his suit personally and ask her himself, she would not dance with him at all. This response seemed to crush at once all Charley's hopes, as he was perfectly sure it would be entirely impossible for Gerald to gather sufficient courage to venture into the presence of the youthful beauty, and fairly pronounce all the words requisite for such a portentous occasion, he being, without exception, the most blushingly diffident youth in his native city. So Charley waited, and coaxed, and flattered not a little, and prayed and conjured, but all to no purpose, until he was fairly wearied, and then he thought he would run away for a moment, find his brother and see what could be done with him, since the lady was so exacting and obdurate, and accordingly he disappeared.

Grace Barclay, who was all the while standing by her sister's side, when Charley fled, ventured to remonstrate with her upon her obduracy, declaring that she had always heard that Gerald Sanderson was overpowered by his diffidence and shyness, and that his case seemed to demand encouragement rather than rebuffs; but, as Grace always leaned to the aggrieved, Georgiana held firmly to her unshaken resolution, and reiterated her opinion that the least Gerald Sanderson could do, was to appear and personally plead his own cause; besides, she said, it would be very beneficial for him to be obliged to make the effort.

Grace Barclay, finding she could do nothing for the shy youth, laughed and strolled towards a group of young things, and assisted them to disencumber themselves of an immense quantity of shawls, cloaks and hoods with which they had been loaded by their over-careful friends. Meanwhile, Georgiana awaited the coming of the brothers, and as she was imagining how Gerald Sanderson, whom she had never seen, but of whom she had heard many strange things, would comport himself, her attention was aroused by a slight movement behind her; she turned and looked upon a face and form which once beheld, could never be forgotten. A tall youth was gazing upon her with the most intense admiration; he seemed to her a man, for he had numbered twenty years; large masses of black, silky hair fell heavily over a brow of great breadth and expansion, a finely chiselled nose, a rather large mouth, with perfect teeth; but the eyes! the eyes were marvellous. There was an irresistible fascination about them; it would have been quite impossible to decide upon their color; indeed they were hardly alike, but their variety of expression, their sentiment, and the flashing light which emanated from them, every one could see and feel.

Tieck somewhere in his fairy tales compares the eyes of his heroine to those of green snakes, and endues them with all the fascination which is said to belong to that tortuous and sapient race. If Georgy Barclay had ever read the German author above mentioned, the same idea would have immediately presented itself to her mind; but at that period, her reading had hardly embraced the Teutonic, and she was just emerging from the everlasting Florian and Telemachus, which teachers persist in inflicting upon their young charges, without the remotest chance of any taste for the French language, or its literature being inspired by their perusal.

This tall youth, meanwhile, never desisting from his ardent and searching glances, bowed profoundly to Georgy, and, with a quiet smile, avowed that he had heard the whole conversation between herself and sister; that he well knew he was entirely unworthy of the honour she had denied his brother's pleadings; but that he could not refrain from expressing his sorrow at the refusal of his request; that he should never more annoy her in the same way, and asked but one thing of her, that she would not forget him; then kissing the tips of his fingers to her, he gracefully glided away.

As the young creature looked after him, in amazement, he suddenly re-appeared, and said, 'I have but one more favor to ask of you, Miss Barclay, and it is, that you will never mention this meeting to my brother; he will surely be offended with me, and I pray you, allow me to rely on your kindness in this matter.' Georgy bowed her assent, and he departed. Soon came Charley, quite breathless in the exertions he had made to find his lost brother, as he called him; he declared Gerald had been spirited away, that, at first, he presumed he had wearied of waiting, and so great was his desire to induce him to join the party, that he had actually gone home for him. Then, not finding him there, he returned and searched all the rooms unavailingly. 'And now,' exclaimed he, 'I find you, Miss Barclay, standing exactly where I left you; you must, I am fearful, think me very, very rude to have permitted you to wait so long for me; but really Gerald is so odd, that, at times, I find him very difficult to manage, and my temper is a little bit tried with his vagaries. Now, to-night Gerald vowed he would not come unless I could persuade you to dance with him, and when I go for him he has disappeared, not even having had the politeness to await my coming. With your answer, it will be a long time before I venture upon another such silly errand for him.'

Then relenting, for Charley dearly loved this much abused brother, he added, 'But after all, poor Gerald is so shy!' Georgy thought she could give, if she would, quite another version of this shy relative, but said nothing, and as Charley was entirely occupied with endeavouring to account for the truant's mysterious disappearance, he did not observe that the lady of his thoughts seemed to have hers equally absorbed. Yet such was the thorough good-nature of Charley Sanderson, that, before the evening was half finished, he had totally forgotten the whole of poor Gerald's misdemeanours, and never remembered to reproach him with them any more.

In any other family than that of the Sandersons this little adventure might have created much amusement; but Gerald had so few pleasures, was so immersed in his books and studies, was so averse to all sociability, having no friend but his brother whom he adored, that, even when Gerald had done his very worst, Charley could never make up his mind to inflict the slightest annoyance upon him; so the whole affair was passed over, as many similar things had been before, without comment.

Charley offered his arm to Miss Georgy, and Grace following them, they all made their obeisances in due form to the amiable hostess, who had given herself the trouble to collect together this youthful party; they then proceeded to the ball-room.

Mrs. Ashley, the lady at whose house this juvenile society was united, had no children, and like many women in the same happy, or unhappy predicament, was immensely addicted to entertaining all the little people in her own particular hemisphere, which, it must be conceded, extended far and wide. She was, as may be supposed, vastly popular, and though many well-judging mothers totally condemned her hospitalities, still they were cried into and coaxed into compliance with the ardent desires and wishes of their darlings. To be present at one of Mrs. Ashley's children's balls was the event of a life, not a very long one, to be sure, and, as the agony consequent upon a denial of this supreme felicity was much more than could be inflicted upon the rising generation, by their wise progenitors, the question was ever, 'Why does Mrs. Ashley give these balls?'

Nobody amongst the mothers seemed duly grateful. It was objected that these balls were too expensively ordered, the refreshments too elaborate, and the dresses too fine, in fact, saving that the heads of the guests, in many instances, but reached the top of the festive board, there was small difference between the 'baby balls' and those with which Mrs. Ashley favoured her five hundred friends who had reached years of discretion on other occasions. Many were the remonstrances made to the lady, but give them she would and did, and, moreover, found plenty of guests amidst the ranks of her most decided opposers.

Charley Sanderson, in all the ardour of his devotions, it is grievous to relate, had totally forgotten Grace Barclay; but Gracy, the darling! little recked she of his obliviousness; he had escorted Georgy, and was not that cause sufficient for not remembering a hundred other pretty little girls? And Grace followed her sister, which, by the bye, was the very best way of distinguishing the two girls apart, as cunning Jane Redmond, an older schoolmate of the Barclays remarked to her brother Robert that very evening, when he was stating his complete inability to say if Georgy or Grace Barclay were dancing with Charley Sanderson.

'You must know,' said Jane Redmond, 'that Gracy so ridiculously worships Georgy that she actually fancies herself a thousand times less beautiful, accomplished and excellent than her sister, and has such a trick of always following her!'

'I thank you for once, sister mine,' replied Robert Redmond; 'I will not forget this precious bit of information.'

'And then,' said Jane, still continuing her gossip, 'how can you know otherwise which is which! Look at Georgy's transcendently beauteous blue eyes!' (Miss Jane was ever prodigal of superlatives), 'and then those long, rich, golden curls are exactly similar to Gracy's, then their undulating and fairy-like forms, and their small feet! Then their height, precisely alike, they certainly are both perfect, and how I do hate them!'

'Hate them!' almost screamed her brother; 'why, I thought you were very intimate with them, and all that sort of thing, Jane; it's quite shocking to hear you talk so violently.'

Mr. Robert was twenty and a little bit over, and imagined himself quite a senior in this assemblage, and had been thinking that both he and his sister were quite out of their own set amidst troops of children, when the appearance of the sisters changed his views.

'And so I am intimate, but do detest Georgy, though I'm not quite so sure that I entertain the same feeling for Gracy; it is more difficult to do so, for she is half an angel at least, the most disinterested person I ever saw; she never thinks of herself.'

'I never demand a reason for any of your unreasonable prejudices,' observed Robert Redmond, and immediately strolled across the room, and invited the 'half an angel' to dance with him, — a very bold manikin that!

Grace Barclay danced with Robert Redmond and with sundry little gentlemen all the evening; enjoyed herself, and imagined that all the admiration she excited must proceed from the fortuitous circumstance of her being Georgy's sister. Although this affectionate young creature was constantly mistaken for Georgiana, even by the most intimate friends of her family, and although frequently, in their childish jests, they could exchange their seats, even in conversation with visitors, and remain undiscovered; yet still she persisted in believing her sister to be infinitely superiour to herself in every way, morally and physically. That this lovely pair should have been pronounced the belles of the evening was not extraordinary, for there were added to their great personal charms goodness, gentleness and sweetness, and remarkable self-possession, and if Georgiana Barclay had a slight shade more pretension than her sister Grace, it was overlooked in favour of her amiability.

There was the most undisguised admiration of their charms exhibited by their attendant admirers, and a vast deal of flattery from the young girls who are often as decided adorers. In fact, nothing is more common among school-girls than the getting up of extravaganzas and partisanship, just as they begin to discard their dolls and kittens, and their superabounding energies and affections must be lavished on something. The dance proceeded, and when late in the night this juvenile party broke up, there appeared to be pretty much the same amount of lassitude and weariness as upon similar occasions when older people do congregate, though proceeding from other causes.

In the first place, they had all remained too late; they had eaten too much of all manner of rich and unhealthful food at an unwonted hour; many had danced until they could not stir a foot, and were utterly incapacitated for any work whatever at school the next day, and more, might possibly feel the ill effects of this unnatural dissipation for weeks. Secondly, though the Barclays and others had danced to satiety, some poor young things had been obliged to sit still nearly all the evening, except when the good-natured and attentive hostess had interfered and protested against exclusiveness; which was, to say the least, rather mortifying to the neglected juvenilities.

The youngest of the girls stoutly objected to being forced upon their reluctant partners quite as obstinately as if they had been older. As to the boys, who declined dancing with these tiny tits, they had, if they had been cognisant of the important historical fact, the authority of no less a personage than the Grand Monarch, Louis the Fourteenth himself, who, in his fifteenth year, pouted and scouted at the proposition made him by his august mother, to lead forth a small girl of twelve, and a princess to boot. Thus it appears that the great and little world have been always the same. 'There is nothing new under the sun,' sayeth the proverb.

Superadded to these objections were the facts, that the children had indulged in strictures upon dress, cakes, and confections, and, worse still, upon persons; costume and character had been criticised alike; and, as amusements are not very abundant, and certainly not extremely various in America, it would appear to be rather the safest plan not to exhaust them too early in life. There is no reason why children should not enjoy themselves, and be made cheerful and happy, but this result can only be attained by simplicity in their pleasures, simplicity in their diet and dress, and early hours. All deviations from these rules create fictitious wants and desires, and encompass with clouds the rainbow in the bright sky of their young days.

CHAPTER II.

'Sparrows must not build in his house eaves.'
SHAKSPEARE.

In the northern part of Boston, amidst dwellings which were, in bye-past days, occupied by its most influential inhabitants, stood a large, square, precise looking house; it was of wood, but painted and sanded in imitation of gray stone; the windows were wide and airy, and their glass panes glittering with extreme cleanliness.

The approach to quite an imposing front entrance, with an immense brass lion-headed knocker, was laid down in square blocks of granite, the sides bordered with boxwood and grass, the stones, the grass and the boxwood all as freshly clean as the window-panes. On the whole, this establishment might well have been called 'a marvellous proper one,' as it frequently was.

Many were the gazers at that old place, (for it had even some architectural pretensions,) who, regarding it most reverentially, would say, in under-toned voices, 'That is the rich Philip Egerton's house.' Such is the magical power of great wealth over the masses, that even the possessor of a fine house is mentioned after a different fashion from his less favoured brethren.

The grand front door of Mr. Philip Egerton's residence, swinging back on its heavy, creaking hinges, presented to the persons who entered, and very few they were, a large, dark and deep hall, with a remarkably handsome flight of stairs ornamented with rich carvings, and having not only broad landings, but permitting two persons to ascend side by side, a little circumstance which would vastly improve many dwellings now, situated in more favoured resorts. On the right-hand side of this hall was a gloomy, square parlour, panelled richly with curiously painted pictures, which artistic work must have been executed at least a hundred years before the date of this veracious description; the furniture; coeval with the panelling, was composed of two small tables, an uncommonly uncomfortable sofa, and precisely one dozen equally disagreeable chairs, all planted so curiously and firmly against the walls that they looked as if they never had been, never could be, and never would be moved. In fact, if at any period a displacing had actually occurred, no one remembered the portentous event, but then they, one and all, chairs, tables and sofa, were polished to such a pitch of perfection as quite beggars description. The carpet on this sombre state apartment was as sad coloured as the plenishing, and very unyielding. The corresponding room on the left side of the hall, contained a threadbare covering on its floor, a square dining-table and four chairs, a huge sideboard and an immense full-length portrait of a remarkably grim and severe looking gentleman, whose face, and, in truth, all his person, would have been decidedly improved by a portion of the scrubbing so liberally bestowed upon the furniture; but, as he was manifestly a very unapproachable personage, nobody had been found bold enough to touch him. The back room on the left was exclusively appropriated to the master of this establishment, and exhibited the same peculiar absence of all enticing provocatives to comfort and luxury; its aspect presenting a very decided impression that a most stiff and stark individual was domiciliated therein, and this view of the case might ever remain unshaken, for no one could be found more perfectly unbending than was the possessor of this ungracious apartment. Most persons luxuriate in the luxuries of the land; Mr. Philip Egerton revelled in its nakedness.

Opposite to this repulsive sanctum was a delightful old-fashioned kitchen, abounding in dark corner cupboards and crannies. Nobody had ever been able to make this spot uncomfortable or gloomy, for its occupants, two ancient servants, would have defied the touch of any fingers besides their own upon its saucepans and brass kettles. An immense fireplace, large enough to niche one's self in, a heavy wooden settle by its side with a quantity of low stools and seats surrounding it, created a picture of warmth and comfort which certainly formed a striking contrast to Mr. Egerton's private room. Every brass kettle was a mirror in which the fairest lady in the land might have satisfactorily beheld her bright face, and as to the warming-pan, it was positively resplendent! A Dutch artist would have devoured it with his eyes, and have been made miserable for months by his utter incompetency to imitate its brilliancy. The tables, chairs and floor were exactly in the condition when all good housewives declare they can be eaten off.'

But however fascinating this kitchen, it was eclipsed and immeasurably surpassed by the garden in the rear of the dwelling. This garden contained no new-fangled, scentless things miscalled flowers, remarkable only for their size and ugliness, but in their place delightful jessamines, sweet-brier, honey-suckle, hundred-leaved roses, lilacs, English violets, and fragrant boxwood perfumed the air with their balmy odors. Then lovely laburnums, laden with graceful blossoms, waved in the breeze, grape vines covered innumerable arbours and broad alleys, and Virginia creepers reached to the chimney-tops, while the lily of the valley sheltered itself in their roots.

Then such Saint Germain pears, brown Beurres and Seckels as ripened in this favoured spot! the latter so hunch-

2

backed that it is pleasant to remember them even now, when it is the fashion to grow them so smooth and well favoured : they may have gained in beauty, but never a bit in sweetness.

This garden, with its dear old trees, its pleasant, shady walks, its hotbeds and gorgeous flowers, to which were added quantities of delicious vegetables, was the admiration of the whole neighbourhood, and well might it so be. In the country a garden is a matter of course, an every-day occurrence, a thing to love, to be sure, but in the town to be adored. Amid the noise, dust, and bustle of a city, it is 'like breathing the gales of Araby the blest' to come suddenly upon a few flowers ; they seem to be quadrupled in value, their perfume concentrated, their colours heightened, their very existence, by force of contrast, a balm in Gilead, harmonizing and elevating the mind, and diverting it from the worldly cares which surround it. As one by one these gardens, these beautiful creations have disappeared before an increasing population, how many have deplored and lamented their destruction ; to the poor they were the only glimpses of Nature their restricted condition permitted. And their fruit, even now where some old plum tree shelters itself in a spot so secluded that no temptation can, by any chance, exist, whereby an axe may reach it, the flavour is pronounced to be incomparable. Would the pomologists had spared the ever regretted Seckels, and allowed them to grow deformed after their own most ugly and approved fashion. Mr. Philip Egerton, the enviable proprietor of this old and favoured Eden, which, like 'the last rose of summer was left blooming alone,' was a gentleman, understood by the whole population of his native city to be immensely rich and proportionably avaricious ; his wealth was said to be colossal, and he himself was sometimes compared to an iceberg, and sometimes to an avalanche, as the case might be. Certain it is, he was uncommon frigid, even for Boston, in his ways, and very haughty in his manners, and, moreover, had very little to say to any one out of his own four walls, and not too much to those who dwelt therein.

Mr. Egerton was a tall, thin personage, with snow-white hair, 'most disposedly worn,' good, salient features, cold gray eyes, an immoveable physiognomy, great quietude of habits, and a thoroughly high-bred air. He was never in the least degree excited, and seemed to be completely denuded of a shade of enthusiasm, or even feeling. This gentleman's dress was in perfect keeping with his character; he always wore a light gray suit, a neckcloth of dazzling whiteness, polished shoes, and stockings and gloves of surpassing purity; indeed, if there were a particle of personal vanity adhering to him, it might be peradventure touching his hands and feet, which were singularly beautiful.

Of the tie of Mr. Egerton's neckcloth, it was stated and thoroughly believed, that it could not ever be made by any other person than himself, such was its extreme precision. To be sure old Dinah, the queen of the chimney-peak in his, or her kitchen, claimed a fair portion of its perfectibility, inasmuch as she certainly bent all the powers of her mind to the bleaching, starching and ironing of the muslin, and was eminently successful in the important operation.

A lady was once told by a gentleman that he considered her education perfectly finished with one exception, and that, after having given profound attention to a certain little volume which he would send her, it would be thoroughly completed; the volume on reception contained thirty-six ways of tying a cravat. The accomplished author of this recondite production, declared it to have been the result of a long life's experience, and it is not improbable that Mr. Egerton may have profited by it also. At any rate, the rich man seemed to have tied up his heart as closely as his neck — if any he had — it was so firmly encased that no one got a peep at it. Mr. Egerton's reserve was natural, and, moreover, seemed to be cultivated, petted and encouraged, for, however narrowly he might be watched, no trace of human weakness ever became visible to human ken. Life with him was compressed into a homœopathic space, as it ever must be where sympathy is absent. Cf all charms in human character sympathy works the greatest miracles. How many do we behold of inferiour persons, qualities and minds, with this Aaron's rod swallowing up every thing! We may bestow the meed of approbation and admiration on brilliant qualities, beauty and accomplishments; we behold with our eyes, but we feel not with our hearts when the one crowning charm is lacking, 'powerful at greatest distance.'

Mr. Egerton walked in his own circumscribed world alone, as he well deserved to do; he had concentrated all his interests in himself; nothing cajoled him, nothing provoked him out of himself; he had polished himself to a Parian marble surface, and all was conventionalism, primness and stiffness, and he certainly had completed a very unloveable character.

If Mr. Egerton looked beyond this world for something unfound here, none knew; all beheld the terrestrial, none saw the celestial. Some tale there was of disappointed affection, as there generally is touching cross-grained old bachelors, which it is rather advisable not to believe at all. There exists no reason why all the faults of every man, who chooses, from causes best known to himself, to remain single, should be laid at the door of poor forlorn woman; she has sufficient, in all conscience, to bear in her earthly career without this unseemly addition. But thus it is, and men always excuse their own vagaries by turning them over to the other sex. If men died of love in glorious Shakspeare's time, and were delivered over to disgustingly creeping things, they have long, long ceased to commit such follies, and abandoned the venture as unprofitable in our commercial country. So, whenever this part of Mr. Egerton's private history was mentioned in polite circles, it was positively vetoed by the fair sex, who, one and all, protested that, having never owned a heart, he could never consequently be said to have lost one. In fact, it must be acknowledged, that, when he became the topic of conversation, he was not very gently handled, he being ever declared miserly, cold and stiff, and his manners, though severely polite, were pronounced freezing and altogether intolerable. When, upon festal occasions, he was recommended by some jesting Benedict as an excellent 'would-be' husband for a young blooming bit of mischief, the proposition was scouted and flouted as wholly untenable, and Mr. Egerton's love passage declared to be a positive myth. Indeed, one very lively lady was heard to exclaim, that she did not concur in all the ill-humour and crabbedness that men choose to assume being ascribed to her sex; they must, she knew by dire experience, have something or somebody on which to throw their ill-natured mantles, and she, herself, was quite sure that, in the event of her decease, her own husband would be obliged to purchase an ape — but then she was an English woman!

Alas! for poor Philip Egerton! But after all, little cared he for sympathy or criticism; the state of his mind disposed him to think woman quite an inferiour part of the creation, ornamental, if you will, but nothing more; therefore, he would hardly have troubled himself, even if he had heard, which he did not, all the eloquent strictures lavished upon his short comings.

Now, this gentleman began his career with a profound contempt for woman and her ways; and it is always noted, that when such a commencement is made, if a man happens to have a sister, she is sure to be visited with a compound interest portion, and Mr. Egerton possessing this relative, she shared the fate of her fellow-sufferers. The immense wealth of this Crœsus, with the exception of his paternal estate, which has been described, was supposed to be locked up securely in bonds, mortgages, and banks, and other unknown and inaccessible places; one thing was positively ascertained,— no one was relieved by it, no one hired it, no one borrowed it, and nobody knew where it was.

Mr. Egerton went early in life to China, was reputed to have there made, amongst that tea-drinking and petticoat-wearing race, an astounding fortune, to have brought it all home in beautifully real gold pieces, and to have securely deposited it in places unknown; and being uncommonly uncommunicative and curt, nobody had dared to ask its whereabouts.

Surely nothing could give a more striking idea of the coldness and haughtiness of the wealthy man, than that this all-important question had never been propounded to him by somebody; but so it was, and it must be reiterated, nobody had mustered sufficient courage to do the deed.

We Americans ask a few questions where money is the topic, whatever we may or may not do on other occasions, and it was surprising! Still Mr. Egerton lived on from day to day in good health, without ever disclosing to people who were dying of curiosity, and publicly declared themselves so to be, one iota respecting his monetary affairs, and these same bags of real gold pieces which he had brought home with him. Many persons privately believed they were buried in some deep and hidden pit in his own lovely garden; and as private belief is marvellously apt to become public, especially if it appertains to our neighbour's concerns, this state of the case came, in time, to be received as a positive fact, and Mr. Egerton derived all the advantages which accrued from such a belief.

In the first place, the glass in his hotbeds was often found broken in the morning, the fences pulled down and otherwise injured, the flowers trampled upon and destroyed, and now and then a large hole was discovered to have been dug by the nocturnal amateurs of gold pieces, the incipient Californians! Secondly, his sleep and that of his family was completely broken up, and what with the arrival and the non-arrival of the gold-seekers, for the charm worked equally well both ways, his very existence was made a burthen to him.

Nobody pitied Mr. Egerton; but there were other members of his persecuted household, for whom his neighbours had more or less sympathy and kindly feelings; so they resolved themselves into midnight watches and all the other means resorted to upon such momentous occasions, and after several months' assiduous exertions, amidst snow-storms and tempests, they succeeded in capturing a remarkably small boy, who was not even white, but black, with a divining rod in his hand. This insignificant individual stoutly protested, with many groans and yells, that he had been employed by some persons, of whose names he was utterly ignorant, to seek for gold buried somewhere in the garden; and as nothing was to be elicited from him, but cries for mercy, he was summarily dismissed, with an impressive injunction to go forth and sin no more.

Notwithstanding the extreme meagreness of this capture, the womenkind in Mr. Egerton's household persisted in remaining in a nervous state of alarm; he, however, heeded not their fears, but decided to dismiss his neighbours with thanks for their kind offices. They were amazingly astonished that he condescended to bestow any thing, and probably, from the rarity of such an unwonted circumstance as the act of giving implied, the performance was sadly deficient in graciousness.

It is now quite time that the reader should be informed of whom Mr. Egerton's alarmed household consisted. That he had a sister has already been mentioned, as being the amiable recipient of a very large share of the contumely he was habitually wont to lavish upon her sex. This relative was a widow, and this was an additional source of discontent, as the bachelor hated widows particularly. She was the mother of Gerald and Charles Sanderson, who also shared the very problematical hospitality of the rich Chinaman's melancholy home. But she, assuredly, merits a chapter devoted exclusively to herself, and shall accordingly have it.

It must be recorded, that Mr. Egerton substituted for his neighbourly night guard a superb Newfoundland dog, and never saw any more divining rods.

CHAPTER III.

> 'He the young and strong, who cherished
> Noble longings for the strife,
> By the roadside fell and perished,
> Weary with the march of life.'
>
> LONGFELLOW.

EMMA EGERTON, early in life, had married General Sanderson; it was a trusting and loving heart she carried to her husband, and nobly and fervently was its tenderness returned; he had a very small patrimony, entirely insufficient for his support; but he was young, a rising lawyer, and an American, who never despairs. Had his life been preserved, he would have carved out a fortune for himself and risen to high trusts, for he had both the character and ability for success; but this, for inscrutable purposes, was denied, and he sunk by the roadside at early noon. A nobler and more manly head was never laid in the dust, as all who knew and loved him could testify. Mr. Sanderson left to his sorrowing wife all he possessed, full well knowing she would minister to the comfort of his orphaned boys, Gerald and Charles, more devotedly than any one else. And he reposed in his lowly tomb, amid the shades of Mount Auburn, and the flowers were planted, and the cypress waved over the hallowed spot to which his bereaved wife turned, for aye, in the midst of her weary years of tribulation and care. At first, Mrs. Sanderson's grief was so overwhelming, that serious fears were entertained for her life; the thought of her bereaved children brought her back to the world and its trials, of which she, the solitary mourner, was doomed to take her fair portion. Emma Sanderson had married just after her father's death, and a short time succeeding her brother Philip's return from Canton; she had been affianced to her departed husband several years before, but, as he was too poor to marry, they had deferred, from time to time, the ceremony. On the decease of her father it was found that he had bequeathed his estate, almost the only property he possessed, to his son, and with the exception of a few hundreds, she was literally pennyless. It was then that Gerald Sanderson and she decided to unite their destinies without any more delay, and to trust to Providence for success. It was granted, for a space, sufficiently for the young widow to possess an oasis in the desert of her existence to which she could fondly turn in after years.

The intimacy, if such it could be called, which had existed between the high-spirited, warm-harted and generous Gerald Sanderson, and the cold-blooded, proud and haughty Philip Egerton, was not very great, or impressive; it was courteous and quiet. When Gerald died, Philip left his sister to herself; perhaps this was all for the best. Some natures demand constant intercourse in their affliction; others, complete retirement to fight the good fight and to quell rebellious spirits. In all cases it is but fitting that the sufferers decide the question; — there should be no interference whatever. This, of course, applies to the first stages of great grief; — there always comes a time for friends and sympathy; — the mind and heart, in most instances, being best brought to entire submission to the Divine will in solitude and prayer. This state, once attained, a healthy reaction ensues, and a degree of outward peace, at least, is restored.

At the expiration of two months Philip Egerton saw his sister; she was perfectly composed, and, after the first ebullition of griefs consequent upon their meeting, she was compelled to be calm also.

'I come, Emma,' he said, 'to offer you and your boys

a shelter beneath my own roof-tree; I can and shall do nothing more. I am thus concise and explicit, as I know no greater misfortune can befall these children than that of being brought up in the expectation of great wealth, I shall consequently hold forth no such inducement for you to cross my threshold. I say exactly what I mean; being an honourable and, as you full well know, an upright man, I propose to endow your sons with a very small sum of money at my decease, and had always intended to do this before their father's death, and his departure makes no change whatever in my views and intentions. My house is very large and commodious; there is ample verge and space for noisy boys, so you can have no fears on my account; they will not annoy me, and when they do, there is always the garden. I freely invite you to come to me, and hope you will decide to accept my proposition. You are asked to enter your father's house; you have a very small income which will clothe yourself and children; for their education, they must be indebted to their native city, which nobly provides for its sons; they must work. This is the age of action; all work, high and low, rich and poor, in America; your children will be both happier and better. I am, myself, a solitary man, with unalterably fixed habits; with these habits you must attempt no interference whatever; you will be a guest in my dwelling, a welcome one, but I shall not permit a single order to emanate from any person but myself. In my domains I am the monarch of all I survey; and, as I care for nothing out of them, I am all the more jealous of my authority being therein usurped. I detest the people here, and will have no intercourse with them, but wish you to see all your friends, as freely in my house as you have done in your own. You can have suites of rooms in the old place, and, as the furniture may not accord with your newly fashioned ideas of elegance, bring your own and make your part of the establishment as home-like as you can.'

This was an immensely long speech for Philip Egerton, and nothing but the exigencies of the case would have elicited it; his style of conversation consisting in short, sharp questionings, and equally curt answers. Emma Sanderson well knew her brother was perfectly sincere in his 'proffers of service' to her; she according thanked him, and told him she would return a decided answer in a week. Then Mr. Egerton, having saluted her by just placing the tips of his stiffly jointed fingers on the end of hers, departed, having contrived to do a rather kind act in the most ungracious and disagreeable manner; but it was a way he had, and a very unpleasant one, indeed!

Poor Emma! she sat shedding floods of tears and uttering deep drawn sighs, when her brother left, as the memory of happy days returned, alas! forever past! This interview with her sole relative had seemed to renew the first agony of her despair, and she had felt herself enveloped in a funeral mantle, in veriest truth, as she gazed upon the clear, cold, gray eyes of Philip Egerton fixed upon her, while he explained to her, in the most dictatorial and sententious manner, his present and future plans and intentions. There arose in the mind of the sorrowing and broken-hearted woman such a yearning for human sympathy, such a longing to lie down by the side of her lost treasure, that she flung herself despairingly on her bed, and for days laid prostrate and helpless, dreading the mandate which must call her 'back, back, to earth.'

Mrs. Sanderson was not a strong-minded woman, which seems to be frequently a synonyme for a thoroughly unloveable person, but a sweetly affectionate and trusting creature, pretty, fragile, and refined. She had a great taste for reading, music, and drawing, and was an accomplished needlewoman; this latter attainment was destined to be an immense resource for her. She had been educated in great retirement, and had made very few acquaintances; and those she had almost entirely neglected during her long engagement to her husband, for hers had been a childish love passage, in common with a vast many others in her country, and, fortunately, more felicitous than they are apt to be. In nine cases out of ten no school-girl marries the boy to whom she has pledged her nursery faith, neither is it desirable that she should. Our views of life, habits, manners and tastes, all imperceptibly change as years pass, in their winged flight, and we do not perceive our own signal and certain metamorphosis until some slight and apparently unimportant circumstance occurs, and we awake from our dream and a change has come over the spirit of it. There is no reflecting person who cannot remember such an epoch in human feeling; we marvel how we could have ever enjoyed this thing, or liked that, and speculate upon, what we are pleased to call, the incongruities of our nature.

Emma arose from this crisis of despair, and firmly resolved that it should be her last enduring weakness, so she accepted her cold-hearted brother's invitation, for what could she do otherwise? The small modicum left by her lamented husband would, as Philip had stated, clothe herself and children; but how were they to be fed, and where, if not in his house? Its having been her father's, immensely reconciled her to this alternative, for had her father died without a will, one half of that old homestead would have been lawfully hers, and this she could not be supposed to forget, and the fact recurred to her mind with additional force in the painful certitude that she must abandon her own dwelling. It was also an advantageous circumstance, that she would not feel the weight of her obligation to her miserly brother so greatly as she might have done, had the dwelling, to which she was on the point of repairing, been purchased with Philip's gold pieces; so upon this subject her thoughts also reposed quietly.

Then the house and rooms were very large, and the garden was delightful; both for her children and herself; and she was sure of having the entire possession of the latter, as, strange to confess, Mr. Egerton rarely entered it, except to see the fruit gathered, confiding the vegetables to the tried honesty of his servants; and the flowers he totally disregarded, caring nothing for them. As to walking in a garden! he never dreamed of such a thing; no gardens for him. He arose by daybreak — it is generally observed that the earliest risers are persons who have absolutely nothing to do — breakfasted leisurely, gave his orders to the servants for the day, and walked, with his head elevated to a great height in the air, to an insurance office, or the Athenæum. Securing a dozen newspapers, secreting some of them under the cushion of his chair, and some in his pockets, and with one under each arm, he began by occupying himself with the 'respectable Daily Advertiser.' Sales, notices, exhibitions, theatres, deaths and marriages were all food for this insatiable reader. It was in vain that all Mr. Egerton's contemporaries, even the most remarkably experienced in such operations, essayed to win this newspaperial race, and, indeed, never renounced the hope of triumphing; in fact, it was the first thing they pondered upon before they arose in the morning, or had even said their prayers; but that gentleman always cunningly contrived to distance them, and won the cup, or in other words, journal.

It must be confessed he was a very uncommon quiet victor, neither singing nor shouting his pæans, but read on forever and aye, until the above-mentioned worthies lost all patience; but, as they diurnally performed this same feat, nobody seemed much concerned at the consequences of 'the miser's' tenacity. In fact, the vanquished had solaced themselves by applying this gratifying and flattering title to Mr. Egerton, and it seem to be their only means of avenging their wrongs. So thoroughly selfish was the possessor of the title, that he carried his egotism even into the newspapers, which certainly did not belong to him, and to which he had no more prior claims than those whom he supplanted. This one thing alone would have created feuds many a time and oft, but it takes two persons to conduct a quarrel creditably, and Mr. Egerton so thoroughly despised his enemies, that he never descended from his lofty and inaccessible altitudes to an altercation, and this added fuel to the flames, for nothing is more offensive to angry men than such freezing neglect. So Mr. Egerton read on.

At two o'clock precisely, the gentleman wended his winding way to his own dwelling, and in half an hour might be seen seated, in great state, in a high-backed chair, at the head of his own board, discussing his repast in a most leisurely and moderate manner. Indeed, moderation was the order of the refection, inasmuch as it was never over-abundant, except in the vegetable season, when it abounded in esculent delicacies. Mr. Egerton never sold the delicious productions of his garden, though his maligners, particularly the losers in the 'Daily' race, affirmed solemnly upon all possible and impossible occasions, that he did. A gentle nap followed the repast, which was always enjoyed in an upright chair in what Mr. Egerton was pleased to denominate his library, though how a room came to bear the blushing honours of such a high-sounding title, in which book there was none, remained to be explained. Mr. Egerton working up all his literature at the public expense, bought no books, hired no books, and subscribed to no newspapers.

At four in the winter, and five in summer, he might be regularly seen in Washington street, solemnly bent upon 'a constitutional walk' to the Roxbury boundary line, an undiscovered bourne from which travellers do return. This he regarded something in the light of a pilgrimage to Hygeia, without the accompanying peas in the shoes, and quite equivalent to the possession of any cardinal virtue extant. In fact, he absolutely believed it to be his duty to impress upon the mind of the only woman to whom he condescended to impart his sentiments on small matters, to wit, his own sister, that she could not be regarded as strictly correct in his eyes, if she did not go and do likewise. Mrs. Sanderson concluded to pay this terrible penalty, and chose another passage-way to heaven when she went forth, which was, however, rarely, except on Sundays.

This grave excursion completed, (Mr. Egerton's vespers,) he returned home, drank one small cup of very weak tea, ate one morsel of dry bread without butter, by way of a salutary example, and immediately retired into his 'library,' with one candle, which, the maligners positively asserted, he always extinguished the moment he shut the door of his sanctum, and was seen no more. At nine of the old clock, which stood on the first broad landing of the stairs — and a treasure of antiquity it was — he ascended, with measured steps and slow, to his dormitory, making his transit as impressive and sonorous as he could, in order that his household might know he had retired.

No pleasant fireside chat for the bachelor!

Soon came the lamented flitting for Mrs. Sanderson, too soon by far; such a distressing parting from even the bare walls, which had witnessed her departed happiness! She left the small, delightful dwelling where her every wish had been gratified, nay, even anticipated, to enter a house to which Catherine of Russia's ice palace was a comfortable residence — for that had lights and fires — to live with an unsympathizing, avaricious and egotistical man, and that man her own brother; thereby duplicating her misfortune. Mrs. Sanderson, moreover, believed that her relative would prove to be no fitting example for her children, for how was she to hold forth to them the merits of the very qualities he lacked? How was she to bid them avoid the very sins their own uncle, every day committed before their eyes? Oh! there were trying moments, when she almost felt she could not do this; she could not enter her late father's house — the sacrifice was too great.

And then she remembered there was another Father's house, even a heavenly one, of which the promise was given, and that He would protect her darlings; and she put her trust in Him. It was necessary to begin her arrangements at the old place before the winter should set in ; and many were the alterations to be made. All clashing with Mr. Egerton's inner life was to be avoided ; the children must be far removed from him, as he could not be supposed to be very tolerant of noisy young things, with drums, fifes, and penny whistles. But here her brother's habits, so very methodically exact, were decidedly in her favour, as she would only be obliged to keep the little boys quiet when he was at home ; when absent, they might run wild about the upper part of the house, in the large chambers and garrets. The children would hardly ever behold their uncle, excepting at meals, and they must be commanded to be orderly and quiet, which was all for the best. Then she must endeavour to give as pleasant a view of Mr. Egerton's peculiar character as she could, always impressing upon their young minds and hearts his great kindness in affording them an asylum when they had no shelter ; and then they must remember how large and commodious was that shelter, and how infinitely charming the dear old garden !

So Mrs. Sanderson made surprising efforts, and had partially succeeded in composing herself, when the hour arrived for her departure, and she found herself once more in her father's house. Alas ! groaned the bereaved young creature, if it were indeed my heavenly Father's house ! and then she looked upon her boys, and mounted the grand staircase, and entered the sparsely furnished and frigid looking chambers. Mr. Egerton was out on his constitutional walk, and would not have omitted his 'vespers' for all the widowed sisters in Christendom.

CHAPTER IV.

'We know not love till those we love depart.'

L. E. L.

It was a cold, dreary and drizzling autumnal evening, with a pestilent east wind blowing in every direction, when Mrs. Sanderson reached the old house. She was met at the grand front entrance by Dinah, Mr. Egerton's black cook, and Peter, the house servant, butler, valet and gardener; they both were over-delighted to welcome her and the boys, whose arrival they had been anticipating with immense pleasure.

'We've ben waitin and waitin hours for you, Miss Emma,' cried Dinah, 'and begun to think you'd nebber come; but massy me, I'm thankful you're all here at last.'

Whereupon Dinah began to hug the little boys, but they would not receive her enthusiastic demonstrations of affection; they were both weary and hungry. Mrs. Sanderson had been busily occupied all the day, and, in fact, for a week, with but one awkward servant, and, of course, all their childish comforts had been abridged, and the last day was like all such packing days, unendurable. Mrs. Sanderson, having been unwilling to forward a single package before her arrival from the fear of annoying Philip, such an awful personage was he, had arranged that all her effects should be sent the next morning in carts and wagons, and had brought but the night gear of herself and children. The French have a proverb that three removals are equal to a fire; Mrs. Sanderson fancied her one a general conflagration, so many were the unlucky mischances attending it. And then she had so poignantly missed the comforting and protecting arm of him who was now powerless! and, with a weight of grief almost too heavy to live and bear, she traversed the large cold chambers of her once beloved home.

In her lamented father's time there had been, in the front chamber, a handsome grate; it was still there, and she asked Peter to bring her some coal, the evening promising to be particularly damp and gloomy. 'None in the house, Miss Emma,' was the answer. 'Could she not have some wood?' she inquired. 'None cut short enuf, Miss Emma.' The truth was, that both of these kind-hearted servants would have rejoiced to make a bonfire for 'Miss Emma,' as they always called their young mistress, but were fearful their master would be angry, especially as he had only ordered the beds to be arranged for her. Mrs. Sanderson, perceiving at once how matters stood, proposed taking her children down into the kitchen; this proved exactly the thing for all parties. The boys were delighted with the old fireplace, the high settle, and the low seats, and were shortly niched in warm corners, with mugs of milk and portions of bread, and there they were undressed and soon fell asleep, and were carried up stairs and comfortably laid in their beds. Their mother, however, felt she could not pass the evening in the kitchen, and she told Dinah she would repair to her chamber, and if Mr. Egerton asked for her company she would go to him, but that she could eat nothing, her appetite having deserted her. Mr. Egerton returned home. She heard him enter the hall; she waited a couple of hours for a summons to join him, sitting in the most disconsolate and melancholy mood on the side of her bed. He neither came nor sent any message; so the bereaved young creature, having commended herself and orphans to the Father of the fatherless, crept into her bed and fairly cried herself to sleep like a little child. And this was Mrs. Sanderson's first night in her brother's house!

The next morning Mrs. Sanderson was awakened by the two boys running into her chamber in high glee. The sun was shining brightly; Peter had procured some coal, and desired his mistress, through Dinah, to order her to make a fire; this was soon executed, and at least they were warmed. Their respective toilettes finished, the young things having been scrubbed and polished most accurately by their careful mother, they all descended to breakfast in the dining-room. Mr. Egerton received his sister solemnly; inquired the state of her health, and noticed very slightly her children, who certainly looked sufficiently askance at him, but had been instructed by their mother not to make the least noise; so things proceeded smoothly. The boys ate their breakfast very deliberately, every now and then casting sidelong glances apprehensively at the tall, thin gentleman, who looked as if he had never bent himself in his life. There is a spirit of free-masonry about the little people; they know instantly who likes them and who does not; so the boys at once perceived intuitively that this grim, severe looking personage was no decided admirer of juvenilities, and governed themselves accordingly.

The meal discussed, Mrs. Sanderson retreated into her own fastnesses, and then soon appeared her own goods and chattels, she having ordered them to be expedited when she was sure of her brother's absence from home. The boys were sent into the garden, and once there, required no protector, four high walls keeping them securely within bounds. They were delighted with this arrangement, and, as their mother snatched a moment now and then from her labours to look tenderly upon her darlings, she felt most grateful to her brother for the precious boon of that dear old garden.

And it was, indeed, a great resource, for she would otherwise have been obliged to take her children out in the streets for air and exercise, and, as she absolutely loathed the idea of seeing or being seen, it was cheering to know that she should not be obliged to exhibit her wretchedness abroad; thus she had a charming retreat in summer for herself and children, and even a pleasant one in winter. As Philip had not permitted her to sell her furniture, she was almost embarrassed with the multitude of her possessions; but they were at last all safely landed in the second story of her new old home without more breakage than usually accompanies such a state of transition.

At dinner Mr. Egerton was politely attentive, asked no questions, and appeared to take no interest whatever in her arrangements; the repast finished, he walked into his library, and Mrs. Sanderson repaired to her chamber. They had tea quite early, after which her brother bade her good night and retired. She heard him ascend the staircase at nine of the clock precisely, and thus was concluded her first day in her brother's house.

And the days sped on in the same monotonous routine, as days will ever, happy or unhappy as the case may be. Mrs. Sanderson made a charmingly comfortable parlour of the front chamber, arranged her piano, books, drawing and working materials in a tasteful manner; the back one was also furnished with her own belongings; the two in the third story were appropriated to the boys for sleeping and playing, and all looked remarkably pretty. Mrs. Sanderson invited her brother to examine her apartments, but he courteously declined, assuring her that he presumed they were very pleasantly arranged from her well known taste, and never was seen to enter them. When all was completed and nothing more by any chance remained to be done, then came a reaction, and it seemed to the solitary mourner as if the evenings would never come to an end. She had ever been in the habit of retiring at midnight, as her departed husband, a little fearful of his matutinal defections, was laughingly wont to say that he finished his day's work and began another before he went to bed. Accordingly, Mrs. Sanderson could not close her eyes before her accustomed hour. And oh! how wearisome were those long, long evenings! there seemed literally to be no end to them. She could not, at that period, take any interest in books, her Bible being the only one in which she ever looked; she dared not touch her piano lest she might disturb the repose of her brother, and was generally disinclined for all occupations. So she passed her time in ruminating on her irreparable loss. The days passed more swiftly as she was engaged in watching and teaching her children; but oh, the dismal evenings!

Gerald, the oldest boy, was a delicate, pale child, who, without being decidedly sickly, required great care and attention, physically and morally, for he was at that early age of seven, a period he had just then reached, a little bookworm, preferring any thing printed to all the toys and playthings in the world. His mother had made every effort to win him from his books unavailingly, and she was, at last, obliged to take away his treasures daily, lock them up, and insist that he should pass the greater part of his time in the open air. Gerald was gentle and affectionate to his mother, but promised to be an absorbed dreamer. Charley, an entire contrast to his brother and two years younger, was blessed with a robust constitution and excellent health, superabounding spirits, and adored his mother with an intensity of feeling that seemed far beyond his years; he was generous and high-spirited, and possessed the most perfect temper and the sunniest smile that ever lighted up the human face. Both these children were sufficiently good-looking and promised to improve; it is not the most beautiful boys that make the finest men, and there is often a striking change, even in the eyes of the fondest mother, from the loveliest childhood to very common looking manhood.

The long winter months passed slowly on; Mr. Egerton altered not, never becoming, more or less, communicative; he was always coldly polite and well-bred; sarcastic he must ever be; but, as he had no intercourse with any one beyond the most formal interchange of common civilities, he had nothing to do with the gossip of the town. He had always regarded his sister as a very weak-minded woman, to whom he should never dream of speaking on any subject in which he was seriously interested; she had never travelled, had never been in England, and consequently knew nothing. The white cliffs of Albion were, to Mr. Egerton, the Ultima Thule of creation; no genuine John Bull, of the purest water, could have worshipped more faithfully his native land; every thing there was right, every thing here wrong; and this was a truthful summing up of his prejudices. Emma knew nothing of passing events, — how could she? She lived within her own four walls and had always done so, and, moreover, had never been in much society, even in her own land.

The topics of conversation, introduced at the meal-time hours, were consequently wretchedly circumscribed; Mrs. Sanderson's timidity and fear of her brother increasing the difficulty of interchange of thoughts and opinions. Mr. Egerton never condescended to give her any information, and France might have had three kings and six presidents, for ought she knew to the contrary, and ministries changed in the land of her brother's adoration, and, in fact, the world turned topsy-turvy without her becoming enlightened touching the facts.

At last, Mrs. Sanderson decided upon taking a very important step, and took in a newspaper; her brother regarded her with slight astonishment when she first mentioned some event which had occurred in his beloved elysium across the blue waters, and thenceforth spoke to her occasionally of what was passing in foreign lands, seemingly having conceived a less unfavourable idea of her intellect from the circumstance of her reading a daily journal. Indeed, she often marvelled that her hypercritical brother did not abandon the land of his birth, which he professed to abhor, and transport himself and his pretensions to a more congenial atmosphere; but this opinion she had hardly ventured to mention in his august presence, apprehensive lest the idea might occur to him that she had an idea of her own.

Mrs. Sanderson was perfectly aware that Mr. Egerton entertained no very exalted opinion of the minds of woman-kind in general, and a particularly small one of hers; so she never ventured upon any thing beyond commonplaces with him; thus he, living with a refined and accomplished woman, knew absolutely nothing about her. Mr. Egerton's table equipage was very beautiful indeed; his father had been a great admirer of old plate, and the house overflowed with it; the sideboard being, every day, loaded with costly and rare articles, emblazoned with the family arms, which having been duly exhibited dazzling with brilliancy, were carefully collected at night in two huge baskets by old Peter, and secreted, in parts unknown, until morning light brought them again into diurnal display. The napery of Mr. Egerton's board was also exquisite from its fineness and its getting up; to this Dinah contributed her important share of skill. The meals were admirably prepared, and however common the materials, the flavouring was excellent and the cleanliness quite perfect; to be sure they were limited to the smallest possible quantity, and it could hardly be asserted that there was a sufficiency, but they were served with extreme care and vast pretension.

Of Dinah and Peter, the two black servants, who have already been mentioned as having received their young mistress, on her arrival, so enthusiastically, all manner of praises might be showered on them; they were up betimes in the morning, and busily occupied all day with their master's concerns; in fact, they seemed ubiquitous, and might have been seen almost, like Sir Boyle Roche's bird, in two places at once; and, at night, they had completed the work of double their number. Perfect treasures, were the pair, of fidelity, honesty and truth.

Dinah, for many long years, had flattered herself that Peter might be induced to tender to her, as a reward for her constancy and devotion, his hand and heart. Somehow this grand event never came to pass, yet she despaired none the less, and went on hoping and trusting, as her sex are apt to do.

Now Peter was a remarkably shrewd and cunning old fellow, and knew, and had known, and would know, for a long time, that he was an immense gainer by this simple delusion of his sable companion; so he did not absolutely bid her despair, but led her on through flowery mazes from year to year, always insinuating, without absolutely asserting, that the pleasant goal might be reached at last. And she, the deceived, permitted herself to be deluded, and served him, and humoured him in all his innumerable caprices, and encouraged his whims until she had fairly spoiled him, as far as she herself was concerned. A slave to the lamp of African Peter was Miss Dinah, and seemed actually to rejoice in her bondage and hug her chains. Peter might rule with a rod of iron, but so Mr. Egerton did not. Dinah thought her master the very first gentleman in Boston, for she asked, 'Was he not doin' most noffin from mornin' till night?' But nevertheless, in her domains, he had no control; he was a terrible personage in her eyes out of the kitchen, but in it 'noffin.' And the gentleman, being perfectly aware of the consideration in which he was held, and comprehending fully the admirable management and economy practised in his culinary department, never ventured to intrude therein; so all things proceeded most smoothly.

The winter wore sluggishly on, and it was in this dreary season that the gold-seeker's emissary had been captured during a thaw, and Mr. Egerton substituted for his body-guard a superb Newfoundland dog, called Tiger, who proved a source of immense satisfaction to the juveniles in his establishment.

At last, the much desired Spring began to appear, if Spring it can be called, which is Summer, for the months set down in the calendar in Massachusetts, as appertaining to the coy goddess, are much worse to bear than those bestowed upon their frosty and snowy predecessors. If, by any process hitherto untried in the alembic of time, the months could be transposed, and May, the poet's delusion, be introduced into July, how pleasantly might we concur in all the glowing imagery and fascinating pictures presented by the verse writers. None can surely forget the days when, the heart and head filled with repletion, with flowery and showery visions, all manner of projects were formed of sallying forth 'a Maying.' The excursion finished, having risen at four of the clock, the perpetrators of this bold deed of high daring, returned home in a state pitiful to behold, with benumbed hands filled with bare willow sticks, and most unbewitchingly blue noses, and popped into their beds, and enjoyed such respectable naps before breakfast.

There remains a small crumb of comfort, however, for the New Englanders, it being almost as difficult to be absolutely certain of catching a glimpse of the 'heaven-born lady' in other climes as here, though, it must be confessed, she nowhere behaves herself quite so ill. In the south of France, she at times conceal herself in a total eclipse; in beautiful Naples, her worshippers are one day treated to a snow-storm, and the next to a sirocco, and are gravely counselled to betake themselves to Athens, in search of the eluding nymph, and once there, 'Living Greece no more,' strongly and impressively recommends Egypt.

With the bursting forth of the leaves, it is hardly worth one's while to be too particular or critical as to the precise epoch, but simply luxuriate in this enchanting season when all Nature awakes to wondrous beauty, and be correspondingly grateful for the blessings received. At this season Mrs. Sanderson found plenty of occupation in the garden, for both herself and children; she procured for them strong working materials, and small as were the boys, they did good service. They were taught to be industrious and useful, and, under the united efforts of mother and sons, assisted by Peter, the spot assumed the most enchanting aspect.

CHAPTER V.

'The life and felicity of an excellent gardener, is preferable to all other diversions.' EVELYN.

THE beautiful trees blossomed in all their affluence of flowers in the dear old garden; Nature smiled and made a bountiful display of all her countless charms; and Mrs. Sanderson's heart and feelings expanded with the gay and vernal season. The children and their canine friend, Tiger, gambolled amid the pleached alleys, and the dog's shaggy coat was covered with snow-white cherry blossoms. The birds returned to their pleasant haunts amidst the shrubbery, and the humming-bird nestled in the lilac; and as the weeks rolled on, fresh gratifications appeared in the luxuries of their simple board, which would never have been seen, but for the favoured spot from which this family derived so many pleasures. Mrs. Sanderson almost lived in the open air, a circumstance which tended to improve her health, and consequently her spirits. She had ever been a quiet gentle creature; so very unobtrusive that no one had taken the trouble, except her departed husband, to discover her many charming qualities; and every one wondered when he married her, how the high-spirited and gay Gerald Sanderson could have chosen so tame a woman. But we are all rather inclined to like our opposites in character; at least, one would imagine this to be the case from the extraordinary freaks played by Hymen. Gerald was perfectly satisfied, and troubled himself little with these animadversions upon his choice. The boys throve wondrously, and Mrs. Sanderson was gathering strength imperceptibly to carry her through another tedious winter and its long evenings.

And where was her brother all this while? Shut up in hot close rooms in the morning, taking long dusty walks to his favourite boundary line, and vegetating in the evening; for he never issued forth on the most brilliant moon-light nights. In vain his sister essayed to lure him into the garden; he would not be tempted. Now and then he walked out on an investigating tour of his premises, sadly alarming Peter, Tiger, and the boys, who, one and all, fled on his approach, and secreted themselves like guilty things.

Mr. Egerton would have been outrageous, had he been told that he was a sad Cockney, but such he innocently was, and there could be no gainsaying of the assertion. He delighted in noise, dust and confusion; he seemed to entertain a certain vague impression that his garden was a good place for fruits and vegetables, and his sister and her children, and may be the dog, but as for any thing else, it never entered his head to interest himself in its contents, beyond the pecuniary results. Any body might have the flowers; he would not sell them, and they could not be eaten, so Peter and Dinah had permission to give them to their friends, as Mrs. Sanderson did not appear to have any; and so they bestowed them upon the neighbours in the most liberal manner.

It may appear remarkable that Mrs. Sanderson should have been so insulated, but she was educated at home by her father; assisted by private masters, he had completed the finishing of her education; and she was really well grounded in all he had attempted to teach her. A scholarly person himself, he rejoiced in her docility and application, and bestowed upon her the closest attention. She was a tolerable Latin scholar, a very good French one, and read Italian; to history and geography and her own language, her father had devoted many years. Few young girls were better fitted to enjoy the fruits of the time passed in acquirements; she was so self-centred and studious, that she richly repaid all his paternal care. Of all this her brother, who was absent at the time, was completely ignorant, and on his return home, finding a shrinking young creature, who evidently held him in great awe, he gave his sister no credit for her various attainments; and this, superadded to his other preconceived ideas touching her sex, was abundant cause for his total neglect of a woman who might have been to him a joy and a blessing in his solitary pathway of life.

But no; Mr. Philip Egerton stalked about with his head elevated above all weak-minded women, and thereby lost a very pleasant portion of agreeable things in this world, which other persons, not so overwise and fastidious, enjoy with vast contentment and pleasure.

But to return to Mrs. Sanderson. She having had no acquaintances before marriage, made only very formal ones after; her husband had no family, and was ever devoted to her, she asked for nothing more; and thus they had lived for each other, and hardly saw any one. This is always injudicious; we are all subjects of sudden casualties which demand assistance, and misfortunes requiring sympathy. When Mrs. Sanderson's dark hours arrived, for none escape, she was friendless. Gerald Sanderson had been admired and respected by his fellow-citizens, and when he departed, offers of kindness poured in from all his friends; as she knew them but slightly, they were refused. She thereby shut her doors upon those who, in after years, might have been of essential service to her orphans.

This was a great mistake; but one that is often made under similar afflictions, and Mrs. Sanderson was doomed to pay the penalty. Then many persons would not have been discouraged by first failures, had she not been removed to her brother's dwelling; but he was so very inhospitable and so haughtily polite, that his patronizing and supercilious manner was absolutely offensive. Nobody likes to be overtly patronized. Nobody wished to approach Mr. Egerton, even if he had desired society, which he certainly did not; so his sister seemed fated to wear away her existence in utter seclusion, in the heart of a city, surrounded by a dense population, and within hearing of its noise and bustle; — this indeed was solitude.

And did she not feel herself alone? Assuredly, and, though she was a person remarkably well fitted for the sort of life she led, perhaps, better than most women, yet, at times, the sense of her own loneliness and friendlessness was bitterly oppressive. The boys were not old enough to be aught but playthings during the daylight, and it was the long evenings she dreaded.

Autumn put on her robes of many colours, than which nothing can be more beautiful in America, and soon stern Winter returned. This season found Mrs. Sanderson better prepared for her position: fortified by the pleasant and pure atmosphere in which she had lived, her strength was increased, her health improved, and her mind more composed and resigned. She had sought and prayed for courage and submission, and the petition had been answered. She began to think that, as Gerald was eight years old and a very precocious boy, it would be well to give him a Latin grammar and rub up her own classics, which she did. Gerald, nothing loth, applied himself vigorously to his tasks; and, indeed, there was no trouble whatever in teaching him, his desire to learn being so dominant that he rather anticipated his daily exercises, than avoided them.

Mrs. Sanderson found the teaching of her son a pleasant and grateful occupation; he came with his books, his lessons learned, and thirsting for more; so that she had but to arrange them for him.

It is to be regretted or not, as the tastes may be, that the same good account could not be given of Charley, for he was never to be found on like occasions; he was off with his boon companion, Tiger, hidden in snow-banks, and foraging for any thing but learning. Then there was such a bewitching old coach-house, in which carriage there was none, after the fashion of the library, minus the books; but it was so charming! All the old trumpery and broken articles which the family ever owned, of the grandiose kind, were there ensconced. Then there was such a collection, as had been rarely ever seen, in the immense garrets of the old house! There seemed to have been brought together under Mr. Egerton's roof every odd article under the sun, collected from all quarters of the globe; he had never even taken the pains to investigate the contents of his own higher regions, which had been amply stored by his late father, who having been an India merchant, had left the relics of his cargoes in odds and ends innumerable. The old gentleman had retired early in life from business, having many scholarly tastes, and had hardly given a thought to the upper part of his dwelling. It was just such explorations as little Charley Sanderson was habitually making to excavate, if such a word can be used, considering it was a garret, all these wondrous things, and every day his mother heard of some extraordinary discovery. Headless figures of Chinese mandarins, Turkish pipes of enormous boa constrictor size, quantities of indigo and synchaws, immense Spanish olive jars, figuring forth the forty thieves, bamboo chairs and sofas and huge fans, Russia duck, and bows and arrows, and other warlike missiles from the Sandwich Islands and the Northwest coast, with countless other things. When the hour for study arrived, it was extremely difficult to find the truant Charley; hornbook and slate were alike undiscovered; both Peter and Dinah assisting in the concealment of their darling, and declaring he was altogether too young for tasks, and too wonderful and too charming 'to ever live to grow up,' and consequently would not require instruction.

When, at last, he was unearthed, his hands must be washed, and his spirits brought into some degree of composure, and Tiger locked out of the room, and he, undignified doggie, scratched and whined at the door all the while the unwilling urchin was puzzling about ps and qs ; so the results were not of the most satisfactory order to his mother. It required to be a mother to do such hard duty.

It is extremely doubtful if women ever receive the meed they certainly deserve for their exertions in small things, for all the wearisome hours spent in teaching rebellious and giddy children ; and it is equally certain that mothers voluntarily take this trouble upon themselves ; it may be, they can find no one to do it for them.

At the end of the winter, Charley Sanderson had learned to put two letters together, which immediately flew apart and never reunited, so that, after all the pains taken to enlighten him, he had made small progress in literature ; but then he had occupied his mother, kept her from herself, and thus far his academical course had been successful. It would be a pleasant thing for victimized maternity, if children could be taught to read by some patent way ; to be sure, there is the phonetic, but then they must be taught twice over, and once is sufficient, in all conscience, for the poor young things, not to even mention their mammas.

That winter a gentleman, who had been a client of the deceased Mr. Sanderson, returned from Europe, and, as he owed his lawyer a few hundreds, duly paid them over to his widow, who placed a portion for each of the boys in the savings bank, and reserved the rest for emergencies.

In a few monotonous and weary years Gerald was entered, quite successfully, at the Latin school, and his schoolmates were quite astonished when they discovered that he had been prepared by his mother.

Charley entreated his mother to send him to a High School, 'for,' said he, 'Gerald will never work, and I must, and cannot spare time for Latin and Greek. I must push my way in merchandise.' So Mrs. Sanderson permitted him to do as he pleased, and Charley entered the High School, and having followed his own inclinations, succeeded remarkably well, his devoted parent having effectually taught him to unite the flying apart letters, and many good things beside.

At school Gerald made no acquaintances; apparently caring for no boy but his brother, his studies wholly engrossing him; there was no need of exciting him in any way; on the contrary, it was almost necessary to divert his thoughts from them, lest he might injure himself. When not occupied in studying his lessons, he was absorbed in castle-building of various kinds, which he sometimes communicated to his mother; this was generally directed to Harvard University, his whole heart being filled with an ardent desire to go to Cambridge, to strive for collegiate rewards and honours, to attain scholastic eminence, to live and die a scholar.

Now this was a sad tribulation for his mother, as she was unable to meet the expenses attendant on a college life, however restricted they might be. She bitterly deplored her inability, but felt the impossibility of gathering together, even with the greatest economy, a sufficient sum for incidental expenses. It may appear extraordinary that desiring, as she earnestly did, to promote Gerald's views, she should not have applied to her brother, but she knew that he perfectly understood the state of things, and that, if he proposed to act, he would make the offer spontaneously, and that by asking she would only subject herself to a rebuff, and be made even more unhappy still.

Mr. Egerton had seen the boy for years, understood his character, perfectly appreciated his efforts, and even sometimes commented upon his remarkable devotion to his books and love for study, never, however, with much commendation, and pressed the matter no farther. Mrs. Sanderson, timid and unassuming, and thinking herself already under immense obligations to her brother, whom she held in great awe, dared not open her lips on this all-engrossing subject; so things remained as they were, and Gerald worked on.

Charley, having, as before mentioned, been well satisfied with his mother's compliance with his wishes, became quite interested in his studies, and was fast becoming a great favourite in his school, and a good scholar. Charley's friends were legion; he was never seen without a train of followers, who seemed quite dependent upon him for their amusements; he had entire control of the coach-house, and that became a place of great resort. Into the garden no foot penetrated, and many were the longing glances directed to that Eden, with its black Adam and Eve, for Peter and Dinah were always, one or the other, keeping watch in its precincts for marauders; so there was no chance for scaling walls, and appropriating, to use a gentle word, the delicious fruits and flowers it contained; the latter, Peter, knowing his master cared nothing for them, permitted Charley to bestow upon his adherents in immense quantities. But what were flowers in the eyes of hungry schoolboys, compared with the delights of brown Buerrés and Seckels? It must be confessed this state of things was very tantalizing for the young revellers, at all times addicted to the luxuries which Pomona had so luxuriantly showered on this favoured spot, who were obliged to look on and be denied the feast.

Charley was the most generous of boys, but this was a point of honour with him, which nothing could induce him to infringe; the rules of the house must be observed, even for a windfall, so his friends devoured with their eyes, as boys will, and the young host lamented in vain his hard fate, and learned abundant lessons of self-denial and probity. One day Charley was mounted upon the high garden wall, near a pear tree, bending under a rich load of luscious fruit just ripened, when a gust of wind precipitated a quantity to the earth. The boys on the outside, seeing this downfall, entreated him to give them just two or three pears. 'That's all, just two or three, dear Charley,' said Robert Redmond; 'pray do, they look so good; the old fellow will know nothing about it.' 'Nothing would give me more pleasure,' replied Charley, 'but my uncle's knowing nothing of the matter will not alter my intentions; I know it to be wrong, as I am forbidden to touch them by my mother, and should not forgive myself if I could be guilty of such a meanness.'

'Oh,' screamed Robert, who was the ringleader and spokesman, 'you will soon be as stingy as your old miserly uncle, if you live as long.'

'Wait till I have something to give, Bob, and then you'll see if I am stingy or not; it's my uncle's fruit, and he has a right to do as he pleases with it.'

Here a chorus of epithets saluted Charley's uncle; he was called an old crab tree, an old Elwes, and a double-refined miser.

'The first bit of money I get,' said Charley, 'I'll treat you all, if you'll cease abusing my uncle, and you shall see if I can't give.'

'Give now,' said a voice behind him. He turned and beheld Mr. Egerton, who, reaching him a few dozens of the coveted fruit, ordered him to throw them to the little outside barbarians; and, moreover, inform them they were the first and the last they should ever have; and that these were only bestowed in honour of his own honesty.

Poor Charley! his was a severe school of youthful privation and endurance, and but for the gentle mother who watched so tenderly over him, would have been sad indeed: as he experienced, even at his early age, a sense of dependence, both irritating and disagreeable, and longed for the time when he should, by his own exertions, be emancipated from his uncle's control, so cold and ungenial.

CHAPTER VI.

'If the stock of our bliss is in stranger hands vested,
The fund ill secured oft in bankruptcy ends;
But the heart issues bills which are never protested,
When drawn on the firm of wife, children and friends.'

LORD SPENCER.

MR. JOHN BARCLAY, the father of the budding beauties mentioned in the first chapter of this book, was the son of a most respectable merchant in Boston, who having bestowed upon him a collegiate education, was unable to do more, having a large family and small means. The son, thrown upon his own resources, applied himself diligently to commerce, and being very judicious and fortunate, amassed a large property. Mr. Barclay, over whose birth some benevolent fairy would have appeared to preside, was gifted with all manner of good and pleasant things. In person he was above the middle size, rather stout and massive, yet very lithe and active, and a perfect type of health and strength; his face beamed with intelligence and beauty, and to these were added a frank, generous and loyal nature, and the most admirable temper. Rich, handsome, and fascinating, every body wondered when Mr. Barclay married Catherine Seyton, a girl whom all the world pronounced to be awkward, ugly, and pennyless. It has always been, and ever will be, a problem to be solved why the joining together of two persons in Hymen's bonds should be a circumstance of such enduring importance to all their friends and acquaintances, who manifestly have nothing to do with the matter;

but so it is, and Mr. and Mrs. Barclay proved no exception to this all-prevalent rule. Indeed, it appeared that they had an unusual portion of attention and criticism, he for his bad taste, and she for her astonishing good luck. A state of wonderment is one most pleasingly adapted to American natures; we have abandoned guessing, in polite circles, and taken to wondering. But even the wisest of seers may be, at times, mistaken, and the awkward and ugly girl became, in a few revolving years, an uncommon fine woman with charmingly graceful manners. Some travelled persons declared this great change to proceed from Mrs. Barclay having gained flesh, for she had been too thin; others that she had grown taller; some said one thing, some another, but all agreed in thinking her very beautiful. She could have revealed the cause in one word — happiness. And truly hers was a blessed lot, the lines being cast in pleasant places indeed. She adored her husband and respected him; she watched over her children with intense care and devotion; she was a firm, true and loyal friend, and a kind neighbour, with a heart abounding in gratitude to her Creator for mercies received; she availed herself of her signal advantages to enjoy them wisely, discreetly and cheerfully.

Three daughters and a son composed this happy household: Georgiana, the first-born, was one year older than her sister, Grace, but this was hardly perceptible, even to the parents, so remarkably alike were these lovely young creatures, who had reached the respective ages of fifteen and sixteen. Kate, the third child, was just fourteen, and certainly possessed none of the remarkable attractions of her sisters; she was a tall girl for her years, running out her head fearfully, rolling round an amazingly black pair of eyes, and perpetually shaking over them large masses of not over-fine black hair, which, by no process whatever, could be kept smooth or in place; then she never, by any chance, stood still a moment, but was constantly balancing herself, first on one leg and then on the other, and, in addition, was a sad romp, with a good heart and high temper. Johnny, the youngest, at ten, was like most small boys of his age, busily occupied in playing and eating, his father having thought proper to send him to an excellent boarding school in the country; he prospered, and, in his vacations, twice gladdened the hearts of his affectionate relatives, when he returned home and when he departed.

Mr. Barclay had one brother, a bachelor, who had lived many years in France. A perfect contrast was Mr. Richard Barclay to Mr. John: the one genial, pleasant and gracious, looking on the bright side of all things; the other rough, burly, and an inveterate grumbler, incessantly trying to conceal his good and endearing qualities under a disagreeable mask. Mr. Richard Barclay could find nothing to like out of Paris; just as devotedly as Mr. Philip Egerton worshipped England, so did this gentleman adore France; but they both agreed in hating each other mortally. Mr. Richard Barclay recounted innumerable anecdotes of Mr. Egerton's nonsensical (he called it) preference for the white cliffs of Albion, and wondered why the old miser did not betake himself to them and leave Boston forever. Mr. Egerton, not to be outdone, declared Mr. Barclay to be Gallic mad, and wondered why the old bear had not picked up a little politeness amidst the well-mannered people whom he so distractedly admired. These pleasant opinions of each other being bandied backwards and forwards to the separate parties by kind and peace-loving friends, added fuel to the never-expiring flames of their long standing feud, and nothing hindered their coming to blows but their never coming together.

Mr. Richard had, to the surprise of every one, highly approved of his brother John's choice, he having discovered the germs of a remarkable woman under the veil of shyness and timidity, which imparted to Catherine Seyton the false semblance of awkwardness; he had appreciated the good sense and the sensibility of the young girl, and knew her to be well read, well educated, and even accomplished.

Mrs. John Barclay never forgot this championship, and richly she repaid Mr. Richard for all the pleasant things he had far and wide disseminated in her favour; she made his brother's house a little paradise for the forlorn bachelor, according him the warmest seat at her fireside, the choicest bits at table, and innumerable other incidental circumstances, touching disruptured buttons and ever altering collars, combined to remind him that she had not forgotten his helping hand in her hour of need. In fact, nothing could exceed Mrs. Barclay's devotion at all times and seasons, and Mr. Richard had a growl for every one, save his sister Catherine; he never called her sister-in-law, and always declared her to be the virtuousest, discreetest, best,—in fact, a model woman.

All this attention to his wants and wishes was the more meritorious, as there was absolutely nothing to be anticipated in the way of the 'root of all evil' from Mr. Richard, he not being one of the American uncles who flourish in the French vaudevilles, and annihilating time and space, arrived with big bags of gold pieces, in the extremity of heroes and heroines, to make two lovers happy. Mr. Barclay's father, it has already been stated, was not rich; he left at his decease a very small patrimony to be portioned out to a large family, the members of which, dying early in life, bequeathed their minute modicums to the two surviving brothers, John and Richard. The former pertinaciously declining to take a dollar of the money, it naturally reverted to his brother, and he went directly to his beloved France, and, once there, though he had always maintained it to be the most economical country in the known world, contrived to spend a vast deal more than he could reasonably afford, and found himself, much against his will, obliged to return home, being unwilling to retrench in his adored Paris.

Mr. Richard was what is usually denominated a strong-minded individual. Now it often happens that this manner of man is exceedingly disagreeable, and the same manner of woman infinitely worse. The possession of this strong mind, being usually demonstrated by hardness of spirit, loud voices which ring unpleasantly on the ears, and dogmatical opinions, so decidedly obstinate as never to be susceptible of change. Mr. Richard was wont to assert that 'he carried not his heart on his sleeve for daws to peck at.'

Mr. Barclay ardently desired that his brother should live with him; but that the gentleman positively refused to do, saying, he much preferred a den of his own to inhabiting a palace belonging to any one else. Finding his resolves unalterable, Mr. Barclay fitted up for him the nicest snuggery imaginable, to which his wife added many feminine touches, which combined to make a very comfortable whole indeed. In this den Mr. Richard growled away his day, longing for the evening when he could repair to his brother's pleasant fireside. In vain his relations urged him to dine with them daily, but he chose Sunday, and to that day adhered religiously.

Somehow his experience of his cherished theory, that man could live alone, was sufficient to himself, and dependent on no extraneous circumstances for enjoyment, was a failure; it was the last thing in the world to be acknowledged, but so it was. To this melancholy fact he endeavoured to blind himself, by holding forth, on all possible and impossible occasions, and expending a vast deal of time and breath on his favourite topic, but in his heart of hearts he doubted, and that dubiousness made him all the more obstinately vehement. This theory was a constant source of discussion between himself and his relatives, who desired most sincerely to behold the happiness of the being whom they tenderly loved; they were thoroughly convinced he was the man to marry, for, assuredly, he was miserable alone, and could fare none the worse with a companion, and the grand experiment was worth trying in such a desperate case.

Mr. Richard had passed through the bachelor's inevitable ordeal of being crossed in love, a perilous passage ever, because a man always thinks to his dying day, that if he had married *the* woman he should have been happier and better. Perhaps, in this gentleman's case, this view of the subject might have proved correct. From the fatal epoch of his 'cross' our bachelor had eschewed womankind, and was evermore showering on the devoted heads of the fair sex a quantity of objurgations frightful to hear; he disliked bread-and-butter girls, thought unmarried ladies of a certain age detestable, and had no words wherewith to express his abhorrence of widows, all and several. A sensible and agreeable matron was then his last and sole resource, and there being no fair mischiefs amongst this class in virtuous America, Mr. Richard led a very respectable life; and yet it often happens that a man may be extremely respectable and very much hated, and this was the gentleman's unhappy plight.

Now Mr. Egerton despised womankind quite as much as his enemy, but then his contempt was too concentrated and condensed for mere words; he contented himself, when he met any of the trio of categories above-mentioned, to hold his white head so monstrously high that he never saw them, and as he never went any where, the world of women was spared his private opinions, nobody but his poor sister being made aware of them, and even to her he was very monosyllabic.

Mr. Richard could not hold his peace equally well, and though he accused the sex of evermore chattering, he was nowise behindhand in this feminine accomplishment. It has been before hinted, that these two worthies never met — if they had, dire would have been the consequences, and great the shock thereof; so they had no means of comparing notes, and there is small doubt but they would have agreed to disagree even upon this, their mutually favourite topic.

As in the case of Mrs. Barclay her brother made an exception in her favour, even so with her children he deviated from his rules, or rather with her daughters; he perfectly idolized them, and was perpetually lavishing upon them all manner of pretty things, adapted to their various tastes and pursuits. It seemed to be an outpouring of all the pent-up treasures of his garnered affections upon their young heads.

Mrs. Barclay was incessantly entreating him not to waste so much money in extravagant purchases, but all in vain. With regard to little Johnny, Mr. Richard declared that no father ever saw his son when he was young, except when he was hungry — and when he grew older, except when he wanted money. This Mrs. Barclay considered truly shocking. The brother, however, left the urchin to his own trap and ball devices, and contented himself with jerking quarters of dollars to him for candies and marbles. And Johnny did not particularly admire his uncle, and habitually shirked his awful presence when he met him in the streets, by dodging round corners and down by-lanes to avoid him; so there was no love lost between them.

The daughters compensated for this absence of affection on the part of the only son, by lavishing caresses on their relative. They thought him, to be sure, rough, and lamented it; but they loved him, nevertheless, with all the fervour and freshness of young hearts, and this, with the devotion of his brother and sister, formed the one green spot in the desert of existence, which the wilfully obstinate man had carefully made for himself.

Nothing is more true than the oft-repeated assertion, that we carve out our destinies with our own hands. The world being our oyster, how do we open it? Awkwardly enough.

Mr. Richard would have been inexpressibly shocked, had he been informed that he in nowise followed the sacred book to which he habitually gave a portion of his time and attention. The fact was, he perused it without digesting its blessed contents, and satisfying himself by so doing, the mere act became in his eyes devotional. In this, as well as in other things, he formed a most striking contrast to his excellent brother, who, reading the Bible, acted out and followed its precepts in his daily walk of life, and beautifully illustrated, in his own proper person, the ennobling and revivifying effects of his healthful draughts at the Fountain of all light and life.

If Mr. Richard had any particular favourite amidst his brother's three daughters, Kate had the best chance; he, however, was rather unwilling to acknowledge this even to himself. Georgiana and Grace every one lauded and praised, but the romp was not, by any means, so much admired as her sisters, and this state of things rather inclined her uncle to show a peculiar degree of graciousness towards her, for him. He had, from some whim, bestowed upon Kate the title of Dolly, at which the whole family, at first, rebelled, and finished by adopting it, the young thing sturdily setting the example by never calling herself any thing else. She was passionately attached to her father, following him every where, like his shadow, sitting always on his knee, and constantly caressing him, her eyes ever seeking the direction of his, and she gave her undivided attention to every word he uttered. In fact, the only time she could ever be declared quiet, was when she was listening to her father. She resembled Mr. Richard in the strength of her prejudices, and her open expression of them, and her impulsiveness was a source of constant apprehension to her mother, who foresaw much trial and suffering in store for her child, if her superabounding energies should be misdirected, and felicitous results in the event of their being led by judicious means into proper channels. She knew that she must be the counterbalancing medium between the father and daughter. It was a hard thing for Mr. Barclay to utter the monosyllable 'No' to his daughters; with his son he was very firm and resolute.

With Georgy and Grace coercion was a thing unknown, because unrequired, but the Dolly was perpetually demanding restrictions, as she reserved to her little exacting self a great degree of latitude in both her actions and opinions. It may seem absurd to mention the opinions of such a young thing, but they were as firmly rooted as if many more years than she called her own, had passed over her head. An indomitable spirit was lying in her little person, and not dormant either, but ever ready to burst forth upon the slightest occasion, so that maternal checks were constantly in requisition. Indeed, Mrs. Barclay was often assailed with the fear that the affections of her daughter might become estranged from her by the obligation imposed upon her of constantly quelling the ebullitions of sensibility and high spirit developed by her child. But no such calamitous result seemed to accrue. Kate Barclay received her mother's admonitory counsels, offered as they were, gently, tenderly, with profound respect and obedience, and just so long as she remembered them they fully answered their intended good purpose; but the difficulty laid in their being very, very often forgotten. She was penitence itself when reminded of her aberrations, and always hoped she might amend, but never could be persuaded to make any promises, declaring she could not trust herself, being perfectly convinced of her own weakness and backwardness in well-doing. Altogether she was a creature to excite constant and incessant attention, for no one knew what she would say or do, and an outbreak might be anticipated at any moment.

Johnny Barclay was her favourite companion and playmate, and during his vacations the nursery was thronged with his friends, a legion, and Kate was constituted mistress of the revels, all their sports and games and plans emanating from her. She openly avowed her decided preference for the society of boys, and thought girls excessively tame and flat, was the proprietor of a sled, and owned a pair of skates.

Kate Barclay's life was April-hued, sunshine and showers of tears; she was always regretting her misdemeanours, and committing fresh ones; but then she enjoyed existence with such an intense zest, and entered with unbounded delight and enthusiasm into every species of pleasure; come what would, she was supremely happy for the nonce.

CHAPTER VII.

'Oh, happiest he whose riper years retain
The hopes of youth, unsullied by a stain!
His eve of life in calm content shall glide
Like the still streamlet to the ocean tide.'

J. T. Fields.

It has already been narrated that Mr. John Barclay had, at a very early period of his life, accummulated a large fortune by prosperous commercial enterprise, which he firmly resolved to enjoy; and, as he could have no pleasure in any thing unshared with his fellow-creatures, it naturally followed that many hearts were gladdened by his prosperity. He purchased a quantity of land and built for himself a most comfortable dwelling, and, at the same time, laid out a pretty square, and filled it with excellent houses, which he rented to his friends, and thus had a small colony of pleasant persons around him, with whom he lived in great harmony, and the most genial, social intercourse, as far as his own efforts could avail towards producing such a desired result.

Mr. Barclay was a good neighbour, in the full acceptation of the term, and was old-fashioned enough in his views to take a proper pride in being so designated; he always declared that, as every one worked in America, no man could be at leisure in the mornings, but his evenings might, with great profit and satisfaction to himself and others, be given to his family and friends. From the first days of their marriage, Mr. and Mrs. Barclay were always at home in the evening, cheerful and happy, and delighted to see pleasant faces around them. This being perfectly understood, and, also from its great rarity, extremely appreciated, there was no lack of visitors. Indeed, no one can exaggerate the value of such a house as theirs had always been in a community where so few are opened in the same way. They conferred a great social blessing on many, who, having no ties of kindred, looked upon their fireside as an oasis in the desert; their house was, also, a resource for strangers; they received all the notabilities who passed through the city, and thereby derived a very signal advantage from foreign intercourse, which does a vast deal, in America, towards rubbing off the rust collected by describing, diurnally, the same circle of opinions and feelings. The house itself was a large, square, unpretending bit of architecture, built more for comfort than show; the first floor contained a spacious dining-room, and a small office where Mr. Barclay received all persons who came on business errands. The hall was large and spacious, and a handsome flight of stairs led to a small ante-room, which opened into a charming parlour fitted up with great taste; the furniture graceful and solid, the paper-hangings and draperies all undertoned in order to bring out an excellent collection of pictures, with which the walls were covered; the dining-room and hall both being decorated in the same manner. These pictures were capital copies of the old masters, by capable hands and originals of the first European and American artists. For talent of any kind Mr. Barclay had a thoroughly appreciative and kindly spirit, and was habitually doing all that laid in his power to foster and encourage it, his house being the cherished resort of his countrymen, who ever found a gracious welcome in it.

This above-described apartment opened into a very large and commodious library, the panelling and book-cases of black walnut, the shelves of the latter being filled with the most beautiful editions of valuable works, unsurpassed in their finish of type and binding; the owner of these treasures always declaring that in them centred his sole extravagance. The book-cases, reaching within five feet of the ceiling, their tops were covered with busts, Spanish and Chinese jars, old armour, and weapons of various kinds. Several niches in the library contained beautiful pieces of statuary, and its furniture abounding in lounges, divans, sofas and easy chairs, was pleasant to behold; a variety of tables, covered with books and engravings, completed the arrangement of this delightful room. Large plate-glass folding-doors connected the library with a conservatory filled with rare plants, and even shrubs, at the end of which was an aviary and fountain. These three rooms laid to the south, and a sort of midsummer dreamland was thus conjured up, even in the aspect of a northern climate. Mrs. Barclay was extravagantly fond of flowers, and devoted much time to their cultivation, assisted by her daughters; her husband encouraged this taste in every way by procuring her every rare novelty in the floral kingdom.

This was a spot in which happiness might seem to dwell, and truly did, to such an extent, that its possessors, when they reflected upon the manifold blessings they enjoyed, declared they trembled for their endurance. There are no such happy persons in the world as those who are constantly contributing to the well-being of others, the absence of all selfish considerations being one of the purest elements of a well-spent existence. In this respect the dwellers in this home were beyond reproach. Every thing was in daily use in Mrs. Barclay's home; she had no one article of table equipage that was better than another, and this saved a world of trouble, time and temper, the two latter of dominant importance in all households; for, if there is a bit of porcelain that excels another, it is sure never to be forthcoming, in an American establishment, when it is most required. Her dinners were excellent, and served unpretendingly, she having no desire to ape foreign fashions with a few servants, and to adopt the affectation of forcing three waiters to perform the service of thirty. If any short-comings occurred, they were never perceived, or commented upon, simply because there was no ostentatious pretension.

Mr. Barclay, being eminently hospitable, invited his friends freely; his wife gave them a gracious welcome, and he a hearty one; and their guests were not confined to the prosperous and those who revelled in luxuries, but embraced poor scholars, artists and others, to whom a well appointed repast was a boon indeed, and the charm of social intercourse, a greater one still. Mr. Barclay's was no debtor and creditor account with feasts; he disliked dining out, and avoided as much as possible all formal entertainments.

Mr. Barclay, from early habit, rose at daybreak, made his own fire, and read a couple of hours before breakfast, but was in nowise bigoted as to the observance of this rule by the rest of his family; he had seen so much positive discomfort produced by the rigid enforcement of over-early rising amongst his friends, that he resolved not to be too strict in his own regulations. It was sufficient for him that his family was punctual at dinner, and probably there never was one more regular in attendance at morning prayers and repasts than his. His breakfast finished, he went to his office, and remained until two o'clock, rode or walked a few hours, and dined at five. Of his brother, Mr. Richard, he saw very little in the morning, but looked forward with great pleasure to his appearance at his fireside in the evening. The contrast between the two brothers was indeed remarkable, the one so handsome, the other so ugly; Mr. John's manners so pleasing, Mr. Richard's exactly the reverse; the one looking at the world through rose-coloured spectacles, the other through darkest green; Mr. John contented, Mr. Richard discontented, — and yet how they loved each other! Knitted together by the most tender ties, they lived most harmoniously, despite the great difference in their characters. Mr. Richard positively adored his brother and all his belongings, and even looked upon John's dog with a more gracious aspect than he regarded many human beings. There was, however, a certain indefinable fascination about this grumbler, and even his ugliness was quite irresistible. If there is no such phrase as a handsome-ugly person, there should be one manufactured, for such was he. His grumbling was ever amusing from its variety of subject, and his very ineffectual attempts at keeping out of sight the sensibility which he was ever endeavouring to conceal, were interesting, and perpetually demanding the attention of his friends. If Mr. Richard was absent from his brother's house for a day, the family lamented his non-appearance, and even the guests could hardly dispense with his presence, he being their sauce piquante.

A certain Mrs. Ashley was his pet dislike, the children's ball-giving friend. On this lady, a very pretty, well-dressed and pleasing person, by the bye, Mr. Richard lavished a vast deal of criticism when she was present and when she was not. The lady, being very amiable, seemed totally to disregard all the bachelor's hints, innuendoes and objurgations, and paid no attention whatever to them, which was very provoking indeed.

Mr. Richard had also a second pet dislike, Miss Serena Tidmarsh, who did not bear her martyr's crown with like equanimity, and repaid him with many a cat-like hit in a very lowed-toned voice, but none the less stringent for that. She was a neighbour of Mr. Barclay's, and her father had been an old friend of his.

With Miss Jane Redmond, another neighbour, Mr. Richard was always at daggers drawn ; they quarrelled famously. She was an overt enemy, unlike her dear friend, Miss Serena ; Jane was open-mouthed, and with a voice in alto answered her opponent fiercely, and gave him no quarter. He rather liked her the better for her candour, if any liking there could be between the discordant pair.

The evening succeeding the children's ball found Mr.

Barclay in his beautiful library by the side of a bright fire, the Dolly on his knee and surrounded by his family, a perfect picture of content and happiness. The Dolly was told, every day of her life, that she was altogether too tall and too old to sit on her father's knee ; but she declared that there were too many good things attached to the position of 'baby of the family' to be readily renounced, and that, until he sent her away, there she should remain, a thing he was very unlikely to do. Georgy and Gracy were not very animated, the ball having sadly fatigued them ; they, however, played a duet or two for their mother, and then threw themselves rather listlessly upon a sofa, and were nearly half asleep when they were aroused by the entrance of Mrs. Ashley. This lady, ever bright and cheerful, entered into a pleasant chat immediately, inquiring of her young friends how they had enjoyed her little party.

'Oh!' answered Gracy, 'immensely, dear aunty, nothing was ever so charming, so delightful; but I do feel so very good for nothing to-night.'

'The natural consequence of unnatural dissipation,' sneered Mr. Richard.

'You cannot propose,' said Mrs. Ashley, 'to feel as brilliant as common, my dear little girl ; you danced the whole of last evening.'

'And will lose the whole of this,' said Mr. Richard.

'Oh no, uncle mine, I do not intend to do any such thing. I confess to feeling a tiny bit fatigued, but Mrs. Ashley will set me all right, as she always does.'

'I do not approve of children's balls,' said Mr. Richard.

'Nor I, either,' said Mrs. Barclay, 'but my friend here with her all-persuasive powers, conquered and carried off my daughters, and it appeared they enjoyed their evening heartily ; it had all the charm of novelty certainly.'

'Yes,' said the Dolly, 'Mary Redmond told me to-day at school, that Jane declared that Georgy and Grace were the little queens of the night, but, in her opinion, they never looked so ill, and were very untastefully dressed. I was dreadfully angry at this, and told her that her sister was always saying spiteful and disagreeable things, and I should like to know what was a dress for young girls if white book-muslin were not. Upon this she said that Jane thought me the most ugly and disagreeable child in all Christendom; upon which I told her I didn't care a rush for herself or Jane either; that Jane was getting quite old, and never having any admirers, was jealous of every one that had.'

'My dear child,' exclaimed Mrs. Barclay, 'pray stop such a torrent of words and listen to me; this was all very improper, indeed. Have I not enforced upon you, time and again, that you must never indulge in personalities of any kind?'

'Well, dear mother, I will try not to do so, but you must let me tell you the whole. I should like to promise solemnly that I would never again reply when Mary repeats what her hateful sister,—oh, dear me! I forgot,—Miss Jane Redmond, says. You can't think, mother, how saucy she was. Mary told me, besides, that I was an impertinent girl, and had no manners, which was easily accounted for, as my mother always kept a pet bear in the house. Oh! I screamed, What a horrid fib! Why, my father has only dear old Nero, Georgy a mocking-bird, Gracy a canary, I a kitten, and Johnny his dandy terrier; the dogs are all kept in the stable, and there is not a bear in the house. "I don't care," said Mary, "you have got a bear, and it's your uncle Dick. Jane heard one old gentleman at table to-day call him so; another said he was Ursa Major, and another Snarleyou, and Jane laughed and declared his motto should be the Baron of Bradwardines, 'Bewar the Bar.'" Upon this, I was in a perfect fury, boxed Mary's ears soundly for calling my dear, dear uncle such abominable names, and was shut up in a dark closet two hours, with a horrid big mouse scampering about all the time, because I would not confess I was sorry for what I had done.'

Having completed this oration, the excited young creature burst into tears. Mrs. Barclay begged her to go to bed and compose herself, and just as she was preparing to obey her mother, Mr. Richard arose and tenderly embraced his champion.

When she had departed, Mrs. Barclay avowed that she had, for a long time, dubitated as to the expediency of sending Kate to a daily school. She was entirely different from her sisters, being remarkably impulsive and very excitable, and the event of this evening had fortified her in her half-formed resolve of retaining her at home and procuring a governess for her. She had perceived no ill effects arising from the course she had pursued with her elder daughters, but this one seemed to require a change.

Uncle Richard, who had always opposed the system of sending girls to daily schools, very much approved of this plan; he had always thought that his nieces should be shut up precisely as were the children in France, and deprecated excessively the custom of allowing them 'to run about the streets.'

Mrs. Barclay, however, had satisfied herself as to the excellence of the schools in her native city, and resolved that her daughters should enjoy their attendant advantages; but in the case of the Dolly, she perceived that another arrangement might be tried beneficially.

Some foreigners, who were travelling in America for the purpose of examining, amongst other things, the system of the public schools, were just then announced, and a very interesting conversation ensued, in which they gained a vast deal of information from their host, who was constantly applied to on similar occasions.

There was a great charm to these strangers in this intercourse; they there beheld an American family assembled together in the enjoyment of domestic happiness, and not tricked out in 'silk attire,' or, in other words, company dress and manners. They seated themselves at the tea-table, over which one of the young and radiant daughters of this household presided, with unaffected grace and modesty; and having partaken of the beverage which 'cheers but not inebriates,' they remained several hours chatting agreeably, and departed, rejoicing in having been permitted to see the interior of at least one family, without fuss and parade.

Travellers worth knowing, who visit this country, come usually for scientific and useful purposes, very few for pleasure; they consequently desire to see the inner life of the Americans, not the outward and infrequent gala-show days and nights, where nothing that they desire to learn can be gained.

CHAPTER VIII.

'Who meets us here? My niece Plantagenet,
Led in the hand of her kind aunt of Gloster.'
SHAKSPEARE.

THERE is a pleasant custom in many American families of adopting Aunts. Some agreeable person, connected with them by no ties of blood, is selected and enacts very successfully her part, the junior members always making the choice. Mrs. Fanny Ashley had received this distinction at the hands of Mr. Barclay's children, and a better or more tenderly affectionate relative could nowhere have been found.

Mrs. Ashley had been a very pretty little girl, and became a very pretty young woman; she was really so, hair, eyes, teeth, figure and face all pretty; and moreover, she was exceedingly amiable.

Somebody of 'man's estate' had said of her that she possessed precisely sense enough for a woman, and to these attractive belongings was added a fine fortune.

Now all these pleasant things had, naturally enough, obtained for her a host of pretenders to her favour, and the young lady certainly surprised immensely all her friends and admirers when she bestowed her hand upon a man almost old enough to be her own father. But she was an orphan and her own mistress, with no one to enlighten her respecting the inner life of the individual she had thus unwisely chosen.

Mr. Samuel Ashley was considered very handsome, even at an age when the fragility of such a possession as beauty is decided ; he had travelled much, and was said to have studied its preservation most accurately in the best of schools for such a recondite science. Mr. Ashley's voice was captivating; he sang, all the women declared, like an angel; he waltzed and danced incomparably, entirely heedless of the sarcasms upon his juvenilities, launched forth by his married contemporaries.

This gentleman was also a good talker, quoted Byron and sighed forth Moore's songs most exquisitely, and had a splendid establishment and great wealth. He had just returned from the East, when he beheld for the first time the pretty creature whom he wooed and won, as he well knew how to do. They were married, and she was installed in his beautiful house to find herself a slave. A greater tyrant never existed than she discovered her liege lord and master to be. His life had been an undivulged secret : the gay, fascinating, agreeable Mr. Ashley proved a miserable invalid, existing only by the perpetual administering of opium, disguised, to be sure, under other names, but opium ever.

No sooner had he secured his prize, than, casting aside all concealment, he appeared before his young wife what he, in truth, really was, — a selfish egotist, vain, cruel and heartless, and, worse than all, jealous. The green-eyed monster had never effected a more perfect lodgment in any man's breast than his : whatever his experience had been in life, it was not flattering to woman ; he had no faith in her. It has been related that he was remarkably handsome. But who can picture the disgust of his wife when she, who had thought his hyacinthine ringlets the most beautiful ever seen, was convinced, by ocular demonstration, that they were put in curl papers, every night, by his own body-servant ! And a precious task had the poor fellow, for this operation was but the commencement of his nocturnal services. This one act alone would have sufficed to disabuse the most enamoured of wives, which Mrs. Ashley was not.

It is true, she had been enthralled; and what was a simple girl to do when an experienced and perfect actor like Mr. Ashley had resolved to win her? He well knew how to spread his net, and the young fledgling was soon entangled in its meshes; she was also flattered excessively by the notice of a man so courted and followed. His slightest laudatory mention of her, the first time he saw her, quite elevated her in the scale of the fashionable circle in which she moved. He pronounced her pretty, very pretty, and every body immediately voted her beautiful. She was dazzled and bewildered by his attentions, and imagining that the delusion under which she laboured was love, she cheerfully consented to place her destiny in his hands.

He began his marital career by commanding her to abandon all her young friends, allowing her to receive them only in the most formal manner: he detested, he said, silly intimacies. Then she was to accept invitations only in certain houses, and those most rarely; he declared his own health to be so delicate that all parties in the evening must be abandoned, a grand and formal dinner being the only amusement permitted. She might sit by his side, if she liked, when he took his daily exercise in a close carriage, but, as to 'running about town,' that was totally inadmissible; his first wife had never done any thing of the sort. So, in default of any thing better, poor Mrs. Ashley entered every day, at one o'clock, a superb equipage and dozed through a drive of six miles, never more, never less, over the self-same road with her magnificent husband, who made a point of never opening his lips. For why should he attempt being agreeable, or give himself any trouble for his wife? A little silly bread-and-butter girl was she when he married her, with nothing but her prettiness and fortune to recommend her, and she must consider herself to have climbed to the very apex of human felicity when he honoured her by bestowing upon her his great name. To be sure, he could not deny, even to himself, that he had been obliged to exercise rather tiresome efforts to gain this young thing, but now he was making amends for the constraint he had been forced to put upon himself.

A wearisome life was hers, and she was fast losing her spirits and health, when death released her from her bondage; and, from being the nurse of a worn-out voluptuary, she emerged, after a decent period of retirement, into the consolatory condition of an immensely rich widow, with renewed health and spirits, and a firm resolve that, if she were ever weak enough to contract another marriage, it should be with the ugliest and worst-mannered man in Christendom.

The first person she sought was Mrs. Barclay. 'My dear Kate,' said she, 'I hope you have not, for a moment, imagined I love you the less for not seeing you; my duties of nurse have been so arduous, that no time have I had for the cultivation of friendship, or even acquaintance. Now I return to beg and conjure you to accord me my old place in your affections, and to allow me the blessed privilege of coming here when I please.' Mrs. Barclay, embracing her cordially, entreated her to return to her old haunts, and sincerely assured her that the more she frequented her house, the better would her husband and herself like and love her. Mrs. Ashley, enchanted by the warmth of her friend's welcome, availed herself of this gracious permission, and haunted, as she persisted in asserting, the dwelling where her warmest affections centred. The whole family were delighted with the gay and pleasant person who conferred so much of her time upon them, and soon adopted her as the aunt of their decided predilections.

Mr. Richard Barclay's pardon must be entreated for not excepting him in the list of the fair widow's admirers: he literally hated her, and often declared she was the only drawback in his brother's house. 'How they could like her, he knew not, a silly flaunting thing; delighted to be rid of her husband, and run wild! Dress and parties, parties and dress, nothing else; her toilettes were exquisite he was willing to concede, but then the time she devoted to them! What could John and his wife find in such a woman as that? Not an idea; he abhorred even the sound of her voice.' And so he grumbled and railed at his enemy, as he called her. Now, this was not at all true; Mrs. Ashley could be no one's enemy, not even Mr. Richard's; she simply thought he was particularly rude ever to her, but then he was the brother of the persons she most loved on earth, and she must bear with his odd and disagreeable ways for their sake. Had Mrs. Ashley been asked who was the man she most disliked in the world, she would have promptly answered, Mr. Richard Barclay. Under the circumstances, she neither betrayed nor concealed her feelings, but avoided any intercourse with the 'bear,' other than what was really inevitable.

This state of things would have been very disagreeable to the friends of the parties, but for the exquisite tact of the lady; and nothing could have been better than her treatment of Mr. Richard's case, for a case it was requiring skilful hands to manage. In vain Mr. Barclay remonstrated with his brother on the extraordinary dislike he had taken to his pretty and pleasing friend; but the 'bear's' prejudices were altogether too deeply rooted for any efforts he could make to eradicate them, so he renounced all hope of effecting an amicable arrangement between them.

Mrs. Barclay was devotedly attached to Mrs. Ashley. The little estrangement which had occurred, she well knew arose from no want of affection on the part of her friend, but the tyranny of her husband; and she was delighted at the frank and loyal manner in which the amiable and affectionately attached woman had returned to her allegiance, and resumed all the pleasant routine of bye-past days. It seemed as if the interregnum had but increased their love for each other: she lamented her brother's whims, and would gladly have reconciled the two persons she so well loved.

On Mrs. Ashley's reappearance amidst her friends, several of her followers began to appear also; the one who made himself the most conspicuous was Mr. Naseby. This gentleman had been rather slightingly treated by dame Nature in every thing, but, as it very often occurs in such cases, the non-recipient takes it into his head that he has been bountifully supplied with all her gifts. Mr. Naseby was perfectly confident that he was a charming poet, a delightful singer, that he danced well, rode well, and gobbled up hearts. To be sure, it did seem extraordinary that he had not been disabused of some of these illusions by the infinite variety of rebuffs he was perpetually receiving. Mrs. Ashley had refused him a dozen times, but he always returned to the charge with renewed vigour, and continued to haunt her steps wherever she went. She declared he was as blind as a bat to his own imperfections, and that there was no way of knocking his conceit out of him.

And he was blind, indeed, for such near-sightedness as had fallen on this unfortunate man no one had ever beheld; the mistakes and blunders he committed, touching the identity of all objects animate and inanimate, were indescribably ludicrous. Although sighing at the feet of Mrs. Ashley, Mr. Naseby was not deterred, by the passionate nature of his attachment, from distributing a few favours, in the shape of verses, flowers and love-tokens in other quarters; in fact, he was a victim to the fair sex, and met with a most ungrateful return. His appearance amongst the young girls, — he being no middle man, and ever meandering between widows and juvenilities — was the signal of instant flight, for besides the soft nothings he poured into their all-revolting ears, he was a perfect terror to them in the matter of their toilettes. Myopia was centred in him: he upset cups of chocolate over rose-coloured tissues, put his big feet into superb blonde flounces, fell sprawling into the ranks of the waltzers, and breathed into the ears of one divinity precisely what was intended for another. Then his two arch-angels comparing notes, vowed vengeance against him for ever and aye; and altogether the 'Cupidon,' as the young tits called him, led rather a troublous existence.

Mrs. Ashley sometimes flattered herself that he had entirely deserted her for some Will-o'-the-Wisp of sixteen, but no such good fortune awaited her; a short respite ensued, and lo! Mr. Naseby made his return known to the lady of his love by breaking her invaluable Spanish fan, upsetting a Buhl tripod with a marble bust of Petrarch's Laura upon it, the nose of the immortal wife, and mother of eleven children being destroyed thereby; or giving Bobby, the mocking-bird, such a big worm that, choking and strangling, he gave up the ghost entirely. The last offence, one of a thousand, the fair widow could not forgive, for Bobby had been taught all manner of touchingly interesting feats, had flown away seven times, and cost her ten dollars for every restoration to his home and perch, besides the original outlay of a hundred.

'What shall I do to rid myself of that incubus, Mr. Naseby?' said Mrs. Ashley to Mrs. Barclay.

'You must not make yourself so agreeable to him,' replied the lady.

'Oh, he is insufferable! I have treated him in the most shocking manner, especially after poor Bobby's death: did you ever hear of any thing so abominable? I have but one hope left, and that is, in the transcendent beauty of your daughters he will be oblivious of what he is pleased to call my perfectibilities.'

'To tell you the truth, my dear friend, I have lately had a suspicion that he has begun to turn his gooseberry eyes in that quarter.'

'I could embrace you with all my heart for the good news,' exclaimed Mrs. Ashley.

And so it was, the inconstant! He had actually promenaded his regards, as the French say, on the two opening beauties, but, unfortunately, could never distinguish one sister from the other. He had proposed to pay his devoirs to the youngest, Miss Grace; but to persons in the full enjoyment of their eyesight the resemblance was puzzling beyond description, then what must it have been to the parcel-blind Mr. Naseby !

Georgy and Grace Barclay had long desired to inform Mrs. Ashley of the partial defection of her recreant swain, but dared not take the liberty. On Mrs. Barclay's hint Mrs. Ashley spake, and then such an amusing revelation as ensued! Georgy had innumerable protestations to record for her sister, and Grace, the beloved one, comparatively none at all. Copies of verses addressed to the divine Miss Grace Barclay had been mysteriously left at the door by small boys, bouquets, countless in number, and a pair of turtle-doves.

The sisters had made a compact never to enlighten the adorer touching their identity, and Georgy enjoyed the joke immensely of repeating Mr. Naseby's platitudes to her sister.

'The wicked young things!' exclaimed Mrs. Ashley, when she heard this recital of adventures; 'but the silly fellow richly deserves all the tricks they have played upon him; at any rate, I shall be rid of his presence at my house for a while.'

But this was a sad mistake of the fair widow's. Mr. Naseby had not the slightest intention of abandoning Mrs. Ashley. He admired her excessively, found her house extremely agreeable, her dinners well appointed and excellent; and what mattered it to him that she had positively declined his matrimonial proffers half a dozen times? He was quite accustomed to such proceedings; refusals were not 'few and far between' in the annals of his life? It would have been well for him if he could have, for once, summed up all his reminiscences of the various defeats he had encountered, and learned a lesson of forbearance and humility.

CHAPTER IX.

'If she undervalue me,
What care I how fair she be.'
SIR WALTER RALEIGH.

YEARS had rolled away, and time had passed sadly and slowly enough to Mrs. Sanderson. Hers was a monotonous life indeed; friendless and alone, she felt the deprivation of social intercourse severely, but possessed not sufficient courage or energy to make any exertion. Gerald had left the Latin school with honours, and had formed a plan and was carrying it through efficiently, to pursue the same course of studies at home that he should have done could he have effected his cherished purpose of entering Harvard University. To this he sedulously applied himself.

Charley had received a good mercantile education, to which had been added French and Spanish, his mother having taught him drawing and music, besides constantly reviewing his studies. At sixteen he had been placed in a commercial house, in which he had conducted himself admirably; he had reached his eighteenth year, and was ardently wishing to do something for himself in order that he might no longer be a burthen to his mother, when, most fortunately for him, he accidentally made the acquaintance of Mr. Barclay. The gentleman was attracted by the energy and industry of the youth, having seen him constantly at work; and when their further intercourse developed all the pleasing and excellent qualities of the young orphan, when he found that, to a high sense of honour and probity in Charley Sanderson, was added the most fascinatingly cheerful manners and pleasing accomplishments, he quite cultivated the society of a creature so gifted by nature.

Mr. Barclay had known Charley's father, and would willingly have paid his mother many delicate attentions, but she was so entrenched behind the barricade raised by her brother, Mr. Egerton, that he had always considered her completely unapproachable. This good man, truly the orphan's friend, had felt some regret, when he first began to discern Charley's attractions, that he had rather neglected these boys, and made all the amends in his power by inviting them to his house. Charley, of course, was perfectly enchanted to accept any proffers of hospitality from such a distinguished quarter; but Gerald, whose shyness and studious and dreamy habits had, by that time, become unconquerable, resolutely refused all overtures for social intercourse. In vain his brother raved of the beauty and amiability of the sisters, the benevolence and graciousness of their parents, the fascinations and attractions of all the surroundings of this family; Gerald obstinately persisted in remaining at home, seeing no one but his mother and uncle, and hardly ever getting beyond the bounds of the garden walls. Indeed, there he took all his exercise, his mother usually walking with him; otherwise, his rounds would have been truly solitary; the rest of his time was given exclusively to hard work, which seemed to be his only pleasure with the exception of music; he played on the guitar admirably, and sang in a masterly style. His mother had greatly encouraged this taste, as it was the only recreation he permitted himself to enjoy; she much lamented the seclusion of her son, but, as she often said, what could she do? Her own means of promoting the happiness of her darling children were so small, that all she could bestow was an unlimited acquiescence in their pursuits, for other gifts she was powerless; and feeling herself so powerless she could not gather sufficient courage to remonstrate with

Gerald on his solitariness. It is true that Mrs. Sanderson was not far-sighted as to the evil consequences which would infallibly ensue from such a course of life, its egotism alone being the rock upon which his whole being might be shipwrecked. Again, if by any chance, her son should be deprived of Charley, his ignorance of the commonest worldly transactions being deplorable, how was he to guide or govern himself? This question she had not asked herself; she had seen so much trouble, and the dullness of her career had been so stupefying, that it had partially obscured her susceptibility to coming events, and she appeared to have settled down into the conviction that sufficient for the day was the evil thereof.

Certainly Charley did his best to push Gerald out into the world, sometimes trying coaxing, and sometimes scolding; at the latter he was, however, no great adept; but if he did not succeed in effecting his purpose in the gairish light of day, he now and then prevailed at night. By dint of great persuasion Gerald would steal forth at midnight for an hour to bestow a serenade upon the sisters whom his brother so rapturously admired, and this to Charley was an immense boon; they sang deliciously together, their voices, from long practice, mingling most harmoniously. Charley, when charged with the pleasant fact of having trolled a love ditty beneath his lady's window by the young beauties, always frankly avowed his participation in the duo, but awarded to his brother all the praises bestowed upon the performance.

Gracy had experienced an intense desire to see Gerald, and often begged his brother to urge him to accept her father's invitation; but he declared Gerald to be an inexorable fellow, nothing could be done with him, he declared, he was so obstinately bent upon living at home and nowhere else; for, said he, 'Gerald will not even serenade you and your sister when the moon is at its full, because he is fearful you might peep out and get a chance look at him.'

'Oh,' said Gracy, 'I do not believe any young gentleman who takes so much pains to hide himself is worth looking at at all. Is he deformed?'

'Deformed!' almost shrieked Charley, 'why he is the handsomest fellow I ever saw in my life, nothing can surpass his beauty; such a romantic air and manner, you never beheld the like, Miss Gracy.'

'Does he wear a minstrel's cloak, or a brigand's hat?'

'Now you are mocking at Gerald.'

'Well, well, I'll not say another word about him, but only ask does he go to church?'

'He does not, but devotes all Sunday to religious exercises; he is very devout.'

By the question 'Does he go to church,' Miss Gracy innocently revealed a little project of seeing Charley's strange brother, of whom wonderful stories were floating amongst the young people, his great learning, his application and total seclusion being considered quite mysterious. The answer put to flight her plan of stealing a look at him. She renewed the subject with Georgy by asking her how she supposed Gerald Sanderson looked.

'Not like other people at all, I imagine,' replied her sister; 'it is said he is a very remarkably handsome person, very poetical and visionary. I am told that an artist, who by chance saw him, has been trying these last six months to induce him to sit to him, but he cannot be persuaded to do so; he may relent, and then, you know, you can see the picture, as you seem to be so curiously inclined.'

'I shall never like him,' said Gracy, 'half as well as Charley, if he is handsome as the Apollo Belvidere.'

'I dare say not, for Charley seems to be the reigning favourite with you, Gracy.'

'I frankly confess he is. I never saw such a loyal, charming tempered, gay creature in my life. How he adores us all!'

'Loves, you mean; the adoration is all for a certain Miss

Grace Barclay. Time was when he paid his devoirs to me, but you have supplanted me entirely in his affections.'

'And surely you had no claim on his affections, for you are, and always have been, perfectly indifferent to him.'

'I agree with you cordially in your estimate of Charley's good qualities, and I really do love him, but as a brother only.'

And true it was, that the youthful swain had at last settled down into a state of perfect adoration of Miss Grace Barclay. This revolution in the tenderness of his feelings had been brought about by the continuous indifference of Miss Georgy, and Charley had turned to another luminary; it was also true, that during the period he wore the elder sister's chains, he frequently mistook the one for the other, a circumstance that often occurred to many persons besides himself. But, he soon began to feel, if he did not see, that there was one who might smile upon him, if the other would not; and accordingly as he had never been perfectly confirmed in his true faith, he abandoned the old shrine and worshipped at the new. And then a long adieu to mistakes; none were made, and Charley became the most constant and devoted of all true knights.

Just after Mrs. Ashley's ball Grace caught a bad cold, which seemed to threaten her lungs. This sadly alarming her parents, they consulted their medical man, and he recommended that she should be shut up in the house all winter, the temperature of which he declared to be quite equable, and, as he did not think change of climate requisite, she remained at home, and took her lessons from private masters.

Georgy went to her daily school, as usual. She, at first, lamented the precautionary measures adopted for the restoration of her sister's health, but, in the end, seemed reconciled, and went forth cheerfully as usual. To Gracy, this was a terrible disappointment; she missed her sister, her classes, her kind teachers, and it could not be said that she bore her deprivation with like equanimity. She declared she could learn nothing well without Georgy; her sister assisted her so much in her lessons, was so much more intelligent and clever, and, in fact, for the first time in her life, was thoroughly discontented. This mood was not of long endurance; her better nature triumphed, as her mother, remonstrating, begged her to remember the blessings with which she was surrounded, and made her fully aware, and also confess, how improper and unbecoming, and even wicked, were these repinings, counselling her to childlike submission, and praying that the cup might pass away. It did, and the spring saw her restored to perfect health.

About spring-time, a good chance occurring, Charley Sanderson, under the patronage of Mr. Barclay, was sent to India. The fact that a situation could be procured on board an excellent vessel with a good commander being made known to the orphan's friend, he spoke to his young favourite, and discovered what he had never before even suspected, that the boy was pennyless. At first, he could be hardly made to comprehend this, having ever seen this young creature so gay and cheerful; he had never surmised that he was enduring all sorts of privations; it seemed to him monstrous that with an uncle, rolling in wealth, there were no means forthcoming, except for a scanty outfit, and that even this resource had been hoarded, in the most economical manner, by mother and son. Charley's outburst of almost frantic grief, when he heard of the project and acknowledged his inability to accept it, was heart-rending; and, as Mr. Barclay subsequently told his wife, being more than he could bear, he had advanced a few thousands, and intended to send him on his way rejoicing.

And on his way he went, blessing and praying for the welfare of his benefactor, every day of his life; the parting from his mother, Gerald, and Grace, was very, very sad, but then it was illumined with the prospect of a prosperous voyage and speedy return. To Mrs. Sanderson the sun shone less brightly when her darling departed; Gerald moped and missed the joyous spirit that had gladdened his existence, and Peter and Dinah groaned and sang ballads, of twenty-four verses each, about horrible shipwrecks and piratical murders in the Indian seas, that were frightful enough to make one's hair stand on end. 'He'd nebber come back alive,' they both declared.

All the Barclays missed and mourned the Charley, he was so constantly with them, and such a bit of sunshine! it seemed hardly possible that the departure of one such young person could leave so large a space unfilled. And Grace found that she loved him with all her heart; 'a light that's fled' was he to her. She had been utterly unconscious of the nature of her feelings for him, until the glittering sail, which she watched from her own window, had sunk below the horizon, carrying with it the light and life of her existence. And many a time and oft went this young creature to that same window, to watch and wait the reappearance of the Indian argosy which would bring back her lover. For this he was, though no one word of troth had ever passed her lips or his, but they had vowed themselves to each other in the depths of their own hearts; and this absence was to put to the proof their constancy.

It appeared also, on Charley's flitting, that Mr. Richard had contrived 'to like the boy too well,' and he spared 'the old miser' not a whit when he descanted upon the impossibility of living with such a good fellow, and not loving him and helping him.

'I always disliked Philip Egerton,' cried he, 'and I do so now all the more. Why, what will he do with his money? He can't carry it with him, of that he must be sure; and what could he have done better than to bestow a bag of the famous unseen gold pieces upon that dear boy? I wish heartily that the divining rod had fished them up, and then somebody would have been the better for them. Where do you suppose, John, they are?'

Mr. Barclay was much amazed at Mr. Richard's condescending, at last, to ask this question, when he had criticised all Boston for doing the same thing.

'It is a mooted point, Dick,' replied he, 'where they are now. He'll found an Egerton Hospital or College with them when he dies, depend upon it.'

'And defraud his rightful heirs,' said Mr. Richard.

'He may marry yet, Dick.'

'Who on earth would have him, John?'

'Mrs. Ashley, perhaps.'

'Oh! John, John, how can you say so? she's a silly thing, I well know, but not quite so foolish as that.'

'I'm delighted, for once, to have caught you defending my favourite and your pet dislike. Miss Serena, then, what say you to her?'

'I give her up, but he'll never ask her, of that I am sure, and am just as certain she would accept him if he did.'

'I had some idea of writing that miserly Philip Egerton,' said Mr. Richard, 'an anonymous letter, just to let him know what all the world thinks of his conduct; but, as I never had done such a mean thing in my life, I was quite sure I should finish by signing my name to it.'

'Mr. Egerton is so supremely indifferent to every thing that can be said or written of him, Richard, that all attacks, overt or otherwise, would fall fruitless to the ground. I must confess I am astonished that Charley Sanderson has not broken through the ice of his misanthropy with his most winning and endearing qualities; and if even my pet has not been able to do this, no one can. I never, in my life, met with a more charming youngster; his very presence diffuses sunshine; 'tis pleasant to look upon his loyal and loving eyes. I often pray that Johnny may become just such another; I shall miss him sadly.'

'I hope, John, he will be one day your son-in-law.'

'Ah! well, my brother, they are both so young, many changes may occur before they can ever think of marrying. I wish my Gracy no better fortune than such a husband, if she can ever make up her mind to leave her mother. One thing I do know, Charley has never opened his lips to her, but came in the most straight-forward and honourable manner to me, and said that he loved my daughter devotedly, and that if I thought I could never consent to allow him to win her, he would never again enter my doors, as his wretchedness would infallibly betray his secret, — a pretty secret, forsooth, which all the household knew. Upon this, I laughed, and told him to let things remain just as they were, and keep his lips closed until his return from India, and then we should see how this grand passion had stood the perilous test of salt water.'

'Oh! John, John,' cried Mr. Richard, 'how many people in this over-wise city of Boston would think you a fool if they could hear you now proposing to give your daughter to a penniless boy; it would quite ruin you on 'Change. So never mention such a thing to any one but your brother.'

CHAPTER X.

LAW. — A rule of action.
JOHNSON'S DICTIONARY.

MR. BARCLAY had many old friends surrounding him, his first neighbour, Mr. Redmond, a man of profound judicial learning and great legal attainments, had experienced the good fortune, early in life, of being able to convince his townsmen of the existence of his gifts, a most important step in any profession, but particularly in that of the law. His career had been one of great prosperity; he had been sent to the West Indies on some business, just after he had completed his studies, and there, besides gaining a large and valuable suit, won the heart and hand of an heiress of great beauty and reputed accomplishments. He returned home, bringing his bride, and having installed her in a very handsome residence, and furnished it in a befitting manner, he immersed himself in his law books, having, apparently, nearly forgotten her presence in it.

Mrs. Redmond was not precisely the sort of person to remind any man very impressively of her existence, much less her absent husband. She was a fine creature, with large sleepy eyes, the lids of which she appeared actually too indolent to raise, and her whole being was so swallowed up in idleness and apathy, that she hardly seemed awake three hours in the day consecutively. She never repined at her husband's neglect, but consoled herself for the loss of his attentions by devoting her time to the perusal of all the novels and romances she could procure. She arose in the morning at nine o'clock, and, as the only thing she did thoroughly was to perform her ablutions, and, as she had a dim consciousness that if she were not then completely dressed for the day, she should never mount the stairs to her chamber again, she made an elegant and elaborate toilette. Descending to the dining-room at eleven, she drank a cup of tea and ate a morsel of dry bread, and then she repaired to the parlour, and installing herself in a luxuriant lounge, she dozed away her time with a novel. It was impossible for her to read Mrs. Austen's works. She heard her admirers laud them to the skies, but two chapters gave Mrs. Redmond one of her soundest naps, and in twenty years she had not finished 'Emma.' Sir Walter she rather liked, but she could not read him forever, and, as she required an immense deal of excitement, she devoured all the yellow-covered horrors in Christendom. Nothing was too shockingly improbable for her taste ; she doted upon brigands and murderers, and strong sensations and pungent situations ; and so she betook herself to the French school, which is surnamed the 'Satanic,' and was tolerably well contented, for every day brought her some new developments of human weakness and wickedness, with the crowning one virtue to leaven the abominable mass of sin, which that seminary disseminates. So Mrs. Redmond dozed away her life, with the interruption occasioned by the birth of three children, a son, Robert, and two daughters, Jane and Mary. The children were left to nurses, and afterwards to a nursery governess, and then to private schools and masters. The boy went to Cambridge, was graduated with honours, and turned out a capital fellow, high-minded, frank and loyal, nobody knew how. He managed these things himself, most people thought.

Jane fared worse. She was critical and satirical from her earliest days, carping and fault-finding occupied her mind ; she despised her mother's inertness and plunged into another extreme ; she was too busy and active, always in a hurry.

There was no repose about her; she flew about like a Will-o'-the-Wisp, resting nowhere. She had most settled and fixed ideas upon all subjects, and, as her mother neither rode, walked nor talked, so Jane, in pure opposition, galloped, ran, and chattered away as fast as she possibly could. Mrs. Redmond looked upon her daughter in as amazed a way as she could compass, and had been heard to declare she could hardly believe Miss Jane to be her own offspring; but this was on some grand occasion, or extraordinary emergency, when even her endurance had been taxed to its utmost capacity.

Little Mary, as they all called her, was gentle and affectionate, but, at times, very ungovernable, from want of good management.

Mr. Redmond had always departed to his office long before any of his family were stirring; he returned to his dinner, seated himself at table, ate a huge meal without knowing whether it were good or bad, spoke never a word, good or bad, and then retraced his footsteps to the same place, and there remained until the small hours, and sometimes just remembered that he had a home at daylight. It was well for him that the quantity and not quality of his food was important, for worse dinners never were eaten than disgraced his loaded board, from the most expensive articles, — no money being spared, — to the cheapest, every thing was either over-done or under-done.

Mrs. Redmond bestowing no attention whatever upon her household, nobody else did, and, consequently, a more extravagant establishment could nowhere be found; fortunately there was wealth, or there would have been shortly an end to the mismanagement. So that the mistress of the house had a few confections at her repasts she was satisfied; retaining in full force her West India taste for sweet things, she always had a basket of candied fruits and sugar-plums on the table by the side of her chair; they rivalled the yellow covers, and as this house kept itself, the pastry cook and confectioner were vastly patronized. Mrs. Redmond had actually so surfeited her children with sweets, that she could not induce them to eat any more ; so she was obliged to bestow her favours upon the Dolly and others with whom she was immensely popular. She found this an excellent plan, as it saved her from talking and endeavouring to entertain young people, which she considered a most wearisome task, and, as she was beautiful and elegantly dressed, they thought her a model woman ; thus she acquired this reputation at a very small cost.

Notwithstanding her sleepy ways, Mrs. Redmond's house abounded in visitors ; she was very hospitable, and, if her friends would only talk to her and expect no answers, she was satisfied ; every one was at home, the hostess permitting her guests to do as they pleased. Her circle was very agreeable, and comprised many pleasing and influential persons, who, meeting others of the same stamp, naturally resorted to a house where they were habitually to be found. Thus it happened that the lady gathered around her a pleasing re-union, when persons of infinitely more attainments and talents were left in solitude. Mr. Redmond, though enjoying the reputation of being a great lawyer, had absolutely nothing to do with this, as he was always invisible ; and Jane, the very antipodes of her mother, would have kept every body away except Miss Tidmarsh, with whom she fraternized in an extraordinary manner, and, in fact, was so ungracious, that the frequenters of the establishment hardly acknowledged an acquaintance with her, and were always pleased when she was not at home. Miss Serena Tidmarsh was the reigning favourite with Miss Jane Redmond, and paid much court to that young lady. Miss Serena, if the truth must be told, was many years older than Jane, but having no friends, she was fain to take up with a much younger person, who, captivated by a similarity of tastes and pursuits, eagerly fell into the net that was spread for her by one much more conversant with the ways of the world than herself.

It was a point gained in Miss Tidmarsh's game of life, to have one house open to her at all times and seasons, and especially a dwelling where she was sure to find pleasant society. She looked upon the lady hostess with supreme contempt, and often puzzled herself to account for the attraction there seemed to hang about her, and which certainly collected very agreeable surroundings. Now, the secret was a simple one after all, thoroughly good-natured people are not so plentiful in society as it could be wished, and when they choose to be the centre of a circle, they can always command one; and if Miss Serena had examined this with half the critical acumen she habitually bestowed upon the short-comings of her own little world, she would soon have solved her problem easily.

Mrs. Redmond disliked her daughter's friend as much as she could any thing but the Barclays, somehow, the only positive opinion which emanated from her lips, being a disparaging one of that family. She, who never was heard to set down aught in malice, seemed in this one instance to fail, and from what this backbiting proceeded no one could tell, but so it was; it might have been that she heard them so universally lauded, except by her daughter and her mature friend. It sometimes happens that even very good people become wearied of hearing other very good people praised. We are but mortals after all.

Robert certainly performed his full part in the pæans that were perpetually chanted in the Barclay chorus, and this was the sole irritative that his mother ever endured. There was, to be sure, a tradition that Mr. Redmond had gone to the West Indies, in consequence of having been refused by Mrs. Barclay in her maidenhood; but this surely could not have been the cause of Mrs. Redmond's prejudice against her neighbours.

The lady fancied that Robert was enamoured of Georgy Barclay, and this seemed an extremely disagreeable subject for her to dwell upon, and, it really being the case, she always dismissed it from her mind as speedily as possible. It would be well if every one would do the same thing, and wiser heads than Mrs. Redmond's might have profited by her laudable example.

With regard to Miss Tidmarsh, Mrs. Redmond was powerless; she, having no influence over her daughter, could in nowise control her, and therefore this disagreeable person came and went at her pleasure and wandered over the house, which might be truly said to contain no mistress, since she could not be expelled.

If Jane's misfortune was the possession of too much energy, her mother's consisted in having too little, or almost none at all. Mr. Redmond had never done any thing towards the formation of his wife's character; she was a childlike, lazy creature when he married her, and so she continued afterwards. His time being so completely engrossed by his legal pursuits, the bestowing of any attention upon the education of his children was out of the question; he satisfied himself that they had masters enough, and he paid their bills. Of money he was profuse; he had received an elegant fortune with his wife, and the income from his profession being very large, there were never any pecuniary difficulties under his roof. In this way he lived perfectly contented, and fully convinced, when he thought of his family at all, that all was right.

Unfortunately there are too many Mr. Redmonds. An ardent desire to accumulate wealth, an overweening love of money, and an undue attention to professional pursuits, connected with avarice and ambition, destroy the better part of man's character in America. Nothing is so uncommon as to find any human being satisfied with his lot and condition, the most prosperous being as clamorous in their repinings as the needy; from the lowest round of the ladder to the highest, all alike rail against fortune. If, by chance, any one pauses and desists in his pursuit of lucre, his name is chronicled far and wide, and the solitariness of the case is amply proved by the wonder and amazement it creates. And even when a man like Mr. Barclay gives a few hours every day to his family, he is considered an extraordinary personage.

It is said that we are born, live and die in a hurry, and most true it is that nearly all the testamentary dispositions of hard-earned wealth are executed in the last agony. When a man comes to die, instead of being able to turn his face to the wall in peace with himself and the world, his thoughts given to his Creator, he is tormented with wills and codicils and lawyers, and terrestrial arrangements, where all should have been not of the earth earthy, but celestial.

And thus it happens that, in a long life, he has not allowed himself sufficient time to dispose of the dross, the accumulation of which has cost him such weary years of toil, anxiety and care, and in the race for which he has exhausted, and prematurely too, all the freshness of his feelings, his heaven-born affections, his sublunary enjoyments, and, awful to reflect upon, perchance his salvation. But over this let the mantle of charity be thrown. It is to be devoutly hoped he has found time and leisure to repent.

Robert Redmond, on leaving college, having taken Mr. Barclay for his model, resolved to be just such a merchant if he could, so he entered himself as a clerk in a large and influential commercial house, with the prospect of becoming, in due time, a junior partner; this view of his case being made almost a certainty by his father's promise of a large sum accompanying the youthful aspirant. And very busily and cheerfully went Mr. Robert to work. It was never reported of him that he actually swept out the establishment, though the time has been, when it was firmly believed no man ever made his fortune without so doing. Young America hires porters to perform this operation.

At any rate, the young man gave great satisfaction to his

employers. He was a youth who sent his thoughts abroad; he was not fitted to plod at the desk, but he did quite as well out of doors, and he was sent to Cuba. There he managed well his commissions, and returned and was sent again. His father seemed rather pleased with his activity and enterprise, and his mother embraced him tenderly when he departed, and folded him tightly in her arms when he was again restored to her; a very remarkable effusion of sensibility on her part. His first visit was always to the Barclays, and his pleasant dinner with them was one of the things in agreeable perspective during his absence. Jane was rather indifferent to his comings and goings; he was a little bit in her way at home; he loathed her bosom friend, Miss Serena, and kept out of her presence as much as possible, and, moreover, expressed to his sister openly his dislike of her associate. This was an unpardonable offence in Jane's eyes, and so she reconciled herself very easily to her brother's departures, and the rather that he always brought her home beautiful dresses of flowered linen cambric and superb Spanish fans; but not all the Cuban sweetmeats which he lavished on his mother ever completely made her smile on his travelling trunks.

It was in his absence that Mrs. Redmond, for the first time, perceived the great value of her son's affectionate devotion to her, dimly, to be sure, but this feeling increased amazingly the second winter he passed away. She remembered so many things he did for her and the house, the latter no unimportant matter; she missed his evenings at home. She had pleasant society, it was true, but no one compensated her for the loss of her Robert. Then there really was security in his presence. Mr. Redmond would have allowed the dwelling to be consumed by fire before his eyes, provided always the firemen did not enter his own bedchamber; and as to asking him to purchase any article for the house, none of its inmates, in their wildest flights of imagination, ever dreamed of such a thing. Sometimes a new servant, who had not been trained to the ways of the establishment, might venture upon such an act of pure folly. Mr. Redmond always responded by presenting his purse, never knowing what might be its contents, or troubling his head about the matter; which might be Peach Mountain coal, the thermometer at zero, or any thing else of equal household importance. Mrs. Redmond then learned, for the first time, that she had owed her greatly increased comforts to the excellent arrangements of her son, whose absence she was made to feel every hour in the day by their disappearance, and to comprehend, in all its domestic bearings and otherwise, her deprivation. This knowledge, however, influenced in no way her conduct; she felt and hourly lamented Robert's departure, but she aroused herself none the more for the consciousness of his loss; she still remained as irreclaimably torpid as ever, praying only that he might speedily return.

CHAPTER XI.

'My comfort is, that their manifest prejudice to my cause will render their judgment of less authority.'

DRYDEN.

'Now this would be perfectly delightful,' said Mr. Richard, one evening when they had all assembled in the library, 'if it were not for one exception.'

'And pray what is that?' inquired Mrs. Barclay.

'Oh! 'tis the wearisome prospect of beholding that ridiculous widow, Mrs. Fanny Ashley, sail into this pleasant family circle and destroy all my comfort. What a bore she is! I am astonished, Catherine, you can have any enjoyment in the society of that woman.'

'My dear Richard,' replied the lady, 'I must repeat, what I have already asserted numberless times, that Mrs. Ashley is my friend, and that I cannot permit her to be so disrespectfully mentioned, even by yourself, who are a privileged person in this house.'

'I assert nothing but the truth,' snarled Mr. Richard.

'I regret to hear you speak in this way of such an estimable person; Mrs. Ashley has ever been to me a true and firm friend in sickness and in sorrow, in weal and woe.'

'And pray what sorrows have you had, Mrs. Barclay?'

'Many; I was a sickly child, nervous and overwhelmed with all sorts of fantastic ideas, and she was my prop and support, she having more self-possession and courage than myself.'

'Boldness you mean,' interrupted Mr. Richard.

Mrs. Barclay proceeded without paying any attention to his remark, — 'and, consequently, she was an immense resource for me, protecting me against the attacks of my schoolmates, and helping me in my early lessons.'

'It must have been in your early lessons, Catherine.'

'She walked home with me to my own door every day, and from that time to this has steadfastly adhered to me and mine. Trust me, my brother, such friends are worth preserving and cherishing.'

'But you might have repaid her, my sister, in some other way than by enduring her frivolity every day. I should go mad to have Mrs. Ashley hanging about me, as she does here, and I wonder my brother John submits to it.'

'Brother John has a pleasant way, all his own, of submitting, and endures his wife's friends, and, moreover, likes the lady in question nearly as well as I do.'

'More fool he,' snarled Mr. Richard. 'What can he see in her?'

'Oh!' said Mr. Barclay, 'I find a great many good things to admire in Mrs. Fanny. Firstly, she loves my wife and children dearly; and secondly, she has a small corner in her heart for your humble servant, which is always a vast recommendation to me.'

'Nonsense, John, you're so soft-hearted, any silly woman can creep into your affections. I should like to see that widow try to do the like to me.'

Mr. Barclay opined that there was not much danger of the attempt being made.

'I detest widows,' resumed Mr. Richard. 'Now here is this woman who never put her nose out of doors in her late husband's reign; no sooner is he dead, than she's every where, — the eternal Mrs. Ashley!'

'Very good reason you have to say she never was seen in Mr. Ashley's lifetime,' resumed Mr. Barclay; 'he never permitted such doings; his was a reign of terror with a vengeance.'

'I wish most heartily that it had continued, John, and that his interesting relic had never enjoyed the chance of dispensing herself every where as she does.'

'But, my dear Richard,' said Mrs. Barclay, 'will you not please to spare my friend, if not for her sake, for mine?'

'I sha'nt promise at all,' replied he, 'for I can hardly refrain from telling the lady myself what I think of her. Even your idol, Madame de Staël, always made a point of informing her friends of their short-comings and defects, so what have you to say now?'

'That great and distinguished as she certainly was, she must have been a very disagreeable person.'

'So you never wish "to hint at faults and hesitate dislikes," my sister, though you are the only woman I ever saw who had so few to be knocked off.'

'I mean to reply, brother, by stating that it is an occupation in which I do not excel. Sometimes, with young people, I venture upon suggestions and reproofs, because I imagine I may do good, but with older ones I should despair of making important changes; and besides, I am inclined to believe there is quite as much good as evil in the world.'

'What Utopian nonsense! I tell you the world is a very bad place, and the people who cumber its surface worse still; and in America where the varnish of good manners is so often found wanting, all the wickedness seems to be duplicated.'

'I am a victim to good manners,' said Mrs. Barclay, 'and will not deny that they have immense weight with me, but if I am to choose, give me the rough bark that I may know what I have to fear. You cannot deny that Mrs. Ashley's manners are good, and I am resolved that you shall, in time, concede that her heart is equally so.'

'Mrs. Ashley's heart is nothing to me, Mrs. Barclay.'

'Take care, Dick,' laughingly cried Mr. Barclay, 'you may succumb yet to the fair widow's charms, and even wear her colors; stranger things have happened than that.'

'Never!' energetically replied Mr. Richard.

'Please, then,' said Mrs. Barclay, 'just be civil when you meet her, and not allow her to perceive how very disagreeable she is to you. I declare I think you evince a total absence of good taste in your very decided disapproval of my friend.'

'I can't help expressing my dislike, and so must talk. What is that woman dancing for at all the balls, and passing her life in dissipation?'

'How many balls do you suppose she numbers in a winter, Catherine?'

'And how many do you suppose she numbers in a season?' queried Mrs. Barclay. 'In her visiting list she may possibly count a dozen balls. Certainly parties are not so superabundant here; and why should she not dance, if she likes the amusement? It is surely extremely difficult for her to find any other kind of recreation.'

'You never dance,' said Mr. Richard.

'Simply because my husband and I have got into a very Darby and Joan way of living, in which we have been greatly encouraged, perhaps too much, by our kind friends, who are so much in the habit of finding us at home that, I really believe, they would now quite resent our absence from our own fireside. You well know how often they descant upon the inestimable advantage, as they are pleased to call it, of having a place to go to in the evening. It is very probable that, if they ceased to come here, we should be obliged to go out ourselves; 'tis dangerous for man to live alone, or woman either. Even Madame de Staël, whom you have just quoted, could not exist out of Paris. She vegetated in her father's dwelling, in the loveliest country in the world, with even the society of the Sismondis, Bonstettens, &c.; so you perceive, the most intellectual cannot get on always ruminating and reading, but require recreation. I forgot to add, by way of strengthening my argument, that this illustrious woman perfectly worshipped her father; and that his little chateau was always filled with her admirers, who were perpetually breathing incense at her shrine, and yet she sighed for a city life. Furthermore, many of these adorers followed her from Paris.'

'Oh! she was a woman, and a French one to boot,' said Mr. Richard.

'I shall not undertake to deny that; but just look at the famous men of your dear continent of Europe; however assiduously they may be occupied during the day, they always devote their evenings to relaxation. Madame de Sismondi arranged every morning some little amusement for her husband's evening; and that he enjoyed better health, and was brighter and more fitted for the labours of the ensuing day, there is no doubt. Tieck gave his evenings to society, and others too numerous to mention; and, to bring the question home to your own door, what would you yourself do without us?'

'Oh! I consider myself at home in your house.'

'But you do not live here, and, consequently, you go out when you visit us.'

At this juncture, just when Mr. Richard was nailed to the floor, the very lady in question entered, all smiles and good nature. Mr. Richard, much to the amusement of his nieces, shrugged his shoulders, and submitted to his hard destiny. Kate laughed outright.

'You seem,' said Mrs. Ashley, 'to be a very merry group, as usual;' and establishing herself comfortably in a lounge, she looked around upon her friends most affectionately.

'Yes,' said Grace, 'uncle Richard was railing at the world, in his old way, and we were all, as usual, amused.'

'I am extremely well enlightened touching Mr. Richard's railings,' said the pretty widow. 'He spares no one, and such general onslaughts do not materially disturb my equanimity.'

'I wish a little more attention were paid to my criticisms,' responded Mr. Richard; 'the world would get on much better.'

'The world treats me very graciously,' said Mrs. Ashley. 'I've no quarrel with it whatever. I should prefer a little more gaiety, to be sure, than is to be found here; fewer lectures and more balls' —

'Hear her,' said Mr. Richard, looking slyly at his sister.

'Yes!' said Mrs. Ashley, 'more balls and fewer lectures. Not that I distractedly admire dancing; but as nobody will give us any thing else, why, I would rather have that than nothing. I do sincerely wish we could have some other kind of amusement. I should like a little SOCIETY, — some place to go to, where I am not forced to dance and eat; where I could have a pleasant chat with agreeable men and women. I am not intellectual, and the word is worn threadbare here if I were; and not being learned, am not ashamed to confess that I like clever people's company better than my own. But, as it seems impossible for me to find this diurnally out of this house, and not having the face to come here forever, why my only alternative seems to be the balls, with, occasionally, a little music, to relieve the tedium of long, solitary winter evenings.'

'I'm quite sure,' said Mr. Richard, 'that if you had this very society for which you declare yourself to be hungering and thirsting, you would still frequent the balls in preference.'

'I will say nothing of the remarkable politeness you display, Mr. Richard, in openly contradicting a lady; but I think, my dear friends, your brother and sister, will confess that I am consistent, at least, and so proved to be, by actually haunting their dwelling, and am astonished they do not tire of me sadly.'

Upon this remark, both Mr. Barclay and his wife earnestly entreated Mrs. Ashley never to imagine she could, by any chance, come too often, and that they both were extremely flattered by the preference she had bestowed upon them. They were the more emphatic in their demonstrations, as they were frequently quite ashamed of Mr. Richard's rudeness to their amiable friend.

'Pray inform me, Mrs. Ashley,' said Mr. Richard, 'why you always mention the long word intellectual so disparagingly; what has it done to arouse your anger?'

'I have heard it all my life,' sighed the lady, very comically; 'my excellent mother held up for example before my eyes, for years and years, a certain young lady, who shall be nameless, as the most intellectual person in the world, entirely dependent on her own resources. This young person never wished to dance, never wished to dress, or to go to balls, talked chemistry, medicine, and all the 'ologies extant; and my mother, in order to improve my mind, so that I might attain the same climax of earthly distinction, forced me to frequent her society. Now, this same young lady rarely walked abroad, and, if she did, never entered a shop; had no taste for music, read Greek, and did not understand French, or draw — I beg her pardon — she squared circles, or fancied she did, and kept her hair in sad disorder. Now, I trust, I have given you my first impressions of intellectual women, and my succeeding observations have not dispelled them.'

'What became of her, — did she marry?' inquired Mr. Richard.

'Oh no! she could never spare time to be courted, or, perchance, there came no lover; she still rejoices solitarily in her intellectuality. You perceive the word grows longer with my story.'

'Courted!' sneered Mr. Richard. 'I'm amazed, Mrs. Ashley, you should use such a common word; it's not fit for good society.'

'And why not? Do you believe any woman was ever won, who was not courted? What system of tactics do you mean to adopt, Sir, when you venture upon the grand experiment of seeking a wife?'

'Heaven forbid!' interrupted the gentleman.

'I should like to know if you propose to throw down the handkerchief for some errant damsel to pick up. Mark my words, you will be obliged to act the offending word, as I believe you would never marry a woman "who could, unsought, be won."'

'Ah, now you adopt proper expressions, Mrs. Ashley.'

'Yes, Mr. Richard, just for the sake of not being tautological, nothing more. I prefer my first expression, and very intelligible it is to all ordinary persons.'

'You are very incorrigible to-night, Madam.'

When Mr. Richard got to Madam with Mrs. Ashley, he always buttoned up his coat, saluted the company, and departed, — which little circumstance, as usual, occurred.

When he was fairly gone — this being well understood by his shutting the hall door with a slightly perceptible bang — Mrs. Ashley said: 'What a pity it is that your brother, Mr. Barclay, is so unlike yourself. He has excellent qualities of head and heart, but seems to take a malicious pleasure in making himself appear entirely the reverse. Mr. Richard takes just as much time in endeavouring to persuade every body that he is the roughest and most disagreeable person in the known world, as other people do to attain the semblance of perfect excellence.'

'That is very true,' responded Mr. Barclay, 'I wish he could get a good wife to humanize him. Pray marry him yourself, and make us all happy.'

'There exists a most important obstacle; the gentleman will not ask me — and if he should, nothing on this nether globe would tempt me to accept him.'

'But think, dear Mrs. Ashley,' said Mr. Barclay, 'what a triumph it would be to make this surly bachelor succumb to your charms; what a blessed influence you might exercise over him; how amiable he would become, basking in the sunshine you would dispense, and how admirably you would elicit all my dear brother's hidden excellences.'

'I am not sufficiently philanthropic to engage in such a forlorn cause, and should prefer a mission to New Zealand to civilize tattooed chiefs.'

'Ah! now you are really too hard on my brother,' said Mr. Barclay. 'I love him dearly; he is the confidant of all my perplexities. I have endured, as yet, thank God for his mercies, few troubles. Richard is loyal, truthful and affectionate, full of generous impulses and deep sensibility. You may look incredulous,—I assure you he makes this roughness a mask to conceal these good qualities.'

'The Americans and English,' said Mrs. Ashley, 'are the only nations who affect these sort of peculiarities. On the continent of Europe every man tries to make the best of himself, and to present an agreeable front to the world. Why should any man wish to be considered a bear?'

'That is a question I do not pretend to answer,' replied Mr. Barclay; 'and I only know that my beloved brother certainly has a slight tendency to that kind of aspiration, and God knows I sincerely lament it. Catherine will tell you how kind he is to her children, how devoted to herself.'

'Indeed will I, with all my heart,' said Mrs. Barclay; 'and I must teach you to think better of Mr. Richard.'

The hour arriving for Mrs. Ashley's departure, she took a kind leave of her sincere friends.

CHAPTER XII.

'In short, by night, 'twas fits or fretting;
By day, 'twas gadding or coquetting,
Fond to be seen.'

GOLDSMITH.

MRS. TIDMARSH, the Barclays' second neighbour, was a widow with one daughter, Miss Serena Tidmarsh. This young lady, like most only daughters, had been allowed to have her own way all her life in every thing, right or wrong. Her father might have proved a salutary corrective, but he had been dead a long time. This state of things growing worse and worse, a species of domestic tyranny was enacted in the poor widow's establishment, quite fearful to behold, Mrs. Tidmarsh being, in truth, a sad victim to her child's whims and caprices, and they were legion. In the first place, their means of subsistence being very limited, Miss Serena wished them to seem boundless; and the consequences of this attempt at deception were so transparent, that though she fancied nobody saw her strivings and contrivings for what she called 'keeping up appearances,' there was not a doubt in the minds of all her acquaintances to the reality of their position, every one peering through the thin veil thrown over the futile attempts to vie with the Barclays, and other rich families.

Secondly, Miss Tidmarsh's temper, naturally not the most amiable, was not at all improved by this mean and petty warfare with her destiny; and her time, at home, was generally occupied in bewailing her miserable lot, and abroad in criticising all the world, and disseminating little and big bits of scandal. Nothing came amiss to her, every thing of that kind being acceptable. She began her day with wearisome and irritating expedients for making the worse appear the better, — turning and twisting, and making old lamps look like new; and then, with a troubled and anxious spirit, sallied forth, and wandered from house to house, in search of something disagreeable or unpleasant, and never desiring to hear the reverse. Being miserable herself, disappointed in her ambitious views, she wished to find every one else in the same category, and as far as imparting all manner of disagreeable and unpleasant truths went, she succeeded admirably.

Miss Serena's pet dislike was the Barclay family; she hated all its members. Doctor Johnson would have admired her, she was such a good hater. Their prosperity and popularity were actual crimes in her eyes. She never stopped to observe how rightfully they were gained; she was satisfied that they existed, and that sufficed to arouse all her malevolent feelings. She would have rejoiced to discover a flaw in Mr. Barclay's character or purse, both being, in her eyes equal. This was exceedingly ungrateful, for the very house in which she dwelt was rented to her by Mr. Barclay, at a mere nominal price, so small as to be hardly worth mentioning, in consequence of his friendly relations with her deceased father.

Georgy and Grace, Miss Serena declared, were not even pretty, and what people could see in them to rave about, as they did, she could not conceive; then Kate was a positive fright, and such a horrid romp! and even little Johnny was a very naughty, vicious boy. He had broken one of her windows with a ball, an unpardonable offence — she forgot to mention that he immediately sent a glazier to mend it. And all this was said in the lowest and softest tones imaginable, but was heard, nevertheless. Mr. Barclay, to be sure, had befriended her father when he was in trouble, but what of that! He had so much money that he would not really know what to do with it, if he did not give it away; and she could never forgive him for advising her deceased parent not to leave the mean little village where he had vegetated, and go to Boston to practise his profession, years before he did. And this was the truth — rather an uncommon circumstance in Miss Serena's narrations.

Mr. Tidmarsh, a country lawyer, respected for his honesty and probity, but possessing small reputation for talent, had been tormented by his wife into leaving his native place and trying his fortune in the city. He had thereby lost an honourable and sufficiently lucrative position in his own community and gained nothing by the exchange; this being precisely Mr. Barclay's prediction when he counselled him not to remove. Mr. Tidmarsh, on discovering the sad mistake he had made, would gladly have returned to his former residence, but this having become impracticable, he was just sinking under disappointed hopes and aspirations, when, by the death of a distant connection, he came into the possession of a meagre patrimony, which relieved his mind from all future anxiety respecting his wife and child. A short time after this event, he contracted a fever and followed his relative. Miss Serena had, in some undiscovered way, adopted very erroneous and extravagant impressions of her father's talents, which she also imagined she inherited, and having been informed that Mr. Barclay had not approved of his removal, and had objected to it many years before the experiment had been tried which proved so sad a failure, she resolved to believe, that if her lost parent had complied with her mother's wishes earlier, he would have won for himself fame and distinction. So, out of this coinage of her own fertile brain, she wove a very touching and pleasing romance.

Miss Tidmarsh had not been more favoured by nature than fortune; she was below the middle size, stooping excessively, which she fancied imparted a willowy movement to her person; was thin and bony; had very little hair, and extremely long scraggy arms ; her neck was singularly elongated, and her shoulders were always uncovered day and night, and were distinguished by large knobs on them which protruded from every dress she wore. These shoulders were always uncovered, summer and winter. To be sure, she had occasionally the pretension of wearing an areophane scarf, or an illusion tippet, but these articles of feminine attire always falling immediately off, the knobs remained visible in their pristine ugliness. These notable charms were always arrayed in an aqua-marine coloured silk dress, the shade never being changed ; this, the damsel's favourite hue, she constantly wore. It so happened that an invalid friend who was going to Paris for six weeks, had, in default of any one else, invited Miss Serena to accompany her, which invitation was rapturously accepted ; she went and returned in the appointed time, not having been permitted to remain longer. This unfortunate excursion filled up the measure of the lady's absurdities, she re-appearing with such a quantity of dippings and bobbings and duckings and French phrases as were perfectly unendurable ; the six weeks in Paris having turned her head completely. Henceforward she could no longer dine without soup, ate her meat *solus*, and changed her plate for every vegetable, and insisted upon her poor mother doing the same things, to whom it was a perfect martyrdom and a sad inconvenience, as they had but one maid of all work, and she was a dwarf and a cripple.

Miss Serena, however, was constant to her aqua-marine fancy, and this costume with newly acquired twitches, starts and contortions, which she imagined to be supremely Parisian, gave to beholders the impression that she was half frozen — so that in all the houses she frequented, on her arrival, 'Allow me to give you a shawl' were the first words addressed to her after the customary salutations had taken place. With her French mosaic she did not long annoy Mrs. Barclay, for that lady, addressing her in a language she herself spoke remarkably well, declared she thought they had much better commune together in a whole tongue than a half one, and Miss Serena, unable to comprehend the observation, stuttered and stammered, and was fain to confess she did not understand its purport, with a very annoyed and mortified air.

But where was Miss Serena's mother all this while? 'At home in her closet, at her studies,' so said her daughter, who affected abroad to idolize her. And so she was, having completed her eighteen hundred and thirty-third sonnet, had numbered it, and pasted it into an immense folio volume, by the side of its predecessors or ancestors — for some of them were very old indeed — and these, never to be too much admired effusions, were awaiting an amiable and accommodating publisher. Now, amiable and accommodating publishers exist, but — oh! that shocking but — they require money, especially when there is a chance that the critical and capricious reading world may not fall in love with their offerings; and Mrs. Tidmarsh had none, and they dared not venture upon the folio without the commodity, so the unfortunate poetess was as unhappy as her daughter.

These sonnets Mrs. Tidmarsh denominated occasional: if they were, she invented the occasions, their subjects being, The first Green Leaf in Spring, the last Yellow Leaf in Autumn, a Mouse running into a Hole, Ditto running out, A Fire-fly, the Belgian Giant, Mr. Barclay's Family, including Nursey Bristow, an important personage in it — Niagara, which she had never seen, and Mary Redmond's Kitten which she had, with hosts of others of equal originality and interest.

It was very cruel, it must be confessed, of the naughty avaricious publishers not to avail themselves of these hidden treasures, but thereby Mr. Barclay was preserved from an infliction — they being dedicated to him — Mrs. Tidmarsh, disagreeing with her only daughter, and worshipping his very shadow. When this important fact was communicated to him, he certainly did pray they might never see the light of day in a printed book, and there was consolation; for the enormous size of the folio precluded all idea of its being 'handed round' in manuscripts to admiring friends and neighbours.

Very few persons ever saw Mrs. Tidmarsh, her daughter keeping her concealed from the rude gaze of the public upon which she so liberally bestowed herself; and, as is often the case, the public, ungratefully regardless of Miss Serena's charms, desired excessively to see her mother; in fact, there was a great curiosity awakened to get a peep at the famous folio, eighteen hundred and thirty-three sonnets being rather a large number for even Boston — 'The American Athens.'

Pleasant Mrs. Ashley resolved she would be tantalized no longer with fabulous histories touching the renowned poetess, but would see her in spite of Miss Serena's precautions. So, one day she happened to meet her careering about in search of a fair, which was operating somewhere; and having perfidiously enlightened her by showing her the place, she left her, fully occupied with screaming dolls and emery strawberries, and repaired immediately to Mrs. Tidmarsh's house. Once there, she gave a sharp ring at the door, and authoritatively demanded of a dwarfish looking pattern of a serving-maid, who answered the bell in a most untidy state, to see her mistress.

'You mean Miss, ma'am?' was the answer, or question.

'Not at all, — your mistress.'

As the dwarf recognised but one in their household, she was rather puzzled, but, extremely awed by the fine lady, she mounted the stairs in great trepidation, and leaving the doors open behind her, Mrs. Ashley derived what benefit there was to be obtained from hearing all the conversation above.

'Oh! ma'am, ma'am, there's a great lady down stairs, with such a splendid velvet hat and cloak! wants to see you, yourself, ma'am.'

'No such thing, no such thing, 'tis my daughter,' replied rather a cracked voice.

'Yes ma'am, I'm all right, I am: she wants to see you and nobody else; nothing else will suit her, ma'am.'

'I can't believe it. Why didn't you say I was out?'

'Because you never are, ma'am.'

A pause ensued, and then Mrs. Ashley heard, 'Perhaps it's Ray's, Gray's and Fay's wife, the great publishers;' Mrs. Tidmarsh, for it was she, forgetting in the confusion of ideas, created by the uncommon circumstance of a visitor to herself, that she had bestowed but one spouse on the firm.

'Well, give me my new green bonnet, and bid her walk up, Sally.'

'So she wears green, as well as her daughter,' said Mrs. Ashley to herself.

A short interval ensued, and the little maid came hobbling down stairs and invited her to ascend. This sprite-like attendant mounted the flight precisely as do small dogs, stopping, turning and watching, and coming to a positive standstill on the landing. Mrs. Ashley found herself in a large chamber scrupulously neat and clean, with a ghost of a fire; it was a very cold day, and there seemed to be no occupant of this room. Looking carefully around, the attendant having disappeared, she presently discovered a sort of closet which had been partitioned off from some other room, as it had but half a window in it; and there sat Mrs. Tidmarsh, her feet immersed in a tub of hot water, the steam enveloping her person, with the famous folio on her knees, a pencil and paper in her hands, and two grass-green bonnets on her head.

Having been extremely agitated by the rumour of a visit to herself, and always wearing a bonnet of the above-described colour, the shade of her green being more matronly than her daughter's favourite tinge, she only thought of putting on the newest and best on such a momentous occasion, and left the old one in its accustomed place. As to her feet, being

10

greatly addicted to soaking them for hours, she had given them no attention whatever.

Mrs. Ashley was obliged to keep her risible muscles under proper subjection — no small task — and then to clear a place for herself and a chair in the closet, as the floor was completely covered a foot deep with little bits of paper, sad scrawls, which she conjectured to be rejected sonnets. She was then obliged to disabuse the lady of the impression that she was the better half of Ray's, Gray's and Fay's firm; and, moreover, to inform her that she had heard such wonderful accounts of herself and her poetical productions that she ardently desired to see them, and had ventured to take the liberty of calling, as she was acquainted with Miss Tidmarsh. She also assured the lady that she had frequently requested an introduction to her from her daughter, but having been unsuccessful in the application, had consequently resolved to effect it herself. Then, by the judicious application of a little well-turned flattery, she persuaded the poetess, nothing loath, to exhibit the folio; and, indeed, so completely fascinated her, that she promised to indite a sonnet to her eyebrow.

Mrs. Ashley, who was fearful Miss Serena might return, felt obliged to curtail her visit; and, with many compliments and thanks, presented her profound obeisances to Mrs. Tidmarsh, and departed quite enchanted with the success of her stolen interview.

Miss Serena was furious when she returned home, and her mother recounted to her the pleasant visit she had received. Mrs. Tidmarsh endeavoured to palliate the offence she had committed in entertaining a stranger, by saying it was only that silly, flirting widow, Mrs. Ashley.

'Silly and flirting if you will, mother,' gruffly responded Miss Serena, 'this ridiculous adventure will be all over Boston before night.' Fancy Miss Serena Tidmarsh, the gentle, delicate-voiced creature! speaking to her adored mother gruffly!

And Mrs. Ashley, who quite piqued herself upon the adroitness with which she had executed her project, certainly did mention it to Mrs. Barclay and her daughters, and just a few, very few other friends, who were immensely amused at her adventure.

CHAPTER XIII.

> 'The world is bright before thee,
> Its summer flowers are thine,
> Its calm blue sky is o'er thee,
> Thy bosom pleasure's shrine.'
>
> HALLECK.

JOHNNY BARCLAY was an only son, a very perilous position for the boy, but his father had resolved that his child should prove an exception to the inevitable rule of 'sole heirs' being spoiled by indulgence, and he very early began to affect a very strict discipline with him. As soon as Johnny evinced the vagrant propensities for which urchins are remarkable, and preferred decidedly the streets to a large and commodious court-yard with plenty of play-ground, Mr. Barclay dispatched him into the country to an excellent boarding-school. At first, the boy was inconsolable, for he was the youngest in the establishment, and on his return home, in the vacation, he vowed to the Dolly, his boon companion and friend, that he would never return. But this high resolve proving abortive, Johnny retraced his steps very sadly indeed, to what he was pleased to call his purgatory.

The second leave of absence found the schoolboy in much better spirits, and quite well contented. The Dolly, inquiring the cause of this sudden revolution in his sentiments touching his seat of learning, was thus enlightened. 'Why you must know, my sister, that when I first went to Mr. Sterling's school I was the smallest and youngest boy there; now, any one, with common sense, would suppose I should have been coaxed and petted and treated kindly ; not a bit ; — I got nothing but cuffs and kicks, and, what was worse than all, little, sharp, short pinches, exactly as if my skin had been caught up with pincers, only they wern't hot; they were the very worst things I had to bear, I can tell you. Well, that whole term I was so miserable I had a good mind to run away, — not home, — for I was afraid to do that; but any where ; I thought of going to sea before the mast; that's what almost all the boys talk about and threaten to do when they're mad with the masters or each other; there's no end to their savage threats.'

'What would my father have done, Johnny, if you had run away, you naughty, naughty boy, to dare to think of such a thing ?'

'Well, well, I can't help that now, you know, for I didn't do it, but I certainly should, as sure as a gun, if something else hadn't happened; why, I was pinched black and blue all over, and sometimes could hardly move for the horrid pain, and couldn't sleep of nights.'

'But why didn't you give the pinches back again, Johnny ? I should have done so in your place, and with compound interest too.'

'Oh I tried, but it was the big boys that pinched. I tried hard to fight them, one and all, and they pinched worse and worse, they said I showed such a right plucky spirit. Well, the next term was awful, and I had just made up my mighty mind to run away, any where, I didn't care where, when Joe Staples—you know him—came tearing along, and tossing up his cap in the air; he was the next oldest boy to me in the school and suffered some, I can tell you, Dolly — Well ! he came and screamed and shouted, " Glorious news ! glorious news for you, Johnny Barclay ! the two Baileys are coming." " What," I screamed, " you don't say so ! well, then I won't run away to sea as a cabin-boy, that's certain." " Why, you don't mean to tell me you thought you would," says Joe. " Oh ! yes, I'd settled the very day, and saved up all my money." "Why, how much have you got?" says he. "A dollar!" "Then give me half for the good news, you little villain," says he. "Well, will you believe it, Dolly, I gave him the whole, for, you know, that was glorious news! capital news! indeed."

'I don't understand at all what you mean, Johnny.'

'Oh, how confoundedly slow you are, Dolly; don't you see, the two Baileys were very small boys, and MY TURN had come, and for every blow, cuff, kick and pinch I ever had, I gave them two — and sometimes three?' said Johnny, as if reflectively making up the sum total in his own mind.

'Oh, Johnny, Johnny, what a sad, bad boy you are! how could you be so cruel, when you knew so well how hard the cuffs, kicks and pinches were to bear?'

'Fiddle-de-dee, Dolly, it was just for that reason that I punished the Baileys, and then if I hadn't done it, somebody else would have pommelled them to death; but, as it was, the big boys gave me my chance, they'd had theirs, and I thought they were proper good fellows for doing so.'

These confidential communications were always made in the nursery, a large, commodious and pleasant room, the windows of which looked down upon the court-yard, and in which the sun shone ever brightly. The room was filled with all sorts of playthings in cabinets and cupboards and shelves, the discarded household gods of Georgiana and Grace Barclay having descended to their sister, who would have shortly demolished them, but for the presiding genius of this pleasant resort, Nursey Bristow. This dear old woman was a treasure indeed; she had lived with Mrs. Barclay from the day of her marriage, and, being a widow and childless, had bestowed all her affections upon the children who were confided to her care, and verily thought them nature's most perfect handiwork. Georgy and Gracy were very much attached to this invaluable person, but having been disfranchised, they had another snug retreat in a little room called their study, so the nursery's sole tenant was the Dolly. In the vacations there might be seen Johnny and his sister holding close and earnest consultations, touching all manner of projects and plans for amusements, none of them of a very feminine character, and Nursey in her low rocking-chair with the cleanest of cap and apron, apparently mending stockings, but looking over her spectacles at her two darlings. It was true, it must be confessed, that she did not altogether approve of all the proceedings, they being, in many respects, exceedingly antagonistic to her preconceived ideas of perfect propriety. 'But then poor Johnny, who was so cruelly sent away to that horrid school all the time, ought to be gratified when he *was* at home;' and she had said this so many times that Johnny felt he was licensed to do exactly as he pleased during his holidays. In Nursey's opinion, the Dolly fully coincided; what her own peculiar tastes had to do with her views she did not stop to reflect.

Every finale of term-time brought Johnny home, fraught with some grand project; as he grew older, theatricals were dominant. And no one can imagine the strivings and contrivings of his sister associate to carry out all the plans for curtains, scenery, footlights and orchestra; nobody could do any thing without the Dolly. It was true she did not perform with the boys, for she was *the* audience, no other person being allowed to be present, — but she certainly was not deceived by illusions and stage effect, as she produced all there was, herself. The girl's greatest trouble arose, however, from the ambitious aspirations of her dramatic corps. They would not rest contented with proverbs and light farces, but sighed after the immortal Shakspeare, and nothing short of Lear satisfied them. She consoled herself, for her lack of influence in diverting their views into other channels, with the certainty that the tragedy was sure to become a farce, and so it did; the passions being torn to shivers in the most orthodox manner. The orchestra consisted of a guitar, played by the Dolly, who also painted the scenery and attired the actors in her own garments when they were required. All this labour she bore with unexampled patience, as well as the rehearsals, where the awkwardness of some, and the want of memory of others 'was enough,' as she declared, 'to try the patience of Job himself.' Theatricals had a great vogue for a long time, and the sister had made grand preparations for the arrival of her brother,—when lo! a change had come over the spirit of his dream; histrionics no longer ruled the hour, but martial ardour reigned in their stead.

Johnny Barclay would be nothing but a soldier. He got up a company, (he called it a regiment,) and from actors the Dolly was elevated to drilling, (the old troupe be it understood,) the youth of her day for defenders of their country's rights—which were not attacked at all. A great mortification awaited her; she knew that her brother had been the principal mover in this military excitement, that he had supplied the greater part of the funds for the vast expenditure consequent upon it; he had given all his own pocket money, and—hers; and what was her annoyance and disgust when, instead of being commander-in-chief of the forces, he would persist in being, notwithstanding all her prayers and entreaties, a drummer! This was positively shocking, outrageous, she declared. 'Johnny had no ambition! he would never make any thing in this world!' But nothing surpassed the drummer's amazement at his sister's anger—'Why, what did I get up the regiment for,' asked he, 'but to make all the noise I could in it? How ridiculous and silly girls are; what absurd creatures!' But, as the pair could not exist apart, they arranged their disagreement amicably, and the Dolly drilled the regiment in the nursery first, and afterwards looked down upon her soldiers from its windows, when they marched and countermarched in the court-yard. Now this company was, or appeared to be, devoted heart and soul to the young girl, who ministered to their gratification so unceasingly. They made Russian mountains and snowy fortifications for her in the winter, and capital slides; and in summer climbed the solitary pear-tree in the court-yard and gathered its ripening fruits. They constantly consulted her upon all occasions, and partook of many nice feasts in the nursery, prepared by Nursey Bristow and their hostess.

The Dolly conceived the idea of presenting to her friends a stand of colours, and upon them she worked untiringly. She had, from her earliest days, possessed an uncommon talent for drawing, and it had been assiduously cultivated; so she executed very many beautiful designs upon the white silk, and plentifully besprinkled the standards with gold leaf and spangles, and altogether produced a magnificent effect in the eyes of Nursey and the soldiers, who watched her operations with intense delight. The colours completed, the day of 'a grand dinner party,' as Nursey called it, was selected for the presentation, as all the family would then be engaged, and the thing might be done without observation; for the Dolly, having prepared a speech for the occasion, was unwilling that any one should hear it but the parties interested. The boys, in the interim, had arranged, under the pear-tree, then in full bloom, a staging which was covered over with variegated horse-blankets from the stable, and some evergreens and flowers, and the effect produced was quite captivating.

Just as the guests at Mr. Barclay's, on the appointed day, had seated themselves at table and were commencing their repast, the Dolly sallied forth from the nursery, carrying in triumph her colours. She was received with shouts of applause by the soldiery, and, as she had made quite an elaborate toilette for the occasion, she really presented a most effective appearance, the costume being imitated from a French print of the Goddess of Liberty, the petticoats elongated. She walked in a stately manner to the pear-tree, and ascending a small flight of steps, mounted the platform prepared for her. The speech was rapturously received, and, after a short pause, she commenced Drake's address to the American flag, and was getting on famously, to the united satisfaction of herself and the military, when, melancholy to relate, the platform gave way, and the inspired declaimer found herself suddenly immersed to the chin in cold water. It transpired that the youthful soldiery might be very good military men, but were not certainly architects, for they had raised their superstructure upon very frail materials, and the Dolly had really and truly fallen into a water-butt. The courageous girl, nothing daunted, waved her colours and finished her poem ; but it was not fated to be heard, for the soldiery, totally unmindful of all the gratitude they owed to their best friend, rent the air with shouts of laughter, and fairly finished by rolling on the ground.

Nursey Bristow, who had been watching from the windows of her retreat this 'grand presentation,' immediately called some of the women-servants, and rescued her darling from her watery prison-house, who forthwith flew up stairs, dripping like a naid. She was disrobed, the bed warmed,— Nursey had great faith in warming-pans, — and then immediately placed therein.

The Dolly heeded, not in the least, her discomfiture ; she rather liked, what she called, the fun of the thing, but she was shocked inexpressibly at the risibility of the soldiery. 'What an ungrateful world is this, Nursey!' sighed she. 'It is sad to think of it, after all the pains I have taken with those good-for-nothing boys, for years ; not one of them ever came to my rescue, but, on the contrary, rolled on the ground, laughing! — Oh! I am disgusted with their proceedings, Nursey dear, and mark my words, from this day henceforth, I will have nothing to do with them, — nothing! Oh! the ingratitude of the world, the in-grat-i-tude!' and the Dolly was soundly asleep.

Nursey looked affectionately upon her darling, hoping and praying she would not catch a cold ; and nothing did the young lady, disgusted with the world, catch, but a nap which lasted unbroken until the next morning.

With the next day came a heavy reckoning for the delinquents, for the Dolly called all the military together, and took, as she said, an eternal farewell of them. She reproached them for their ill manners and their ingratitude, and told them she hoped they would miss her forever. The military were completely overwhelmed with this unexpected blow, and pleaded for mercy in most abject terms, but the young damsel was inexorable.

As soon as they had departed, the Dolly said, 'Now, Nursey, I intend to turn over a new page in my life. I play no longer with boys; they are a heartless and unfeeling set, and I have done with them. I am constantly told that I am an untameable romp; that may be true, but I've finished my games with the boys. Only think, Nursey, I'm fifteen next month, — it's quite time, you'll allow.'

And the Dolly kept her word sacredly. Deputation upon deputation waited upon her, and begged her to reconsider her promise, unavailingly. She was the first person to relate her ridiculous misadventure, and, accordingly, made an excellent sketch of it, and presented it to the family at dinner, that same day, and related the occurrence with great spirit, and also her intention of abandoning her old friends. The latter part of her communication was received with great commendation by all but Johnny, who was very unhappy on the occasion.

> 'A change had o'er his spirit come,
> And he was sad indeed.'

CHAPTER XIV.

'There is something very mortifying to pass one's life in a struggle to make way in a particular path, and not to believe that one neither does, nor can succeed or advance in it.'

AUTOBIOGRAPHY OF SIR EGERTON BRYDGES.

THE Barclays received the pleasing intelligence of the arrival in America of a family in which they felt a great interest, and from which they had been long separated. Mr. Augustus Gordon had lived with his wife and children in Europe, many years in diplomatic situations, and by some remarkably strange accident was permitted to retain them in the various changes of administration, which, in the interim, had occurred; and he certainly never ceased speculating upon this anomaly in his career, and never fully comprehended it. Some one suggested to him the probability that his government had forgotten him.

At last, came the hour of his recall, and he was replaced by another minister. He had fortunately possessed a small patrimony, or he would have revisited his native land a beggar. His salary having been entirely insufficient for the support of a wife and family, he had consequently encroached upon his own small fortune, and thus he found himself without any advancement in his profession — a legal one — and with limited means, thrown upon the wide world once more.

It is a subject for grave speculation for all travelled Americans, how men can be found willing to accept these diplomatic missions. In many cases, it may arise from sheer ignorance of what they will be obliged to endure on reaching their destination. Seduced by the outfit, which is a mere trifle, they find the salary, on their arrival, just covers their house-rent in the great cities of Europe — if house they have — and their lives are passed in petty mortifications and annoyances. And these are duplicated if men carry their wives with them; there being no republican simplicity of attire for women in courts, they must dress, and dress well, or stay at home, which many of them do. There is no reason why America should not be properly represented at her embassys, as well as other nations, and there is nothing to be done but to increase the salaries of her Ministers — and teach them French.

The Gordons had won their way along — he with great learning and talent, she with tact and good-nature — and they had been obliged to make sad inroads into their own small property, and had only, after this sacrifice, lived very quietly indeed. They felt the necessity of economizing in their situation much more than they would otherwise have done, as it prevented their offering to their countrymen hospitalities which would have very much gladdened both parties. Indeed, Mr. Gordon often asserted that he, in his long residence abroad, had never seen one American, who, when he beheld the state of things, so mean and denuded, contrasted with that of other powers, did not loudly declare it must be changed, but opined he forgot all about it on his return home.

When the Gordons revisited their country, they entered their oldest son at the law school, and, as Mr. Gordon intended publishing an important legal work, he thought they should find Cambridge an agreeable residence, and so they did. There is a remarkable equality and evenness in the condition of all the society connected with the university, which completely extinguishes all striving for what is perpetually in the mouths of our people — style and fashion — these two unattainable things being scrambled for by one part of our population and railed against by the other. The latter raise a great outcry and opposition, and are asked by those, who really have seen the things, where they are to be found. To those who desire information pleasantly conveyed, the revelations of that most amiable and excellent deceased pastor, Mr. Colman, in his valuable work, will truthfully and fairly exhibit what is meant by these two sadly misapplied words.• The all-important basis of style and fashion being service, and we having none, as such, it necessarily follows that the pinchbeck substituted is pinchbeck indeed, and the alarmists, who deplore its real presence in our midst, are wofully mistaken. There is something very attractive in the transplantation of the simple-hearted clergyman, from his own solid and substantial mode of life, which is, as yet, thank Heaven, dominant in Massachusetts, to the lordly palaces and castellated halls of England; and the glowing pictures he has given us of what he saw, are sketched with great exactitude. The book might be made of incalculable advantage in this country, and if read aright, would teach us the extreme folly of aping ducal establishments, with sixty real servants, in houses of twenty-five feet front, and six 'help.' We are indisputably a discontented, aspiring race, and if we adopted some less ambitious standard in our own households than that of the nobility of proud Albion with their princely fortunes, we should become, in process of time, both wiser and happier. England, with her long line of ancestry, her wealth and entailed estates, does the thing, and does it gloriously: whereas, our prominent short-comings are both absurd and ridiculous. Let every true-hearted American woman look to this, and govern herself accordingly; let her resist all innovations which cannot consistently be carried out; let the means and end agree, and she will do more good in her day and generation than she will ever effect by aspiring to command ships of war, and lifting up her small and weak voice in the Senate of these United States.

The Gordons, fresh from the splendour and magnificence of foreign courts, preferred the quiet simplicity of a Cambridge life to the more pretentious and hurried one of a city. They had a fellow-feeling for the professors of the University, whom they consider to be as badly paid as they themselves had been, their salaries being as objectionably small. There are collected together in Harvard University, a band of men, remarkable for their various accomplishments and great attainments, but in nothing more than their spirited devotion to their Alma Mater; and, during the Gordons' stay in Cambridge, several of these professors were offered double their salaries and houses annexed, if they would leave for other seats of learning, and refused. Of all the noble endowments made to the oldest institution in America, nothing has been given for the enlargement of the incomes of men who devote their energies and lives to it with such enthusiastic devotion. They should certainly be absolved from all the petty annoyances attendant upon small and insufficient means.

Much of the pleasure incidental to a Cambridge residence depends upon those who reign in the Presidential mansion; and the Gordons were peculiarly fortunate in finding a large family, whose cultivated tastes, refined habits of thought and feeling, combined with purity of heart and charm of manner, quite captivated them.

Mrs. Gordon was, at first, kept in constant commotion by the incomings and outgoings of the 'help.' She behaved admirably; but having been exempted for so many years from these annoyances, she resolved to take high ground when they endeavoured to intimidate her by threats of immediate departure, and dismiss them on the instant. This, in the end, proved quite effectual. The result of her experiences in this chapter of her life was sufficiently characteristic to be narrated.

Mrs. Gordon having been recommended by her friends not to employ, in any event, an Irish servant, she accordingly inclining to her own people, determined to engage only American 'help;' and as she had returned home with an earnest desire never to eat another 'made dish,' she imagined she might probably discover a good plain cook. Her first essay commenced with a young lady, who sentimentally informed her that 'the dream of her life was the possession of a turtle-shell comb, a linen cambric collar, and, may be, a pair of long kid gloves!' What the damsel required the comb for, Mrs. Gordon could not well comprehend, seeing that her head was nearly bald. Three days after her advent, she rushed into the library, where Mrs. Gordon was sitting absorbed in a new book, and most summarily commanded her to dismiss her waiter, James, declaring indignantly, that 'he had been too sweet upon her.' On being asked in what way, she replied, he had dared to call her 'My dear!' She was informed she might immediately depart.

The next venture, in nearly the same space of time, perpetrated a similar act, with this difference — the man James was declared, in the most violent language, to be the 'crossest wretch ever seen!' She was invited to follow her culinary predecessor. The third on the list entered the house, retired to her bed, and remained two consecutive days in an apparently felicitous snooze. The fourth quarrelled with all and several, excepting the man James, whom she rather patronized, but he abhorred her. The fifth was extremely disgusted that the family should speak any English, she vowing 'the only recommendation it had in her eyes,' (she meant ears,) 'was the hope that she might catch from it the French language,' she having preparatorily armed herself with a remarkable thin pamphlet, purporting to teach that pleasant tongue in six lessons, without fail. The sixth came cityward for sea air, lobsters and clams; and the seventh informed Mrs. Gordon 'that, for a woman who pretended to have seen furrin parts, she liked remarkably plain fare.' Now, not one of these errant misses had entered the house with the remotest idea of obeying its mistress in any one thing, or remaining a moment beyond her own capricious will, — kitchen rangers all!

There is something so totally repugnant to all service in the American breast, that it is perfectly wonderful our people ever attempt such an obnoxious operation. In a country where every man is looking forward to being President of the United States, and every woman may be his wife, it is wholly impossible for service, in any liberal acceptation of the term, to exist; and whatever doubts Mrs. Gordon might have had on the subject were summarily dispelled by dire experience.

It is gravely asserted, that the organ of reverence is absent, on leave, in American heads; and truly, it was nowhere to be found in the above-described New England non-serving company.

All things come to an end in the magical number seven; so by the time Mrs. Gordon's list had reached this numeral, the neck of her native Americanism was fairly broken, and she then presented herself a holocaust to the tender mercies of the exiles from that gem of the sea, the Emerald isle, and certainly never regretted the measure. From that benign period she enjoyed a quiet, well-ordered household, nay, even more, an attached and devoted one, and could never be induced to confess she repented her abandonment of her own people — as 'help.'

There is a dreamy sort of existence attending all college life; and the environs of 'halls,' cloistered or not, are redolent of repose and quiet. Mrs. Gordon often marvelled at the absence of the fine manly sports, games and exercises she had beheld in other climes, when she saw the numerous students taking only short and often solitary walks, looking as if they were 'dragging their slow lengths along,' from a sense of the imperative necessity of some sort of exercise, or an apology for it, rather than its actual enjoyment. She renewed her intimacy with the Barclays; and, entering into it with great zest, derived much pleasure from her occasional visits to Boston and their agreeable home, where a warm welcome ever awaited her, their manner of living being very congenial to her tastes and views. She vainly sought in other houses for the pleasant evenings of the continent, where, without form and ceremony, friends meet and partake of social interchange of feeling and sentiment, and love each other the better for it. She regretted this state of things all the more that her own limited means would not admit of the expenses attendant on grand entertainments; and she perceived that she should not be able to dispense any hospitality whatever, if she did not, on her return to Boston, exercise more moral courage than she was aware of possessing.

CHAPTER XV.

'In faith and hope the world will disagree,
But all mankind's concern is charity.'

POPE.

'I SAW this morning,' said Mr. Richard Barclay, 'an immense quantity of barrels of flour, sugar and coffee, with many boxes of tea and other things, tumbled into your cellar, brother John. Are you proposing to open a grocery shop?'

This question was asked one day, just about the blessed Christmas and Thanksgiving time. Mr. Barclay, looking slily at his wife, replied, 'Not exactly, Richard; at least, there will be no pay. Catherine has a bad way of never sending any beggar from the door; and as she never gives money, I think buying these staple commodities by the wholesale decidedly the most economical plan.'

'Nonsense!' replied Mr. Richard; 'there can be no worse way adopted of dispensing charity than giving to street-beggars; 'tis against all rules. I am astonished, Mrs. Barclay, that a woman of your sense should' —

'Please stop,' interrupted the lady addressed. 'Whenever you commence a speech to me, brother Richard, with that prescribed formula, I am always perfectly sure you think me remarkably silly; so I will e'en save you the trouble of pronouncing such a verdict, and confess myself guilty, to satisfy you!'

'All political economy condemns totally such weak proceedings, my sister.'

'My head, brother, has never been able to receive these dicta; you well know I never had any capacity for abstruse sciences, and I sum up in one word political economy, and call it *hard-heartedness.*'

'Hear her, John, I pray.'

'Yes, I hear very well,' answered Mr. Barclay; 'but when you get a wife, Dick, you will find it much better to let her have her own way in some things.'

'My wife shall never give to street-beggars, John.'

'When shall we see this rara avis, uncle?' queried Grace.

'Your wife, Richard, will then never be wrong,' said Mrs. Barclay, 'as those who never give can never be deceived. Now I would much prefer to be cheated twenty times by false pretences, than lose the chance of serving one really distressed person, deserving or not. I very well comprehend that this is against all that is laid down in the books, but the heart is often as good a guide as the lucubrations of frigid reasoners. My kind husband, at least, throws no obstacles in my way. I was brought up to give; my mother did so before me.'

'A bad bringing up,' said Mr. Richard.

'Of which your brother has enjoyed all the disadvantages, just as our people say they enjoy a *bad state of health.*'

'Women never know how to reason,' said uncle Richard, 'and never will.'

'Not even your wife, that is to be?' said the Dolly.

'Let her open her lips if she dare,' said he.

'I'll teach her,' said Georgy.

Uncle Richard held up a threatening finger or two.

'I confess,' resumed Mrs. Barclay, 'that my deepest sympathies are not aroused for merely the poorly poor; they incline vastly towards the class that has seen better days. Physical sufferings, that can be relieved with a bit of bread, have not the same weight with me as moral ones; and all my exertions are made for the poverty that hides its abashed head. The head that was once uplifted as high as any in the land, now fallen by the adverse fortunes of commercial ventures, fills my heart with compassion, and many a one there is. My life has not yet reached its common verge, and yet what changes have I not seen!'

'Well,' said Mr. Barclay, 'I think it always best to leave the hearts to the women; they will have them, whether we will or no; and I am not quite sure that we are any the better for being so scientific in our charitable operations, or so overwise in our generation.'

'The best method is, for all people who have tender consciences, to follow out their own devices,' said Mrs. Barclay. 'Those who have not, may require "flappers," and societies are excellently well adapted for them. Many would do nothing if they could not associate themselves with others for benevolent purposes; the thing is, to do good. We hold various ideas on this subject; but if we all resolve to do our work upon earth well, it does not much signify *how*. It is much the same with different sects and religious creeds; faith and works lead to the same haven at last, however we may disagree as to the roads.'

This was a season of great and pure enjoyment to the young people of this family. They were the almoners, and were daily packed by their mother in a hackney coach, — she would not permit her own carriage to be used, lest it might be known, — and with Nursey Bristow, carried all manner of delicacies and substantial comforts belonging to this blessed season to the very quarters where her interests were centred. They always left the vehicle at some distance from the house, and creeping quietly along, with their baskets and packages, just pushed them in at the doors and instantly retreated. Nothing could exceed the dexterity with which they executed their missions, and certainly nothing surpassed the happiness they enjoyed, except that which they imparted. Many in this way received relief, who would not for worlds have had the fact known, but who, nevertheless, were intensely grateful. The certainty of possessing unknown friends is a source of great happiness and contentment to broken fortunes and spirits preserving self-respect under adverse circumstances.

Mrs. Barclay diverted uncle Richard from his projected controversy by informing him of the (to her) joyful intelligence, that the Gordons were about to leave Cambridge and to settle in Boston, and had taken a house that very day in her own neighbourhood. To this Mr. Richard assented with all his heart. He had a great admiration for Mrs. Gordon, and her husband was an old friend of his; so the arrangement pleased him exceedingly.

A few weeks saw that family comfortably installed in a pretty dwelling, not very large, but filled with works of art and taste, collected during a long residence in foreign lands. Mrs. Barclay claimed Clara Gordon, her friend's only daughter, as her guest during the transition state, and would gladly have had all the members of the family, but Mr. and Mrs. Gordon could not consent to such an invasion.

Clara they found a charming inmate, remarkably well educated and very accomplished — enthusiastic and warm-hearted. The demonstrations of her affections were very decided, and seemed almost unreal, from their ardent character; but were notwithstanding perfectly sincere and constant. The younger members of the family were devoted to her, and on leaving them she expressed her warmest acknowledgments for the hospitality and kindness she had received. Mrs. Gordon was soon visited by all the notabilities of the city, and invited to many balls and a few dinners.

To the latter she was happy to go, but the former rather militated against all her preconceived ideas of *pleasure.* Still, as she had lived long abroad, and had there contracted fixed opinions, she was not willing that her daughter should make her entrance into society without the protection of her mother, and, consequently, resolved to accompany her. She had beheld with amazement, that none of her own contemporaries ever went into the gay world with their daughters, and had condemned their practice of remaining at home. She had remonstrated, and had been told that they were not even *invited*. To be sure, her friends informed her she was asked because she had declared she would not allow Clara to go without her, and that a fashion existed from which there was hardly any deviation, of leaving out the mothers who had daughters, and asking the women who had none — an even distribution of party favours, which Mrs. Gordon had great difficulty in comprehending. Indeed, she hardly knew what to make of such a state of things. And truly her first ball was melancholy enough. About half a dozen women with the hostess, composed the matrons ; the rest of the immense crowd were children — or what she had always considered as such in Europe — half a dozen old bachelors, who liked to be seen in youthful society, and hardly any other men ; of boys, there was no end. As she was beautifully dressed in her foreign gear, and, moreover, extremely animated, an amiable youth, the son of one of her friends, invited her to dance. She answered this request by saying, 'My dear, if you will find a partner for your mother, I will accept your invitation ;' and, as she laid a peculiar emphasis on the affectionate part of the speech, he retired in disgust.

Meanwhile, Clara, a very pretty and engaging girl, simply attired, attracted no attention whatever, and with a number of poor young creatures, passed the evening in wishing — as she could not dance — that she might be at home. Clara was not at all mortified at this neglect, for she imagined that she was not asked to dance because she was not known, but her mother, with her keen perception, discerned the cause immediately. Clara had been educated to follow, and not to lead. She was timid and retiring in her manners amongst strangers, and, therefore, had no decided air, and was thought quite a failure by the leaders of the youthful *ton* ; especially so when the great advantages she had enjoyed were summed up. To be sure, the few ladies present thought Clara Gordon charming, and Mrs. Ashley determined to present some of her young friends to her; but these minute gentlemen afterwards declared that *she had no conversation*, which was, assuredly, most true as far as they were concerned, being entirely ignorant of the names and qualities of the guests.

At last the good-natured and indefatigable widow discovered an 'American Methusaleh' of seven-and-twenty, who, having just returned from Europe, and, of course, not wishing to dance, was willing to be presented to a young lady who had travelled; so Clara had an escort to supper, and shortly after returned home, declaring the only pleasant thing to herself respecting the ball was its short duration.

'Why, mother,' said she, 'we went at ten and are at home at twelve, and yet the whole thing seemed infinitely longer to me than the *fêtes* in Europe, where I have remained eight hours and more.'

'If the evening seemed long to you, it was never-ending to me,' replied Mrs. Gordon. 'I really and truly believe that we women were as weary of the sight of each other as we could possibly be, for we soon exhausted all our small talk, and the noise of too much music in not over-large rooms drowned every thing like conversation.'

'How I wish I could never go again,' said Clara.

'But you must, my dear daughter, and try to become acquainted with the young people with whom you are to pass your life.'

'They will never care for me,' said the girl. 'They seem to be broken up into sets and only talk to each other, and I — having no subjects in common with them — shall never get on.'

'You must make the effort, nevertheless, my dear child.'

'I will do as you bid me, mother; and now, good-night, for I am half asleep.'

Mrs. Gordon communed with herself long after her child was gone: she thought that, perhaps, it would have been better if she had been educated in her own land; but, then, she said to herself, 'I could never have borne to see my daughter a leader of fashion before she was nineteen, exhausting life ere it had begun, enjoying no childhood, and losing the best hours of her existence in profitless amusements. Now she is a tolerably good scholar, possesses a few accomplishments, and what is better than all beside, is docile, obedient, and well-mannered. I will not then complain, but endeavour to reconcile her to what, from my experience of to-night, seems to be her destiny here — unrecognised good qualities. And so Mrs. Gordon, looking upon herself very much in the light of a martyr, resolved to accompany her daughter into the picayune world of fashion. The next evening she went to Mrs. Barclay's with Clara. Soon after their entrance, Grace asked the young lady how she had been pleased at the ball.

'Not at all,' was the reply.

'How very extraordinary,' exclaimed Gracy, 'I thought every body enjoyed balls immensely.'

'I certainly did not, for I knew no one, and, as all the company, which was almost entirely composed of extremely young people, took very little note of me, I had rather a dull evening, and enjoy myself much more here. My mother wishes me to go into society, that I may not seem alone in my native city; but I hope she will soon change her mind on this subject, and as I know she is sacrificing herself to me, the sooner she does so, the better.

Kate, who heard these remarks, cried, 'What, not enjoy a ball! I could dance forever from morning till night and never tire of the delightful amusement. That comes of being educated abroad: you are spoiled for every thing in your own country.'

'Not at all,' replied Clara, 'I went out into society the winter before my return home, for the first time, but I always sat at my mother's side. She was the point of attraction; she was the belle — if you will. The men only danced with me because they wished to please her; they never talked with me; they looked upon me as a little bread-and-butter girl, and I was all the time really pining to get home, where I heard the girls had so much liberty and such fun. You know I never was permitted even to walk out alone in Europe — my maid always accompanied me; that at least I can do here, and enjoy it immensely. But, it seems, that if there I was too young, here I am too old.'

'Well,' said Kate, 'you've made out a pretty good case, but it won't deter me from accepting every invitation I can procure. Gracy won't go into society because Georgy does not, and says she can have no pleasure independent of her sister. They ought to have been twins; it was a great mistake, but just let me get a chance, and my mother's situation as a chaperone will be no sinecure, I can tell you — I shall lead her such a gay life, a perfect fandango!'

'I don't think Mrs. Barclay will consider it in the same light,' said Clara, 'if she is not to enjoy herself any more than my mother did at Mrs. Lorimer's ball. I only wonder why they called it hers, for she did not seem to have had a chance to invite more than a dozen of her own friends and contemporaries, and such an immense crowd too.'

'No room, my dear,' said Kate, 'no room for old people; they've had their day, and must clear the way for the young.'

'But my mother was not considered an old woman in Europe. She was quite admired and sought for there, but here they look upon her as an antediluvian — fossil remains, if you will. She is clever and amusing, and across the waters they think a vast deal of such things — they like to be entertained. I think my mother very agreeable, and Mrs. Barclay also; indeed, I fancy them to be very much alike, and imagine they must have been so from childhood.'

'Mrs. Ashley is the only woman,' said Grace, 'who

always gets on well; she never seems to lose her popularity; it appears she will never be considered old.'

'Oh yes,' said Clara, 'that's all true; but then Mrs. Ashley is an exception to all rules; "one swallow makes not a summer," Gracy.'

'Ah!' cried the Dolly, 'it's young America rules the land now; every person over seventeen is in a total eclipse; you're an old, old maid, Clara. Just let me break forth upon the all-astounded little world of fashion, and you'll see what a noise I shall make in a Maria Louisa blue brocade, embroidered in pomegranate blossoms and ditto coloured ribbons to match in my bonnie black hair! I never, never intend to renounce the hope that I may yet possess such a divine dress; and let me once have it, and you will behold a leader such as the round globe ne'er saw.'

'And the Chinese tails!' whispered Grace, slily.

'Oh! the hideosities!!' said the Dolly, at the same time bestowing upon the offending braids a terrible twitch, and waltzing out of the room.

CHAPTER XVI.

'I'm twenty-two, I'm twenty-two,
They gaily give me joy.'
N. P. Willis.

Mr. Bradshaw, 'the American Methusaleh,' who had escorted Clara Gordon to the supper-table at Mrs. Lorimer's ball, called the next morning upon her. He was twenty-seven or eight years old, and considered by all the assembled juvenilities of the preceding evening as verging towards an antediluvian stage of existence. This gentleman had been travelling in Europe with great advantage to himself, having improved his time judiciously. He was a sensible, well-educated man; a thorough American in all his feelings and opinions; and although he had found, in other climes, much to admire and approve, and regretted the absence of many pleasant things in his native land, yet he loved his home, and the soil on which he had drawn his first breath was dear to him. Here were centred his heart's affections and sympathies. He had, however, one great defect; he was vastly sententious and very prosy. Mr. Bradshaw was not a very demonstrative person, and the picayunes thought him dull, and did not hesitate to call him so. He had imagined, pretty much as Mrs. Gordon had done, that it was fitting and proper for him to show himself, lest he might be accused of neglecting his friends for foreign reminiscences. So he sallied forth, and, after two or three children's balls and experiences amidst the disbanded nurseries, he had resolved that it was impossible for him to make any more sacrifices in that way, when he made the acquaintance of Miss Gordon, and that event changed his determination of abandoning the little world of fashion. Mr. Bradshaw was much struck with her quiet and ladylike manners, her deferential bearing towards her mother especially; and his farther intercourse confirmed his first impressions. He was convinced that the best thing a man can do in America is to marry, otherwise, knowing not how to pass his evenings, he may fall into club habits; and so Mr. Bradshaw, without being desperately enamoured, and perfectly able to give his future wife a pleasant establishment, decided that he would pay his court to Miss Gordon, and forthwith commenced operations. Now this sort of beginning is never generally very successful, the suitor entirely mistaking the character of the object of his admiration, and beholding in her a composed and self-possessed manner, fancied her to be well-balanced mentally, and not remarkably impressible; but 'under still waters currents lie,' and little wotted he of their existence when he made up his mind touching the character of Clara Gordon.

The restrictions to which the young girl had been subjected during her European life had left their impress, and, though having been two years in the land of liberty, she still submitted her most trifling actions to her mother, and, as Mr. Bradshaw saw more of her, he was astonished, at the same time greatly approving, to observe this respect and deference. The gentleman naturally concluding that such an obedient daughter would make an equally compliant helpmate, was enchanted to have made the discovery of such a treasure, and determined to avail himself of it immediately. Meanwhile the object of his mild passion was wholly unconscious of her conquest. She perceived that Mr. Bradshaw sought her constantly, that he was ever hovering near her, but this state of things she attributed wholly to their mutually isolated condition; that he sympathized with her on her loneliness in the balls she acknowledged, but then 'fellow-feeling makes us wondrous kind,' and he really had so few persons to whom he could speak, that he was actually driven to take refuge with her.

One morning, at breakfast, Mrs. Gordon said to her daughter, 'I am excessively weary of holding up the walls at these apochryphal festivities, Clara, and having exhausted all my small talk with the very few unfortunate mothers, who, in my predicament, have decided they must accompany their young progeny the first season, I have marked out to myself a plan which I propose to pursue. I have peered about, and, in my explorations, discovered that in all the houses we frequent there are sundry nooks, crannies and corners, in which are secreted some card-tables, to which a few superannuated worthies resort in order to kill their long evenings. I intend to present myself as an applicant for the honour of making a hand at whist with these aforesaid octogenarians. They will be half frightened out of their wits by my humble request, I know, but I don't care a rush about that. I must, if I keep my promise, and my word is as good as my bond, do something, and shall therefore adopt the "old lady-like accomplishment" of whist.'

'But, my dear mother,' interposed Clara, 'you know next to nothing of the game; they'll not accept you, I'm afraid, and, really, I wish you would not sacrifice yourself to me, for I had much rather go to the Barclays any time.'

'Never mind, my child; I promised to go out this season, and have, at last, devised a plan to make my martyrdom palatable by learning whist; so do you purchase for me, this very day, the best and most recondite treatise you can discover in the city of Boston, on this important science, and I shall begin this evening at Mrs. Allen's, — I beg her pardon, — Miss Allen's ball. I know that I must not trump my partner's trick, and that I must play the third hand high, and the rest shall come by intuition.'

'I pity your partners, my mother; they will be obliged to exercise an immense deal of patience; and another important thing, how will you be able to keep silent?'

'You're a saucy thing, — I have great confidence in my own resources.'

That evening, then, having been provided with the treatise, and having looked it carefully over while her maid was dressing her hair, Mrs. Gordon found a partner, and bestowed herself in a small room at the top of the stairs, and abandoning her place at her daughter's side, it was immediately occupied by 'the Methusaleh' who was sedulously watching all their movements. Miss Jane Redmond occasionally condescended to peep out from the loop-hole of her retreat, influenced by her overweening curiosity respecting the affairs of the world, and preferring, on some momentous occasions, to say I *saw* to I *heard*. She was generally invited, though considered to have passed her grand climacteric entirely; but she had contrived to inspire the picayunes with such a wholesome terror of her tongue and its animadversions, that they thought it much the best plan to keep the peace with her; and, as they invited Mrs. Ashley for her agreeable qualities, so they asked Miss Redmond for her disagreeable ones. In fact, they were all horribly afraid of her.

Jane strolled up to Clara, who was standing, guarded by Mr. Bradshaw, and begged leave to present to her acquaintance Mr. Hugh Maxwell, and then disappeared. And a handsome bright-eyed and mischievous looking person was this young gentleman, and being very gay and animated, he entered forthwith into a half confidential conversation. After inquiring how she liked America, — for he said he had a right to ask this national question, she having lived so long out of her country must be regarded in the light of a stranger, — he begged to excite her compassion. 'Look at me, pray, Miss Gordon, and commiserate my forlorn condition, "I'm twenty-two, I'm twenty-two," and like "the last rose of summer am left blooming alone; my mates of the garden lie scentless and dead;" that is, Miss Gordon, the plain unvarnished English, for every man I know having taken unto himself a spouse. If you but knew how solitary and wretched I am! pity me, I conjure you!'

Miss Gordon admitted that his sad case demanded sympathy.

'Alas!' said he, 'miserable enough am I, without a friend in the world! They are all occupied with their babies, and have no leisure to bestow upon such a wretch of an old bachelor as I — oh! Miss Gordon, bestow one sympathizing glance upon me. I've a claim "on a blink of your e'en," for I made the excruciating exertion of adorning myself this evening for the sole and express purpose of being presented to you. You perceive that your fame has reached my hermit's cell; "turn, Angelina, ever dear," and hear that I propose to be your slave just so long as you show yourself in "the gay and festal halls;" for I honour your moral courage. Ages gone by I made my appearance in the fashionable world, with a deliciously charming band, garlanded together with wreaths of perfumed flowers, of which not one remains. I beheld them disappear in agony of spirit, and then retreated myself, — for what could I do? The places that knew them once, know them no more, and in their stead several generations have flourished.'

'What melancholy reminiscences,' said Clara, quite amused by her companion's nonsense; but Mr. Bradshaw, who detested nonsense, looked unutterable things at Mr. Hugh Maxwell, and certainly wished him back in his hermitage.

'But,' said Mr. Maxwell, 'you have not yet inquired how I was particularly informed of your advent in these fascinating latitudes, Miss Gordon.'

'You have a sister, I perceive,' said Clara, regarding a most fragile young thing whom she had always observed to be dancing with a small boy, to whom she had heard she was affianced.

'Even so, Miss Gordon; but will you promise not to be

offended if I just venture to hint how I collected this, to me, invaluable information?'

'I will assuredly promise not to be offended, Mr. Maxwell.'

'Well, then, be it known to the travelled and accomplished lady, that this very morning I was asking my little relative how the war was carried on in her own peculiar circle; and, after giving me the history of the divers engagements existing between all these children now jumping up and down before us, Miss Carrie Maxwell, that is, my respected sister, declared that all things were proceeding harmoniously. But, I rejoined, have you no old people about now? and she answered very few, indeed, only two. I inquired the names and styles of the victimized pair, and she replied — Now, Miss Gordon, will you promise solemnly not to be offended?'

'I promise,' said Clara.

'Well, then, she replied, — my sister, I mean, — she answered that the only old people about were — Miss Jane Redmond and — Miss Clara Gordon.'

Upon this revelation, such a ringing laugh as fell upon Mr. Bradshaw's ears! He was positively shocked, being very critical on the subject of laughter, and very angry with Mr. Maxwell for provoking this indiscretion.

'And will Mr. Maxwell,' said Mr. Bradshaw, for the first time joining in the conversation, 'please inform me in what light I am considered, if Miss Gordon is designated as old?'

'Most willingly,' answered the gentleman addressed, 'my sister, Miss Carrie Maxwell, has a long, long while voted you to be a second grandfather Whitehead! I beg not to be made responsible for her opinions; if you propose to call any one out, — for you look sufficiently indignant to perpetrate an honourable murder,—please apply to the little gentleman with the huge cravat, so assiduously paying his court to my respected relative, and I've no doubt he will be enchanted to give you all necessary and unnecessary satisfaction.

Why, Bradshaw, how owlishly solemn you look! I'm absolutely alarmed. Miss Gordon, I place myself at your feet, and will put a girdle round the earth at your bidding, but just now will leave you and your redoubtable champion, and return when he is in better humour.'

Thus saying, Mr. Maxwell made a profound obeisance, and departed.

Suddenly he returned and said, 'I forgot entirely to inform you, Miss Gordon, that I came here this evening for the sole purpose of seeing you and finding a CONTEMPORARY; but perceiving you are guarded like the golden fruit in the Garden of Hesperides, I am constrained, altogether against my will, to abandon a half-formed project of re-entering the world, and bid you a solemn and eternal adieu.'

'What a ridiculous popinjay!' exclaimed Mr. Bradshaw.

But, after all, he thought to himself, this may make a good opening for me, and he asked Clara if she were not fatigued, and would not prefer to be seated; so she placed herself on a sofa, and Mr. Bradshaw composedly disposed himself beside her. Now, it was very true that Mr. Bradshaw had worn to the lady of his love a very *paternal* guise, not exactly that of a grandfather; but there was ever a very fatherly atmosphere enveloping him, and Clara Gordon felt it. He was too wise and too good for daily bread; he made long speeches and delivered virtuous homilies upon the degeneracy of the times and the backslidings of the people, and preached too much on week-days altogether. He was an excellent individual; there was not an objection to be made to him morally, and he was only, as a matter of taste, rather too demonstratively good. And, as Mr. Bradshaw had not hidden any of these admirable requisites for a perfect helpmate from Clara Gordon, it is wonderful how she could have been so blind to them and his desire to make her the sharer of his manifold excellences; but so it was. She felt neither, and saw not at all. He was sitting beside her, and, turning towards her, lowered the tones of his voice, which in any way should have been drowned in the noise of the music and the talkers, and he whispered :

'The absurd fooleries of Mr. Hugh Maxwell are very disagreeable to me, and I hope also to you, Miss Gordon, but as he was pleased to do me the honour to mention my unworthy name in connection with yours, I will venture to affirm that I devoutly hope it may ever so remain. I have long desired to mention a subject lying next my heart; and, as he seems to think we are left by all our contemporaries alone, his impression evidently being that of others also, will you allow me, dear Miss Gordon, to ask you to accept my heart and hand? I have perceived a very great sympathy in our tastes and feelings, and presume this has also been made evident to the bystanders, since they have conferred upon me the high favour of connecting my poor name with yours. I can place you in a home as comfortable as the one you leave, and solemnly promise to make it as happy as it is in my power so to do. I know that, to all young ladies, an offer of marriage is an important event in their lives, requiring mature reflection, and demanding the advice and counsel of their friends and advisers, and presume you will be no exception to the general rule, and require sufficient verge and space for profound cogitations upon my words. My professions bear the seal and stamp of perfect sincerity, and I have profound regard and respect for your character, in which I behold many things to admire. I also dwell with great satisfaction on your numerous accomplishments, as tending to enliven a home in a superiour degree; and I sincerely hope for an acquiescent response to this exposition of my unwavering sentiments, for which I now wait with impatience.'

Poor Clara! She listened with dismay to this never-ending oration, with its repetitions and involved sentences, and was all the time thinking how she should manage to rise from the very, very low Louis the Fourteenth sofa on which it could not be said she reposed in peace; she had tried many times, during Mr. Bradshaw's peroration, ineffectually.

'Permit me to assist you to rise, Miss Gordon; I know full well you will wish to confide this event to your mother. I entertain small doubt of her being propitious.'

'I have no present intention,' said Clara, provoked beyond expression at his pertinacious obstinacy in believing there could be no obstacles any where, 'of consulting any one; and have but to reply to your proffers, that I most positively and respectfully decline them.'

'Impossible!' exclaimed the gentleman, 'you cannot surely refuse me!'

'I certainly do; and nothing can ever force me to change my irrevocable intention of declining your addresses.'

'This being such an extraordinary proceeding, Miss Gordon, I must forthwith see your mother.'

'It will avail you naught, Mr. Bradshaw.'

Upon which Mr. Bradshaw left Miss Gordon and saw her mother, whom, in his excitement and indignation at her daughter's conduct, he called from the card-room, and confided to her her child's delinquencies. Mrs. Gordon informed him that she could not control her daughter's affections, which, it appeared in his case, were not fixed upon him. She regretted his disappointment, but it was evident he had not touched her child's heart, and that all expostulations would be useless. Mr. Bradshaw became vexed with both mother and daughter, and took, as he told Mrs. Gordon, an eternal farewell of them.

Mrs. Gordon was not very sorry at Clara's rejection of her suitor, though he was certainly an eligible match, and she rather agreed with the picayunes, in thinking him a tiny bit prosy, his conversation being rather tiresome, though unobjectionably wise,—but she was astonished at the exhibition of bad temper he had made, which she, however, attributed to mortified vanity, he having been so remarkably sure of his matrimonial prize.

Indeed, Mr. Bradshaw could never be made to comprehend the cause of Miss Gordon's rejection of his suit.

CHAPTER XVII.

'Dark lowers our fate,
And terrible the storm that gathers o'er us.'
JOANNA BAILLIE.

It was just at this period when Mr. Barclay found himself in the complete enjoyment of his eminently prosperous existence, in the zenith of his manhood, adored by his family, surrounded by steadfast friends, and environed with countless blessings, for which he was aboundingly grateful, that a dire calamity befel him. A calamity which probing him to the heart's core, and rudely dashing the overflowing cup of his happiness to the earth in one dark and dreary moment, dissolved into thin air the peaceful fabric of his existence, never again to be restored. A cloud, black as Erebus, broke over his devoted head. And this sad affliction dwelt in the person of his child, his first-born, his idolized daughter, Georgiana. She sought him in his own private room, and closing the door carefully, fell at his feet in a paroxysm of grief and remorse, and confessed herself to have been secretly married.

On listening to this astonishing revelation, Mr. Barclay imagined it to be the result of sudden delirium, of hallucination, and he could only be persuaded of the truth of her story by her repeatedly reiterated asseverations.

'And to whom?' demanded her almost distracted father.

'To Gerald Sanderson,' she answered.

'To Gerald Sanderson!' he exclaimed, 'the young and dreamy enthusiast and hermit, of whom I have heard his brother speak so frequently, loving him devotedly, but ever regretting his half-monastic habits,—how got he access to you, my child? when and where? I have always understood he constantly remained in his study, at the top of the old house, eschewing all society, and devoting himself to abstruse and philosophical speculations.'

'Oh! my father, I dare not look in your dear face for very shame and agony of spirit; I have most grievously sinned against you and my beloved mother, and deserve no forgiveness whatever. I have hoarded up this fearful secret until it became utterly impossible for me to retain it any longer, in accordance with Gerald's earnest prayers and supplications, he having conjured me to allow him to bear the brunt of your well merited indignation, and assured me he would not permit any one to be blamed but himself, and now that he returns not home, I can bear this no longer. Alas! I full well know how much more criminal I am than he; he has never experienced your exalted goodness, your indulgence, your devoted watchfulness, whereas I, sinner that I am, have offended against yourself, my mother, and my Maker. Oh! what a load of misery is on my soul; how ungrateful, how disobedient, have I been; what disgraceful deceptions have I not practised, when all around me was truth and honour! My father, my father, I ask not for forgiveness; punish me as you best think fit; no penance can be too severe for me to endure. Oh! the weight on my brain is too great to bear and live; my whole life is banned and marred forever!'

Mr. Barclay, with parental kindness, essayed to calm the violence of his daughter's feelings, to compose, in some degree, the fever of her mind. He then asked her where she had first seen Gerald Sanderson. She replied, 'In the cloak-room at Mrs. Ashley's children's ball,' and narrated, what the reader already knows, her refusal to dance with him. She then stated, that her sister's cold confining her to the house during the winter, she had no companion in her daily walks to school, and that, very soon after the ball, she began to meet Gerald Sanderson. By degrees, insensibly she encountered him more frequently; that at first she had not mentioned his constant appearance in her path, simply from a species of timidity, arising from a complete subjugation of all her feelings which that youth had established over her, from the very first moment she laid her eyes upon him. She compared this feeling to sorcery or witchcraft, or any other undue fascination; *unholy* she called it, for had she not been led into undutifulness and hypocrisy by giving up her whole soul to her lover? In the beginning all was a dream, but soon came a change. She longed for his presence, voluntarily met him, and took long walks with him in bye streets, avoiding the frequented haunts where she might chance to encounter familiar faces. He wrote her long, impassioned letters and verses, gave her serenades, sent bouquets and little novelties of various kinds anonymously. Of these the family had taken no notice, such things constantly occurring from other quarters. He had haunted her presence day and night, she said, having passed a great part of the latter under her windows; he said the watchmen, on their beat, knew him intimately by sight, and took no note of him. He played and sang divinely, and Gracy had jested with her, after Charley's departure, upon Gerald's serenades, but had not the most remote idea that she had ever seen him. He had forced her to swear she would never divulge her secret, even to her sister; it was not to be thought of. At last, he had told her he must depart as his brother had done and seek a fortune, to marry her; that his uncle would never leave him any thing, and that he must work as Charley had done, in order to give her the same comforts she possessed at home. She must always live in luxury, he said. So when the time arrived that he was to depart he urged a secret marriage, at which she revolted. It took a long, long while for him to induce her to consent, but weak and powerless in his hands, he succeeded. They entered a house where she found a clergyman and a gentleman, whom Gerald declared to be his best friend, — not a young man, by any means, — and they were married. The ceremony concluded, — (it was short, — she remembered it very indistinctly, — it was all confusion in her recollection) — she and Gerald left the house immediately. They parted at the corner of the street, — she never saw him more ; she had reason to believe he passed that night under her windows. The next day she received a large bridal bouquet, a few hurried and passionate appeals to her constancy, her affection, and he was gone. All these events occurred in such rapid succession that she had no time for reflection. She knew she had done a great wrong, committed an unpardonable offence against her parents, but, in some unaccountable way, she seemed not to regret it as such. She was composed and quiet, assured that Gerald would return. His absence appeared to produce a certain relief to her overcharged spirit ; she stilled the voice of her conscience, and pursued the even tenor of her way unmolested. He did not write, and yet she was not unhappy ; she trusted in him, but she could in no manner comprehend her quietude under the infliction of his absence. She had regarded his injunctions of secrecy as merely fanciful ; he was of a romantic and visionary turn, (she had a little of the same character herself,) and the whole thing seemed a pleasing romance in her eyes.

This state of affairs lasted a long while. She had never appeared to acknowledge to herself her position, but, as time rolled on, and Gerald made no sign, she began to apprehend misfortune, even death, and a film appeared to pass from before her hitherto blinded eyes. She supposed she had become more matured in her judgment : she had looked upon her position in a totally different light. Conscience, once fully awakened, would no longer be hushed, and her sufferings had become perfectly unendurable, the more intense, from the obligatory concealment ;

so, in a frenzy of despair, she had arisen from her prayers to God for assistance, and gone to her father to make a completely frank and truthful confession, and to beg and conjure him to pardon her, though she felt she had no right to sue as a petitioner for mercy, when she stood in his presence.

Of course, all this was extracted bit by bit, and it seemed that her heart would break under the trial, and her father, totally unused to menaces, or even reproaches, treated her with kindness and tenderness, and comforted her; instead of harshness and contumely, she received consolation. This was even more than she could endure; so paternal was his bearing in her eyes, that she mourned her dereliction from her duty all the more, and her duplicity towards her inestimable and priceless father seemed more heinous than ever. Georgiana had been so tortured by remorse, that the full disclosure of her appalling secret had, in some sort, relieved her harrowed mind. She felt that the crisis of her fate had arrived; the ordeal was passed; she had poured into the sympathizing bosom of her all-pardoning parent the tale of her misery, and he had deigned to breathe words of hope and encouragement to his erring child. Then came to both father and daughter, the distressing thought of the mother and wife! She was to be informed of the blow which had fallen on her household; how would she bear it? A worshipper of truth, having devoted her days to the instilment of its healthful principles into the minds and hearts of her children, how would she receive the mortifying intelligence that her untiring efforts had been unavailing? Here was an acted lie in the very heart of her own family, the place of all others in which she would have least expected to find it! How discouraging to her must be this failure of her exertions to prove and perfect the character of her daughter, the oldest, — the one to whom she looked for the fruition of her educational plans, to say nothing of the example which she had ever prayed this child of her affections might exhibit to her sisters and brother.

As these reflections arose in the mind of that child, she shrunk with fear and trembling at the melancholy task which her father had taken upon himself, the imparting this story of her humiliating disgrace to her mother. It was to be done, and no one but he could properly break the wearisome tale, and again and again, how would she receive it?

Mr. Barclay supported his fainting daughter to her chamber, and closing the door, left her with her misery. How long he was gone she knew not. It seemed an age of torture; she listened intently to every sound with checked and fevered respiration; she hardly dared to breathe; cold chills crept through her veins, and in after-times, as she pondered upon those appalling moments, it was with an intensity of suffering sad to reflect upon. Indeed, she often marvelled that reason had not sunk under that mighty trial. At last approaching footsteps were heard; slowly and solemnly they fell upon her ear; the lock was turned, the door gent'y opened, and her father appeared. If he had come without her mother! She attempted to rise from her chair; a choking and overwhelming sensation obliged her to re-seat herself; — an instant, and her mother had folded her arms around her, and was whispering in melting tones forgiveness, mercy, — blessed and revivifying words! Mr. Barclay left them together, and over the scene, in which the repentant young creature poured forth her whole soul on the bosom of her parent, a veil shall be drawn. The father then sought for Grace, and imparted to her the events of this miserable morning. She was overwhelmed with astonishment and grief; she had never, in the slightest possible way, suspected aught to her own perfect sister's disparagement, and could hardly be made to believe what she heard; and surely, from no other source, would she have given credence to such an astonishing revelation. She declared that lately she had perceived a change in her sister, which daily increased. She rather shunned society; had wakeful nights; was excessively gay when in the presence of the assembled family, and moping and melancholy alone. She had always endeavoured to rouse herself when she had entered the room and found her in these moods, but very shortly relapsed. Grace also said that she had been some time thinking that her sister's health was declining; but, as neither her father or mother seemed to perceive it, she forbore mentioning her own suspicions lest she might alarm them. Now all was revealed, she felt the most intense commiseration for Georgy; and so accustomed had she ever been to regard her sister in the light of a superiour being, that it was with great difficulty she could bring herself to express what, in any other case, she would have openly avowed, her entire disapprobation of her proceedings. Still, Grace was obliged to confess that her idol had deviated from the path of her duty, and that with such parents the error was all the more reprehensible. There was no way of glossing over her conduct; she had been both undutiful and ungrateful, and this was a source of exquisite suffering to the tender-hearted and loving young creature.

The Dolly received this sad news with an outburst of sensibility, almost alarming from its violence. She wept, wrung her hands, and bewailed her sister's fate with irrepressible emotion. She raved at Gerald's folly, at Georgy's, and finally threw herself into Nursey Bristow's arms, and fairly cried herself to sleep. Nursey laid her gently in bed, from which she did not arise until late the next morning.

Mr. Barclay sent immediately for his brother, who came and betrayed the deepest and most intense sympathy in his sorrow, but took a cheering view of the case. He said he hated Philip Egerton, and knew absolutely nothing of Gerald except his disgraceful conduct in relation to his niece, but that his father was an honourable man, universally respected; the mother, a good, weak creature; and no very great harm, he thought, could ever arise from a connection with the scions of such a stock; so he was disposed to look favourably on the marriage. Again, Gerald was so young, so unworldly and so romantic, that many excuses might be urged for his conduct, which, under other circumstances, would admit of no palliatives whatever. Mr. Richard was quite sure that Charley would never have committed such an act, not he; but then he was a complete man of the world compared with his brother. He knew, for certain, that his young favourite was dying in love with Gracy, and yet had never revealed his passion. 'Now,' said he, 'the best way for you, John, is to go to-morrow morning and see Mr. Egerton, state the case to him, and have every thing settled satisfactorily. Revolve over the whole affair in your own mind this evening; arrange your plan for storming the miser's stronghold, sleep upon your trouble, and awake like a giant refreshed, and attack Mr. Egerton and his treacherous nephew. I beg your pardon, I will never again call your son-in-law hard names. God bless you, my brother, and good night; for I intend to leave you to your own reflections until to-morrow, when I sincerely hope things will assume a different aspect.'

Mrs. Barclay remaining with Georgy, her husband paced his hitherto delightful library with heavy and mournful steps all that long evening, every visitor being refused; and Gracy creeping closely to his side accompanied her father, oppressed with grief. This being the young girl's first introduction to sorrow and suffering, she longed for the morrow, for change, imagining that the light of another day would bring healing on its wings. So impossible does it seem to convince youthful minds of the continuity of affliction; and why should it ever be attempted?

Mr. Barclay, before he retired to rest, sent a servant to Mr. Egerton's to inquire if Mr. Gerald Sanderson had returned home, and learned that he was at his uncle's house; at which information he felt slightly relieved, as he thought the sooner the whole thing was settled and arranged, the better.

CHAPTER XVIII.

'Wait! for the time is hasting
When life shall be made clear,
And all who know heart-wasting,
Shall find that God is near.'
CHAUNCEY HARE TOWNSEND.

THE next morning, after a wretched and sleepless night, Mr. Barclay ordered his carriage and went to Mr. Egerton's. He raised the ponderous knocker, and, at this unwonted sound in that establishment, Peter rushed to the door, followed by Dinah, who kept a little in his rear. Mr. Barclay inquired if Mr. Egerton were at home, and if he could see him. Peter opened the best parlour door, with great ceremony, and ushered him into Philip's state apartment. There stood, nailed to the wall, the old chairs and sofa, and the one solitary table, all looking as if they had not been removed for a century, stiff and formal like their owner, — the grate not having seen a fire since the late Mr. Egerton's decease. The room was intensely cold, and, although the visitor's feet were almost frozen during the long time he awaited his answer, he hardly seemed conscious of the atmosphere in this incipient ice-house. Mr. Barclay was quite sure that Mr. Egerton was at home, having arrived early in order to secure an audience. In the excited state of his feelings the minutes seemed hours to the unhappy father, and he longed impatiently for the reappearance of the black mercury. At last, when he had begun to think of once more storming this old castle of dullness, by repairing to the hall door and attacking its lion-headed knocker,

Peter arrived, and with many bows and grimaces assured him his master would be happy to receive him. In this the black plenipotentiary had remarkably stretched his powers, inasmuch as Mr. Egerton, after walking about the room an indefinitely long period, had made a sort of assenting sign that his most unexpected guest might enter his sanctum.

When Mr. Barclay found himself in 'the Library' without books, in the presence of two hard chairs and a large square table, so polished he could have arranged his toilet in it, very little fire, and the immensely stately, pompous possessor of this private elysium, his courage nearly failed him, every thing appeared so frigid, so unimpressible. Mr. Egerton arose from his high-backed chair, and coldly bowing, desired, in measured terms, to be informed to what fortuitous circumstance he owed the honour of a visit at such an unwonted hour, from a gentleman he so rarely had the pleasure to see. This was any thing but encouraging, it must be confessed. Mr. Barclay, however, recovering himself, stated that he had come on an errand of considerable importance to himself, and trusted Mr. Egerton would also be interested in it. That gentleman, instantly perceiving that there must be some momentous event to be announced, from the agitated manner of a man whom he had always not a little envied for his prosperity and equanimity, begged Mr. Barclay would take a chair, and, seating himself composedly, awaited its disclosure. Mr. Barclay immediately began, and, in a plain unvarnished tale, recounted the sad story which has already been related. As he proceeded, although at times his voice almost failed him, the Christian spirit breathing through his words, his patience and forbearance, and the charm of his simple and natural manners failed not to produce upon his listener a somewhat sympathetic effect. Mr. Egerton was an honourable man, and deeply felt his nephew's treachery. Then his own good name was, to a certain extent, involved in this nefarious transaction, the pure blood of his family tarnished, and poor Emma, his sister! — what had become of her? And then there was a satisfaction, no, not exactly that, but something near akin to it, that in his presence, and before his eyes, he beheld the only man he had ever condescended to envy, in his whole natural life, bowed down with grief and shame for the dereliction of an idolized child. For, however Mr. Barclay might brave the coming storm, disgrace it was, and emanating from a source which the unhappy father had always regarded as pure and undefiled. Unspotted had his daughter ever been, and what was she now? A creature for the shafts of envy and malice to be expended upon?

Mr. Egerton's feelings softened towards Mr. Barclay, the tones of his voice altered, and while he expressed his honest indignation at Gerald's misconduct, he begged him to accept his sincere sympathy in his tribulation. The two gentlemen, after a long and most intensely interesting conversation, debated the best means of apprising the delinquent of his turpitude, and then dispatched Peter up into the young offender's quarters in search of him.

Gerald, who was just then deeply engaged in solving some abstruse mathematical problem, and looking marvellously unlike a lover, quite resented the black's intrusion into his eyrie, which was certainly a very unwonted circumstance. The excitement produced by the arrival of a visitor at any hour would have completely upset poor Peter's brain, — but at nine in the morning! he had not an idea left in his head, and accordingly bounced into the student's presence without even knocking.

'Pray what do you want, Peter?' cried Gerald, in no very gentle tones; 'what means this sudden intrusion?'

'Oh Massa, Massa Gerald, Mr. Barclay, the great Mr. Barclay, is down stairs in my Massa's library, and wants to see you; so take off dat ole dressin gown and put on your bess bettermost coat, and run down right off, dis minute.'

'I shall do no such thing,' replied Gerald. 'Mr. Barclay and I can have nothing to say to each other, I am positive.'

'Oh yes, Massa, Massa; good deal, good deal, I guess.'

'And what do you know about this matter, Peter?' said Gerald, gradually awakening from what Peter called his 'brown study,' in which he had been intensely engaged previous to the astounding news of a visit from the great merchant.

'What can he want?' said Gerald to himself.

'Guess he want someting strange, berry strange, Massa.'

'How do you know? you old villain!' cried Gerald. 'I really believe you've been at your vile trick of listening at the door.'

'And if I had, what harm, Massa? Der nebber cum to dis house noffin; and when de biggest bug in de whole town come bang-whanging away at de ragin lion's head, spose I goin to wait til he be gone to know his bisness? No, Massa, no!'

''Tis a very bad habit you have contracted, Peter, and should be immediately corrected.'

'Yes, I berry well know it's all wrong. Missus hab told me so often enough for dis ole coon to member. But den, you all know I nebber tell any ting out ob dis house.'

With this salvo for his conscience, the old servant was perfectly satisfied with what he had done; and as Gerald did not inquire what the secret was, — at which he was immeasurably disappointed, — he applied himself most diligently to making the young man presentable before he entered, what Peter considered to be, the august presence of the 'biggest bug' in the town.

Gerald descended, slowly and measuredly, the stairs, seemingly occupied in arranging his scattered thoughts, before this grand audience should take place. At the library door he stopped and hesitated; he had never spoken to Mr. Barclay, and had rarely seen him. This meeting evidently agitated and alarmed him. After one or two unsuccessful efforts to turn the lock, he effected his purpose, and stood in the presence of his enraged uncle and afflicted guest.

Mr. Egerton, totally forgetting his dignified and imposing ways, fell upon the young culprit unmercifully. 'What have you been doing?' exclaimed he, — 'you disgrace to my blood! you traitor! who have stolen, like a thief in the night, into this good man's house and taken away his daughter! Shame on you for a recreant, as you are, to your name and to your station! What will my poor sister and your devoted mother say to the tale of your dishonour and perfidy, which I shall have to narrate to her? This horrid story will go far towards re-opening wounds in her lacerated heart, which religion and time have been healing. Answer me directly, — How dared your noble father's son commit such an offence against good faith and morality?'

'Of what offence do you accuse me, uncle?' said Gerald, in the calmest manner possible.

'Of having lured away Miss Georgiana Barclay!' thundered forth Mr. Egerton, 'from her duty; of having turned her head with your absurd poetry and music and flattering lies, until she consented to become your wife, unknown to her excellent parents, whom I believe to be unexcelled in their tender devotion to their children.'

'I never, my uncle, spoke to Miss Georgiana Barclay in my life,' replied Gerald coolly.

'Hear him! hear him!' cried Mr. Egerton. 'God help me, he is adding falsehood and hypocrisy to the already horrid catalogue of his wicked doings!'

'My father's son,' said Gerald solemnly, 'never lies.'

'Oh, the viper! the young villain!' exclaimed Mr. Egerton. 'I will send you out of this house before this day is well over; you shall get your bread in other ways than studying astronomy — calculating the stars, forsooth! I will send you on a voyage round the world, in which you shall have plenty of leisure to repent you of your misdeeds; — a fellow that I have supported and harboured, — faugh!'

'I am perfectly willing, Sir,' said the young man, who had become thoroughly aroused and angered, 'to leave this old house, which has sheltered me, and very little else, during many years. For your hospitality, such as it has been, I am sufficiently grateful; but I entirely deny your right to order me any where; and I tell you, in your teeth, I will not be sent to the Sandwich Islands or the Northwest Coast, by you or any one else. I know,' he resumed, 'that those long voyages are considered to be, by yourself and others, the schools of reform for all wild youths, and also that you have counselled many a father to do this same thing, to the utter degradation and ruin of his son. One case came under my own immediate cognisance, where a youth of great refinement and sensibility was banished, for some very venial and juvenile offence, from a luxurious home to a forecastle; and what with the contamination of its atmosphere — which, I grant, he had not the moral courage to resist, that quality being rare in the spring-time of life — and his own despair, he entirely succumbed. I saw him the last week even, a vulgar, degraded wreck, — and that was your own doing, Sir. I never saw a China merchant, who did not firmly believe in the efficacy of this plan; and I now reiterate my assertion, — I will not go!'

Mr. Egerton's amazement at this outpouring of resentment from his quiet, unobtrusive nephew, completely bereft him of words. He literally had nothing to say. Mr. Barclay, who had until then been unable to make himself heard, spoke. He asserted, that he could in nowise comprehend why Mr. Gerald Sanderson should so positively deny the charge brought against him; for this he must be answerable to his own conscience. He averred that he believed his daughter's assertion before the asseverations of any one; that he was disposed, for many good reasons, into which he would not then enter on the discussion, to look more leniently upon the marriage than Mr. Egerton, and that he would make the proposition that they should all repair to his own house, and in the presence of the young lady herself settle the question at once.

Mr. Egerton acceded immediately to this measure, and Gerald respectfully signified his complete willingness to accompany him. The drive was passed in perfect silence by the whole trio. On arriving at their destination, Mr. Barclay, hastily jumping out of the vehicle, ushered Mr. Egerton and his nephew into the library, and then left them. They passed the time during his absence in carefully avoiding each other; Gerald's uncle being still too much overwhelmed to renew his accusations, and the nephew remaining reserved and sullen.

Mr. Barclay found Georgiana more composed than he had anticipated. Her mother, whose gentle attentions and melting kindness had effected this change, looked like a martyr, as she was.

'My dear wife, and daughter,' said he, 'I have brought Mr. Egerton and his nephew with me; you must endeavour to compose yourselves sufficiently to receive them. You, dear Mrs. Barclay, your son, — and you, my daughter, your husband; — all, all is forgiven! Life is too short to be filled with the misery we can evade by our own exertions; want of fortune is nothing to me; the all of life is not money, and provided Gerald Sanderson turns out a good fellow, I shall thankfully receive and treat him as my own son. I do not regard the offence, when I look upon my beloved child, in the light his uncle does, who is outrageous at his breach of faith. I know you to be very attractive, dear Georgy, and he very young and romantic, and I remember my own boyish days, when I thought myself a man.'

Mrs. Barclay looked upon her husband as if he were superhuman, — and Georgy, throwing herself into his arms, wept abundant tears of joyful gratitude for his forbearance. Some time elapsed before they were sufficiently composed to descend the stairs, and many were the pauses made.

Mrs. Barclay could not so decidedly imitate the superiour

goodness of her husband. She thought Gerald a traitor, and could not excuse him on the plea of his youth. She believed that his brother Charley would never have so conducted himself. She had long perceived his passion for Grace, which he had never, by any word or sign, revealed to its object, and she felt there was a vast difference between the brothers. Mrs. Barclay knew Charley to be the soul of honour, and she hoped that Gerald, having lived with him, might still retain the germs of a quality for which nothing can compensate. Mr. Barclay had not mentioned to her Gerald's obstinate denial of his marriage, because he so thoroughly disbelieved him; and although this was certainly truly shocking in his eyes, yet he trusted, — for he was ever hopeful, — that time, good example, and the influence they should all mutually exercise over him, would eradicate any bad qualities he might possess; and with these benign views he gave his strong, supporting arm to his child, and, Mrs. Barclay following, they entered the library.

Mr. Egerton, looking inexpressibly relieved, arose, and coming forward, entirely screened Gerald Sanderson. This was well arranged, as it prevented the shock of a sudden interview between the youthful pair before he had signified his approval of their union, which he proposed formally to do. Mr. Egerton received his niece elect with a stately, but, for him, remarkably softened manner. He was evidently much struck with her extreme loveliness, and he cordially welcomed her into the bosom of his family, at the same time lamenting that in the excitement of their departure from his own dwelling, he had neglected to bring with him his sister, Mrs. Sanderson, who certainly had the first right to embrace her. Mr. Barclay was rejoiced to perceive the evidently agreeable impression his child had made on this hitherto imperturbable personage. Georgiana received his modulated gratulations and felicitations modestly, timidly, and with downcast eyes and mantling cheeks she thanked him for his courtesies.

Indeed, nothing could surpass the attraction of the sweet young girl, as she stood in the bloom of her charms, at seventeen, with the radiant curls encircling a brow polished like Parian marble, a voice redolent of sweet sounds, a fairy-like figure, and enjoying a character for unsurpassed amiability, but above all, for the possession of such parents.

Mr. Egerton had always conceived a very decided prejudice for what he called a 'good stock;' and inwardly rejoiced that he was to be allied to John Barclay and his excellent wife; at the same time he could not help thinking that the young rascal, his nephew, did not deserve such a rich prize in the matrimonial lottery for having so pertinaciously denied his marriage. Then he remembered that this was Gerald's first offence, and it was better to forgive and forget.

But where was Gerald? As this question arose in his mind, he changed his position, and presenting his nephew to Georgiana, said to him, 'Let by-gones be by-gones, Gerald; we will never more remember what has passed between us to-day. Now let me see you embrace your lovely wife, and God bless you both.'

At this juncture Georgiana Barclay, raising her eyes for the first time, with a piercing and heart-rending shriek, exclaimed, 'Oh, God, this man is not Gerald Sanderson! this man is not my husband!' and fell senseless on the floor.

CHAPTER XIX.

'In the judgment of right and wrong, every man has a self.'
WATTS.

WHEN Mr. Egerton and Gerald left Mr. Barclay's melancholy abode, the former, true to his established habits, wended his way to his beloved insurance office as usual. It is, however, certain that there was a shade less of haughtiness in his bearing; his head was less elevated, and he was, for a wonder, wrapped up in something besides himself.

Rochefaucault has asserted that there is something not unpleasing to us in the misfortunes of our best friends. How many a time and oft has this saying been quoted, and it is not yet worn out, false or true as it may be! Mr. Egerton, assuredly, in that memorable walk deplored the overwhelming calamity which had befallen such a thoroughly estimable person as he was fain to confess Mr. John Barclay to be, and he certainly wished that this terrible affliction might have been averted from the head of a man whose whole life had been so unspotted, and so filled with the milk of human kindness towards his fellow-creatures. But then Mr. Egerton had no weaknesses for his fellow-creatures. He entertained a very bad opinion of human nature, and consequently could not sympathize with those who looked upon it more leniently, or excused the short-comings of their neighbours. He had ever considered Mr. Barclay a rather weak and silly philanthropist, giving himself a vast deal of trouble for very ungrateful recipients of his labours.

Then there was, unacknowledged even to himself, a slightly envious feeling, mingled with his other sentiments, touching this gentleman. Not that Mr. Egerton would have admitted the fact for worlds, but so it was, and could not be gainsayed; and thus it happened that the Frenchman was right in this case. Mr. Egerton certainly then hugged himself in his single blessedness, and thanked his stars, over and over again, that he was not cumbered with children to entail upon him such an accumulation of misery. How he congratulated himself that he had never married! but this he had done many a time and oft, before it had been suggested to him by Benedict acquaintances, (for *friends* he had none,) that he was immensely grateful for remarkably small favours. Still, as it has been stated, Mr. Egerton did not walk quite as erect and self-sufficiently as usual. The little sympathy he felt did not, however, prevent his entertaining the whole assembled worthies in his favourite resort, maligners and all, with a succinct and clear account of the sad scene he had witnessed that morning. To do him justice, he did not relate this unpleasant tale from any gossipping motives; his being deeper and better founded, he considered himself bound to exonerate his nephew from all suspicion. Mr. Egerton, being an honourable man, wished nothing that appertained to himself to be suspected, and, moreover, Gerald's name was most unpleasantly mixed up with this melancholy adventure.

The tale was heard with breathless attention and deep sympathy by many. Many who were parents thanked God for his mercies, that they had been spared a like affliction; some persons sneered, and declared that pride must have a fall. To this a majority demurred, insisting there was nothing but a proper self-respect about Mr. Barclay. Others asserted that girls should be shut up and not permitted to run wild about the streets, even if the schools were so excellent. Being asked what they did with their own daughters, it turned out they had none.

Generally, the feeling excited was a true-hearted sentiment of sympathy with the afflicted parents, and a profound indignation against the young villain who had assumed the name of Gerald Sanderson for his own nefarious purposes; and joined to this was an ardent desire to discover the offender. In this Mr. Egerton most sincerely participated, and resolved to leave no means untried until it was effected.

The whole history of Miss Barclay's sad love-passage was so unfathomable in its mystery, that there seemed to be no bounds to conjecture; and certainly, under no other circumstances, could a like calamity have occurred. But for Gerald Sanderson's secluded and monastic habits of life, no person would have dared to assume his name in such a bold and daring manner. Mr. Egerton felt that he had not been blameless in this case, in permitting the young student to bury himself alive in the midst of a populous city, where even his very person was unknown; and his existence would have been equally so, save for the charmingly social and genial qualities of his brother Charley. To this conclusion he was not suffered to come alone; for the maligners were disposed to attack him with all sorts of annoying remarks, and pelted him with wise sayings and saws innumerable. Mr. Egerton also could not fail to perceive that Gerald's reputation would be tarnished, at least in a degree, by this occurrence, for garbled reports would be circulating every where, in which his share must bear a distinguished part: and that, in fact, the story would never be told without producing a certain injurious effect upon the reputation of his nephew. So Mr. Egerton resolved to have a long and stringent conversation with the young gentleman, and point out to him the error of his ways, and urge him to abandon them; and as his own assimilated in a very remarkable manner to Gerald's, this colloquy promised to be very like the extracting of the mote from his nephew's eye while the beam remained in his own. It was, however, fated never to take place.

Most men on leaving Mr. Barclay's gloomy abode would have proceeded directly home to impart the sad tidings to sympathizing wives, mothers and sisters, but this magnificent Mandarin held the whole tribe in peculiarly small acceptation, and 'poor Emma' as he called her, least of all; so he waited until a short time before dinner, and then communicated to her the events of that all-wretched day.

Mrs. Sanderson was inexpressibly shocked; it was true she had no personal acquaintance with the excellent family, so suddenly precipitated from the apex of human prosperity to an abyss of sorrow and shame, for she could not deny, even to herself, though most unwillingly, that shame was indeed there, — but she knew all its members from Charley's animated and glowing descriptions. Now, making all due allowance for youthful enthusiasm, heightened by gratitude for boundless favours, she had become thoroughly imbued with a high sense of the intrinsically excellent qualities of all the members of Mr. Barclay's family, and totally unbiased from her own isolated condition by its wealth and position, she imagined she had formed a correct judgment. Strange to relate, Mrs. Sanderson's first thought, on recovering from the agitation created by this sad intelligence, was for Charley, and not for Gerald, who seemed, certainly, to have been the doomed victim of an abominable plot. She was fully aware that Charley, young as he was, had an enduring affection for Grace Barclay, which would cease but with his existence; whereas, apart from Gerald's love for herself, she did not deem him sufficiently of the earth earthy, to be touched by human suffering in any way. He had lived in a little world of his own, peopled it might perchance be, but not with living, moving, sentient beings; and she, therefore, naturally concluded he would remain passive on this occasion, and she knew that Charley would suffer intensely from the misfortunes of his friends.

The mother concurred fully with the uncle in the opinion,

that the time and the hour had arrived for effective remonstrance, and that the setting forth to Gerald, in proper colours, of the dangers he had incurred himself, and the misery he had innocently, but surely, brought down upon the devoted heads of the Barclay family, would not fail to produce a signal reform in his habits. Mrs. Sanderson also resolved to aid her brother in his good work towards her children, and was even very much astonished that he had deigned to impart his intentions to her, it being certainly one of the longest communications she had ever received from Mr. Egerton, and came nearer to being confidential than that gentleman ever permitted himself to demonstrate to 'poor Emma.' 'Poor Emma' was completely aware of the mean impression entertained of her abilities by her brother. Mrs. Sanderson lamented she had never presented herself at the Barclays. She so longed to fly to them — to offer assistance, if necessary — to pour forth her abounding sympathy — to tell them how sincerely she grieved for their afflictions; but how could she do this? — a stranger to them and theirs!

Mr. Egerton, who had never, by any chance in his arrogance, thought himself wrong, seemed to have caught glimpses — uncertain and flickering, to be sure — that his own example might have contributed to foster Gerald's natural taste for solitude; but if he could judge himself critically, what was she, the mother of this son, to do? Bitterly did she lament she had not availed herself, early in Gerald's life, of her maternal influence to wean him from the overstrained indulgence of his anti-social habits; that she had not offered herself as a sacrifice, and even accompanied him into the world. This world had been shut out from her own eyes and her child's, and she now feared, that if he yielded to her entreaties and went forth, he would be blinded by excess of light; for there could be nothing to interpose and shield him from the effects of the twilight gloom, in which he had hitherto been suffered to exist, and its shadows would continue to hang around him, and colour his future days.

She also thought, that if Charley were but at home, he might exert great influence over his brother, in this emergency, and be of signal importance to the unworldly Gerald; and sadly she missed the bright and cheerful spirit which had ever illumined her path, and who was separated from her by wide wide seas.

Mrs. Sanderson seated herself at her brother's board without the power to eat a morsel, the melancholy intelligence he had imparted to her having deprived her of all appetite for her meal. Not so Mr. Egerton. He discussed his repast precisely as if nothing had occurred, and, when the cloth was removed, recommenced his conversation with his sister. He told her that Gerald had hastily quitted him on leaving Mr. Barclay's, and he counselled her not to be alarmed at his non-appearance at the repast; he would doubtless return when he had gotten over the ebullition of his anger, and his astonishment at the harassing scenes through which he had that day passed; and that he would probably be thereby convinced that there was another mundane sphere, besides the one in which he had always thought proper to sojourn — a little more worldly, to be sure. But Mrs. Sanderson could not be diverted from her own sad reflections even by the unwonted occurrence of her brother's loquacity. Her thought was of Gerald. What would he do? How meet this momentous event in his life — the first — and certainly remarkably extraordinary in its complexion! Then, what was her son to do? — his habits broken up; his mind in a chaos of ideas, and contending emotions overwhelming him with their intensity. Mrs. Sanderson regarded her brother with a species of envy, that he could so quietly and coolly talk over the troubles which had befallen the child, who was apparently the least able to bear the assaults of fortune.

How would Gerald ever be able to stem the current of the busiest of communities? How was he to win his way along, coming, as he naturally must, in constant collision with the peculiarly wide-awake people, whom he would ever meet in the daily walks of life? Alas! these were questions she had often propounded to herself before in a helpless sort of way; now they arose in fearful legions before her affrighted imagination, and she marvelled how she had lived so long without comprehending their vital importance. Mrs. Sanderson reproached herself again and again with her own inertness and want of activity and energy. She considered herself to have been criminally negligent, and bewailed the absence of stringent measures in her conduct towards the children she adored. In fact, so acutely alive had she become, in those few passing hours, to the defects in her management, that in floods of bitter tears she wept her own deficiencies, and — many will concede — washed them away.

Since the death of her husband, Mrs. Sanderson's life had assumed such a monotonous complexion, that this was the first grand event which had occurred, and portentous did it seem to her in all its bearings. There was no way in which she could regard it without blaming herself, and possessing naturally a very tender conscience, she certainly spared none of her own short-comings, but, in fact, exaggerated them immensely. Then arose before her eyes a vision of the young husband, so early lost! had it pleased God to spare his life, how differently would these objects of her devoted affections have been educated! Gerald would not have been allowed to pursue his own way in such a decided manner — his enthusiastic love of learning would have been tempered with discretion; the father would have checked its immoderate indulgence, and looked to his physical nurture with care and attention. Whereas, what had she, the mother, done? Nothing — absolutely nothing! And now, for aught she knew, her son, her beloved Gerald — whom no one valued, no one appreciated, save herself — might be ruined by base suspicions and dark surmises, impossible to fathom or to answer. It was too distressing to dwell upon this constantly, so she tried to divert her thoughts from dwelling upon the dark and gloomy pictures she had conjured up; and then they reverted to Mr. Barclay's distressed family — alas! a sadder refuge.

Mr. Egerton, after the unwonted exertion of unbosoming himself to any one, and that person a woman, retired into the library, and seating himself in his high-backed leathern inconveniency, ruminated for a while; but the more he reflected, the more puzzled he became as to the person who could so boldly have perpetrated the outrage on his family name. This with him was an unpardonable offence. The world pronounced him to be a haughty, pompous, disagreeable, mean man, but no accusation had reached his *honour; that* was untarnished ever. Finding the chair extremely uneasy, (a fact which had been always apparent to all his family,) he arose and paced the room for hours — an unprecedented act in his life — and Peter informed Dinah late that very night, that 'a berry 'strawdinary affair had happened to Massa; he had not sat down the whole evening!'

With Mr. Egerton an excitement was such a novelty, and one growing out of a partial interest in the affairs of others, that a sort of *caviare gusto* adhered to it; and after revolving the whole story over in his mind repeatedly, he actually commenced taking a deep and deeper interest in it, until, at last, he quite finished by making it almost his own. And, again, he was rather sorry he had spoken so roughly to the ever meditative and gentle Gerald, and was vastly amused at the lion spirit he had aroused within him. For Mr. Egerton to confess to himself twice in one day, an interest in any one, and a tiny bit of repentance, was a miracle, indeed; *he* — the infallible personage! But even so it was. He tried to remember what he had really said, in his fury, to his nephew, which had produced such an ebullition of temper, and recollected that he had treated him very much like a boy, and thereby had discovered he was a man. 'Well,' soliloquized the bachelor, 'I may make something of that young fellow yet, there is ringing metal in him. He showed fight remarkably well.'

Altogether the day had not proved long; on the contrary, quite short. Mr. Egerton, being generally troubled with the duration of his waking hours, cultivated sleep assiduously. With absolutely nothing to do and very little to reflect upon, life with him was rather 'up-hill work,' so he was quite pleased on looking at his watch, to find it past ten o'clock.

When Peter went his nightly rounds to see that all was safe on the premises, in which he was always accompanied by Dinah and the dog, he discovered with amazement that Massa Gerald was not at home. 'What's going to happen next?' exclaimed he—'ole Massa up 'til ten, and young one out! nebber knew such doins afore. You go to bed, ole woman, and I'll wait up till he cum.' Wait and watch he did, until morning light dawned, and no Gerald appeared! Where that young gentleman was must be reserved for another chapter.

CHAPTER XX.

'I slept and dreamed that life was Beauty ;
I woke and found that life was Duty ;
Was then thy dream a shadowy lie ?
Toil on, sad heart, courageously,
And thou shalt find thy dream to be
A noonday light and truth to thee.' — Anon.

The moment Gerald Sanderson parted with his uncle, after the distressing scene of which he had been an agonized spectator, he sallied forth into the country with a rapidity of movement and a heart-stricken expression that arrested the attention of all he met; but little recked he of the piercing glances he received from the passers-by, — their doubts and surmises, — to all was he insensible. Suddenly, even before he was aware of the distance he had traversed, he found himself at the gates of the Mount Auburn Cemetery, and rushing through its solemn mazes tenanted by the dead, he reached his father's last resting-place, and, throwing himself beside it, wept a flood of tears. These tears, the first he had been able to shed, greatly relieved his overcharged heart, and there he remained for hours holding stern communion with himself. And bitterly did he then lament and deplore the passages of his short life, and grievously bewail its mistakes, its egotism and self-indulgence, which had not only injured his own well-being, but darkened and sullied the future of the lovely creature whom he had just left. Had he not been immured within his own four walls in the spring-time of life and enjoyment, the catastrophe which had brought shame and desolation to the hearth-stone of the best of men, would have been averted. He was the primary cause of this sad tale, and on his own devoted head must the blame fall. When he reflected that, but for himself and his follies, all would have been sunshine which was now darkness, he shuddered to think even death might ensue. His brain was on fire, and, maddened with remorse, he gnashed his teeth and wrung his hands in the depths of tribulation.

Strange to say, he had never, until that fatal morning, seen Georgiana Barclay, — never beheld the fair form of one whom his brother knew so well, and loved even as his own sister. He had heard Charley dilating upon the charms of the two objects of his affections until the very sound of their names, instead of creating a desire in his mind to behold these paragons, had filled it with a complete distaste for them, so superiour did he consider himself to the weakness of admiring any young girl whatever. This feeling had, at last, risen to such a pitch that he formally requested his brother to drop his ever-interminable discourse upon the perfections of the sisters, as it had become extremely tiresome for him to listen ; and, as is often the case, having reached this point, his aversion to the subjects of Charley's extravagant eulogiums became more and more decided. His brother, always conceding to him disputed opinions, had almost renounced all mention of the Barclay family in his presence, and made amends amply for his abstinence in that quarter by never ceasing to laud them to his mother, who lent an attentive and sympathizing ear. That Gerald Sanderson had become a little wayward and capricious from the indulgence of his whims at home, there was no question ; and, as Charley and his mother regarded him in the light of a prodigy of learning and accomplishment, these unpleasant defects were making great inroads into his character and marring its original excellence. Thus it happened, that when the beauteous vision of Georgiana Barclay appeared before him, claiming him for her husband, he was overwhelmed with the magnitude of her charms, and his whole nature seemed to experience an entire revolution in the short space of time which he had passed in her presence. Then to this was superadded her despair at the treachery which had been practised upon her; and the creature who had fainted at his feet, a very statue of Parian marble, seemed destined to fill up with her host of attractions, the measure of his existence. The first burst of feeling exhausted, he knelt and prayed for strength to begin a new life, to cast aside the visionary dreams in which he had revelled, lived, and had his being, and to substitute, in their stead, lasting and enduring duties. This fervent invocation finished, he vowed to devote himself to Georgiana Barclay forever, to defend and protect her through all the manifold trials, which he well knew awaited her in the vale of tears into which she had entered. 'I have been,' he exclaimed passionately, 'a weak, romantic boy; I will go forth from this hallowed spot a man. As my folly has destroyed the happiness of a woman for whom I would willingly lay down my own useless life, it is but meet that I should watch over her and protect her. From this moment my resolution is firmly taken; it shall be sacredly kept.' And Gerald Sanderson walked slowly and composedly home, and stood in his mother's presence a sadder and a wiser man.

Mrs. Sanderson was inexpressibly shocked at his appearance. Such an astonishing change had the occurrences of one day produced. She begged him to be seated, to take some slight restorative, for she was absolutely terrified at his exhausted condition. This he declined, but said he should soon be better; that the melancholy and exciting scenes through which he had passed had completely unmanned him, and sleep would be the best thing for him.

Gerald then proceeded to inform his mother, that, in consequence of the insulting and reproachful manner in which he had been assailed by his uncle in the morning, he had decided never to pass another night under his roof. Mrs. Sanderson was inexpressibly shocked at this determination, but on hearing a detailed account of the interview, she also made up her mind that her son could no longer accept the hospitality, such as it was, of her ungracious brother, and consistently with his own self-respect must leave the house that very evening. After some moment's reflection, she remembered a quiet and comfortable boarding-house kept by a poor widow whom she had formerly known, and having bestowed upon her afflicted son innumerable little attentions which served to compose his excited nerves, and bring his thoughts into a sufficient degree of order to make arrangements for leaving, she proposed to accompany him and engage lodgings. To this he cheerfully acceded. They soon reached their destination, and found a comfortable chamber, large and airy, which, from being in the third story of the house, was comparatively quite cheap. This was a very important object, for the mother's purse was but too scantily filled, and the son had so little that the most rigid economy would be required.

To this new abode Gerald repaired that night, and thus it happened that poor old Peter watched and waited till morning light for the young Massa, his mother having totally forgotten to inform the worthy servitor of the change in her son's destination. For this there certainly was sufficient excuse in the agitating scenes through which 'poor Emma' had passed. She, so unaccustomed to excitement of any sort, was amazed, when she summed up the events of the day, to find that she had actually been out of her own dwelling and ventured into another. She, however, passed a sleepless night, and when her son came to see her in the morning, she conjectured he had also done the same, from his wearied and worn appearance. She determined not to notice it, or in any way to advert to his sufferings. Hers was the task to pour balm into his bruised spirit. She fully understood, from the half-uttered confessions of the preceding evening, that he required all her tenderness and care; and when, on that day, he poured forth all the tale of his misery and despair into her bosom, she conjured him not to dwell upon this wretched theme until he could do so without such an undue degree of excitement. Mrs. Sanderson did not regret so much the view Gerald had taken of his innocent share in Miss Barclay's misfortunes, for she at once perceived that it was destined to be the source of a great revolution in his habits and feelings, and promised to be of essential importance to his future welfare. So she essayed to allay the outbreak of sensibility with which he accused himself of his complicity, but at the same time did not deny what was self-evident in his case. She admitted that, if he had lived like other youths of his age, he might have prevented the assumption of his name by an arch-deceiver, who had basely availed himself of his known peculiarities to insinuate himself into the confidence of the young lady who had so severely suffered from the treachery. At the same time she avowed she did not consider Georgy blameless, which it appeared Gerald did, and could not even endure to hear this part of the story adverted to. Mrs. Sanderson declared she thought Georgy's extreme youth a most extenuating circumstance — her romance of character another; but her first duty belonged to her parents, and she could not herself forget the deceptions practised, neither could she forgive them. 'When she reflected,' she said, 'upon the tender devotion, the unbounded love and indulgence of Mr. and Mrs. Barclay towards their children, and, moreover, their admirable management, and above all their example, she had small forbearance left for the girl who could have been so completely blinded to the priceless advantages she enjoyed.'

To this Gerald replied in no very logical manner, by declaring that he was alone to blame, that in his presence no man or woman should be permitted to advance aught in disparagement of his paragon, that it was his decided purpose to defend her character and reputation at all hazards, at all times, and on every proper occasion.

Mrs. Sanderson was thoroughly convinced that no true knight of old had ever been more completely imbued with this spirit of chivalrous devotion to his ladye-love than the tall, inspired youth who stood before her, — his eyes flashing fire, his whole graceful form breathing of spirit and enthusiasm. She was truly amazed at the change which had come over the spirit of his dream, and the velocity, (no other word could be used to designate the metamorphosis,) with which the whole had been so suddenly effected, — and one brief day had done this work! But what cannot one short day do?

Her mind was entirely at rest regarding Gerald's every-day concerns, as he had informed her he should give a week to the prosecution of his researches for Miss Barclay's husband, and then would commence a life of unremitting labour in his profession; always bearing in mind, however, that his first duty was the defence of the fair young girl, and the discovery of her treacherous husband. Evidently Gerald had nerved himself to his great work. His whole bearing was a picture of what may be done by man for man. His very step was firmer and bolder, and he already looked like a being of fixed purpose. His mother watched him from her window when he departed, — as mothers will, — and admired, with deep-felt expressions of gratitude, the air and bearing of her son as he receded from her view.

Mr. Philip Egerton, after a remarkably excellent night's rest, (he was not usually a good sleeper,) arose much refreshed and in uncommon spirits, descended to his breakfast, and was informed by Peter that his sister had already discussed that meal two hours before.

'Bless me,' exclaimed he, 'I must have overslept myself, — how extraordinary!'

Peter imagined the sky was about to rain larks; for this

late repast, superadded to all the other marvels, had nearly upset his not over well-balanced brain. However, he fidgetted about, having something more wonderful still to relate, but his master seemed determined to take no notice whatever of his varied attempts to commence a conversation, and he began to think he should never have a chance to impart his intelligence. Suddenly Mr. Egerton remembered he had not seen Gerald, and felt rather inclined to ask him one or two questions respecting his affairs, his colloquy with 'poor Emma' having opened the flood-gates of all the eloquence he possessed, so he ordered Peter to call him. This was the moment for that worthy's long desired explosion; but when it arrived, the good and affectionate creature was so overpowered by his sorrow, that, instead of answering, he burst into what the boys call a 'boohoo,' and blubbered and sobbed in a whirlwind of griefs.

'What in the name of heaven is the matter?' cried Mr. Egerton. 'Is Gerald Sanderson ill?'

'No, Sir, no, Sir,' stammered Peter.

'Well, what then?' asked his master.

'He's gone Sir, gone clean away, Sir, the young Massa, I'se always tended since he would make nasty dirt-pies, — to be sure, nebber so many as Massa Charley, nebber so uncommon many, but he's gone for all that, — and left ole Dinah and I, and his mother, nebber to come home agin, eben to hab his best coat brushed. Oh! oh! who will ebber do it as I hab, or clean his shoes! To be sure, he nebber dirtied 'em much, he nebber go out much, and now he'll nebber come back again. Oh, Lord! Oh, Lord! what will his mother, Dinah, and ole Peter and the dog do? Lord, Lord, what will become of Dinah and me and his mother! trunks and all gone! Oh, dear! oh, dear!'

Mr. Egerton, convinced that no information was to be obtained from this mourner, was repairing to his sister's apartment, when, on the front staircase, he found Dinah, — a second Niobe, — all tears and lamentations, sitting with her checked apron over her head, and holding Tiger's successor in her arms, bewailing the loss of young Massa. Dinah had got thus far, in her ascension to Mrs. Sanderson, when she declared she felt such a swimming in her old head, she was obliged to sit right down on the grand staircase — a liberty she had never allowed herself to take with the grand staircase before — but every thing went wrong that day, she said.

Philip began to think he should never reach his sister and learn what had really happened in his household; so, telling Dinah she was an old fool, though he really did justice to the faithfulness and devotion of his servants, he found 'poor Emma,' who, frightened out of her wits, had to impart the reasons of Gerald's disappearance. Having calmly heard her story and also her approval and acquiescence in her son's projects, he coolly told her he thought this might prove in the end the very best thing that could possibly happen to Gerald. His removal from his sky parlour, and his descent from the regions of morbid imaginations to the commonalities and realities of existence, might effect a radical change in his life; and, whereas he would never have done any thing or made any thing of himself, he now stood a chance of becoming a valuable member of society. 'In fact,' resumed Mr. Egerton, ''tis the very best news I can possibly hear of that remarkably silly boy. He actually roused up yesterday, like a young lion from his lair, and I hope he may continue to feel precisely as he now does. For myself, I don't care a rush for his anger, or indignation, — I'm only glad he's departed.'

This was a long peroration for the Mandarin to make at one sitting; so, having delivered himself of it, he quickly repaired to his old arm-chair in State street and his dozen newspapers, and spoke never a word more that morning.

Mrs. Sanderson descended to the kitchen, and did her best to assuage the unlimited bewailings and howlings of the sable pair in their own favoured spot; but finding they insisted upon nursing their grief, she left them to the ample enjoyment they seemed to derive from their luxury of woe, at the same time, thanking them sincerely for their heartfelt sympathy.

CHAPTER XXI.

'The glories of our earthly state,
Are shadows, not substantial things.'
SHIRLEY.

MR. BARCLAY, raising his insensible child from the floor, bore her tenderly in his arms to her chamber, and laying her carefully upon her bed, instantly summoned his servants, and sent in every direction for medical assistance. The stricken father was quite assured that this terrible shock would produce the most dangerous results, and so it proved; for as soon as Georgy was restored to consciousness, her brain seemed literally on fire, and for hours, ravings and faintings followed each other in rapid succession. At night, when it was pronounced to be a brain fever, the mother took her place at the bedside of the sufferer, and watching over her in intense anguish of spirit, prayed that this bitter cup might pass away, and the life of the beloved object of her affections might be spared. An experienced nurse, who had been employed, vainly essayed to urge Mrs. Barclay to take some repose, but the next morning found her on the same spot, worn with fatigue and sorrow. The medical men, in their consultation that day, declared that the patient was in a most critical state, and that no opinion could be pronounced for many days, or even weeks; that the malady being a moral one, as well as physical, was all the more difficult to treat, and the more uncertain to decide upon its future course; that time could only answer the anxious questionings of the half-distracted parents. With these opinions the members of this family were fain to remain in a state of heart-rending suspense.

As the most profound silence was enjoined, no one but the nurse and one other person was allowed to remain in Georgy's chamber, her poor father every now and then creeping to the bedside, and taking just a hurried look at the sufferer. Mr. Barclay could not be persuaded to leave the house. He however received all his friends, who gathered around him in deep sympathy with his affliction. Several of these sympathizers, with the very best possible feelings, suggested that the whole truth of the sad story might not be revealed, and that the marriage had better not be avowed. As they rather urged this course, he replied, — 'I could never consent that there should be any concealment whatever, and that the whole truth and nothing short of it should be given to the public. For,' resumed he, 'you may depend upon what I say, the people here never believe any part of a story where one half of it is left unrevealed; but, let them at once know the whole truth, and they will immediately begin to find excuses and apologies for almost any thing, and especially for the errors of extreme youth. I have known,' he said, 'the most wretched falsehoods adhere to whole families for half a century, when, if at first all the incidents of the cases had been freely communicated to the public, the whole thing would have dissolved itself into thin air in a month. No, no, my dear friends, I sincerely thank you for your kindness, but my mind is made up on this point.'

Mr. Richard Barclay, who had evinced the most profound sympathy and sorrow on learning the sad story of his beloved brother's calamity, was foremost in these entreaties for silence; but on listening to Mr. Barclay's opinions, he said: — 'I don't know that you are not all right, John, after all; for of one thing I am perfectly sure, nothing could be concealed from the American people; they ferret every thing fairly out, sooner or later; so perhaps it is best to give the whole story at once; for, if you do not, as they are very imaginative in this sort of affairs, they will finish by making it twenty times worse than it is.'

'Alas! my dear brother,' replied Mr. Barclay, 'that seems to me just now quite impossible.'

'You will think differently in time,' rejoined Mr. Richard. 'You must let things take their accustomed course, John; the nine days' wonder of talk will inevitably occur; you well know how the public revels in disagreeable, melancholy and horrid events, and how it delights in disseminating the story of them. Who ever hears a pleasant bit of news here? Nobody. But if there is any thing so shocking it absolutely makes one's heart ache to listen to it, somebody must needs put on his seven leagued boots and come to spoil one's dinner with the recital thereof. Nobody ever told me an agreeable thing in my natural life, and nobody ever will. Why, I've heard, between the pirouettes in a quadrille, talk about a horrid murder or shipwreck, which would go far to making your hair stand on end. It's our way, and a mighty disagreeable one it is. Why can't we be smiling and gracious like the French? It all comes of our descent from that Melpomene-loving John Bull. I wish most heartily we had possessed another grandfather.'

And thus Mr. Richard scolded on; the affliction which had befallen his brother not having tended to sweeten the acerbity of his temper, he always choosing to regard misfortunes in the light of personal aggressions. This certainly might not have appeared to be an opportune occasion for the expression of such strong and decided prejudices, but they belonged to his overloaded faggot, and he had been so long grumbling, that it had become an inveterate habit, of which he could not rid himself, and, to do him all imaginable justice, of which he was quite unconscious. This over-critical and carping personage would have regarded just such a declaimer against things, all and several, as himself, an intolerable bore, and would have found it quite impossible to endure his presence even an hour; but Mr. Richard Barclay was no exception to the general rule of man's blindness to his own peculiarities.

These criticisms upon men and things in his own country, had grown by what they fed on, until they had assumed extravagant proportions, and had been so mingled with Mr. Richard's daily conversation, that, however deeply interesting, and even poignantly so, as in this case, the subject might be, it was evermore sure to be garnished with a few nettles, and very stinging they were, as the reader well knows. Here was a man, his heart actually bleeding for the woes of his best friends, and which might assuredly seem all absorbing,—and yet, such was the tyranny of a bad habit, that he could not abstain from it, even upon the most momentous occasions. Truly do we build around us impenetrable walls of hewn granite, prison-houses from which we cannot escape.

On that day Mr. Barclay received Gerald Sanderson, who, after walking hours before the house, at last ventured to ring the door-bell, and request an audience. Poor Gerald was entirely overwhelmed with affliction when he beheld the father of the woman whom he had solemnly sworn to defend and protect. Mr. Barclay himself, so affected he could hardly give him an audible welcome, listened in wrapt and mournful attention to the outpourings of the youthful enthusiast, as he detailed the misery he endured, his sorrow and grief. Indeed, as soon as he had mastered his own emotion, he applied himself vigorously to soothing the sufferings of the sorely stricken youth, who poured out his feelings in the most affecting terms. When some degree of composure had been secured, Mr. Barclay assured and re-assured Gerald Sanderson that he considered him entirely free from blame—and begged him to think nothing of the unhappy circumstance, and conjured him not to dwell any longer upon it. To this Gerald replied, that it was entirely impossible for him to do otherwise, it being his daily thought and nightly dream; and that, while the life current flowed in his veins, so should it ever be. That he was imperatively called upon to be Miss Barclay's champion, and had vowed himself to her cause, as truly and devotedly as ever did knight of old; that nothing should deter him from trying to drag to light the usurper of his name, and expose his falsehood and treachery, and he should never again sleep in peace until that was effected.

This interview was not without its beneficial effects upon Mr. Barclay, who found himself thus obliged, in his own misery, to minister to the 'mind diseased' of another. He comforted and soothed his half-distracted young friend, and having retained him several hours, begged him to visit him as often as he could.

The intense sympathy which Gerald had shown for the sufferings of himself and family, had greatly interested the unhappy father, and he perceived that he was indeed one who could probe the veriest depths of their afflictions from the intensity of his own.

Mr. Barclay also beheld a sensitive and shrinking nature, united to great tenderness and manliness of character, awaking from a species of torpor which had encompassed it, avowing its nobleness and chivalry; he beheld it with a feeling of deep interest mingled with a strong sentiment of gratitude. And how could he but choose be grateful to one who, in the sincerity of his heart, had sworn allegiance to the 'bruised reed,' now lying perchance on her bed of death?

Mr. Barclay's piety was of a healthful, cheerful character, and confiding nature; he knew that 'whom the Lord loveth he chasteneth,' and this conviction was, for him, a source of perpetual consolation and gratitude. He regarded his present affliction as no special punishment, he beheld the rain fall alike on the just and the unjust, and he knew the ways of Providence to be dark and mysterious, but ever wise and merciful; he acknowledged that he had enjoyed a larger proportion of prosperity than usually falls to the lot of mortals, and so believing, he bowed himself submissively before, what would seem to be the law of man's nature, partial suffering and sorrow.

Mr. Barclay's life had been one of faith and works. To the best of his ability he had husbanded the talent confided to him, but he had seen good men and true, whom he, in his humility, considered infinitely superiour to himself, exposed to long trains of afflictions and privations; and he resolved, come what would, to bear his cross meekly, patiently, and await the final hour when all things should be revealed. With this state of mind this good man mingled no complaints or repinings, for he was devoutly grateful for the blessings he still retained.

And night found the patient restless, fevered and delirious, not even recognising the gentle touch of her grieving mother, who, hovering around her pillow, was ever administering unavailing remedies. And day succeeded to day and week to week, without any material change for the better; to be sure, the phases of her complaint varied, and at last typhoid seemed to be rooted in her exhausted frame; to this was added such complete prostration that every moment threatened to be her last.

When Georgiana Barclay was first taken ill, her father had only entered her room to give one look at his suffering child, but as the malady gained ground and the symptoms changed, and she becoming every day weaker, he was required to lift her, which doing so gently and firmly she seemed to prefer his aid to that of any other person; then he began to pass the nights by her bedside, forcing his wife to take some needful repose the while, for she was nearly exhausted with fatigue from constant watching. And thus Mr. Barclay came to guard and protect this young creature in the still hours of the night, and his spirit sank within him as he looked upon the attenuated form of his idolized child, and communed with himself upon her probable future destiny, should it please God to spare her life. And a thorny path was in this perspective; narrow and rugged the way. The mystery of her marriage, were it revealed or not, promised nothing but misery, for surely the wretch, who could have thus deceived her, was utterly unworthy to be claimed as her husband, even should he prove to belong to the most virtuous family in the land; and if he did not, what was he? — who was he? Soul-harrowing questions were these for a parent to ask of himself, with no possibility of being answered. Mr. Barclay firmly believed in his daughter's statement; he knew her to be the soul of truth and honour, but could he ask the same reliance on her testimony from others? She was henceforth, in the event of her restoration to health, to walk through life, bearing a blighted name; enshrouded in darkness, unenlivened by a ray of light, if her husband were not discovered, and if he were, the deepest obscurity might be preferable. How truly then would Georgiana require the strong arm of her father to support her fainting steps, and her loving mother's sympathy in this profound affliction, to which would be superadded the harrowing conviction that all this trouble had been caused by her own imprudence and misconduct.

The father also trembled for the accusations which her overcharged conscience would perpetually elicit, and the reproaches of this inward monitor he conceived would be ceaseless. What a sad picture of human suffering was presented to his imagination, — and who was the victim? his beloved child, — his first-born, who had awakened in his heart the first enthralling sentiment of paternity.

Oh! the dark, dark hours of those protracted vigils! they contained months of torturing reflections, unresolved doubts, and soul-searching bitterness, which nothing, save prayer, could mitigate or assuage. On the first revelation of this affliction he had thought of abandoning Boston and all his pursuits, and retreating into the country, there to bury his daughter's shame and sorrow; but, after mature reflection, he became convinced of the impropriety of such a proceeding, as it might give rise to more suspicions than already existed; so he resolved to remain. There were doubts to be removed, and he trusted in Providence that his child's innocence would be proved; for he knew that, if human efforts could effect this, he and his numerous friends would, in the end, discover the mystery.

And surely man was never blessed with more ardent and enthusiastic supporters than was Mr. Barclay. They vowed never to desist from the search for the wretch who had assumed Gerald Sanderson's name; and one and all declared they should never be satisfied until they had dragged him to light.

Mrs. Ashley had almost lived in the house during the long illness of her darling; refusing all other engagements, she installed herself every morning in the library, ever ready to be occupied about the patient, who sometimes appeared to derive comfort from her presence.

Mr. Richard had evinced the devotion and tenderness of one of the sex whom he had always affected to despise, and though he was not exactly the person to be found serviceable in a sick room, he could give his unrepressed sympathy. He was constantly running all over Boston, and sending to New York for delicacies which his poor niece could not touch when they arrived, and moreover, he entirely forgot to find fault with his pet dislike, Mrs. Ashley; the strongest proof he could possibly evince, of the all-absorbing nature of his grief; also he made no comments upon Miss Tidmarsh. Mrs. Gordon, ever active and energetic, employed herself assiduously in assisting Mrs. Barclay, whose patience and fortitude seemed absolutely undying; and even Mrs. Redmond aroused herself sufficiently to insist upon doing something, though what that something was to be, nobody very well comprehended.

Georgy's young friends actually besieged the house with proffers of aid from their parents and themselves, and every thing was done that kindness of heart and feeling could suggest to alleviate the suffering family.

At last, there appeared a change for the better; at first so slight as to be hardly perceptible, but slowly every day increasing, and yet the medical men, in attendance, would pronounce no distinctly favourable opinion. In time, however, youth rallied and conquered, and Georgiana Barclay was raised from her deathlike prostration, and pronounced out of all danger. With what intense feelings of grateful devotion her father and mother received this joyful intelligence, there is small occasion for recounting. Suffice to say, they poured forth their surcharged hearts in earnest and solemn thanks to the Source from which emanated this great and abounding mercy, and asserted that all was well with them. They would bow, they declared, with childlike submission to the infliction which had been sent in the secret marriage of their daughter, — for was she not spared unto them? all other misfortunes had paled before the harrowing thought of her death. Nothing was remembered but her restoration from the fell destroyer, and they thanked God for his signal mercies, and repeated and reiterated that all was well with them.

CHAPTER XXII.

'There's not a look, or word of thine
My soul hath e'er forgot;
Thou ne'er hast bid a ringlet shine,
Nor giv'n thy locks one graceful twine,
Which I remember not.'

MOORE.

MRS. REDMOND was sitting, dozing over a yellow-covered novel of the worst possible sort — its cover as dirty as its contents — and every now and then taking a peep through her torn lace curtains at the Barclay house, when Jane and Miss Tidmarsh rushed in. Miss Serena resembled, on this momentous occasion, an overboiling cauldron, and Jane was so breathless with the news she had to impart, that she could not speak for several minutes.

Mrs. Redmond, at last, becoming conscious by unmistakeable signs, that there was an explosion somewhere, aroused herself sufficiently to inquire what it was; so she said, 'What have you to tell, girls? what has happened?'

'Oh,' almost shrieked Jane, 'such an adventure at our neighbours the Barclays; such a story! such a hubbub!'

'Ah!' said her mother, with a sort of half-awakened, half-bewildered air, 'any thing wrong there? — any mischief?'

'Mischief, and to spare, my mother,' was the reply; 'there is Georgiana Barclay, who, it appears, has been married a long time, as she thought, to that bit of dream-land, Gerald Sanderson; and having, only yesterday, confessed her wicked doings to her parents — though why she did it now nobody can tell — this has naturally created the most intense commotion. Now, you perceive what your model is, I hope — the girl you have always held up to me for example! Well, Mr. Barclay instantly, on the reception of this terrible communication being made to him, posted down to Mr. Egerton's, saw the old miser, who vomited forth fire and flames in his anger — and between the two, poor frightened Gerald was dragged down from the upper regions of the old house, where he studies the stars; and, both abusing him at once for his treachery and duplicity, placed him in a carriage, and went, as fast as the horses could carry them, to Mr. Barclay's.' Then Jane made a solemn pause, and looking her mother in the face, appeared to enjoy immensely her great excitement.

'Oh, this is too, too shocking to believe,' cried Mrs. Redmond; 'how very sad indeed!'

'I can yet tell you something worse still,' said Jane:— 'Lo! and behold! when Gerald Sanderson was confronted with George Barclay, they had beheld each other for the very first time in their natural lives! He was not the right man! some one else had assumed his name.'

Then Jane Redmond, having produced the unheard-of circumstance of thoroughly arousing her dormant parent, indulged in a loud and malicious burst of laughter.

Mrs. Redmond had never been charged with an overflow of affection for her neighbours; but she was a mother, and she felt that this was a load of grief and suffering almost too great for human endurance. She exclaimed: 'How can you be so hard-hearted as to laugh and mock at such misery as the Barclays must suffer? Shame! shame on you, my daughter.'

'La, mother!' cried Jane, 'you seem to have changed all of a sudden, it seems to me, and have begun to stand by that disagreeable family; for my part, I rejoice that pride has had a downfall.'

'And I also,' chimed in Miss Tidmarsh.

It seemed, at that moment, as if Mrs. Redmond had, for the first time, comprehended how culpable had been her neglect of her child, and how much she had to answer for at the great tribunal, where all are weighed in the balance. Here was a creature, confided to her charge by the Almighty, who had been permitted to foster such evil passions as made her own mother's blood curdle in her veins; her eyes opened to the total want of care in her management of this child, her own indolence and apathy, and her own consequent unhappiness. 'Jane,' said she, solemnly, 'can you possibly forget when little Mary laid insensible; when we had all renounced even a shadow of hope; when I, her mother, who never despair, had made up my mind that I must resign my youngest born, — can you forget, I repeat, that Mrs. Barclay, with energetic confidence, almost breathed the breath of life into your sister by her innumerable applications and frictions, — how she watched over her day and night, until she was pronounced out of danger, and then crept silently out of the house to avoid our acknowledgments? Thank God, I, at least, expressed my undying gratitude to that woman for her kindness.'

'Miss Serena Tidmarsh,' said she, addressing her particularly, 'you will please to walk immediately out of my doors, and never do you re-enter them again. I have long thought your society was a great injury to my daughter, whom I devoutly hope is not as malicious as she seems to be. I therefore desire her to hold no further communion with you.'

Miss Serena forthwith made her exit, in a very crestfallen manner, which, to say the least, was very different from her entrance. Mrs. Redmond then ordered Jane to her chamber for the day, which command the young lady sullenly obeyed, and, once there, cried heartily from mere spite, but having exhausted her tears, recommenced her accustomed operations of watching the Barclays' house. The fact was, that Jane Redmond's incurable fancy for knowing and settling other people's affairs, and her insatiate thirst for scandal, which had been encouraged by her bosom friend, Miss Tidmarsh, had so completely vitiated a heart naturally none of the best, that no favourable impression could be made upon it; at least by her mother, whose inertness and indolence she despised.

Thus Mrs. Redmond even reaped as she had sowed, and finding that she possessed no influence whatever over her daughter, she, that very day, resolved that Mary Redmond, a promising girl, should be instantly removed from her sister's contaminating presence, and this was shortly effected. Mary, incessantly domineered over and thwarted by Jane, was delighted to hear that she was to be sent to a good boarding-school. There was but one drawback to her happiness, and that was her separation from her friend Kate Barclay, whom she really loved, though now and then she teased her a little. She crossed the street, imparted to her this pleasant intelligence, and embracing her again and again, took an affectionate farewell of her.

When Robert Redmond returned home to dinner, his countenance well betrayed his feelings; not a morsel could he swallow, and at last, fairly overcome, he left the table. His mother immediately following him, he threw himself on her neck and wept like a child. Mrs. Redmond loved her son, now she respected him; so great was the contrast between him and his hard-hearted sister. She informed him that she had literally turned Miss Tidmarsh out of doors, and also imparted her determination to send Mary to school, and to this plan he gave his unqualified approbation. Apart from his knowledge of the pernicious influence exercised over Jane by Miss Tidmarsh, he was greatly relieved by her banishment, for she had lately taken into her silly head a project of enslaving him, which she seemed disposed to carry into effect by main force.

Poor Robert! he certainly did consider this an infliction, and often asked himself what great sin he had committed to merit such a punishment. Wherever he went he was sure to find Miss Tidmarsh; she was certain to be returning home at the precise moment he went to his meals, and ever just about to take a walk as he left his house. She literally haunted his steps, and actually made him, at times, quite nervous. It being extremely easy for her to know all his movements from Jane, who never dreamed of her friend's projects, she was always at the right moment in the right place, in her own view of the subject; Mr. Robert Redmond being of a totally different opinion.

It may be asked where was Mr. Redmond on this day when his best friend's home was filled with grief and sorrow. He came to his dinner and received the sad intelligence with sundry ejaculations, evidently not comprehending it at all; his head being filled with a patent case, he was revolving machinery, and arranging all its knotty points. One week afterwards, the suit being decided in his favour, he had leisure to feel quite sorry for Mr. Barclay's affliction.

In the evening, Robert Redmond held a confidential conversation with his mother, in which he imparted to her his long cherished affection for Georgiana Barclay. 'He could hardly,' he said, 'remember when it began, and he felt, now that she was lost to him forever, immeasurably wretched.' He was greatly indignant at the author of her misery, and declared he would give ten years of his life to discover her husband. Never for a moment doubted he the truth of the unhappy young creature's story, nor did his mother; they well knew she was truthful and honourable. Mrs. Redmond, who felt grieved that she had permitted herself ever to believe aught in disparagement of her valuable neighbours, or to entertain any prejudice whatever against them, dwelt with feelings of gratitude on Mrs. Barclay's kindness during Mary's recent illness, and the attentive devotion it had elicited. Indeed, that day proved an era in her existence, dispelling many disagreeable thoughts and awakening many profitable reflections. The next morning Robert Redmond called on Mr. Barclay, and told him in a straight-forward manner, that having learned he had no objection to speak upon the melancholy event which had occurred in his family, he had come to offer his services in endeavouring to discover the wretch who had destroyed, in such a mysterious manner, its peace and well-being.

Mr. Barclay answered him kindly, even affectionately, and declared himself to be greatly obliged to him, and most willing to accept his proffered services in the dire extremity to which he was reduced. Robert Redmond then inquired about Miss Barclay's state of health, and her father informed him that she still laid in a state of partial insensibility, and that he entertained strong doubts of her survival of the shock she had endured. This sad communication completely unnerved the young lover, and he found it impossible to repress his sensibility, and, seating himself, remained some time quite overcome.

Mr. Barclay was much affected by this demonstration of feeling, and spoke openly to him of his own sufferings, and expressed his gratitude for the sympathy exhibited towards his child.

'Alas! my dear Sir,' said Robert, 'I have so long loved your daughter, that I now find much difficulty in remembering the commencement of my interest in her. Imagine then, I pray, my distress when all my long-cherished hopes are blasted, and in such a cruel manner. I could submit with some degree of patience to this infliction, if I could be assured of Miss Barclay's happiness; but when I reflect upon the indignity offered to you and yours, my blood actually boils with resentment and anger.'

'We are in the hands of the Lord, my young friend,' said Mr. Barclay, 'and whatsoever he chooses to inflict we must bear with submission.'

'Allow me to say, Sir,' said Robert, 'that the whole community sympathizes with you. My mother's heart bleeds for Mrs. Barclay; indeed, she is aroused in a most remarkable way.' He then sorrowfully and respectfully withdrew.

Robert Redmond returned to his mother, and communicated to her the state of Mr. Barclay's family, and she instantly wrote a note, overflowing with gratitude to Mrs. Barclay, for her devotion in her own child's extremity, and begged to be allowed to make some slight return. She offered to watch day and night, and declared she should never be satisfied until she was employed in her behalf. Mrs. Barclay sent Kate with a kind message of thanks that Mrs. Redmond's proffers of aid would be gratefully accepted when needed, but that, at present, they were overwhelmed with like requests.

The reaction had been very powerful in Mrs. Redmond's views of her opposite neighbours; she watched their house still, devoting all the time she could possibly spare from her novel reading, but, happily, not with the same carping and critical spirit. Indeed, it is extremely doubtful if the lady would have overlooked them at all, had not her lounging-chair been placed near the window. Where there really exists a good heart, however overgrown it may have become with rank weeds, let but one ray of sunshine enter, and another invariably follows. Mrs. Redmond was actually enjoying the effects of such a felicitous event.

Robert Redmond wandered about the town despairingly; he could fix upon no occupation; his mind was a chaos of contending emotions. He now comprehended that all hope for him had fled, and bitterly lamented he had not essayed more openly to win Miss Barclay's affections. The truth was, that he, in his humility, although much older than the young girl, had considered himself so immeasurably beneath her, that he had never ventured to address her but with the commonest courtesies of every-day life. Then Jane was so disagreeable, that their home had few attractions for very young people, and Mary, though pleasing, was too juvenile for any members of the family, except Kate.

Mary Redmond was a very good little girl, and, as it sometimes occurs in such disorganized domestic elements, she stood forth quite prominently in this discordant family; more, perhaps, by force of contrast than otherwise.

The good example of the Barclays had a great share in colouring Mary's existence, and her brother's also, and their beneficent influence became every day more visible. Robert Redmond revolved over perpetually in his mind who the wretch could be, who had so essentially destroyed the happiness of the family he so dearly loved. He could not remember to have ever seen Georgiana Barclay with any one with whom he was unacquainted, but once. In vain, did he try to recall the features of this individual. He recollected thinking, at the time, he was a stranger, but, as his friends were always receiving foreigners, he paid no attention to the circumstance.

In all his reflections, and amidst this maze of conjectures to which there existed no clue, never did he, for a moment, blame Georgiana; she remained in his eyes, as ever, faultless, nor would he permit any one else to blame her. Fiercely resenting any criticisms on her conduct, he was ever ready to do battle with any one in her defence; and no true aud loyal knight of old ever held his ladye-love in deeper, higher, holier consideration than the sorrowing youth, who, from morning till night, fretted out his days in repining for the treasure he had lost. Robert's love seemed rooted all the more deeply in his heart that he had never revealed it, and to this conclusion had it come at last, that it was the absorbing interest of his life. No other woman, he repeatedly avowed, should ever occupy Georgy's place in his affections.

Mrs. Redmond, becoming extremely absorbed in the afflictions of her friends, her son beheld, to his immense satisfaction, the disappearance of the tawdry looking volumes he so much disliked, and perceived his mother had substituted for them some embroidery. This he considered a salutary change, for he entertained an unmitigated disgust for the would-be fashionable gentry she patronized; not even to mention the bandits, brigands, and robbers, whom she liked better still. This change, however, only lasted during the beginning of her excitement; she soon returned to her old friends with renewed vigour. Robert Redmond suddenly found himself, to his astonishment, leaning on his mother, — the slight and frail reed that mother had ever seemed to be to him! And now she was all the world. Weak, indolent and frivolous as she was, Mrs. Redmond's sensibility awoke after her own fashion, at the call for sympathy from a son whom she had loved, but was too inert to make any decided demonstration, and she responded to the appeal warmly and devotedly.

And thus it is, man may wander about, seeking for counsel and support in other quarters, but he returns to his mother at last. Surely, Robert Redmond's parent would have seemed to be lamentably deficient in all the requisites for grand emergencies; but maternal love had lighted a lamp in her heart, if it had failed to do so in her brain, and she seemed to him a very tower of strength. And indeed she was; she comforted, soothed, deplored and caressed, and truly did just as well for him, under the circumstances, as if she had been the wisest woman in all Christendom.

Robert discovered that, at the very moment he lost his mistress, he had found his mother; that she was an equivalent might be questioned, but she contrived to dispel, by her tender attentions, a vast deal of gloom and despondency which prevailed in the heart of her son; and, this being the case, it was of small import if Mrs. Redmond were silly or wise. And then how that mother rejoiced with her son at the glad tidings of Georgiana Barclay's restoration to health!

CHAPTER XXIII.

'Some falls are the means the happier to rise.'
SHAKSPEARE.

AND Georgiana Barclay arose from her bed of pain and suffering, pale, wan and exhausted. The lily of the valley was not more colourless than her delicate cheek, nor more disposed to hide itself from human ken than was this crushed flower, swept to the ground by merciless blasts. Rude winds had visited the blue-veined brow, over which rich masses of golden curls flowed in graceful beauty, but the eyes that, heretofore, had beamed on all so lustrously, were dimmed: their downcast lids seemed doomed ne'er to rise again; their light was quenched indeed. A creature, shipwrecked on the sanded shores of life, ere that young life began, was this sweet bud of promise; she had loved, hoped, trusted, and, alas! all too early, had won the guerdon of woman's destiny; and she was to bear her cross through her apppointed days courageously, fearlessly, or perish. The future on earth was dark and sombre. A blight was upon her fair fame, never to be effaced; with this heart-rending conviction she beheld the sun rise and set; her nights were passed in tears.

A weight of woe was upon her almost too heavy for human strength to cope with, but she was young, and youth can never be entirely divested of hope; a portion of this blessing will ever cling to early days, even under the most adverse fortunes. Women of maturer years, as it has been demonstrated in many cases, sink under even the slightest, faintest breath of scandal affecting their honour; they understand all the concomitant wretchedness and misery attendant upon it; they full well know that, like the Venetian mirror of old, it must not be approached, — and they sink. It is a wise dispensation of Providence that the spring-tide of existence is buoyant and hopeful, — 'Hope on, hope ever,' its motto. Life is made up of contrarieties which admit of no explanation; and that woman, redolent of benevolent and tender sensibility, should have no charity for the frailty of her own sex, is the most extraordinary of all; but so it is, and has ever been. And, even more, she gives no quarter, — she allows no extenuating circumstances to change the fiat of her cold decision; the nearest approach to mercy she can reach is not to believe in the existence of guilt, is not to listen to the sad tale of its misery and despair. No sterner *Daniel come to judgment*, than is woman to woman. Of all this a girl of seventeen is fortunately ignorant, and however she may deplore in bitter tears of contrition and repentance the course of events which have covered her with a shroud of suspicious gloom, she knows not the deep profound of her misfortune, its appalling and enduring quality, its tenacious and abiding nature. For the possession of the rich sources of wealth, locked up in the ardent and devoted affection of her parents and family, Georgiana Barclay poured forth her whole soul in thanks to her Creator; she had been saved from entering the dark valley of death, and she resolved that the rest of her days should be given entirely to them, and them only. Should the husband who had so treacherously won her hand, re-appear, she would never again behold him; she considered herself perfectly justified in adopting this course and adhering to it. In fact, she had conceived an irrepressible disgust with every thing appertaining to the recreant to truth and honour, who had so wickedly misled her youthful imagination, and lured her away from her allegiance to her parents and friends; the sight of him would have been hateful to her. The more she reflected upon her own misconduct, the more rigorously she blamed herself, and the more odious she became in her own eyes. She believed that no sacrifice she could ever make would suffice to atone for the load of misery she had brought upon all she held most dear in the world. She thought no penance which she could perform, no sacrifice she could make, would be any atonement for the grief and even shame she had brought down upon the head of her revered father; and for the mother who had untiringly and perseveringly watched over her day and night through wearisome months, she dared hardly to raise her eyes in her presence. A tender conscience had Georgiana Barclay, an excellent thing in man or woman. It was Mr. Barclay's desire that his daughter should, on her convalescence, re-appear in her own little world, as if nothing had occurred to disturb the even current of her young days; and this wish being communicated to her in writing, (for he could not trust himself to speak,) Georgiana registered a solemn vow that all its requirements should be fulfilled, let the cost to herself be what it might. And dreadful was the conflict of her agonized feelings when the evening arrived wherein she was again to rejoin the circle once to her so genial, so fascinating and endearing. It came all too soon: she had counted the days, and, as they swiftly departed, she had bitterly mourned their absence, and would gladly have availed herself of any plausable excuse to evade the dreaded moment when she should again behold the assembled group. Alas! what a mighty change had come over the spirit of her dream of life since the last time she had stood amidst her family and friends! Then, though she was threatened with the storm which had now broken over her devoted head, yet she had seen it only in perspective, and had never until now fully comprehended its magnitude and its fearfully momentous consequences. So thought this young creature, but little she recked, comparatively, what these consequences were to be, — 'A blindness to the future kindly given.' At any rate, she nerved herself to the task, and found herself once more restored to the apparently unchanged communion with her tried and faithful friends; but she felt there had been a change. There was a shade more of tenderness in their greeting, and a deeper intonation in their pleasant voices, which fell upon her ear gratefully yet sadly.

Miss Edgeworth has a heroine who would have submitted to any other infliction than pity as a punishment for her short-comings ; and true it is, that this quality is often mixed up with worldly feelings, which engender disturbing doubts of its native purity. Not that any thing so base had entered the charmed circle of which Georgy found herself the centre ; but she was, for the first time in her life, a victim to suspicious doubts, and so henceforth seemed doomed to remain. Indeed, from the peculiarity of her situation, how could this be otherwise ? and suspicion was already added to the weight of the burthen which her overladen spirit was to bear.

Uncle Richard 'for this evening only,' forgot to grumble, and contradicted Mrs. Ashley but once, that pleasant lady being all smiles and gaiety as usual. Mrs. Gordon was in her most entertaining mood, and her daughter, wild with joy and excitement, never took her eyes from the beautiful picture of her restored friend. Kate literally danced for joy ; and Gracy declaring that, if she would tread a measure, she must have music, played a waltz ; and the volatile creature twirled round poor Johnny until he fell flat on the floor from dizziness and exhaustion, not being accustomed to such saltatory movements, and, moreover, a tyro in the act of dancing.

Quiet, after strenuous efforts, being restored, and all beginning to be soberly happy, several other persons arrived with congratulations at the re-appearance of the invalid ; amongst these were Gerald Sanderson, Miss Tidmarsh, and two or three foreigners of distinction who had been recently presented to Mr. Barclay.

Gerald, entirely overcome by the intensity of his feelings, stammered forth his sincere satisfaction at once more being allowed to see Miss Barclay, and then retreated to the conservatory; remaining there a few minutes, he returned, and seating himself in a distant part of the library, fed his eyes upon the object of his idolatry. Miss Serena devoted herself, after having paid sundry insincere compliments to Georgy, to a young Frenchman, and invited him to accompany her to one of the tables, where she entertained him in her patchwork French with all the scandal she had managed to collect during the week.

Now Johnny Barclay happened to be drawing at this table, and this youth was a naturalist; an incipient one to be sure, for his researches were entirely confined to the feline species. And woe unto the unfortunates! their tribulations, as far as he was concerned, being legion; in fact, he never allowed a cat to enjoy her existence any length of time in his latitudes, and waged against that amiable race an exterminating warfare. Many old women in the neighbourhood had almost determined to enter a protest against Johnny's murderous propensities, having missed their favourites and pets from their accustomed haunts, and had only been deterred by their respect for his father, whom they could not bear to disturb with complaints. It so happened that Johnny asked Miss Serena some question touching a foreign city of which she and her companion were speaking, and Miss Tidmarsh, being ignorant and not wishing to proclaim her want of knowledge, pretended not to hear him. Upon which Johnny, raising his voice above all drawing-room conventional regulations, reiterated his demand. The lady answered in her lowest whisper, and the turbulent child, roaring loud enough to be heard at the end of the street, bawled out, 'Why don't you speak as loud as other people, Miss Serena? you can; it's only before company you're such a mouse in a cheese. I heard you this morning when we boys chased a glorious tom-cat up your pear-tree, and poor dirty little lame Sally only came to the door to see the fun, — I heard you bellow and use awful naughty words besides!' No one knew what to do or to say upon this explosion; nobody could pretend to deafness — all the assembled company having been stopped short in their colloquies by the uproar.

Mr. Barclay immediately ordered his son and heir to bed, — the boy's most condign punishment, — and Miss Tidmarsh really did, for that time, take French leave, having precipitately left the room as Johnny finished his peroration. Johnny retreated to that refuge of the destitute and distressed, Nursey Bristow's quarters, and there it is lamentable to state, (but the truth must be told,) he recounted his exploit without evincing a single demonstration of repentance; but wickedly avowed his satisfaction therein, and his fixed resolve to do the same thing again whenever he got a good chance. Nursey, shaking her head and combing his, bewailed his naughtiness in melting terms, which produced no effect whatever upon the little sinner.

Uncle Richard behaved no better than his hopeful nephew, for perceiving the absence of Miss Tidmarsh, he burst out into the most uncontrollable fit of laughter, in which he was joined by all the assembled company, except the heads of the house, who, it must be confessed, had much difficulty in restraining their mirth. Even Gerald, who had so long thought he should never smile again, was fairly overcome, and betrayed his mirth in no measured terms. Mr. Richard's second pet dislike being Miss Serena, (he never renounced his first,) he was highly pleased that her deceit had been thoroughly exposed; he having always regarded the delicacy of her lungs, of which she was perpetually complaining, as a complete myth with which that young lady favoured the public. 'And now,' exclaimed he rejoicingly, 'we shall hear no more of the ridiculous creature's pretensions to morbid affections of the chest.' But he was mistaken, — her bad habits were as deeply rooted as his own, and she was sure, in a few days, to forget the young scapegrace's rebuff, and be more absurd than ever.

Georgiana, though not very strong, had crept out after

Miss Tidmarsh, whom she hoped to find in the hall; but the delicate pretender had vanished, having totally forgotten her hooded cloak which remained pendant on the hat-stand, and singularly resembled its owner. Mr. Barclay privately informed his wife that he proposed punishing Johnny, and only hoped he should perform the operation without laughing. Mrs. Barclay replied that she wished he might avoid such a catastrophe, but had her own doubts whether the offender would not coax his father out of all such retributive justice. Mr. Barclay was altogether too indulgent to his children; his wife made strenuous efforts to counteract the pernicious effects of such a course, and the consequence was, that they ever held her in much greater awe than their father. He could not behold, in any degree of peace, a frown on the brow of a child; he must immediately chase it away; he frankly acknowledged his weakness, and declared that he left all the wholesome disciplining of his family to his wife. In this respect he very much resembled all indiscreetly fond fathers, in which America abounds.

CHAPTER XXIV.

'A rich man may have carved by the mere success of his enterprises a right to be heard, having been tested by that success.' — ANON.

MR. BARCLAY, after many interviews with Gerald Sanderson, became extremely interested in that young man's fortunes, and firmly resolved to do him some solid service. Gerald, captivated by the sympathetic nature of his newly acquired friend, felt that he almost haunted his footsteps, and yet could not persuade himself to renounce the happiness it imparted. Gerald unveiled to Mr. Barclay all the most secret recesses of his heart; his abandoned dream-land and visionary projects; and communicated his earnest desire to effect a complete metamorphosis in his habits, and to school himself severely in the busy marts of men; his plan being one he had long revolved in his mind, — to enter himself at the law school at Cambridge, where he thought a year would suffice, as he had already studied three at home, and then find a place in some distinguished lawyer's office in Boston. All this was judiciously arranged, but the means whereby this project could be carried through were wanting, his small modicum being entirely inadequate to the disbursal of his daily expenses. He had been told of the hope deferred, and the sickened and fainting hearts of aspirants for legal fame; but nothing dismayed, he determined to pursue his course, and try to find some occupation which would gave him bread while pursuing his studies. These sad reflections cost him many hours of serious thought, and were the only subjects of his matured plans which he failed to reveal to Mr. Barclay; for, had he not assisted his brother? There then seemed to be no one to whom Gerald could apply, for, in the days of his most amicable relations with his uncle, he would never have ventured upon any proposition for aid, and in their disseverment it was entirely out of the question. So, poor Gerald pined away his days in repentance of his past follies, and beheld his plans for improvement passing away from lack of power to execute them, and he actually seemed in danger, notwithstanding all his good resolutions, of fast falling into his old and pernicious habits of castle-building and melancholy reverie. From this state he was most opportunely and joyfully aroused by a note from a gentleman, whom he only knew by reputation, requesting him to call at his office the next day at twelve o'clock. Little slept he that night, and arising at break of day, he thought the long, long hours would never come to an end; but at last he beheld the desired meridian, and found himself precisely at the appointed time in the presence of a large, red-faced, burly individual, who, greeting him freely and heartily, desired him to be seated, and then entered upon business immediately, by saying: 'A mutual friend of yours and mine, Mr. Sanderson, has often spoken to me of you, and thinks you are exactly the person I want. He says you are the soul of honour and probity, and that implicit reliance can be placed on you; that you are a good French scholar, and will be able to conduct satisfactorily a commercial correspondence in that language, respecting some business which demands profound secrecy. Don't be alarmed, there is nothing wrong about it; but I have discovered a way to make a round sum of money, and am determined to keep close, and have all the cakes and ale for myself and children. Now, if you will undertake this affair for me, and I understand, in the end, that you have not breathed a syllable to any one respecting it, I will give you a thousand dollars a year, and should the enterprise prove successful, you shall have a bonus besides.' It need hardly be doubted that Gerald gladly accepted this proposition, the more so, when he discovered that the work might be executed in three days of each week. When Mr. Barton, that being the name of the gentleman, informed Gerald of this fact, he declared he thought the remuneration altogether too large for the services to be rendered; but the merchant answered that he was paying for character and not work, and persisted in his offer. Gerald inquired who the person was who had kindly interested himself in his welfare, and heard, without surprise, Mr. Barclay's name mentioned, — for what other friend had he in the world? Mr. Barton was a tolerably liberal man, and was very willing to pay for specified moralities, (he wanted them,) but not exactly a thousand dollars a year. He thought six hundred ample, and Mr. Barclay supplied the deficiency under the seal of secrecy.

Gerald Sanderson entered that very morning on his functions, and his employer seemed well satisfied with the zeal and intelligence he evinced. Mr. Barton perceived that he comprehended at a glance the important bearings of the business, and applied himself assiduously to unravelling all its intricate parts. They passed many hours together, and parted mutually pleased with each other, Gerald being convinced that he could give satisfaction to his employer. That evening Gerald consecrated to his mother, and a blessed one it was. She was made happy in the certainty of her son's independence and his ability to pursue his legal studies, she having always earnestly desired he should adopt his father's profession. She also thought that this training under a thorough business man, like Mr. Barton, whom she knew to be an able financier, would be of immense service to the young dreamer. Mrs. Sanderson had always thought if Gerald could be once aroused and completely disenchanted of his illusions, he would never again relapse, for she knew there was a fund of practical good sense lying unrevealed under his dreamy qualities. What would the delighted mother have given to be able, on the instant, to impart this agreeable intelligence to her brother? but he was immured in his library, with never a book, and no one could put foot therein unless formally requested to do so. Now, instead of pouring forth her excited and overjoyed feelings in fraternal intercourse, she called up the two sable friends she possessed in the kitchen, and told them the pleasant tale of their young master's prosperity; to which Gerald added a bank note a-piece, the first he had ever had the happiness to be able to bestow upon them. The pair, when they did not laugh, always cried on grand occasions; that evening they celebrated by doing both; and Peter, after descending into his own domains, gave a slight touch or so of heel and toe, and declared that next to the return home of Massa Charley, this was the very best bit of news he could ever hear.

The next morning Gerald Sanderson called on Mr. Barclay before breakfast, and attempted to thank him for his unexpected kindness; but, in his own estimation, signally failed, so greatly was he overpowered by his grateful feelings. He, however, managed to invoke the blessing of the fatherless upon his head, and, as the Italians say, blessings never fall to the ground, they must have rested there. Mr. Barclay requested Gerald to remain and breakfast with him, and soon his lovely family was assembled together in the library, the servants following. Mr. Barclay read impressively a short household service, and concluded with a fervent prayer for their welfare. This finished, the greetings of the day commenced affectionately, and they then repaired to the dining-room, where, around a cheerful board, graced by youth and beauty, the heads of this home looked as if sorrow and suffering might not enter there; and yet, alas! it had.

Gerald walked to Cambridge three times a week to the law school, and the rest of his time was devoted to Mr. Barton, that gentleman, however, not requiring his presence in the evening, he was a free man; but not once, in the whole course of that year, did he open a book disconnected with his legal pursuits. When wearied with hard work and study, he frequented the concerts and theatres, and kept up by practice his own fine voice, and accompanied himself on his guitar, and went to Mr. Barclay's as often as he dared. Mrs. Barclay's hospitality was unbounded to him. With a woman's keen susceptibility to love-passages, she had instantly perceived the state of his feelings, but she thought he would eventually conquer his passion for her daughter, in view of its utter hopelessness; she felt his solitariness and the great advantage he would derive from his communion with her family, and so she welcomed him warmly to their fireside.

Mr. Barton having begun to take a decided liking to his diligent amanuensis, one day invited him home to dinner, in order, as he declared, to make Mrs. Barton and his daughters acquainted with him. Gerald accepting the invitation, accompanied his patron, and found himself in an elegant house, furnished in shockingly bad taste, glaring and flashy; in very truth, his eyes were almost blinded by the variety of ill-assorted colors, which met them on all sides.

The Misses Barton, showy and ambitious girls, were just half educated, knowing a little of almost every thing; they drew a little, played a little, and sang a vast deal, with remarkably unmusical voices, and talked immensely of all the 'ologies, to which were superadded chemistry and medicine.

Mr. Barton, in describing his daughters to Gerald, had mentioned with pride their vast attainments, and said that subjects were discussed at his table, and to all appearance definitely settled by these young ladies, that would puzzle the most profound philosophers to unravel. 'But,' said he, 'I have paid so much money for their schooling, that I presume I am getting my money's worth, and the gist of the matter lies there, after all.'

Mrs. Barton, a good housewifely creature, received her

guest with great deference; the daughters paid small regard to their parents in any thing, evidently considering them quite an inferior order of persons.

There was one thing which appeared to Gerald Sanderson to be very remarkable, and it was, that the Misses Barton, having paid such strict attention to the acquisition of various foreign and dead languages, should have so singularly neglected their own vernacular, in which they were sadly deficient.

The dinner was excellent and well cooked, and Mrs. Barton, to the undisguised disgust of her daughters, was quite willing that Gerald should comprehend she had taken a large share in the confection of certain pastries which she strenuously recommended to him. The servants were ill trained and excessively awkward, and the hostess very fussy with them, giving various orders and hints quite audibly enough for all to hear.

To his great astonishment he heard not one word of the dreaded 'ologies, the young ladies being completely absorbed in obtaining all the information they could from Gerald, respecting the Barclay family, and he shortly made the discovery that his gracious welcome was entirely to be attributed to his known intimacy in that quarter.

Now, how shall it be written? That the Bartons were not of the same rank as the Barclays, — no such word as rank in democratic America. Not of the same class, — that will never do. Not of the same standing, — worse and worse. The fact is, and the truth must be told, it is very hard, indeed, to describe certain things in a Republic. Were the Bartons then not fashionable? Travellers say we have no fashion; then how in the name of common sense is this awkward affair to be managed? Well, then, for want of something better, the Misses Barton did not visit in the same houses with the Barclays. Then, were they or the Barclays 'our first people?' But this is getting to be too abstract a question, and the best way is to let it alone, and, moreover, by far the safest. The result was, that the families were unknown to each other; and though the Barclays had never seen Gerald's friends, it appeared they had been carefully scanned in all public places, and particularly on Sundays. Miss Julia Maria Barton begged to know if Gracy's hair was really golden; and Miss Araminta Cora Barton asked if the sister's eyes were black or blue. Kate and Johnny were entirely neglected; their fame had not penetrated into the Barton circle.

These questionings and Gerald's answers broke all the ice of ceremony, and a conversation ensued, if thus it could be called, which was composed of interrogations and responses, and made them all seem quite sociable. The young ladies did not touch upon the debatable ground of poor Georgy, for there sat facing them the principal personage in the story; though he fancied they were really dying to do so, but, fortunately, they spared him such an infliction. The visit pleasantly enough ended, he rose to take leave, when they all entreated him to return very soon; 'the oftener the better,' said Mrs. Barton. Mr. Barton, who sallied forth with him, declared he had not enjoyed such an agreeable meal for a long time, never having heard a single word about that nasty Liebeg, or his decided aversions the 'ologies, while Gerald was in his house.

Gerald was much amused with this new phase of things; and, as there was nothing of which he liked to talk better than the Barclays, the sound of their names being to him a breathing and subduing melody, he resolved rather to cultivate the acquaintance of persons who took such an intense interest in them, no matter what the motive.

Mr. Barton had begun life in a very small way, and his early career had been unprosperous; he had failed in business, but, with the characteristic courage and energy of his 'Down-East' race, — for he came from the State of Maine, — he, nothing daunted, looked adverse Fortune sternly and defiantly in the face, and dared her to do her worst.

Failures in other lands are wearisome and melancholy enough, there would seem to be no recuperative qualities in the sufferers; but in America a man falls but to rise and take a bolder flight. A few years soon saw Mr. Barton re-established, having gathered a rich harvest of experience from his previous commercial disasters, and, what was greatly to his honor, having paid off the principal and interest of his debts. This time the fickle goddess continued to favour him, and he made by speculations an immense fortune; and then he performed a remarkably wise act,—he settled one half of his rapidly gained wealth on his wife and children, declaring they should never again be made beggars. For himself, he averred, that, as occupation was the main-spring of his existence, and he should die of atrophy without it, he must work, and so he did just as assiduously as if his daily bread depended upon his exertions, looking carefully after the smallest sums in a very searching manner. Occasionally he gave to charities, incited by Mr. Barclay, who had great influence over him; but this was rather to behold his name by the side of a man's whom he greatly admired and respected, than from any real sympathy with the wants of others.

Mr. Barton took great delight in recounting his early adventures; he prided himself immensely on having battled with poverty in its most pinching and griping aspect, and on having conquered the enemy, and was rather vain of his signal exploits. Not so his daughters; they, blushingly, interrupted him, and always endeavored to divert his attention from the subject of his early days, and conjured their mother to do the same; but the good creature answered that, if it made her husband happy to do this, it was all she desired in the world. It was wonderful the efforts were so perpetually made, seeing they were so constantly abortive; but then the Misses Barton's father always began his graphic descriptions when they had their very best acquaintance with them. Now, this may faintly shadow forth where the

Bartons were in society, for the truly very best persons in the land would have listened with interest and pride to the detail of their countryman's struggles, from which, it appeared, the young ladies' 'upper ten thousand' turned their heads in mockery and disgust.

Mr. Barton's baptismal name was a peculiar one, to say the least, he rejoicing in the appellation of Nicodemus, and choosing to have it emblazoned in black letter upon his door-plate, and also visiting cards, that being the latest fashion. It was in vain Miss Araminta Cora advised him of the pleasant fact, that all the small boys in the neighborhood had christened him 'Old Nick,' and even proceeded to append a portrait of the real Simon Pure, horns and all, on the back-gate of his dwelling. The father remained obstinately impervious, and vowed he would never forswear his birthright for all the little vagabonds in Christendom; and that they had brought the war into his camp, because he had warned them, with their confounded balls, off the court in which he lived. He was not to be scared out of his name, a good family one, by babies, not he. So his daughters were obliged to resign, for a time, all immediate hope of a change in their father's patronymic; but as they inherited his never-dying spirit of tenacity of purpose, they never despaired.

CHAPTER XXV.

'Something the heart must have to cherish,
Must love and joy and sorrow learn,
Something with passion clasp or perish,
And in itself to ashes burn.'

HYPERION.

BUT does not the reader wish to hear something of the whereabouts of the dear Charley? He has never been any where but in his bereaved mother's heart and mind, morning, noon and night, since his departure. Gerald has pined for his joyous brother; Peter and Dinah have obstreperously lamented his absence; and Mr. Egerton has said never a word of the favourite, good or bad. The voyage was long, tediuos and monotonous, for every one but Charley, who was the life and soul of the whole ship's company. Mrs. Sanderson had given her son a Bible and Shakspeare; these he read, the first solemnly and attentively, the second eagerly drinking in its beauties, and, by turns, enacted, for the gratification of his shipmates, almost every character in it.

A great talent, had Charley Sanderson for histrionic accomplishments, which he had but sparsely exercised on shore; but it was then brought out for the amusement of others, as time moved slowly and tediously on — and where does it lag more wearily than at sea? There was one exception to the general favouritism that the dear boy enjoyed, and that was in the person of a dark, atribilious, disagreeable man, — a passenger who seemed to think smiling an offence, and laughing a crime, — and who had, from the first moment he laid his ugly grey eyes on the youth, apparently hated him. If Mr. Johnstone had been asked why, he could not have satisfactorily answered, even to himself. It was generally believed by the lookers-on, that he disliked to see such a joyously happy creature crossing his own unhappy path. At any rate, he took no notice of the 'popular member,' and always snarled at all the praises and commendations bestowed upon him; to this Charley gave no heed whatever; he thought the ship large enough for them both, and went on his way rejoicing and working, for he set himself to learn navigation, and studied assiduously.

Some time before they reached Calcutta, Mr. Johnstone fell dangerously ill of a contagious malady, and, being universally disliked, no man on board thought proper to risk his life for such a 'disagreeable animal.' He would have undoubtedly suffered from total neglect, and might have died, but for the very person whom he had flouted and scorned, Charley Sanderson. The dear boy entered his state-room, proffering all the assistance in his power, watched over him day and night, and fairly brought him round, so that he recovered his health, but not entirely his strength, before they landed. Charley himself was unscathed by his wearisome exertions, as he richly deserved to be; he also won golden opinions from his shipmates, who, one and all, declared that he had behaved like the glorious good fellow he was. 'Such benevolence and such a forgiving spirit,' they cried, 'were rarely seen.' This sickness unto death was, for Mr. Johnstone, a signal mercy. He had begun his career in a mean and sordid way, believing in nothing and in no one, and with an intense craving for human sympathy, had, by his morose, unsocial and forbidding manners, cast away from him his fellow-men. Without family, or connections, he had wandered to India, and there, under its burning sun, led a self-concentrated existence. Without interests or affections, he had, after many years, returned to America, and finding no one to care for him in his native land, he resolved to retrace his listless steps, and finish his days in Calcutta, since there was nothing to live for at home. Besides, he had found life perfectly intolerable in Boston and elsewhere, his habits having been revolutionized by his Indian residence, so back he was going, when a passage to eternity seemed much nearer to him than one to Calcutta. Now, then, was exhibited to this unbeliever in humanity, a new phase in his previous conceptions. Here was a mere lad, whom he had purposely avoided, for no reason on earth, and for whom he had most savagely betrayed a sentiment of contempt; and this young creature had devoted himself, with the most perseveringly untiring efforts, to the salvation of his life — and wherefore?

There was no wealth to tempt, no apparent goodness to seduce; on the contrary, surliness and ill-nature; and yet he had risked even his own existence for that of a bad-tempered and disagreeable man. This was surely a most remarkable thing, and gave abundant food for reflection. This carrying out of the doctrines of our Saviour by one so young, completely humbled and changed the ill-conditioned character and temperament of Mr. Johnstone; from believing in nothing, human or divine, he prayed that he might become exactly like the youth who had set him such a noble example of forbearance and forgiveness; he would immediately take him for his model, and this he told Charley; for once the ice-bound barrier dissolved which severed them, the restored invalid seemed to delight in baring his whole soul to his preserver. But Charley conjured him to do no such thing, to take no such frail reed as himself for a model, but seek and he should find in the inspired volume which his mother had given to him at parting, even the Bible, for greatly had he been shocked to discover that Mr. Johnstone was not the possessor of a solitary prayer-book. Certainly no missionary ever laboured with more pious ardour and enthusiasm in the good work of bringing an unbeliever to the blessed light of the gospel, than did Charley Sanderson, and his efforts proved eminently successful; particularly during the watches of the night, when Mr. Johnstone, unable to sleep, was extremely impressible, and consequently more open to conviction. Charley, imagining that his newly-acquired friend was not prosperous, offered him any pecuniary assistance his own limited means permitted, and begged to share and share alike when they reached their destination. At last, the long wished-for land appeared, and, amidst the noise and confusion attendant upon all arrivals, the passengers trod the shores of India. They all repaired to the same hotel, and Charley had ordered a modest chamber, when he was informed by the waiter, that Mr. Johnstone, whom he seemed to know very well, had provided one for him, to which he was immediately conducted. On entering it, he was surprised at its size and elegance, and contemplated remonstrating with his friend on his extravagance, but, as he had ordered it, he concluded to remain in it at least one night. Having changed his garments, he was thinking of just taking one peep into the street before dinner, when a servant informed him that Mr. Johnstone requested his company in his own parlour. Charley, descending one flight of stairs, found that gentleman in an elegantly furnished room, and a table beautifully arranged for two persons, at which he invited him most graciously to seat himself. The dinner was very luxurious and capitally served. Mr. Johnstone, now a changed creature, gay and evidently very happy, did the honors of the repast with remarkable spirit. Charley thought his friend a little beside himself, for the nonce, but determined to have every thing set right by the next day, otherwise he should be ruined; he, however, made no comments that would damp, as he thought, the excitement attendant upon the first dinner on shore.

When the fruit appeared and the servants had retired, Mr. Johnstone addressed him thus: 'You are, no doubt, immensely surprised, my dear young friend, at finding me, as you may naturally enough suppose, squandering away the little money I have. Now, permit me to set at rest all your apprehensions. You must henceforth regard me not in the light of the poor Mr. Johnstone, but the rich one; for rich I am, thank God, and can thereby endeavour to repay you for all the immense debt of gratitude I owe you. Henceforth you are to be my guest.' Observing that Charley was about to object to this arrangement, he resumed: 'You must not say one word in opposition, I am obstinately bent upon this, and will have my own way; but for you, your wondrously noble kindness, I should have been fathoms deep in the sea, but through your efforts, under Providence, I am now a regenerated and totally changed creature. I feel there is nothing I can do for you that will in any way prove an expression of my gratitude, so you must receive whatever my paltry wealth can effect. Of what avail was all the dross I had hoarded, when I had lost my own soul? Through you, I repeat, I am in a hopeful way of being brought to salvation; and since the wretched day you entered my state-room, looking like an angel of mercy, a great revolution has been wrought in me. But why should I call it a wretched day? — rather say blessed. Now I am, and ever have been, a man of few words and fewer good deeds; you must allow me to make a beginning, and with whom can I do this so effectually as my preserver, temporarily and eternally;' and, finishing, he actually wept like a child. To Charley, who, following the true instinct of his own excellent nature, had, in his own eyes, only performed a simple act of Christian kindness, this ebullition of feeling on the part of his, so lately saturnine friend, was, indeed, extraordinary, and he knew not what so say. He disclaimed, however, the great merit attributed to him, and declared he should consider himself the obliged person.

The next morning he wished to commence his operations immediately, but Mr. Johnstone said he had other views for him, in which he could essentially serve him, and he must await his pleasure. He desired his young friend should see the city thoroughly, and, in the interim, he would arrange for him something which he thought would exactly suit him. This was effected, and Charley, instead of making several India voyages to and fro, was installed in a mercantile house for two or three years, the head of which desired to establish a branch in America; and all this was done through the influence of Mr. Johnstone and his rupees. Of the latter part of this transaction, Charley was kept completely ignorant. He knew that his friend had been engaged, at one time, with this house, and supposed they had taken him to oblige Mr. Johnstone. It was a sad and melancholy sacrifice for him to abandon his dear mother, brother and friends, but he knew full well he could never be justified in renouncing such an excellent chance for preferment, and that the only hope he had on earth of obtaining Grace Barclay, his heart's treasure, laid in the success of his apprenticeship in this India house. It was a golden venture, and no considerations, however sentimentally imperative, must bid him forego the positive fact, that he might in time become sufficiently important to his employers to induce them to bestow upon him their patronage in his native land. All this he wrote, in a joint letter to his mother and Gerald, and also in another to Mr. Barclay, by the same ship in which he went out.

Mrs. Sanderson was greatly afflicted when the vessel arrived without her son, though she had already received an overland duplicate of the letter, and she was thoroughly prepared not to see him, yet there had ever lingered a hope that something might occur which would prevent his stay in India. But he came not, and in lieu of the Charley, she beheld a Cashmere shawl, of surpassing beauty, in a camphor-wood box, a present from a man whom she had never seen, and a letter, detailing most frankly and circumstantially, such a grateful narrative of her son's admirable conduct, as made her eyes rain tears of heartfelt joy. It was then she reaped the fruits of the good seed she had sown, and a proud and happy mother was she that day!

Mr. Barclay was delighted with his young favourite's cheering prospects, and Gerald carried to him Mr. Johnstone's letter, which he read with intense pleasure, and begged permission to communicate its contents to his family. It can safely be imagined how enchanted was Gracy with this missive, and how she gloried in her choice, when she heard all she loved, praising in no measured terms, the Charley. She felt that she loved him a thousand-fold more, now that such admirable qualities had been developed in him, and she was quite sure all her family sympathized with her, which they certainly did.

Mr. Richard said that, for his part, he was in no wise surprised at Charley's good conduct, and he thought the very best thing Mr. Johnstone could do was to adopt him, he having neither kith nor kin, and give him a portion of his vast wealth, the more especially, since the boy had taught him that there was something better to worship than mammon. The old fellow was a brand saved from the burning, but better late than never, he had known him when the bark was rougher.

Mrs. Ashley exclaimed, when Charley's letter was read to her, 'How charmingly romantic! Quite an Arabian Night's tale, and all true, nevertheless!' Miss Tidmarsh said, that 'There was always something happening at the Barclays; she supposed that they would then no longer object to a match between Grace and Charley Sanderson, as there was a good prospect of wealth; though she had heard they had hitherto violently opposed it.' And this was just as near the truth as that veracious person ever came. But she was not deterred by her ever-recurring, ungracious opinions of her neighbours, from frequenting their agreeable house, and constantly bestowing upon them her disagreeable presence. In this Miss Redmond, agreeing with her friend thoroughly, yet found it convenient to do the same thing.

There were too many pleasant people clustered round the Barclays, for the amiable pair to renounce visiting where they were constantly to be met. As soon as they heard of Charley's good fortune, they sallied forth to verify it, and both entered Mrs. Barclay's library at once ; the one striding along, and the other half sliding, half swimming. Jane Redmond informed Mrs. Barclay that her father had been employed by Mr. Johnstone in some legal business, and that Mr. Redmond was far from thinking that gentleman very wealthy, and conjectured Mr. Charley Sanderson must be mistaken.

Mrs. Barclay made no reply to this speech ; she was only amazed that Jane had been able to extract so much information about any one from her restricted paternal intercourse. Mrs. Gordon, who was present, begged to know Mr. Johnstone's age. Upon that question being propounded, Mrs. Ashley, in high glee, declared she had caught her friend at last. 'I am surprised,' she exclaimed, 'that you, dear Mrs. Gordon, of all persons in the world, should inquire the age of any one, after all your criticisms upon our habits, and having heard you frequently declare that you were never an hour in American society without listening to this question ; I repeat, I am astonished.'

'That's very true,' replied the lady, 'I make no denial, and am fairly entrapped. You remember the "evil communications" of our copy-books, and also have not forgotten good Mr. Burlington's habit of always diminishing the fortunes of his friends, and adding to their ages, so that what he substracted from their wealth he piled on to their years. A very innocently dangerous person was he. Age is a favourite topic in our country. I lived abroad many years, and never heard the subject mentioned, and, for aught I knew to the contrary, might have been sweet seventeen, but now the nearest approach I make to receiving a compliment is, that I wear well, hold my own, and bear my years. Thus, however flattering may be the intentions in the bestowal of these very apocryphal favours, they come to me in a decidedly neutralized state. You may all laugh as much as you please, I don't believe the men like this sort of sugar-plums any better than the women. An old friend of mine told me, that he was sitting in the reading-room of the Tremont House, last week, when two men, having glowered at him an immense long while, crossed the floor and asked his age, in a respectful manner, it must be stated. "Upon which," said he, "I flew at them in a violent rage, and asked them what, in the devil's name, they wished to know it for? I being bald, half-blind and lame." So, you perceive, the other sex, even at an advanced period, is as techy as we are on this debatable ground, and the fewer remarks you make upon my comments, the better. And, permit me to assure you, my good friends, that no one will find me encouraging the idle curiosity of the little Pedlington school, by divulging the number of cycles which have gathered around my head, unless an immense heritage is to be gained by the confession.'

'And you are perfectly right, Mrs. Gordon,' said Mr. Richard. 'What impertinent and futile curiosity! I don't think that even I myself would like to confess my age any better than your old friend, who was made so furiously angry by those ill-behaved fellows. But it's just the way here always; it's every body's business to know every body's business. Give me a country where people are unacquainted with their next-door neighbours, I say. What a terrestrial paradise such a land must be, no Mrs. Grundy extant; she has always lived in all the streets I have inhabited, and exercised full sway. Did you ever hear the definition of age in the "Man of the World's Dictionary?" — "Age, the only secret which a woman religiously keeps; and touching this grave subject, we know many men — who are women."'

CHAPTER XXVI.

'To-morrow you take a poor dinner with me;
No words — I insist on't — precisely at three.'
GOLDSMITH.

ONE evening, after dinner with the Barclays, Mr. Egerton, who had now become quite domesticated in their establishment, — that is, for him, — arose to depart, for he never remained in the evening, and solemnly invited the whole family to dinner with him in one week from that time. Mr. Barclay, quite taken aback, in a nautical way, accepted on the spot, and would probably have done the same thing the next day, so touched was he by this demonstration of good-will from the pragmatical and inhospitable personage. As this event occurred soon after Georgiana Barclay's restoration to health, the kindness of this unwonted proceeding was manifest, and it was evident that Mr. Egerton had decided upon this grand experiment in his life from the most delicate motives, decidedly wishing to evince to the whole community his entire belief in the truth of Miss Barclay's melancholy story.

Mr. Egerton walked in solemn state round the assembled friends, and personally requested the honor of Mrs. Ashley's company and that of Mr. Richard Barclay. The lady graciously assented, and the gentleman did not decline, to the utter amazement of his brother and sister, who were just as much astonished at the invitation, as at its prompt acceptance. This ceremony completed, Mr. Egerton begged, as a particularly personal favour, that Kate might be allowed to join the party. At this proposition both her parents demurred, pleading her youth, but on his strenuously persisting, they consented.

No sooner did the assent fall upon the Dolly's enraptured ear, than she rushed like wildfire out of the library, and skipping up four stairs at a time, bounded into the nursery, embracing Dame Bristow again and again, and then waltzed round the room till she fell exhausted into a chair.

'What is the matter, deary?' cried Nursey.

'I'm invited to a dinner-party, Nursey. What do you think Mary Redmond will say when she hears of it?'

With both hands upraised in wonder, Nursey Bristow regarded her child for a long time before she could regain her speech, and inquire 'Where?'

'Guess, Nursey, guess; I'll give you one, two, three, and even four hours to discover; and you'll never do it then.'

'I can't wait, darling,' said that bewildered and worthy woman; 'I can't indeed. Where can it be? Who could have been so silly as to ask such a child as you to a formal dinner-party with grown-up people? I shall never guess, if I go on forever; so pray tell me, that's a dear.'

'Well then,' said the Dolly, rising from her recumbent position with the most important air imaginable, and drawing herself up to her utmost height, 'I am asked to dine with the redoubtable Mr. Philip Egerton, Nursey mine.'

'You'll never be permitted to go, deary.'

'But I am already; and have obtained, not the unqualified consent, to be sure, of both my respectable parents. Just think of that, ma'am, as long as you please; contemplate the subject, Nursey, and revolve it over in your own perspicacious mind, — please do.'

Nursey rolled up her old eyes over her spectacles, and exclaimed, 'Well, well, miracles will never cease, my darling; the world is certainly coming to an end.'

'Not before we have had our grand dinner, I hope.'

'When did the old miser invite you, my child?'

'Even just this minute, Nursey. I tore up to tell you,—I mean to say, walked up,—now that I am bidden to feasts and to sit at great men's boards.'

'All, all invited? asked Nursey. 'And Miss Georgy, will she go?'

'I hope and pray she may; for, do you know, Nursey, it's my private opinion that this grand and unheard-of demonstration is made in her honour quite entirely.'

Nursey agreed with her darling completely, and felt the attention. It would have hardly been one from any one else but from Mr. Egerton, who had never been known to give a dinner in his life—it was extraordinary! So Dame Bristow resolved, mentally, never again to call Mr. Egerton 'the old miser.'

'Now, Nursey dear, what shall I wear to this grand banquet?' asked the young romp, in a most excited manner. 'Oh dear! how I wish!——'

'What's the use of wishing, deary, for any thing you've not got? for you know, perfectly well, your mother will never allow you to wear any thing but a book-muslin.'

'Oh! now I do wish, Nursey, that all the book-muslins in the world were at the bottom of the deep, deep sea. What I, Miss Kate Barclay, do want, and am literally dying for, is a magnificent Maria Louisa blue brocade, embroidered with superb pomegranate blossoms, which I stood an hour—disobeying my mother, who charged me never to do such things—admiring at a shop-window in Washington street. If I could but possess it! Do you think, Nursey, it was named after the charming Louisa of Prussia, or that horrid Austrian woman, a disgrace to her sex, who abandoned her husband, and left him to die alone on the rock in the wide ocean?'

This being an historical doubt which Nursey was unable to solve, she only nodded her ignorance.

'Do you think I can have it for this dinner?'

'I've already told you, Miss, that you can't. What absurd nonsense for you to desire such a dress as that; its positively ridiculous for you to think of it. You can't carry it off; you're not old enough.'

'Put me into it, Nursey, and try me — you'll see if I can't.'

'And it was very wrong of you, Miss, to stand staring into shop-windows, when your mother forbade you to do so; and as to its being for an hour, I do'nt believe a word of that — for how could you keep still so long?'

'Oh, never mind all that, Nursey dear; if I could but have that dress, what a happy creature I should be. At any rate, I must have some new ribbons for my sleeves and my sash.

'Why, you've plenty of sashes, Miss.'

'Yes; but if I cannot be the ecstatic possessor of that unsurpassed brocade, I must have pomegranate-coloured ribbons for my "bonnie brown hair."'

'Your bonnie brown hair! Why, it's as black as a crow's; and I was just thinking how very becoming would be the long tails with the brocade.'

The Dolly, planting herself directly before Nursey, said: 'Now, Nursey, you can't seriously imagine that I'm to sport those two execrable Chinese appendages at my first dinner-party!'

'Why not then, deary?'

'Because I propose to obtain the royal permission, that the abominable objectionables shall be disposed around my all-beauteous pericranium like a coronal, Dame Bristow.'

'A what?' demanded Nursey, extremely puzzled to follow her birdling into her amazing Johnsonian flights.

'Why, a crown imperial, Nursey; in plain parlance, I mean they shall form a diadem. Who knows what inroads they may make into "the old miser's" heart of hearts. I can't help thinking I've made an impression even now, he was so urgent for my august presence at his festive board.

And then the ribbons! Who knows, Nursey, what they may do? —

> "A pomegranate flower bear
> In blossom to my love."'

'Oh!' cried Nursey, out of all patience; 'your sisters never ran on, Miss, in such a way. Why don't you take a leaf out of their good books, and behave yourself. They never gave your mother, or I, half the trouble you do, — we're both obliged to be eternally watching you.'

'Well, well, I know all that, just as perfectly as you do; but then they "never loved, like Nathalie, her goosy, poosy" — and you know it. Now, what I ardently desire is, to coax you to coax my mother to issue a royal mandate, that *the* hair which, but for your admirable management would never have been brought into order, — you having made things straight which were never intended so to be — shall be elevated to the top of my head, and never again left to fall in straight lines. Hogarth's curved ones for me forever! Do you hear, Bristolinda?'

'Oh yes, I hear — but don't believe she will consent.'

'Now if you'll do but this one thing for me, I'll hug all the breath out of your old body. How I wish the same accident that occurred to poor Rachael Taylor might happen to me. She and her mother bewailed it in dust and ashes, and ate earth on the occasion.'

'What was it?' inquired Nursey.

'Oh! she went to a panorama of something or other, either of the Nile or a whaling voyage, I forget which; and you know all such places are pokerishly dark "abysses profound," and when she came out, her two magnificent John Chinamen were missing. Some amiable philanthropist — I wish I could meet with him — had despoiled her of her hirsute possessions; and how she mourned their loss, no tongue can tell. Mrs. Taylor has not done fretting yet, and never will until bounteous nature supplies the deficiency. Now, I should have considered it a benevolent exploit on the part of the operator; the mother took a totally different view of the subject, and called him or her "a horrid thief."'

'It was a melancholy loss,' sighed Nursey.

'Oh, I dare say you would never have got over the calamity; but please don't forget to broach my all-important affair to my mother to-morrow morning betimes, darling.' So saying, she embraced Nursey tightly, and descended to the library, six stairs at a time, and resumed her accustomed seat.

'Don't you begin to think,' said Mr. Barclay, 'that a young lady who is bidden to banquets, is too old to sit on her father's knee, my Dolly?'

'Suppose then that you put me down, my father; such a positive case of abandonment may be imagined.'

This not being done, the conversation turned upon the marvellous event of the invitation from Mr. Egerton. Mrs. Ashley declared she did not believe in it at all; it was a myth; and if they really went, they should find it a Barmecide's feast, — and then she inquired of Mr. Richard how he, who had until lately eschewed the gentleman, should have permitted himself to be seduced into a doubtful allegiance by the first temptation of the arch seducer, Mr. Philip Egerton.'

'I think,' answered Mr. Richard, 'that my brother John will explain this to you at some more convenient period. I am free to confess that I have much mollified my recent opinions touching that gentleman, even to the acceptance of a dinner, and actually went the length of calling upon him formally last week.'

'This is quite marvellous,' resumed the lady; 'but I remain still doubtful respecting the banquet.'

'Perhaps you would be more credulous if you had listened to a short interlude I enjoyed with Mr. Egerton,' said Mrs. Barclay, 'just before our own meal to-day, when he consulted me about his projected hospitalities, and, moreover, invited me; thus I was the first person asked.'

'We shall see!' said Mrs. Ashley, 'and seeing is believing, though I have even heard obstinate persons declare it was not.'

'Why should not Mr. Egerton give a dinner?' inquired Mr. Barclay.

'Because he never has,' replied the lady.

'There exists no reason why he should not begin to adopt hospitable and pleasant ways, even at the last hour,' said Mr. Barclay.

'I confess to an unusual proportion of curiosity,' said Mrs. Ashley, 'about this forthcoming repast, and would willingly have renounced all my future engagements for the chance of fulfilling this one, and am really glad he asked me. How I shall surprise all my friends, when I can say, carelessly, I dined on such a day with Mr. Egerton, and we had thus and so; and shall astonish them quite as much as when I mention my elephant, which I keep in petto for grand occasions.'

'Now, dear Mrs. Ashley, pray tell us of your forest friend,' said Georgiana; 'I think I never heard you mention this before.'

'When I was in Geneva, in Switzerland,' said the lady, 'there came down a man from Paris to that curious old town, with Mademoiselle Djeck, the elephant, whom I believe had figured in this country also. After exhibiting her ladyship a few weeks, the keeper ran away, and left her to the tender mercies of the authorities, and remarkably tender they were; they're a saving people, the Genevese. They ordered her to be placed in a dry ditch under the ramparts of that locked-up city; but finding she consumed an immense quantity of food, they decided to slay her, for economy's sake. This was accordingly done, and her flesh sold in the market-place, and most eagerly purchased; and will you believe me, I tasted a tiny bit, that I might astonish people when they were boasting of having eaten odd things, just for a show-off.'

'How did you relish your tempting morsel?' inquired Grace.

'Not much,' answered Mrs. Ashley; 'it tasted like coarse beef. I was soon, however, at a large dinner party, composed of natives of various lands, and many of them great travellers; they were all narrating their numerous experiences in gastronomy. One had eaten buffalo, one snails, another Chinese dogs, &c.; but I distanced them all by gravely avowing my own experiment. You should have seen how they looked at me! They were quite mortified at being eclipsed by a woman, and thought me an ogress besides.'

'Not a very frightful one, at least,' said Mrs. Barclay.

'Now,' resumed Mrs. Ashley, 'perceiving I have made an impression, I shall depart; but must add that, some time afterwards, I met a Genevese surgeon, who assisted at the massacre of the big innocent, Mademoiselle Djeck, and he informed me that nothing could have been more affecting than her execution. At first, the soldiers who were employed to destroy her, missed fire, and the poor animal, supposing this to be the word of command her late master was in the habit of using, actually went down on her knees to be killed. Of one thing I am perfectly sure, I should not have tasted the morsel of her flesh, had I heard this account before it was offered to me. So good-night, my friends.'

Mrs. Ashley departed. 'What a pleasant person she is!' said Grace,—'always having some amusing reminiscence.'

'She is a remarkable instance,' observed Mrs. Barclay, 'of what may be done, with a good temper, kind heart, keen eyesight and retentive memory. There are many women, vastly better educated in every sense of the word, who are not half so companionable or agreeable. Mrs. Ashley never gives us any strong-minded looks, and really entertains a rather inferior opinion of her own abilities, as such; but what she has seen she remembers and describes most agreeably. Mrs. Ashley is neither any great reader of solidities, but as we have so many who devote profound attentions to incomprehensibilities, it matters not.'

'I'll defy any of the class you refer to,' said Mr. Richard, 'to use a longer word than that; but I observed, my dear Georgiana, a decided negative in your expressive face when Mr. Egerton invited you. Please accept, I pray.'

'I cannot indeed, my dear uncle Richard.'

'I must not hear you say this, Georgy; there are many considerations which will arise in your mind, on reflection, and induce you to change your opinion, I hope.'

'Say yes, my child,' said Mr. Barclay, 'and confer a favor on your mother and myself, as well as your uncle Richard.'

Georgy not being proof against these entreaties, consented.

'Now you are all in the mood of granting melting petitions,' said the Dolly, 'do please let my Chinese tails be gracefully disposed around my brainless head on that momentous occasion. I've hardly heard a word of the conversation this evening, for thinking of being obligated to wear them hanging, dingle-dangle, to my first dinner-party. All the energies of my being are concentrated in the obtaining of this one favour, and its denial will make me unutterably wretched; so relieve me of my weight of woe, I pray.'

Both Mr. and Mrs. Barclay laughed heartily at the Dolly's 'Misery of human life,' and promised that she should be gratified, and, even more, that she might ask Nursey Bristow to commence operations the next day, so that the offending elongations might be brought into proper order before the dinner, the permission extending no further. So the Dolly retired to her dormitory, and nearly annihilated Nursey in her ecstasies of delight at the completion of her wishes; fell fast asleep, and dreamed they were cut off, — and awoke, crying heartily because they were not.

CHAPTER XXVII.

> 'Now each mechanical man
> Hath a cupboard of plate for show,
> Which was a rare thing
> When this old cap was new.'
>
> OLD BALLAD.

THE next morning, after his dinner at Mr. Barclay's, Mr. Egerton propounded to Mrs. Sanderson his intention of giving to Miss Barclay a grand feast; and this information was imparted in such a solemn manner, that it occasioned a vast degree of astonishment in the person to whom it was addressed. But if the lady was amazed, her servants' delight was unbounded. As the conversation occurred at breakfast, Peter heard it almost unbelievingly, but nevertheless ran out, as soon as he had finished his service, and cried out, 'Oh, Miss Dinah, Massa's goin' to gib a hightop dinner — a Bethazzar's feast — to all the bigwigs; noffin was ever like it, or ever will be again. Do you hear, ole woman? Why don't you answer?' Peter might well ask this question, for the cook was speechless. In time, however, she regained her voice, and poured forth such a volley of questions! — Who was coming? What were they to have to eat? and last, not least, What was she in the varsal world to do? How could she ever manage a grand dinner?'

'Oh! nebber give yourself any concern whatsomdever in this matter, Miss Dinah; you're not to touch the dinner. I heerd my Massa say the great Miss Thompson was to be sent for, and the great Mr. John Leander Pitts with all his men. I tell you, ole woman, I thought I should drop down right back of my Massa's chair, I'se so glad and so proud the ole house is to be opened agin. I nebber spected to see any more grand company here, Miss Dinah. Oh! the good ole times!'

Peter, like all his race, was excessively fond of society, of feasts and gay shows, and this unexpected event had actually turned his old head, as he declared, 'insidout.' Miss Dinah's mind, being happily relieved from the Atalantean weight of a grand dinner, could take in Peter's rhapsodies very comfortably; but it was in vain for her to attempt to follow him in all his flights, which were accompanied with the cracking of his fingers, and a touch of heel and toe, as he recounted the glories of old Massa's time.

If there were commotion in the kitchen, there was also excitement in Mrs. Sanderson's quarters, for she began precisely as did the Dolly, with wishing she had something to wear befitting the occasion. It was not exactly a Maria Louisa brocade, embroidered with pomegranate blossoms, but still a dress was required. She immediately occupied herself in overlooking her long-forgotten finery, and was surprised to discover many beautiful articles which had been lying hidden in divers coffers. Mrs. Sanderson's young husband had always admired pretty things on women, and had more than surpassed his small means in making expensive purchases for her, which, as he was laughingly wont to say, was throwing away his money, for she never wore them more than once. In truth, they were altogether too elegant for her small establishment, yet she could never bear to tell him this, and accepted them in the same gracious spirit in which they were presented.

There was one dress, an emerald green velvet, a great favourite of his, lying in its folds, as fresh as the day it was purchased, and as men, when they buy women's gear, always get yards and yards too much, she soon had the waist and sleeves remodelled, and it turned out, as it really was, most beautiful and very becoming.

Peter and Dinah recommenced operations instanter, and cleaned over and over again all the plate in the house. The massive chests on being opened, revealed such treasures! and such a magnificent display as was made of things that had not seen the light for years, quite beggars description! Then Dinah carried tubs and tubs of hot water into the china closet, and washed its contents, as if they had never been touched before.

But this china-closet demands a special notice. In the first place, it should have been denominated a cabinet, so ample were its dimensions, and so rare and costly its contents; in fact, the sight of it was sufficient to drive a collector of curiosities quite mad, and to arouse all manner of envious feelings in the breasts of porcelain hunters. Every variety of the old burnt china, so valuable even in its own land, the curiously cracked, with the rare colours, and the transparent biscuit were all there. Whole sets of these, separately arranged, many of them with the arms and initials of the family, graced the broad shelves, interspersed with green dragons and blue cats. There were dinner services innumerable and tea to match, and such superb desserts! In fact, there was no end of the beauty and value of these treasures. Now, it cannot be truthfully asserted that the presiding guardian of this closet, Miss Dinah, was aware of their intrinsic worth, but they were, nevertheless, her household gods, for had they not belonged to 'ole Massa!' and no care that she could bestow upon them was sufficient. Whenever she was missing, Peter always declared she would be found in that 'china-closet,' a-cleaning the crockery.

The eventful and long wished-for day arrived for the feast. Mr. John Leander Pitts walked into the dining-room, with his men, and Mrs. Thompson stalked into the kitchen. She found every thing in order for her operations, and the great John Leander stood, spell-bound, before the above-mentioned wonders of porcelain which Peter exhibited in the most vain-glorious manner, inquiring every two minutes, 'if he had ever set his two ole eyes upon de like;' which John Leander was fain to confess, much against his will, he never had.

At five of the clock the guests were assembled punctually. They were ushered, with all manner of indescribable scrapes and bows, by Peter, into the library, which served for the time as a cloak-room, and thereby was avoided the disagreeable necessity of mounting flights of stairs, which universally exists in American city houses. To persons entertaining a pious horror of the treadmill, this is a serious objection to all the parties given. Then Peter marshalled the company into the best parlour, which, it cannot be denied, was quite as stiff and formal, though not so cheerless and cold as usual.

The half hour before dinner is proverbially stupid, and this was no exception to the general rule. The imperfect light, from a blazing fire in the grate, served to give flickering glimpses of the assemblage, and the rather low and whispered tones, in which a sort of meteorological conversation was held, was rather appalling, and then the chairs and tables nailed to the wall, nobody daring to move a seat, it looked so forbidding.

The Dolly, in a white book-muslin, with pomegranate-coloured ribbons in her sleeves, and such a love of a sash, and above all, the Chinese tails bound around her well-turned head in magnificent profusion, really looked very pretty; but then she wished herself, in that solemn interval, fairly at home, with Nursey Bristow and her pet kitten, at least fifty times. All things come to an end, dreary and otherwise, and Peter entering with a magnificent low bow, which he had practised before one of the large mirrors, many a time, and which was unfortunately lost in the obscurity, announced dinner. Then came a change indeed, a blaze of lights, exquisite flowers, and such cut-glass and old plate as decorated the board, the latter of such rare workmanship and splendour as attracted all eyes. Tongues were then let loose in their natural tones, and the genial influence of the scene produced a corresponding feeling. The party consisted of Mr. Barclay, his wife, and three daughters, Gerald Sanderson, his mother, Mr. Richard Barclay, Mrs. Ashley, Mr. Meredith, a young clergyman, Mr. Naseby, Mr. Rosevelt, an officer in the navy, and Mr. and Mrs. Gordon, and their daughter Clara, and her eldest brother.

When the guests had found their places, which were indicated by a small card in each plate, Mr. Egerton requested Mr. Meredith to say grace, when there fell upon their pleased ears such a voice, so musical in its tones, and which, once heard, it was impossible to forget. Indeed, Peter, in giving to Dinah a glowing description of Mr. Meredith, reported his voice to be 'the Melodeon of the spears.' There was at once undisguised admiration expressed for the old plate and china, Mrs. Gordon declaring herself really tempted to be envious at the sight. All this praise was not unacceptable to the host; he certainly quite prided himself upon these among his abundant possessions, for there was a different service for each course.

The Dolly found herself seated next the Rev. Mr. Meredith, who, addressing to her some slight remarks, was extremely amused at her answers, and became quite interested in his young neighbour. The Dolly informed him that this was her very first appearance at a dinner-party; that she could hardly conceive how she had been permitted to enjoy such an exquisite pleasure by her father and mother, and she was vastly obliged to them; that at first she had found she must acknowledge the best parlour odious, and wished herself at home; but now, every thing being changed, she should like to remain until midnight. That this was a very natural young lady the gentleman soon perceived, but he entertained rather a decided prejudice for her class, there being so many little men and women about. It was indeed refreshing to meet with a child, though rather a tall one; so he asked her many questions and received satisfactory answers, enlightening him with her own little history. The Dolly was enchanted with her companion; for he did not regard skating in the court-yard a sin, any more than the proprietorship of a sled, and most particularly liked dogs, though he did not equally affect kittens.

Mr. Naseby sat next to Miss Georgy Barclay, and mistaking her as usual for her sister, Miss Grace, whispered in her ears all manner of soft nothings, in his would-be mellifluous tones; she, adhering to the old fashion of never disabusing her sister's devoted swain. There seemed no end to the blunders he committed. He invited Mrs. Gordon to drink wine with him, calling her, in the most pointed manner, Mrs. Ashley, of which mistake the lady mischievously made him cognisant; he then upset a glass of claret over Miss Georgy's dress, which, not being white book-muslin, was irreparable. Then, in endeavouring ineffectually to remove this injury, he dropped his napkin, and, in reaching for it, tipped over and lost his eye-glass. These little playful occurrences rather diverted his attention, for a time, from the suppositious lady-love at his side; but he shortly overcame these misadventures, and returned to the charge with renewed vigour. Gerald sat opposite to Georgy Barclay, and contented himself with looking at her whenever he thought she did not perceive him. He had been invited to meet his friends very unexpectedly, and gladly availed himself of the permission, and also made himself generally agreeable.

The grand dinner was very successful; a pleasant flow of chat and thought pervaded it. Mr. Egerton was, assuredly, not a person to give an impetus to pleasurable things, but he really did make astounding efforts at unbending and unstarching upon this occasion. With the fruit appeared the host's invaluable specimens of porcelain. Mrs. Barclay, examining her plate, said, 'I never comprehended the great value of this china until I went to Europe. We are all surrounded, in this country, by such quantities of the material, and, accustomed to see it from our childhood, we really do not appreciate it as we should, until we behold what a value is set upon it across the water.'

'Women are china-fanciers ever,' said Mr. Barclay, 'and mistress of herself when china falls, has been poetically stated to be the highest point of excellence in your sex.'

'Yes,' she replied, 'by a bachelor, but you surely remember the tiny cup and saucer which I showed you in Dresden, where it had just been sold for five-and-twenty dollars. I began then to think myself very rich, with a couple of dozen.'

Mr. Richard Barclay interposed to declare, 'There was no comparison between the French and Chinese, the former being incomparably superior.' This leading to a discussion on the different degrees of excellence of various countries in the article, Mr. Rosevelt and Mr. Meredith slipped in, agreeably enough, many interesting anecdotes. Mr. Meredith laughed heartily when the Dolly, totally forgetting his clerical position, invited him, jestingly, to conceal a remarkable bit in his pocket for her, declaring, that when a little child, half her pleasure in having a nice thing, consisted in stowing it away in a receptacle of the same sort. Mrs. Ashley, seated on the left hand of Mr. Egerton, was gay and chatty, and Mrs. Sanderson seemed almost to recall the days of her past happiness in such engaging and congenial society.

A dinner-party is either insufferably stupid or very agreeable, there is no medium; a chance discussion, light and flowing, like the one related, often breaks the ice, and, setting all tongues in motion, leads to other things of more importance. Mr. Egerton's china effected this pleasant purpose, and his guests enjoyed themselves exceedingly. When the ladies retired their host arose, and in his grandest and most imposing manner, bowed them out of the dining-room, and then Mrs. Sanderson invited them into her own apartments.

On entering her sitting-room, Mrs. Ashley — who had dreaded 'the best parlour' quite as much as the Dolly — having established herself in a comfortable lounge, exclaimed, 'What a charming room! home is written all over it in golden characters — books, music, drawing, flowers and knicknackeries, and then so quiet and retired! I absolutely adore these old houses, they are so large and commodious; my own little dwelling seems quite a wren-box.'

'Had you not better compare it to a musical box, dear Mrs. Ashley?' said Grace.

You're a flatterer!' answered the lady.

'Ah!' said Mrs. Sanderson, 'the old house is but an heir-loom, and melancholy enough has it been to me these latter years. Were it not for this part of it, I know not what I should have done, or my dear children either.'

'These rooms must have been a resource,' said Mrs. Gordon, 'for, to speak frankly, the rest is gloomy enough; we have had a gay dinner to-day, but, generally, I should imagine, you would find it, Mrs. Sanderson, a little bit dull.'

'Most truly do I find it gloomy,' replied the lady.

'What a beautiful dress you have on, Mrs. Sanderson,' said the Dolly, 'it's almost as handsome as a brocade I saw the other day.'

'It is, indeed,' said her mother, 'and recalls to my mind a modern Italian picture of great merit, in Florence, of Tasso reading to Leonore his own poems. The princess wears a dress of emerald green, and I was so enamoured of it that I resolved to purchase one exactly similar, when, suddenly I recollected my unlucky complexion, and that — like the milkmaid, in the story-book — green would be positively unbecoming to me. Now, for you, Mrs. Sanderson, the hue is charming.'

'This reminds me of an anecdote about myself,' said

Mrs. Ashley. 'I happened to tell a young lady, one day, that on seeing a new fashion, for the first time, I could generally trace it to some picture of the old masters I had beheld abroad, so she reported, that Mrs. Ashley said she always dressed herself after all the old pictures. Heaven help me, how I should look! But I shall assuredly never forget my first visit to the Borghese Palace in Rome, when, being accompanied by a very handsome young man, and a most prim and antiquated damsel from our Quaker city of Philadelphia, we suddenly found ourselves in a small room, containing fourteen Venuses, in Mount Olympus disarray, all having been entirely oblivious of sublunary garments — save one — and she had donned, for the occasion, a Spanish hat and feathers. You may well imagine that we beat a speedy retreat. My ancient friend's steps were very zig-zaggish, indeed. She came extremely near unto fainting, and solemnly entreated, that no "pretty young fellows" might ever again accompany us in our explorations.'

'My husband,' said Mrs. Sanderson, 'had an English friend, who would never accept a story — however good it it might be — singly. He persisted in receiving pairs of — ear-rings, he called them. Now, I think I can give you a pendant, Mrs. Ashley, for your young Miss, with her peculiar ideas of costume. Mrs. Reginald Gardiner, whom you know, was one day very politely asked, how she could wear pink ribbons, at her advanced time of life, (American fashion;) and she very prettily replied, "I have an old apple-tree in my 'wee bit garden' in New York, which puts forth pink blossoms every revolving year, and I shall wear my cap-trimmings of those roseate colors, just so long as my dear old tree continues to bloom." A few days afterwards comes a lady to Mrs. Gardiner, and says, "Oh! I heard *such* a charming speech of yours." "Pray, what was it?" "Oh! I heard you said you had an old apple-tree in your garden, and had all your caps made precisely like it."'

Mrs. Sanderson, in showing some rare gems, led the ladies to speak of diamonds, when Mrs. Barclay jestingly declared she never wished to wear less than fifty thousand dollars' worth.

'Very modest indeed in your pretensions!' said Mrs. Ashley.

'You may laugh, if you please,' said Mrs. Barclay, 'but I assure you, nothing looks so mean to me as a few diamonds. I saw women in Europe wearing diamonds to the amount of half a million of dollars, who did not seem to be overloaded; other precious stones in the same quantity would be perfectly frightful. Jesting apart, however, and always excepting heir-looms, I think the spending of money in such things, in our country, every way absurd. I like harmony in arrangements, domestic and otherwise, and think the unities should be preserved; and confess it would grieve me excessively, to be obliged to take off ten thousand dollars' worth of diamonds, and descend into my Plutonian region — the kitchen — to lard a partridge, and compound a Bavarian cream — which many a time and oft I have been obliged to do in the interregnum created by the sudden and causeless outgoing of one high and contending priestess of the culinary art, and the incoming of another.'

'A crabbed old man,' said Mrs. Gordon, 'once told me that our women, when they congregated together, never talked of any thing but dress and servants; so, fortunately, here come the gentlemen to their tea.'

They entered, and music — in which Mrs. Sanderson joined — inviting Grace Barclay to preside at the tea-table, in her stead, whiled away the time until Peter, with a sublime bow, which, on that occasion, was not lost for lack of light, announced the carriages; and thus ended Mr. Philip Egerton's grand dinner.

CHAPTER XXVIII.

> 'What call'st thou solitude? Is not the earth,
> With various living creatures of the air,
> Replenish'd, and all those at thy command,
> To come and play before thee?'
>
> MILTON.

THE evening succeeding Mr. Egerton's dinner Mrs. Ashley came, as she declared, to talk it over. Mr. Rosevelt and the Rev. Mr. Meredith both presented themselves, and also Mrs. Gordon and her daughter. They were all professing the pleasure they had enjoyed in their visit to the bachelor, when Miss Tidmarsh and Miss Redmond joined the circle. These two ladies had heard of the unwonted proceedings at 'the old miser's,' — things are circulated rapidly in Boston, — and the two damsels were dying of curiosity to know if Mr. Egerton's guests had actually seen any edibles at all; a question they had permitted themselves to moot in various places. And they were really made very uncomfortable, for the Dolly had intense satisfaction, which she openly avowed, in making them almost expire of envy at not having been present, and filled their unwilling ears with an entire and complete description of the glories of the plate, the splendour of the porcelain, and the super-excellence of the dinner, and gaiety of the party. Miss Serena, not being able to contradict this statement in the presence of so many eye-witnesses, responded with rather incredulous ohs and ahs. Getting weary of hearing praises bestowed, — laudations of every kind being positively hateful to her, — she turned her attention to the gentlemen, or, as she was pleased to call them, the beaux. Now if it had not been for the chance of seeing those beaux, she would never have crossed the threshold of Mrs. Barclay's doors.

The gentlemen were very ungrateful, not paying any regard to her amiable advances, or evincing any admiration of her bare and knobbed shoulders. Miss Serena always looked like a person pinched with the cold, and that evening more than ever; and if she wore this guise at the Barclays, who were noted for the warmth of their dwelling, how did Miss Serena appear in cooler latitudes? It afterwards transpired, through Clara Gordon, that Mr. Rosevelt had asked her this same question. Nothing abashed by her total want of success, Miss Serena changed her seat, and entered into conversation, if the bald and disjointed sentences she uttered could be so denominated, with Miss Gordon; thereby interrupting a degree of intercourse between her and Mr. Rosevelt, which appeared to her to be altogether too interesting to the parties. This was a plan the amiable Serena invariably adopted and thoroughly enjoyed, being one too many, a thing all the world exceedingly dreads and avoids.

Finding she made no impression on the handsome young naval officer, she moved towards Mrs. Barclay, and began informing her she thought it extremely probable that Mr. Naseby was about to be engaged to Jane Redmond, and inquired what she thought of the match. Mrs. Barclay answered, she was always glad to hear of happiness any where, and of matrimonial engagements when they were officially announced, but permitted herself to give no opinions whatever upon mere conjectural reports. Which answer Miss Tidmarsh translated, after her own peculiar fashion, to mean, that the lady was very angry at the report, hoping to secure Mr. Naseby for one of her own daughters, and bored every one she met with her own malicious constructions. Georgy and Grace never very well knew what to do with Jane Redmond, for she regularly contradicted all their assertions, however incontrovertible they might be; and as she was older than they, she regarded them in a remarkably inferior light, and took no pains whatever to conceal her opinions. They generally proposed music as a safety-valve, and, as she played well and liked to be invited, they contrived to get on smoothly. They sometimes did wish, it might be avowed, that Mrs. Redmond had not the right to come and go at her pleasure in their father's house, but a friendship of long standing had existed between Mr. Barclay and Mr. Redmond, who, however he might forget the rest of his friends and acquaintances, never neglected his college chum. Mrs. Barclay had long desired to renounce all but formal intercourse with her two neighbours, and would have done so, but for the other members of their respective families, and was glad to find that her daughters liked neither Jane or Serena any better than she did herself. When the music was finished, the twain, having drank a cup of tea each, and seasoned them with a little scandal, retired, leaving behind them, as usual, a disagreeable impression.

It being just then the moment, there was always a mysterious signal given to the Dolly by Nursey Bristow that her hour had arrived to depart, she made her salutations and left the room. A second ensued, when she re-appeared, having jerked her shoulders entirely out of her frock, and brought her long hair into precisely the fashion of Miss Tidmarsh's head gear; she sailed into the room, dipping and bowing, and then curtseyed herself out backwards, in Miss Serena's best style. So perfect was the imitation, that every one was convulsed with laughter, except her mother, who never encouraged any of these proceedings.

'She is perfectly incorrigible,' said Mrs. Barclay.

'Impossible not to laugh,' cried Mr. Richard, 'I wonder how you can look so grave, Catherine.'

But the lady addressed looked graver still, and the Dolly was well lectured the next morning; but, somehow, though she professed to be sorry for her misdemeanours, and really was, she was constantly in the habit of commencing a fresh score.

'Surely,' said Mrs. Barclay to her husband when their guests had departed, 'I have been spoiled by Georgy and Grace, for Kate gives me more trouble in one week, than they ever did in their natural lives, in these small matters. I wish, John, you would not laugh at her, she is greatly encouraged by your mirth.'

'How can I help it?' replied Mr. Barclay, laughingly, 'the imitation was so perfect.'

'Ah!' said his wife, 'you will spoil that child, John.'

'Girls bear spoiling remarkably well,' answered he.

The next evening Mrs. Sanderson and Gerald made their appearance. This was her first visit, and she had preferred to make it informal, rather than ceremonious. She came, she said, to thank them for their kindness in honouring the old house with their cheering and agreeable presence, and she also brought her brother's acknowledgments, who, but for a cold, would have presented them himself.

Mrs. Sanderson was greeted with great cordiality, and before the evening was half finished, she had lamented she had not paid this visit years before. Georgy and Grace conducted her into the conservatory, and, once there, enjoyed a charming chat respecting their mutual favourites, the flowers and birds. She was much delighted with the taste displayed in the arrangements, and afterwards joined them in duets and some concerted pieces of music, and played admirably.

Mr. Richard was extremely attentive and courteous to her, and Gerald followed all their movements with his eyes. What contentment did he not experience in beholding his beloved mother once more entering into a little society, and communing with kindred spirits! Hopeless as was his own case, and wretched as he must ever be, for thus youth always exaggerates, he still could feel great interest in his parent's welfare, and was overjoyed that a prospect of change and variety was opening to her in an intercourse with this charming family. Gerald had, since the abandonment of the dream-land in which he had been enthralled, experienced many unpleasant hours in addition to his other perplexities, on the subject of his mother's total seclusion. Mrs. Sanderson was a great reader, it was true, and she also possessed many accomplishments, but there is nothing like a collision with one's fellows, to rub off the dust collected in the brain by solitude and clear away its cobwebs. We are too prone to overrate our own individual importance when we live alone, to magnify the value of our own opinions, and also to think ill of a world into which we never enter.

Gerald Sanderson had eaten of this bitter fruit, in his early seclusion; his own soul was filled with poignant remorse, that, but for his own insane folly, the woman he adored might have been spared a life of misery. He beheld her battling with her destiny, and bearing, with a martyr's fortitude, her cross, while, again, and again, he reiterated, in agonized despair,—'This, this is my work.' These sad reflections made him all the more anxious that his mother, now that her sons were unavoidably separated from her by their occupations and pursuits, should gradually be alienated from her recluse habits of existence, and he hailed with delight the vista of a pleasant social life now presented.

Zimmermann has written a thick volume on the charms of solitude, and has finished by avowing and confessing that we must all have some one person to whom we can exclaim, 'How charming is this solitude!' An old author has said, quaintly enough, 'The mind requires dusting, and, as this is a process we are not inclined to perform ourselves, it must naturally enough be done by others.' The world is a much better place than its scorners imagine, who peeping out from the loop-holes of their disagreeable retreats, scowl and rail at its inhabitants, and covering them with the panoply of their own virtuous indignation, bedeck them with all imaginable and unimaginable vices. That we are not wholly good, or wholly bad, is most true, unmitigated villains being rare. It assuredly behooves these patterns of excellence, who believe they possess 'all the cakes and ale,' to come forth and suffer themselves to be admired, as, at present, they are hardly even desired.

It is pretty well conceded now, that, to do good and effect beneficial reforms, pleasant faces and cheerful voices are required; the reign of the sour-visaged and dingy saints has passed away, and forever; the present generation must be lured into straight-forward paths, not coerced and driven. The modern brothers and sisters of charity must don no conventional and gloomy garb; they must insinuate themselves in cheerful garments, into the hearts and souls of their converts, bit by bit; long homilies are out of the question; no one in our ever curiously busy land, having time to listen to a second chapter, not to even mention, a forty-ninth.

Many of the people, most inclined to do good, commit the grand mistake of forgetting that a mighty page has been turned over in this last century and added to the great volume of the universe, and that gentler handling is required. To those who have looked on, and added their own small mite to the general welfare, this has become a self-evident fact. In these times children are made to do many pleasant things, not precisely duties, by cheerful precepts and examples which were unknown to our rigid forefathers. A milder and more genial race has succeeded to a sterner one, but there is yet much to be done. All duties should be rationally enforced, but the pleasant amenities of life may be very much cultivated in a cheerful atmosphere. The children of the poor particularly, may be taught 'to look through nature up to nature's God,' and allowed occasional glimpses of the beautiful things which He has provided for mankind, with great advantage to themselves and the rich; thereby bringing them together in closer bonds, and breaking down the iron barriers which separate them.

On becoming more acquainted with Mrs. Sanderson, Mrs. Barclay counselled her to interest herself in some of the charitable institutions with which Boston abounds; she being a person who required to be aroused, and to have other thoughts directed into useful channels, and for these, societies are great blessings. The lady, agreeing with her adviser, promptly set herself to work, and became thereby obligated to bestir herself, and was consequently much happier than she had ever been. She found these institutions demanded both care and much time, and she was induced to devote a portion of her leisure to them. These things also brought her into connection with many deserving persons, whom she had not before known, and extended her several relations and sympathies.

Gerald encouraged his mother in all her little plans and projects, and even persuaded her into an excursion to New York, and once there, she went on to Washington. The preparations for this expedition exceeded, by far, any arrangements for an expedition to Nova Zembla, and Mrs. Sanderson could hardly forbear laughing heartily at her own luggage, and its multifarious variety of articles. But having once perpetrated a journey, and returned home in comfort and security, she began to think it was not such an arduous undertaking as she had imagined.

CHAPTER XXIX.

> ' One glance from her my soul loves best,
> In the soft grace of beauty drest,
> I would not change and wish to live,
> For all this boasted world can give.'
>
> IGLESIAS DE LA CASA.

MR. BARCLAY had been gratified at receiving in his house the young clergyman, Mr. Meredith, whom he had met at Mr. Egerton's, having heard an excellent report of him from several mutual friends, and finding him pleasing and genial. He invited him to join, whenever it suited his pleasure, his family circle; he also asked Mr. Rosevelt, Mr. Barclay, having a partiality for the navy, and thinking a gentlemanly sailor a rather fascinating sort of person. He was always inclined to receive him hospitably, and ever admired his straight-forward, frank and loyal nature, as well as his generosity. To be sure, he sometimes smiled at his susceptibility and childlike simplicity respecting womankind — angels all, as he religiously believes them to be — and sometimes sympathized with him in his disappointments.

Mr. Rosevelt seemed fated to follow in the footsteps of his impressible class, for he fell desperately in love at first sight with Clara Gordon. Sailors are all Romeos, very Shaksperian. In this case, the gentleman rover found a Juliet, for that young lady romantically responded to his passion, and, moreover, fancied she had done a very wise thing; thus the sea swallowed up the 'American Methuseleh.' It was not more than a month, or less than a week, after their first meeting, that the enamoured Lieutenant poured forth the tale of his love at his lady's feet, and that she confessed her perfect willingness to share his destiny.

When this important intelligence was announced at home, it met with a very decided opposition from her parents. They could not at all consent to part with their only daughter, to become for the rest of her days a wanderer on the face of the globe; then they objected to the long, irremediable absences which an officer's wife must endure, the separations so difficult to bear, and, in fact, both Mr. and Mrs. Gordon smiled not upon the pretender to the favour of their daughter. Clara Gordon flew in utter despair to Mrs. Barclay, and begged and conjured her to intercede and pray for the consent of her parents. Mrs. Barclay counselled her young friend to wait a year, and then, if she were of 'the same opinion still,' it might possibly be obtained, they being shocked by the suddenness of the whole thing. But Clara declared her lover would hear of no such dilatory proceedings; that he would be unutterably wretched, and thought he should never survive a refusal; and that she herself was miserable. After an interview with the lover, Mrs. Barclay, finding all reasoning out of the question, and both parties being in a most despairing state, and happening to be acquainted with the gentleman's family, which was an excellent Southern one, and knowing that he had a small private property and good expectations, and having learned the most important part, that his character was excellent, she concluded to try and do something for the unhappy pair.

So Mrs. Barclay saw Mrs. Gordon, and smoothing away many difficulties, and making her friend and her husband cognizant of many pleasant facts which she had, moreover, gathered from the Commodore of the station, — undoubted authority, — she managed to bring round the Gordons, and they bestowed their consent to the union of the pair, and, as they said and firmly believed, they were made supremely happy. Clara nearly smothered her friend with kisses, and her sailor lover looked as if he would also like to do the same thing.

Then came all the busy note of preparation for the wedding. Grace Barclay was invited to be first bridesmaid, and a handsome young officer was first bridesman, and, as a matter of course, became enslaved by the superlative charms of his associate, though he was not so fortunate as his friend, Mr. Rosevelt. In a marvellously short period, almost beyond belief, had he belonged to any other profession, Miss Grace Barclay received her first offer of marriage — a most momentous occurrence in a young girl's life, — smiles she, or frowns she, — and this offer the damsel becomingly refused, but in such a gentle manner that the rejected suitor continued to be her fast friend. It must be confessed, however, that, notwithstanding his despair and tribulation, he lost his heart again the very next year, and Gracy heard of his nuptials with intense satisfaction; for she, in her youthful simplicity, had felt very sad at witnessing his sorrow, and almost imagined he might succumb under its weight; but he had lived on, and she was greatly relieved of her anxiety.

But to return from this short and hurried digression, very indicative of salt water, Miss Gordon was married in church, the bridegroom in full uniform, looking admirably. The bride was attired in a pure white silk high-necked dress, and a bewitching French hat, filled with orange blossoms, and such a veil! — a present from Mrs. Barclay, — it nearly covered her whole person. The bridesmaids were charming, though, of course, they are never permitted to eclipse the bride, and the church was filled to repletion with young persons; and the Dolly thought the whole thing went off admirably, and was capital fun, as she privately informed Nursey Bristow. And most especially did she incline to Mrs. Nichols's delicious wedding cake, her very best handiwork, of which she had a portion passed through the bride's ring, and pinned up in white paper with the bride's pins;

and this arrangement being effected, the little parcel was placed carefully under her pillow, and she dreamed 'never a bit of any body or any thing,' she said, and added, half crying, 'that this was very provoking indeed.' The happy couple, after a charming breakfast, departed on a visit to Mr. Rosevelt's family, and to the Barclays, who had been kept in a perpetual state of excitement for a month, the whole of this engagement and bridal seemed like the embodiment of a dream.

Georgy and Grace deplored Clara's departure bitterly, and the Dolly thought every thing vastly dull. Mr. Richard pronounced the Gordons to be fools for consenting to such hurried doings. Miss Serena Tidmarsh opined no good would ever come of this hurried marriage; and Jane Redmond said, 'Who would have imagined that any girl could find a husband at Philip Egerton's?' Mr. Barclay roundly asserted that his young friend had made a good match, and that all would agree with him in time; but then Mr. Richard said, his brother John had always a weakness for 'the buttons,' and his opinion did not carry as much weight as usual, on this occasion. Mr. Richard Barclay never heard of marrying, or giving in marriage, with any great degree of equanimity; he generally snarled more or less on such occasions. Mrs. Ashley said, 'All's well that ends well,' and 'We must wait, for this whole thing has been carried through in such a hurry-scurry, that I have not had time to breathe, and, besides, I am very sorry to lose Clara, and cannot be expected to give my unqualified consent.' So they all said their say, but, as Mrs. Barclay quietly observed, 'the subject of these remarks was "married and awa'," and all they could do or say would not alter her condition.'

The bride and bridegroom returned, after a month's absence, having had a delightful warm-hearted Southern reception, and intended remaining a few weeks with Mrs. Gordon, preparatory to their going to Norfolk, where he was ordered.

Shortly after their return, the wife of the Commodore of the station issued invitations for a ball on board a seventy-four in the harbour, and the Gordons, Rosevelts and Barclays were all invited. It being a delicious season of the year, every thing favoured this pleasant fête. Mr. Barclay, who admired excessively a ship of war, instantly persuaded his wife to accept the invitation. Georgiana peremptorily declined, but Grace was extremely pleased with the idea of seeing the beautiful vessel in a gala dress, the more especially as all her friends were going. The Dolly was in a frenzy of despair at being obliged to stay away from this 'entrancing party,' and coaxed and pleaded and induced Uncle Richard to pray for her exemption from general rules, and, at last, between the pair, a consent was extorted; and even Johnny was smuggled on board, nobody knew how. Mr. Rosevelt was strongly suspected of having introduced this small contraband article, but there he was, and no one pleaded guilty, not even the youthful aspirant for marine festivals himself.

On a delicious afternoon in July, the Barclays departed, 'on pleasure bent,' from their own house, and reached 'the stairs,' where an orderly inquired if they were for the ship, to which they responded affirmatively. A young midshipman assisted them down these stairs, and a handsome lieutenant placed them carefully in a twelve-oared barge, the linings of which rivalled the whiteness of the women's dresses. In a moment they were upon a world of waters, enlivened by the songs of the seamen in the surrounding shipping, and the plashing of oars, — a delightful contrast indeed, to the dust and brick walls of the city. The seventy-four's barges were plying to and fro for the guests, manned by sailors in their prettiest of all costumes. At the ship's side, on a carpeted platform, they were received by two officers, who helped them up the ladder, which, on this occasion, were transformed into good and broad steps. They were then ushered into a scene of perfect enchantment, a ball-room which Aladdin's lamp might have produced in the good olden time, when we believed and luxuriated in the Thousand-and-one Nights, — a ball-room of two hundred feet in length, adorned with the flags of all nations, and presenting such a gorgeous harmony of colouring as quite dazzled their bewildered eyes, enchanting the artist as well as the amateur. The tri-color of France, the bold lion of England, and the stars and stripes of our own land, all mingled together in peace and harmony, as it is hoped they ever will be. At one end was an orchestra most tastefully decorated in the same way, and, at the other, the top of the Commodore's cabin was carpeted and draped with flags and filled with luxurious seats, from which they looked down upon the beauteous ball-room below. The hatchways were surrounded with stands of arms, each musket bearing an innocent wax-light! a great relief to many of the female part of the assembled company, who held in terror muskets without either stock or lock. Coloured lanterns were disposed amidst the draperies, looking like emeralds and rubies.

The Barclays were presented to their lady-like hostess, and the Commodore, all graciousness, conducted them over his ship, even down into the orlop-deck. The cleanliness and purity of the vessel might be gathered from the fact, that the white satin shoes of the young girls were spotless. They then peeped out of sundry loop-holes, and beheld a sun-set such as was never surpassed at Venice, where the majesty of light is predominant. As the twilight shadows gathered around, the illumination of this enchanting ball-room commenced, and when it was finished and an air from the opera of Gustave issued from the orchestra, it surpassed in beauty the famous last scene of that production in Paris.

Just then the ship's bell sounded, and Mrs. Barclay declared she was alarmed lest it might be the stage manager's call, and the whole would, presto, disappear, so perfect was the illusion. The company was composed of youth, middle-aged, and even some old people — a very memorable event. Philadelphia had sent to this ball its golden-haired Peris, Milton its beauties, and Boston its lovely daughters and lovelier mothers, in the 'mezzo giorno,' on whom the rich, warm rays

> 'Of mid-day sun shone with a summer power.
> Queen-like they moved with pure and lofty brow,
> And, redolent of thought, life's wide-expanded flower
> Had so remained unchanged.'

Sweet Tasso, the poet of the matrons, has said something like this. 'What a pity the mezzo giorno does not show itself oftener!'

The dancing was spirited, and interspersed with frequent visits to refreshment-rooms and many visits to the gun-deck. Hundreds of cannon, bristling and fearful, lined this deck, which was half-lighted, presenting, by a refinement of good taste in its partial illumination, a severe contrast to the oriental splendour above; and in truth it seemed a remarkably popular part of the ship, the sailors grouped in amongst the guns, adding to the lights and shadows of its immense perspective. The officers devoted themselves to the guests, and every woman present imagined herself an exclusive object of attention, an impression that the 'buttons' are very apt to give to the fair sex. At midnight, after giving a dozen or more last looks at the ball-room, the guests departed, delighted with every arrangement, and as the ship receded from their view, the bright moon above, the blue calm waters below, she looked as she was a thing of life and beauty.

To attempt to describe the Dolly's raptures would be impossible. She was soon discovered by the midshipmen to be an admirable dancer, and accordingly her partners were countless, and she flew about like a lapwing, and was surrounded by admirers. She gave her mother warning next day that she must not expect her to be rational for a month, and was answered that if she were it would be for the first time in her life. Johnny had contracted a violent friendship with a middy who was just out of leading-strings, and seriously meditated an immediate entrance into the navy, but was admonished by his father that he had better wait a few years and ruminate upon his project. Shortly after this never to be forgotten ball, the Rosevelts left for Norfolk, and were sadly regretted by all their friends.

CHAPTER XXX.

'If, despising all visible decorations, they were only in love with the embellishments of the mind, why should they borrow so many of the implements, and make use of the most darling toys of the luxurious?'

BERNARD MANDEVILLE.

SHORTLY after Gerald Sanderson's first visit to Mr. Barton, he received from him a huge embossed card, in a saffron-coloured envelope, requesting the honour of his company at dinner, and forthwith accepted the invitation. A week's notice prepared him for a grand entertainment, and on the appointed day he sallied forth, in full dress, to dine with his patron. Punctually at five he reached the house, and being ushered into the 'best parlour,' found that he had arrived half an hour too early, his watch having misled him. In the interval, before the appearance of the ladies, and his host, whose apparelling was not finished, he had plenty of time to examine, at his leisure, the plenishing of these halls of beauty.

Louis the Fourteenth has many misdeeds for which to answer to posterity, but if he could but see the abominations, in the matter of furniture and upholstery, perpetrated in his honour, and falsely bearing his name and style in these United States of America, he would consider his punishment great indeed. Really nothing was ever so odious as the sprawling tables and comfortless chairs and sofas, which, covered with gilding and brocade, encumbered those small rooms, and all so low that no one could rise from them without risk of life and limb. Immense mirrors with ponderous frames, enormous clocks, and huge figures, bearing candles so tall that they almost reached the low plaster of Paris ceilings, all cold and naked. The walls were covered with the gaudiest of paper-hangings, and sprinkled over with pictures, great and small, the lines all broken at the base, and looking as if they had been thrown there at a venture.

The catalogue of this collection of the fine arts was absolutely astounding in its nomenclature — two Raphaels, four Correggios, almost as many as grace the Dresden Gallery, three Claudes, &c. Now, considering that the love-lorn King of Bavaria purchased the last d'Urbino to be found on sale in all Europe for twelve thousand dollars, and a small one too, it was really marvellous where such inestimable treasures had been found. Not a single native artist had been, by any chance, admitted into this distinguished society. Oh, no! On the other hand, there were loads of knicknackeries, puerile and ridiculous enough. Presently the ladies dropped in, one after another, and were enchanted to renew their acquaintance with Gerald and their inquisitorial researches into the Barclay family. To all their demands upon his time, Gerald exhibited the most remarkable and exemplary patience, it being an ever-gracious theme to him, the mention of his friends. The Misses Barton informed him they were to entertain on that day a most select party, with only one exception, and that was their father's country cousin — Mrs. Hastings, of Hastingsville — who having most inopportunely arrived the evening before, they had been obliged to invite, sadly against their will.

'I told her,' said Miss Araminta Cora, who rather liked Gerald, and threatened to do even more, 'that she would not in the least enjoy herself, and begged her to come tomorrow, when we would get up a snug little party of her old friends for her, but she would not hear of this arrangement, declaring she wished to see our new ones; and as there are expectations, she being very rich indeed, we were obliged to submit. Now,' resumed the young lady, quite confidentially, 'though I should like exceedingly to have you to sit beside me at dinner, I must renounce the gratification, and beg you to do me the great favour to lead our cousin of Hastingsville down stairs; for if she gets near any other of our guests, she will so shock them with her commonplaces, proverbs, and homely saws.'

So Gerald promised, and received in return the most gracious of smiles from Miss Araminta Cora.

The party consisted of twenty-four persons, a world too many for enjoyment. None of them seemed to be acquainted with each other, and Mr. Barton persisted in introducing them. Now, as they were all Bostonians, this was in bad taste; and Gerald was just thinking that the several parties were much annoyed, when one gentleman rebelled, and fairly told his host that he declined the acquaintance of the person to whom he was presented. This was a terrible stroke, but it transpired that there had been a deadly feud between the two gentlemen, all about a cargo of saltpetre, in which neither was to blame except that they would not listen to reason, and of which Mr. Barton was entirely ignorant, this being a new phase of society to him. This, it must be confessed, was a most discordant commencement of festivities, and as ill-luck prevailed, the twain were seated next to each other at table, and discoursed gunpowder slantwise. Indeed, it was discovered that almost every one had been mismated on this grand occasion.

Gerald thought he was especially favoured, for just before the repast, Mr. Barton, taking him suddenly by the button-hole, and at the same time destroying a moss rosebud which his daughter, Miss Araminta Cora, had bestowed upon the youth, begged him to place himself at his right hand. 'For,' said he, 'my girls have insisted upon giving a thorough French dinner, and I don't know the name of a single kick-shaw, so you must promise to tell me.' Poor Gerald! his post of favourite promised to be rather wearisome, but he slipped out of this dilemma by advising his friend not to attempt offering any thing whatever, but to order the servants to do so. 'What a horrid time I shall have,' said Mr. Barton, 'not being able to offer any thing; how very inhospitable I shall seem. Those confounded girls will be the death of me with their foreign nonsense; I wish I had never consented to such a grand parade.'

Gerald, faithful to his promise, escorted Mrs. Hastings to dinner, and shortly heard the Misses Barton holding long arguments on their favourite studies with the two saltpetre guests, who, for once, though not addressing each other, seemed to be of the same mind, opining that one or two 'quarters' of chemistry, geology, medicine and anatomy were worse than useless; and one of them, avowing he had dabbled a little in the sciences, thought a whole life would hardly suffice for the acquisition of chemistry alone. Mr. Barton, who supposed his talented progeny had learned all these things thoroughly, was amazed beyond expression at this discovery, and after a long pause, he turned to Mrs. Hastings and said, 'Well, cousin, what do you think of all this?' The lady, who proved to be a strong-minded woman, declared she had given no attention to the sciences, seeing that it required an age to get any knowledge of them whatever, but was devoting all her powers to getting a homestead bill passed, and was resolved to see if women could not be exempted from taxation, — an abominable imposition upon the sex, which she hoped to see set right before she died. There should be no taxation without representation; for her part she did not desire to represent any thing but herself, but she would not be satisfied until that thing was changed.

Gerald, finding his host had sprung a mine unawares, endeavoured to change the conversation by inquiring of the lady how she liked the country.

'I should like it very well,' she replied, 'if I could ever discover it in America. Where I live there is more aping of what my neighbours are pleased to call "style and fashion" that in any city in the Union. I hear divers complaints here of the same thing, but do you come and stay with me and see how the rule works at Hastingsville. Why,' said she, 'none of the farmers' daughters make butter and cheese now; they are all learning exactly what cousin Barton's girls do, and talk in precisely the same ridiculous manner of things they know nothing about. Cousin Barton can afford to allow his chits to waste their time, but the country people must have somebody to do housework and look after the dairy; all the world can't be idle ladies and gentlemen. The fact is,' she resumed, 'the spirit of unrest is rampant in our country; nobody is satisfied; even I, with my eyes wide open to this crying evil, have two objects which must and shall be accomplished, and I should not be an American if I had not.'

Gerald was much amused with his neighbour, and heard her opinion of the guests with a hearty laugh. 'The old friends,' she declared, 'were much the most interesting; they had subjects in common with cousin Barton, and were not set up and stiff like these people. The old dinners were vastly pleasanter and better; for her part, she liked to know what she was eating; nobody could tell what these Frenchmen did when they once got into one's kitchen. And then, cousin Barton, a good creature enough, and his wife even better, were thrown away upon the "upper ten thousand." They despised them, and melancholy to relate, by courting these people they had lost all their old friends. Now if you could have seen Nick at his own board years ago; he was such a happy fellow! urging every body to eat his good things, and enjoying himself hugely; now he looks all curled up into a heap.' Then peeping down the table, she reported Mrs. Barton to be in precisely the same condition. 'This all comes,' said she, 'of spoiling children. My cousin's daughters are all the time tutoring their parents, and have deprived them of all their pleasures. When I am here I have some influence, and use it to make my kind-hearted relatives more comfortable with pleasant chats about old times, for I should think this eternal bothering about Pinnock's catechisms would weary them out of their senses. I am sure I take leave of my own sometimes, here and at home, with all the nonsense I hear. You perceive I speak plainly.'

'I am afraid, Mrs. Hastings,' said Gerald, 'you will disabuse me of all my ruralities by the account you give of country life, and the falling off of the present generation from the good fashions of their forefathers.'

'I am sorry to disturb your illusions,' replied the lady, 'but if you could see my neighbours in their silks and finery, you would soon cast aside all your preconceived opinions. There are no milkmaids now; they went out with the spelling-book which chronicled the well-filled pail. The young ladies are afraid of cows. Eggs are no longer counted; and all the wools sorted are German, out of which country damsels manufacture — not socks and stockings, as of old — but nondescript animals and cabbage-headed flowers.'

'Have you no influence?' queried Gerald.

'None at all: the fact is, I get angry and lose all my persuasive powers — if any I ever had — which I doubt.'

The dinner was excellent, and admirably ordered, and well served, and Mrs. Hastings was fain to confess that the coloured gentry, who conducted the arrangements, were capable and much better trained than the old scrambling set who formerly served her cousin's table at the repasts she so much regretted; but then the guests, she persisted in declaring, were not half so pleasant or agreeable.

The company all leaving the dining-room at the same time, music was introduced, the Misses Barton regaling their circle with some very questionable melodies. When they had finished, Gerald was entreated to favour them. So he obligingly sang some delicious airs from 'Lucretia Borgia,' accompanying himself with a guitar, and received the most enthusiastic thanks. His style was unambitious, his rich manly voice, soul-searching, penetrated into the recesses of all hearts, and his auditors seemed never weary of listening. When he had finished, Mrs. Hastings was exceedingly voluble in her praise, and informed him that she had puzzled her poor brains all dinner-time, to understand what situation he held in the family — she having been told he had one — and now she had discovered he was the music-master, he could be nought else.

Gerald, laughingly, assured her that he had not the honour to teach the young ladies, and that such was not his vocation. Then how can he play and sing so well, queried Mrs. Hastings, if he is not a teacher? The carriages being shortly announced, the guests departed, and when the last vehicle rolled away, Mr. Barton, giving himself a congratulatory shake, and unbuttoning the lower part of his waistcoat, plumped himself down into a Louis the Fourteenth, as if he hoped to rise from it nevermore, and exclaimed, in most joyous tones, 'Thank heaven, it's all over.' 'Why father!' screamed the triad of daughters, 'how can you say so? every thing so elegant, so well arranged, such good taste, so *recherché*.'

'I don't know what that last word means, if it be not stupid,' said he.

'Oh dear! oh dear!' screamed the three in concert.

'Well, my old woman, what do you say?' said their father, addressing his wife, 'what do you think of this hard day's work?'

'Why, my good husband, I had nothing to do with cooking the grand dinner, and that I liked very much. I've seen the time when I was so thoroughly worn out making jellies, custards and pastry, that I hardly had any strength left to put on my best gown, and was half-asleep all dinner-time.'

'But,' interrupted Mrs. Hastings, 'did you have a pleasant meal to-day?'

'To be sure,' replied Mrs. Barton, 'to be sure I did;

there was not even one dish put on the table awry, and that was really charming!'

Mrs. Hastings, of Hastingsville, smiling contemptuously at her simple cousin's idea of a pleasant dinner, then inquired if Mrs. Barton had enjoyed any improving conversation with the gentlemen who sat at her side, she having observed that they talked very fast across their hostess.

'Why no, not exactly,' she answered, 'they almost distracted me with talking about things I could not understand. They had a furious dispute about steamboats going to England, and quoted Dr. Dionysius Lardner, Mrs. Heavyside, and a vast many learned people besides.'

Mrs. Hastings, casting a half glance at Gerald — who had been especially requested to remain — said, 'I perceived they had almost forgotten your presence, which I consider very rude indeed; there is surely a certain respect always due to the hostess. Cousin Nick,' said she, 'I do not think you have got at the right people yet. What's the use of talking of books forever? I want to know what a man thinks himself, and desire to get at the kernel of these big nuts. Now, there are in Boston and its environs — if they could be collected together, which I am told is very difficult — very agreeable people. Then why don't you try? It would be richly worth your while. Almost every body likes good dinners. Yours are splendid. Then why have them eaten by such disagreeable stiff creatures — so full of airs and pretensions, and apparently having no regard for you whatever.'

'Shocking, shocking!' cried the young ladies.

'I think,' said their father, 'she is perfectly right; but I had rather have my old friends than any others; there's a heartiness about them I like.'

'Then, why not invite them?' asked Mrs. Hastings.

'Because the girls have so showed them the cold shoulder, that they will not come if we were to go on our knees to them.'

'If there is one thing I have to be more thankful for than another, it is that I have no daughters, cousin.'

'Thankful for small favours,' sneered Mr. Barton, who did not like to hear his children criticised.

'Do you know any man satisfied with his condition in this country?' asked Mrs. Hastings, suddenly turning to Gerald.

'I think I do.'

'Who is the happy person?'

'Mr. Barclay.'

'Will you introduce me to him?'

'I can hardly take that liberty, madam, having so lately made his acquaintance myself.'

'I shall then call upon him shortly, as I am really anxious to see a contented individual.'

'Have you none in Hastingsville?

'The last place in the world for a search! All my acquaintances there are dying to go to town, and I can hardly have my own way in any thing — every body quoting "city fashions" — that's the pet phrase. I wanted, last week, to get some large logs cut for rustic seats, and I was credibly informed that nobody sat upon logs in the city, and, if I would, I must have stuffed cushions.'

Just then, Gerald discovered Mrs. Barton in a sound sleep on the most comfortless of sofas, and, being fearful if the lady remained much longer in her crooked position she would catch a stiff neck, he arose to depart. Mrs. Barton awoke, and was greatly shocked to perceive she had reclined upon the brocade — 'ten dollars a yard.' How she sighed!

As Gerald wended his way home, he reflected, in a species of agony, upon the prospect of Mrs. Hastings's visit to Mr. Barclay, and this under the cover of his own name. What should he do when he saw her enter, some pleasant evening, the charmed circle where all his ideas of elegant refinement centered? This question he repeatedly asked himself, and regretted having answered the lady, when she inquired where a contented man was to be found.

Mrs. Hastings, of Hastingsville, was an enterprising woman, priding herself upon a strong mind, very much given to fiercely enforcing her doctrines — in other words, cramming them down other people's throats. Her personal appearance also added some weight to her arguments; for she was a tall, masculine woman, with remarkably big, uncovered bones, a loud voice, and — being near-sighted — wore spectacles, sometimes, even green ones. Mrs. Hastings's dress, however, was unlike that of her sisters of the strong-minded class, being remarkably rich and elaborate; and, although not certainly prepossessing, her air and manner commanded respect. Yet still Gerald Sanderson was quite nervous at the idea of her presenting herself, at what might seem to be his instigation, in Mrs. Barclay's house; so he resolved to explain the matter in that quarter, lest the lady might fall upon her unawares. His fears of the threatened invasion for such a curious purpose, were shortly removed by hearing Mr. Barton regret that his cousin had been suddenly called home by the illness of her husband; and Gerald was thereby made aware of the existence of such an individual as Mr. Hastings — a gentleman, whom Mr. Barton averred, was very little seen and rarely heard. This did not surprise Gerald, as he had concluded, that if there existed a person enjoying a marital title in the lady's household, he must be very secondary indeed.

CHAPTER XXXI.

'Of all the gay places the world can afford
By gentle and simple for pastime ador'd,
Fine balls, and fine concerts, fine buildings and springs,
Fine walks and fine views, and a thousand fine things.'

BATH GUIDE.

MR. BARCLAY, amidst his pleasant possessions, had never made the acquisition of a country-house. He declared himself to be a bit of a cockney, liking his city life extremely well, and varying it in the summer heats by excursions to the sea-shore and watering-places. The latter he had not recently frequented, as he had thought his daughters too young for such gay places.

Mrs. Barclay, who ever jestingly asserted that she had not the housekeeping bump sufficiently developed in her cranium to keep up two establishments suitably, preferred to retain one in excellent order, and enjoyed these snatches of change greatly, but always returned, with renewed pleasure, to her own charming home. Both parents, however, thought that an entire revolution in Georgy's habits and feelings would be eminently beneficial, and resolved to take her with her sisters to Saratoga. To this arrangement she made a decided resistance, and pleaded that neither her health nor spirits demanded it; that she was perfectly contented in her father's house, and required no change whatever; but in the end consented to go, to gratify her parents. For herself, she anticipated no pleasure whatever, but true to her resolve of doing every thing, henceforth, for them, she determined to adopt the semblance of satisfaction at least. She was so conscious that her melancholy story would be known and commented upon, that she dreaded an entrance into a world of strangers; but this display was entirely obviated by the extraordinary resemblance between herself and Grace, and, as no one could very well distinguish one from the other, she thereby avoided all embarrassment.

Mrs. Ashley accompanied them on this excursion, and Mr. Richard declined. He said he detested watering-places, and once a day was quite sufficient for him to see the silly widow, without being obligated to dance attendance upon her for a month. Mr. Richard might have spared himself these fears, and have enjoyed many pleasant hours with his friends, instead of dozing away his time at home, earnestly praying for their return, and railing against such absurdities as families leaving their own comfortable dwellings and running about in search of pleasure. Indeed, at one moment, he was almost tempted to follow them, so heartily wearied was he of his solitariness; but then his consistency was at stake, and obstinacy forbade any change of purpose.

The amiable grumbler might have truly spared himself any apprehensions with regard to Mrs. Ashley, pleasant people being wanted every where, and in no place more than Saratoga; the lady was followed and courted to her heart's content. And a charming party they were, when they first appeared; all the inmates of the United States Hotel congratulated themselves upon such an addition to the beauty and grace of the household. They soon made many acquaintances, and the younger members contracted indissoluble friendships with other young creatures whom they had never seen before, and there was the accustomed interchange of trinkets, bouquets, locks of hair, and model attachments, which commonly occur upon such momentous occasions. The sisters were quite worshipped, so beautiful and so engaging, their music entrancing all ears with harmonious strains! The Dolly considered herself, she said, in a terrestrial paradise midway between heaven and earth, and even had not time to remember if 'the tails' were bound round her head or not; the more especially as certain Spanish girls, to whom she had vowed an enduring constancy, allowed theirs to float on the breeze with endless yards of coloured ribbons.

Mr. Naseby had followed his adorations, and, just one week after his arrival, the following occurred.

'My dear Grace,' said Georgy, rushing into her sister's chamber, 'such a scene as I have had! I think I shall hardly be able to recount my absurd adventure, for laughing.'

'Pray what is it, Georgy? I am dying with curiosity to hear.'

'And so you should be dying to know it, for you are, in truth, the heroine, though I flourished in your stead.'

'Please tell me directly then, dear Georgy.'

'I was just running through the garden piazza, from a friend's room to my own, when my steps were arrested by a hand gently and lightly laid upon my arm, and a voice whispered softly, "Give me but one moment, divine Miss Grace, — a kingdom for one moment." At first, I was bewildered by the suddenness of the movement, and, as it was twilight, hardly knew by whom I was addressed; but shortly perceiving this importunate swain to be one of your waifs and strays, Mr. Naseby, I became instantly possessed of a little of my old mischief, and resolved to leave him in his delusion, he being always in one, you well know, so I stopped and received the most impassioned declaration of love and adoration, and, over and above all this, a positive offer of his hand and heart, house, carriages, jewels, &c., &c.'

'Capital!' exclaimed Gracy, 'what fun! and what did you say?'

'Why, I ventured to put a very pretty negative on all these demonstrations. Was I right?'

'To be sure. What! I marry Mr. Naseby! heaven forbid.'

'But he would not receive the negative, and insisted that his devotion, his love, demanded quite another response, and even suggested — you understand his consummate vanity — that you had, in some sort, favoured his suit; that he had seen certain indications of preference, not to say, affection. I thought I should have laughed outright when he asserted his having *seen* any thing. Imagine his adopting that phrase, under the circumstances; it was like a blind man talking of light. I confess I was irritated when he hinted at your having betrayed a preference for him, and that made me even more decided than I should have been, and I reiterated my refusal very pertinaciously. Upon this, he declared himself to be a very ill-used person, saying that you had never given him reason to think he was displeasing to you, and that even your father and mother had also smiled upon him, as well as Miss Georgy Barclay, and that he had, for some time, considered himself quite assured of the concurrence of all your family. I replied that he must receive this denial in good faith, and must never again resume the subject, and upon that ground only would he be permitted to renew his intercourse with my relatives. Mr. Naseby then became quite angry, and declared he should complain to my father, and reveal to him the manner in which his daughter encouraged her admirers, and then rejected them. I told him that course would be of no avail, we were quite spoiled with indulgence, and, being always allowed to take our own way in these things, he would absolutely gain nothing by such a procedure. Finding me most unrelenting, — though I cannot think the measures he took were very persuasive, — he departed in a furious mood, choosing to regard himself as a most remarkably injured individual.'

'How very, very happy I am,' cried Gracy, 'that you received his declaration in lieu of myself, you answered the silly fellow so much better than I could have possibly done. What can he call encouragement? I really have almost had scruples of conscience when I have thought of the mischief we have concocted together, and all the naughty tricks we have played upon Mr. Naseby. I shall never experience any more twinges, I can assure you.'

'Oh! no,' said Georgy, 'have no compassion at all upon him; he has sadly misbehaved this evening. I am not quite positive that I have been able to make my account of this adventure very lucidly clear, for there was such a confusion of persons and things in my mind.'

'Pray make no apology, dear Georgy; the only wonder is, how you managed to do so well, and save me so much trouble. I shall never think of that garden scene without laughing. What a Romeo! Why worlds would not induce me to marry such a buzzard, and so vain and conceited! I hope he will not be so silly as to appeal from your decision, or mine, — which is it?'

'He may, but if he does, he will gain nothing, and my father and mother both well know that you have always refused to listen to his declarations, and that I have done the same thing. Now, Gracy, as it is evident he cannot distinguish his charmer from her sister, what a confused story he will have to tell; and you can affirm that you never received the proffer of his true love! This is really delightful!' And Georgy positively laughed, after her old fashion, in a way that gladdened the heart of her sister, in which merriment Gracy cordially joined.

That evening, at the ball, Mr. Naseby avoided Gracy, but certainly did appeal to Mr. and Mrs. Barclay, representing himself as a much aggrieved personage. They assured him that they had never perceived the least apparent liking for him in their daughter, but would inquire the next morning how matters stood. This they accordingly did, and were immensely amused when they listened to the little farce which had been enacted on the garden piazza.

But how to reveal to the gentleman his mistake? The Gracy had no mercy upon him, for she thought he had hoped to implicate her, and Georgy was resolved he should know what he had done, as she thought this knowledge would prevent any recurrence of like adventures in future. So, Mr. Barclay was deputed to inform Mr. Naseby that he had offered himself to the wrong sister, and, though this office was performed in the kindest spirit imaginable, it proved any thing but acceptable to the unfortunate recipient. Mr. Naseby would not, at first, believe he could have been so deceived, and Mr. Barclay was obliged to remind him of the imperfectibility of his vision, tempered with the acknowledged resemblance between his daughters. This softened the matter a little, but he keenly felt all the ridicule attendant upon such an absurd incident, and commented, with great severity, upon Miss Georgiana Barclay's assumption of her sister's name and style. This part of his proceedings Mr. Barclay advised him to withhold and keep to himself, and, moreover, counselled him to bury the whole affair in oblivion, as the part he had played in it did not certainly redound to his credit, and, by blazoning it abroad, he would only publish his own discomfiture. Whereupon, the indignant and defeated pretender to Gracy's hand took the advice so kindly proffered, and departed the next day, having lost all the pleasure he had proposed to himself in his excursion to Saratoga. Gracy was enchanted when she learned that her true knight was gone, 'over the hills and far away,' to Niagara. She now entered freely into the amusements of the place, as before the recent event in her history, Mr. Naseby had so followed and besieged her that she had preferred to lock herself up in her own chamber, rather than encounter, at every turn, the sentimental squire of dames, who was perpetually pouring into her unwilling ears, in the blandest of tones, honeyed words and speeches, which both cloyed and annoyed her.

'And how many more yards of ribbon do you propose to wear, Miss Catherine?' said Nursey Bristow.

'Just as many as Carmencita de Dolores and the other girls, the delicious darlings! If you could but see, Nursey, their beautiful black eyes, and hear their melting voices!'

'As if I do any thing else all day long. Are they not forever and ever in this chamber, rolling about on your bed?'

'I grant that; but then you will not acknowledge their superlative charms, their overwhelming attractions.'

'I'm looking at their tumbled frocks, Miss.'

'Oh dear! Oh dear! I wish I could make you see them as I do, — so fascinating, so bewitching!'

Kate had loved Mary Redmond, but every thing paled before the passion she had conceived for these Spanish girls. Their broken English and pretty ways had captivated her, and she poured forth on their lovely heads a volcano of enthusiastic admiration. Nothing was ever so fascinating; they were called the inseparables, the trio. They walked together, sung together, and would have danced together, if young America would have permitted them; but this was not allowed, Kate being a famous belle among the waltzers. So much for youth, the pleasant meetings, the bitter partings. It is the season designated for enjoyment in the programme of existence, but it is questionable if even in after years more scalding tears are shed, than when young hearts twined together in an inconceivably short space of time, are sundered — and some old ones too.

Though set down in the books as a resort for the very gay and frivolous, there is always at Saratoga a substratum of clever and studious men, who resort to this watering-place for relaxation, and they, with their pleasant families, give an elevated tone to the society. Casting aside all the cares attendant upon professional pursuits for the time, these men look as unlike the American of the city as possible, and impart to this watering-place an additional charm.

While their children amused themselves, Mr. and Mrs. Barclay found very many interesting persons, with whom they cultivated an agreeable intercourse, and whiled away a few weeks acceptably to themselves and others. Then came the partings, and these were heart-rending to the Dolly. She imagined she should never survive the separation from her Spanish beauties; and such protestations and vows of eternal friendships were hardly ever before registered, and such a voluminous correspondence as was threatened, in order to alleviate, if possible, the agonizing pangs consequent upon the wide waters being placed between herself and the objects of her idolatry.

And they returned home. The Dolly resumed her studies, wafting many sighs to her friends for a long while, and certainly betrayed a remarkable degree of constancy in her adherence to the memory of their piercing black eyes and broken English. Mr. Naseby withdrew himself from Mr. Barclay's house, and rarely visited Mrs. Ashley; he had absented himself on account of his wrongs, and betaken himself to other haunts, amongst which Mr. Barton's house was one.

Mr. Richard was overjoyed at the return of his favourites, and railed in good set terms against all such expeditions for pleasure, when persons had comfortable and luxurious homes. But his brother responded, that they loved this home all the better for beholding how very inferiour every thing else was in comparison with its attractions. Mr. Richard declared his belief that Mrs. Ashley was at the bottom of this expedition, its prime mover, and disliked her all the more.

Georgiana devoted herself to her father and mother. Their forbearance and kindness demanded her deepest and most abiding gratitude, and she asked for no other boon than the power to minister to their welfare and happiness. And Grace was wrapt up in love and admiration of her sister; as Georgiana refused all invitations, so did Grace, and in their home was centred all their pleasures. The Dolly insisted that

> 'They sat upon one cushion,
> Sewing of one seam ;'

and that, in her opinion, Grace was an absurd creature not to shine forth at the balls, which she was so fitted by nature to adorn and beautify. 'No sentimental considerations shall ever induce me to forego such enchanting pleasures,' cried she. 'I should like to annihilate time and space, and become old enough to sally forth and enjoy myself, and really believe I am ; and if I could but persuade my mother of this important fact, and extort from her a permission to exhibit myself, would'nt I have that Maria Louisa brocade !'

Gerald Sanderson was a most constant visitor, as well as his mother, whose spirits were much improved by her intercourse with the Barclays and others, for the recluse was no longer immured within her own solitary home, but walked abroad and interested herself in her fellow-beings, from which course she derived signal advantage. Gerald worked sturdily on, and began, in course of time, to command the attention of others besides his employer. Mr. Barton being thoroughly satisfied with the management of his affairs, soon threw a vast many other things into his hands, and Mr. Barclay also gave him business, and sent him clients, and he prospered even beyond his most sanguine anticipations.

And there was outwardly sunshine, once more, on the heads of the Barclays. The world seemed to have become oblivious of Georgiana's sad story, no one reverting to it, save Miss Serena Tidmarsh, who was very unwilling to resign her hold upon it ; but things pass so rapidly in succession in America, that, if it were not for the unfaltering efforts of a few Misses Tidmarsh, almost all the skeletons in the country would be buried, and their memories never resuscitated. But these amiable Serenas have a great tendency to adhesiveness, and grasp tightly and hoard up all scandalous waifs and strays. Johnny Barclay came and went back, with sorrowing steps and slow, to his seminary for polite learning, sometimes bringing home good reports and oftener the reverse, and 'had,' as he said, 'capital fun with the Dolly,' who studied not at all when her brother and playmate was at his holiday exercises, and which certainly did 'exercise' Nursey Bristow.

So time sped and years passed gently and quietly on, — they were not the happy ones of by-gone days. The sense of security from the shafts of adverse fate had vanished, and dread of ills which 'we wot not of' would hover around and oppress at times the beings on whom these shafts had descended. To be sure, their gay friend, Mrs. Gordon, assured them that, amidst the pleasant people with whom she had lived, she never had heard of this foreshadowing of evil. They enjoyed the goods of this life without anticipation of troubles, which they could not, in any event, avert, and died not many deaths in fearing one. And she thought this plan decidedly the best, but at the same time believed it to be a characteristic trait in the minds of her countrymen, the looking on the shady side of things. At any rate, there was no danger of Mrs. Gordon's perpetrating the same mistake, for she added, by her cheerfulness, a vast amount of pleasure wherever she appeared; and, as she greatly frequented the Barclays' house, she was the source of much happiness to them.

Suitors came to Gracy, but she remained constant to her first love-passage, and smiled not at all on the pretenders to her favour. News often came of the dear Charley, who was making rapid strides towards promotion, and gave very agreeable accounts, in his letters, of his favourable prospects, and hopes of return to his friends. And this family 'kept the peaceful tenor of its way,' uninterrupted by any startling events, united and tranquil.

CHAPTER XXXII.

'I will not warn thee not to set thy heart
Too firmly upon perishable things ;
In vain the earnest preacher spends his art
Upon the theme ; in vain the poet sings.'
SOUTHEY.

MRS. BARCLAY had received several little presents from Mrs. Rosevelt, accompanied by short and most affectionate notes, breathing a grateful spirit, but there had recently arrived a very interesting letter from that lady, which she read to her family with great satisfaction.

'NORFOLK, ——.

'I pray you may not consider me, dear Mrs. Barclay, a sadly ungrateful creature, wholly unmindful of the all-important part you took in procuring for me the consent of my parents to my union with my beloved husband, and I entreat you to believe I shall never forget your kindness. Having occasionally sent you a little memorial of my existence, I now proceed to explain why I have not written more elaborately before.

'You well know what a hurried marriage was mine, my dear friend, and how many times a certain musty proverb was quoted, which is always served up on such occasions. I hate proverbs. I therefore resolved, from the first, not to give you any positive information respecting my position and feelings, until I had been a wife a sufficiently long period to impart stability to my statements, and to warrant their immediate acceptance. Faithful to this high resolve, I

24

have awaited the termination of this period, in order to give consistency to my account, and now solemnly aver that I am perfectly happy; indeed, I rather think I love my husband better now than ever, his excellent qualities having been greatly developed since I first knew him. Having thus satisfied you touching my welfare, I must inform you, that on arriving here we repaired to an antiquated building, surnamed the castle. In this large establishment, presided over by a dignified and charming old Virginia lady, we found a nice parlour, chamber and dressing-room prepared for us, and which we have ever since occupied with great contentment.

'This house is filled with naval officers and their wives. We meet at meals, and in the evening occasionally, in a large parlour, where there is a piano. The society is excellent; the lodgers, all arriving from different parts of our country, and all having seen the world, have abundant sources of conversation, both pleasing and instructive — and all the common gossiping about our neighbours, which you so thoroughly despise, is thereby avoided. To be sure, my husband and I much prefer to pass our evenings together in our own parlour, but we occasionally mingle with the boarders, to avoid all semblance of singularity: and when he is on duty, I go to the ladies, and play for them to dance and also sing, they professing to like my humble efforts in either way. There are here some charming Mahonese women, who have taught me their beautiful embroidery, and I am busily employed in working two lace shawls — one for you, and another for my dear mother.

'You will smile, my dear friend, when I assure you I firmly believe the naval officers' wives to be the happiest women in the world. The fact is, that their husbands never remain long enough at home to become wearied of their society; and then a sailor always fancies all women to be angels — may he never be disabused. Certainly the separations are shocking. Just imagine a three-years absence! What shall I do when my hour arrives? I tremble while I write. There is no end to the amount of sympathy demanded here for the outgoings and incomings; this very morning Mrs. Captain Barrett, an excellent friend of mine, is bewailing the departure of her liege lord in an agony of tears, in my parlour; and precisely at the same time, Mrs. Lieutenant Carter rushes in with the joyful intelligence that her husband has reached the Ripraps, — so I demand of the twain, Am I to laugh or to cry? Nothing can surpass the kindness of the officers to the families of their absent shipmates; they are even excellent nurses. We have had a case of sickness and death here, where the attentions were of the most delicate character; where men, who had faced the cannon's mouth, watched over a little child like women, and thoughtfully ordered from the pastry-cooks jellies and confections for the sufferer; and when he died, laid him tenderly and feelingly in his coffin, and covered it with flowers.

'The towns-people are very hospitable and kind, and have the most agreeable fashion of sending us, by comely blacks, the most delicious lunches, and immense baskets of odoriferous flowers, and they also give gay and pleasant balls and dinners. Thus you perceive, dear Mrs. Barclay, how very pleasant are the places in which my lines are cast.

'I send my devoted and enduring love to your daughters, my respectful regards to your husband, and pray you to believe me, as ever, your most affectionately attached

'Clara Rosevelt.'

Mrs. Barclay was highly pleased with the good news of her young friend's welfare, and expressed herself accordingly. 'The end thereof has not yet arrived,' said Mr. Richard. Gracy bounded to him, and closing his mouth with her hand, conjured him not to say one word in disparagement of her dear friend's marriage.

'Now just suppose,' said the Dolly, 'if I should take it

into my head or heart to give you a handsome young officer for a nephew, what would you do, uncle mine ? '

' I would immediately lock you up, Miss.'

' But I may yet, for all your threats.'

' Who would think of you having a lover,' said Mr. Richard, — ' a baby like you, eternally on your father's knee. Pshaw ! you are not yet out of leading-strings.'

' But I have had,' cried the Dolly ; and then, overwhelmed with confusion, she hid her head on her father's shoulder, and nearly cried from mortification.

Mr. Richard living, as he did, so entirely in this family, and daily beholding its members, did not perceive that the youngest daughter had o'ertopped her sisters, and actually appeared to be older than they were. And true it was, moreover, that a foreign traveller, of good family and large fortune, had demanded her hand of her father, after the fashion of his country. Mr. Barclay had courteously refused this alliance, and had hesitated as to the propriety of informing the Dolly of this important conquest. On reflection, he concluded to tell her. She heard him with profound attention, and informed him that she was exceedingly obliged to him for refusing the gentleman's offer. She confessed she had a prejudice for being differently won, and would never marry any man, even if she died an old maid, who did not ask her consent before her father's. The next time she met her rejected suitor, she made it a point to turn her back upon him most indignantly, which demonstration did not appear to annoy him in the least, and at this the Dolly confessed she was vastly surprised. Mr. Richard, who had not heard this passage in his favourite's life, was very much amused at her spirited answer, and declared that, notwithstanding his love for her sisters, he really believed, if he possessed a fortune, he should make the gipsey his heiress.

Mrs. Rosevelt's epistle proved most satisfactory to all her friends and acquaintances, except Miss Serena Tidmarsh, who having, Cassandra-like, prophesied that Clara's marriage would prove unhappy, was consequently much annoyed that her evil omens had not been verified. However, she consoled herself with saying, 'Well, Mr. Rosevelt will be ordered to the coast of Africa shortly, I've no doubt,' — and thereupon took especial comfort. But Mr. Rosevelt had already enjoyed, before his marriage, a cruise in that engagingly fascinating region, and contracted an irritation of the nerves of his eyes, which, though not at all disfiguring, was of sufficient importance to warrant an application for a constant absence from the shores which had proved, fortunately for him, not so disastrous as they commonly are.

The Reverend Mr. Meredith, the young clergyman who had been presented to the Barclays at the same time with the young officer, was a man of remarkable purity of thought and action, and was noted for his particularly conscientious discharge of his parochial duties. His talents were good, his delivery most simple and impressive, and, at times, even affectingly touching. He was not reputed to be a brilliant writer, yet his followers were perpetually enchained by the unaffected naturalness of his style and the almost apostolic grace of his manner, to which his expressive face and noble bearing added additional charms. From his earliest days Mr. Meredith had devoted himself to Gospel teaching; and having completed his studies, he was invited to preside over a rather fastidious parish in Boston. This call was but partially accepted, as he insisted on being granted the permission to preach one year before the closing step should be taken in his ordination, which would bind him and his people irrevocably together, — he dwelling solemnly on the importance of this measure, as tending to perfect the intimate relations between himself and the people over whom he was to preside.

The parish was rather unwilling to grant this request, as he was considered well qualified to satisfy all its various requisitions; but he persisted in modestly adhering to his primal resolution. At the expiration of a year, in which his popularity had increased tenfold, Mr. Meredith informed the parish that, in the interim, he had, very unexpectedly, come into the possession of a large fortune from the demise of his grandfather; but that this accession to his temporalities would in nowise interfere with his previous arrangements, his life having been always consecrated to the ministry. This state of things would then produce no change in either his vocation or feelings, and he had but touched upon it in order to ask leave to associate with him, as a colleague, a young friend, whose share in the ministerial duties would naturally lighten his own labours, and thereby allow him more time to devote to his people.

Mr. Meredith declared, that he thought a vast deal more good might be effected by social intercourse with his parishioners than by the most elaborate discourses; that his own highest aim in his relations with them was to understand, as far as in him laid, their wants and requirements, and to respond to them in the truest spirit of devotion. By associating with him his friend, he was assured of a corresponding acquiescence and a perfect similitude of views and opinions, and, far greater than all beside, of acts. He said he had long conceived it to be almost an impossibility for a clergyman to write in such a manner as to perfectly satisfy his parish, and at the same time to see his people freely, in all their hours of need; that if he were obliged to choose between these two alternatives, he should decidedly adopt the latter, as eventually proving the most useful and beneficial.

Upon this request being granted, Mr. Meredith assumed the responsibilities of his position in the most solemn and impressive manner, and devoting all the energy of his soul and mind to the discharge of his sacred mission, became to his people their pastor in the most perfect acceptation of the word. His was no violent manifestation of zeal expending itself in froth and fume, but the lucidly clear and gentle current flowing securely, refreshing and revivifying its banks as it passes along slowly and pleasantly. It was some time before the apparently unimpressible style of Mr. Meredith's manner was appreciated ; but once allowed to take firm hold on the listener, its grasp was adamantine, there was no recoil from it ; the hardest of hearts were softened, the rather that his eloquence was insinuating from its extreme gentleness than from its brilliancy or profound reasoning. Mr. Meredith's mission on earth was to persuade sinners to walk in the right way, not to force ; and in this he was eminently successful.

The young clergyman soon found Mr. Barclay's house a great resource in his hours of relaxation. He was remarkably social and genial in his feelings, and the society he met therein satisfying him completely, he consequently became a frequent guest.

The Barclays all, with one exception, were delighted with this valuable acquisition ; and the only person who did not appear quite captivated by the gentle graces of the young pastor was the Dolly. This juvenile Missey had, at first, quite admired Mr. Meredith, but suddenly rather avoided him, declaring him to be all too good for her. She said he looked, breathed and discoursed goodness, until she was fairly wearied.

Mr. Meredith, however, took small note of this dissentient voice, and was uniformly polite and attentive to her, but she rejected his overtures rather significantly, and held herself quite aloof from the gentleman's attentions. The Dolly's dislike on this occasion was not very demonstrative, — hers usually were, — she rather avoided the source of it by evading all advances to conversation and intercourse. She did not, in her accustomed way, express it openly, but only now and then gave expression to it.

Mr. Richard Barclay had lately become extremely captivated with the persuasive powers of the youthful divine, and had actually purchased a pew in the chapel, in which he was constantly seen, a most assiduous attendant upon the service. The Dolly and Nursey Bristow were often formally installed in this pew, the Missey declaring she much preferred Mr. Meredith's preaching to his talking; his crowning virtue, in her eyes, being the shortness of his sermons. Nursey Bristow thought every thing he said and did, perfection.

CHAPTER XXXIII.

'But I, I seek thee in my heart of hearts,
Where none thine image sweet can see,
My hidden love, my secret faith that parts
Not with my life, my gentlest girl, from thee.'
TASSO.

MRS. SANDERSON pined for her beloved son. She had received letters in abundance, setting forth his prosperity, Mr. Johnstone's unvarying kindness, and his own certainty that the time would soon come when he should once more retrace his steps to his native land, and behold all he held most dear on earth. Then, then could he claim the hand of the delicious young creature to whom he had devoted his heart's best affections, then could he ask her to share his lot and bestow upon her all the luxuries of existence. And although no tryst has passed between Charles Sanderson and Grace Barclay, the pure faith was deep rooted in his bosom; he believed in her, his trust was unshaken. Mrs. Sanderson contributed greatly to this state of feeling by her unvaried assurances of her firm belief in the young girl's constancy, and she kept her son advised of all the indications of deep interest manifested by Grace on the reception of bits of intelligence imparted not positively to her, but to all her relatives.

In this manner the far distant exile was comforted and consoled under his privations, and the time, which would otherwise have dragged so sadly and slowly along, was bereft of a portion of its weariness by the ministering hand of the mother. And this was of signal importance to Mrs.

Sanderson herself, by reason of keeping her mind occupied, and interesting her intensely in the proceedings of various suitors for Grace Barclay's favour, which the beautiful girl's attractions gathered around her, and to whom she evinced the most perfect indifference. As these pretenders to the hand of the young girl appeared and disappeared, Mrs. Sanderson busied herself in advising her son of their rebuffs, and communicated to him the most exquisite pleasure. At last, after many disappointments and hope deferred, sickening the mother's heart, there came the joyful and blessed intelligence that the Charley was on the eve of returning, having effected a prosperous arrangement with the India house to transact its American business in Boston, and was also to bring with him Mr. Johnstone, who proposed to fix himself in the city.

And soon the long-expected son arrived, looking outwardly quite like another creature, but ever the same dear Charley internally. Though the India sun had embrowned his skin to such an extent, and the addition of a most imposing moustache, with nearly a foot to his height, had made him almost unrecognisable, yet was he still the selfsame joyous creature. And such a jubilation as his arrival created! His mother, in a trance of delight, could not take her eyes from him; his brother, beside himself with rapture; Peter and Dinah, oblivious of all proprieties, laughing and crying, dancing and singing; Tiger's successor scampering about and barking tremendously; and Mr. Philip Egerton touching, almost imperceptibly, Charley's expanded palm with the tips of his frozen fingers.

Then such loads of presents, scarfs, shawls, muslins and sinchaws! Mrs. Sanderson knew not what to do with her treasures, so numerous were they, and Gerald had cashmere cloth sufficient to make him forty dressing-gowns and as many waistcoats. In the evening Charley begged his mother to accompany him to Mr. Barclay's, in which request she joyfully acquiesced, Gerald accompanying them. They were greeted most cordially, and the Charley received many complimentary notices of the great change which had transpired in his personal appearance, with the hope that none had been made otherwise. The family were all content he should return exactly the same pleasant individual that he departed. To one and all the traveller brought some memento, some curious India stuff or rarity. He seemed to wish that all should share his happiness and prosperity. No one was forgotten, Johnny's fireworks were amazing from their variety and beauty, and even Nursey Bristow had been remembered. Mr. Richard declared his present to be the very best of the whole collection, and was truly overjoyed to see his favourite once more. On being questioned as to the whereabouts of his 'convert,' Charley declared he had left him at the Tremont House; he having totally refused to accompany him home, but hoped shortly to have the pleasure to introduce all his friends to him, and particularly begged Mr. Barclay and his brother would call upon him, which they agreed to do the very next morning.

Charley spoke of his new friend in terms of unbounded gratitude, and could hardly have been more enthusiastic had he known all that Mr. Johnstone had done for him; that gentleman having kept concealed a large portion of the benefits he had conferred upon his young friend. This he was able to do by making all the extraordinary preferment and advantage appear to proceed from the head of the India house; whereas, certain bags of rupees had very miraculously facilitated the sudden gradations in the rise of the young merchant. In fact, 'the convert' had become so devotedly and earnestly attached to Charles Sanderson, that he could not live without him, and had followed him home. Having had no family ties and no friendly relations in this life, his pent-up feelings, which had been lying dormant for so many long, long years, were now gushing forth like perennial springs, watering and refreshing the soul of this solitary man to such an extent, that he felt himself waxing better and better in body and mind as time rolled on. Now, all this amelioration in his condition he acknowledged was to be attributed to the genial and blessed influence of Charles Sanderson. Time was, when Mr. Johnstone would not have believed in the existence of a creature so perfectly true and disinterested, as the boy whom he had found on the sluggish waters of the India seas, and who was ordained by Divine Providence to conduct him to the Source of all light and life, a repentant and erring sinner. Now, all was changed, he had become a new man and a regenerated one, looking upon things terrestrial and celestial with other eyes than the jaundiced vision of by-gone days; existence had become to him a boon, for had he not something to love, something to interest him? How different was his condition, in these awakened moments, from the morbid torpidity of his previous life! Then he was encompassed with darkness, and yet endured the torture of compunctious visitings in that benighted state; now he beheld in the perspective a bright and shining goal, which, with careful perseverance, he hoped, in process of time, to reach, and there present himself as a burnt offering in humiliation and supplication.

And Grace, — how did she feel on the re-appearance of her child lover? She had heard of his projected arrival, and knew precisely the time he was expected to come, and watched and waited at the window which looked out upon the waters of the bay, seeking to distinguish the white canvass which would waft home the youth whose image had never been supplanted in her breast. And how had her remembrance fared, meanwhile, in his heart of hearts? This was a question she asked herself every hour in the day, How would he look upon her? The first glance would decide this oft mooted point, — the first glance alone. And that one soul-searching look sufficed; she knew he had been constant, 'as the sun-flower turns on his God when he sets, the same look which he turned when he rose,' so came that glance to her, and she was content withal. It had been a love-song without words, the passion of these young people, even such as German composers have given to enraptured ears, none the less eloquent for lacking sweet voices. No tryst had been made, no promise given, no vows pledged, yet were they perfectly assured of the constancy of each other from the rapturous moment their eyes met.

The next morning Mr. Barclay and his brother called upon Mr. Johnstone. They found him overflowing with grateful reminiscences of his first meeting with Charles Sanderson, which succeeding years had not diminished; indeed, he declared he should never have re-visited his native land but for that meeting. He now hoped, he said, to finish his days in his own country, and he considered his having encountered that youth to be a signal interposition of Providence in his own behalf. He wished to know his family and all his friends intimately, to form new social ties, to enter freely into a world he had obstinately and blindly rejected, being now convinced, through the teachings of his youthful friend, that it was not the hateful place he had morbidly pictured it to be. He desired to live with his fellow-men, to share their sorrows and their joys, and was convinced that this was the supreme will of his Creator, otherwise he would not have been sent on earth. He owed this revolution in his sentiments to the benign and genial influence of his preserver, — for thus he should ever continue to call him, — and he hoped and trusted to profit most beneficially from his farther intercourse with all that young man's friends.

The brothers were greatly pleased with this interview, and entreated Mr. Johnstone to visit them freely, and to make himself at home with them, which he promised to do, and shortly availed himself of their proffered hospitalities.

Mr. Johnstone went to see Mrs. Sanderson, and gladdened her heart with good tidings of the excellence of her son, his pleasant prospects, and the confidence which was placed in him by his commercial correspondents abroad. He begged permission to be considered quite a member of her family, and declared that, having so long possessed the inestimable treasure of Charles Sanderson's companionship, she must not engross too much of his time, or he should be made quite wretched. Mrs. Sanderson promised to award to him a full share of her darling's leisure, and they parted mutually pleased with each other.

Mr. Johnstone immediately purchased an elegant house in the vicinity of Mr. Barclay's establishment, and furnished it in a style of oriental magnificence; and, as he had brought home with him some native servants, the illusion seemed quite perfect. How the poor creatures were to withstand the inclemency of the winter season seemed extremely dubious; but, after gathering up a large quantity of snow, which they called white wool, and crying their eyes out because it melted, and freezing their fingers besides, they concluded to remain in the well warmed house, and never more stir abroad. To this resolve they religiously adhered, and prospered accordingly. Mr. Johnstone immediately commenced giving a series of beautiful dinners, which proved extremely popular, and as he had a storehouse of India rarities at his disposal, and was, moreover, very generously and gallantly inclined to bestow them upon the ladies, there seemed to be no bounds to the favour he found in their bright eyes. And all this he seemed to enjoy with intense delight, and entered into the spirit of the entertainments as if he had never been present at any before, which was, in fact, the case, so that they possessed for him all the charm of novelty. Mr. Johnstone insisted that Charles Sanderson should always assist him in performing the duties of a courteous host, and would fain have enlisted him as an occupant of his little palace; but to this arrangement the young gentleman objected, as he declared his mother would be actually jealous if he abandoned her.

And Mr. Philip Egerton even condescended to honour Mr. Johnstone with his august presence at the festivities proffered by such a generous and hospitable host, even though he made no return, his own wonderful exploit, in that way, having satisfied him for the rest of his natural life. Mrs. Sanderson was drawn out also on the plea of 'its only being a bachelor's party,' but to this was superadded her gratitude for all the kindness the host continually showered upon her son.

Mr. Johnstone devoted himself to Grace Barclay, making her the most magnificent and costly presents, and distinguishing her, upon all occasions, above her peers. A short time after Charles Sanderson's return, he waited upon Mr. Barclay, and, in his accustomed frank and straight-forward manner, declared his undying love for his daughter; that it had never faltered for a moment, during his long absence; that the hope of obtaining her hand had been the beacon-light of his India life, and the primary cause of all his exertions; that he had solemnly adhered to his promise, and never breathed one word of his entire devotion into her ears. He begged permission, now that his prospects were bright and cheerful, and that he felt he could bestow upon this idol of his soul the same luxuries she enjoyed at home, to be allowed to speak to her, to ask her to share his lot. Mr. Barclay, who, when Charles Sanderson was pennyless, had resolved to give his consent to his union with his daughter, withheld it not, but graciously and frankly accepted him as his son, and bade him try his fortune with Grace immediately. This being speedily effected satisfactorily, the youthful pair, looking supremely happy, presented themselves before the contented father and mother, and received their fervent benedictions.

Mrs. Sanderson declared that the measure of her satisfaction was entire and complete. Gerald was enchanted, Mr. Richard delighted in the welfare of his favourite, and Mr. Egerton forgot himself, on this felicitous occasion, into the expression of something very much like 'capital match, good fellow, pretty girl, excellent stock,' pronounced in a most formal and emphatic manner, but clearly enunciated, as Peter and Dinah could have testified, had they not themselves been assiduously engaged in making, what the Poles call an hurrah's nest, in such a loud and furious manner, that a respectable thunder-clap would have passed over their black heads unheeded. Indeed, the young gentleman, the hero of this uproar, was almost torn piecemeal by his warm-hearted humble friends.

CHAPTER XXXIV.

'The lust of gold succeeds the lust of conquests,
The lust of gold, unfeeling and remorseless,
The last corruption of degenerate man.'

JOHNSON.

MR. EGERTON had been indisposed several times during the season, and there had been reports of sudden seizures with cramps and violent pains, which he strenuously denied, and, in truth, dragged himself slowly down to his accustomed resorts, when he had really no longer strength and power to do so, in order to prove that he was not an invalid. In vain Mrs. Sanderson begged and entreated her brother to remain at home, and take some little care of himself, but he always refused distinctly, and seemed to receive all hints respecting attention to his own health in the light of personal affronts.

Mrs. Sanderson knew not what to do. Gerald had never renewed any intimacy with his uncle sufficient to warrant any interference in his affairs, and Charley, keeping himself as much as possible out of Mr. Egerton's presence, dared not open his lips to him. The secluded life of Mr. Egerton precluding all access to him, Peter was the only medium through which his sister could obtain any positive information of his state and condition. It appeared, on inquiry, that Mr. Egerton had very sleepless nights, accompanied with great suffering, which he had for a long time alleviated with opium, but that failing to produce effect, his pain had become intense, yet all the while he would have no medical assistance. At last, the accounts of his servant becoming more serious every day, Mrs. Sanderson resolved to speak. Mr. Egerton was excessively offended at her venturing to give any advice whatever, and declared his fixed resolve not to apply to the family physician. He said he had no faith in medical men, and would not see any of them.

This state of things continuing, greatly to his sister's sorrow, she knew not what to do, when one morning Peter called her before daylight, and informed her that he had been watching all night at his master's door, having heard him groan at eleven o'clock, and not daring to enter, he could endure the suspense no longer, and had come to beg her to go and discover the cause of his illness. Mrs. Sanderson arose, and hastily throwing on a dressing-gown, reached her brother's chamber to find him insensible. She sent immediately for medical assistance, and in a short time several of the faculty made their appearance, and having applied all necessary restoratives, pronounced Mr. Egerton's case hopeless. They said he had suffered for years with an internal complaint which was incurable; that it had reached its crisis, and that no one could tell what he must have endured of pain and agony. It appeared that he had always understood the exact nature of his malady, and believing that nothing could relieve him, had never tried any thing. On being restored to sensibility, the sick man asked how long he might live; and said he had been for years awaiting his final hour; that he was prepared, and desired only to see Mr. Barclay. His question of the duration of his life was answered by the doctors that he might live a day or two, not more, and with this assurance and some palliative remedy, the gentlemen took leave. Mrs. Sanderson remained at her brother's bedside, and after a quiet sleep of an hour he awoke, seemed quite relieved of pain, and again desired to see Mr. Barclay. She sent instantly for him; he came, and she left them together.

Mr. Egerton was very weak, but calm and collected; he

welcomed his visitor, and requesting him to be seated, he said: 'You are, my dear Sir, the only person I respect sufficiently in this world to invite to my deathbed, to hear a species of confession, which, if I were a Roman Catholic, would be made to my confessor; and, in fact, you do now stand very much in that position towards me.'

Mr. Barclay interrupted Mr. Egerton, and entreated him not to tax his strength by commencing any long narrative, but he replied, 'He must do this now or never.' He resumed, 'You well know, my dear Sir, that my deceased father had expended nearly the whole of the remains of his once large property before he departed, having lost in manufactories immense sums, the proceeds of India ventures, which he had invested, as it proved, injudiciously. In point of fact, my father left little else than this estate, yet, as he imagined me to be immensely wealthy, this gave him no uneasiness, being convinced that poor Emma and her children would never want for any thing while I had the means to provide for them. When his will was opened, it had been executed many years previous; it was found that he had bequeathed this estate to me, and the residue of his property was to be divided between my sister and myself. Now, there was next to nothing left besides the old house, and Emma and her husband acquiesced in my opinion that this state of things should be kept a profound secret, and so it was, and has been, up to this moment. I came home, after many years' absence, with the reputation of being a Crœsus, a false estimate often made of returned Chinamen, and finding that the renown of my reputed gold had penetrated into the heart of my native city, and that all I could do, or say, my people would never be disabused of their belief in my wealth, I tacitly consented to their bestowal of a colossal fortune upon me. There was something so captivating to my perverted imagination in hearing, even the small boys whisper, as I passed along the crowded streets, "There goes the rich Mr. Egerton," that I could not persuade myself to renounce the gratification it afforded me. I believe scholarly attainments and literature have more dominant power in Boston than any where else in my country, and that we are even apt to over-rate what we possess in that way; but wealth, all-glittering wealth, is still worshipped, — alas! all too much, and, as I now lie here, the world receding from my view, I deplore, in anguish of spirit, my own insane love of even its shadow. None other have I ever possessed than a vain show; for my fortune, even while in Canton, had been over-rated, and just before I returned home I lost two valuable ships, one on the North-west coast, and another on her passage to America, which gave nearly the finishing blow to my finances. But when I once more trod my native shores, and discovered what a personage the fancied possession of a large fortune had made me, the respect with which it environed me, and the great consequence it imparted to my position, I, who had no scholarly tastes, or literary pursuits, and no decided talent, succumbed under the temptations offered me by the above state of things, and consented to be a living lie. Would that I had died ere I thus degraded myself.

'And this has been to me a living death. My downfall was terrible. A man of honour once, I felt myself an impostor; I looked no honest man fairly in the face, and not being willing to bear the outward semblance of a cheat, I vowed to hold my head higher and more haughtily than any one else in the community, and hide my degradation from mankind if I could not from myself. And thus, just in the ratio that I was lowered in my own private estimation, did I appear cold, haughty and defiant to the world. I have held small intercourse with my fellows, have denied myself the gratification of all social and genial intercourse, which, I really believe, I should have greatly enjoyed, and absented myself even from your charming abode for this same reason. The weight of my own duplicity presses too heavily on a once honourable spirit. And, alas! what has not been lost, — lost to me by my voluntary alienation from poor Emma and her noble boys. This alone seems to me priceless. Knowing I could do nothing more for them but secure a shelter under the old roof-tree in the dwelling which, in fact, partly belonged to them, and being unwilling to behold their many wants and privations without possessing the power to gratify them, which under the circumstances was impossible, I withdrew from their presence, and, retreating into my den, in a corner of the old house, left the rest of it to my heirs. Thus I continued to dwell within myself, — no pleasant domicil, I can assure you, — and closed up all the issues of my heart; for I have one, whatever may be asserted to the contrary.

'My heirs, forsooth! poor fellows, I sicken at my own delusion! And what have I gained by it? Scandal and detraction, — "The old miser" my title. Oh! many a time and oft, have I longed ardently to throw myself on my dear sister's neck, and reveal the sad tale of my internal sufferings, — God knows, I had bodily enough, — but they were as naught, in comparison with the mental. I absolutely, at times, hungered and thirsted to hear her sympathizing voice pouring the balm of commiseration into my soul. But pride, indomitable pride, has coloured and distorted my whole career on earth, and, instead of a deathbed surrounded by loving hearts, breathing forth prayers for my salvation, I am doomed to depart, unmourned and unregretted. When I reflect how different might have been these my last hours, but for the leviathan absorbing my whole being; when I think that, but for the contemptible renown of possessing filthy dross, I bartered away my soul to the prince of darkness, I bow down my once loftily raised head, and, in sackcloth and ashes, repent me my sins. I am even willing, reserved and retiring as I have been, as a slight extenuation of my offences against God and man, to point a moral and adorn a tale as a beacon-light to my countrymen, — "the proud man's contumely" has disappeared.'

Mr. Egerton's 'confession' was not made without many interruptions, and almost as soon as he had finished, another violent attack occurred, and then he fell into a drowsy state, in which he remained many hours. Mrs. Sanderson, her sons, and Mr. Barclay surrounded his bed, but could not perceive that he in any way recognised them. Peter and Dinah they were necessitated to order out of the chamber, so obstreperous were they in their demonstrations of grief at 'the Massa's illness.' At twelve that night he breathed his last, so quietly that none knew when his spirit took flight. Mrs. Sanderson remained with the body until morning dawned, and then retired to her own room, but not to sleep. She retraced all the steps in her past life, and pondered over them; she tried to remember if she had ever, in word or deed, given cause for the evident estrangement of this dead brother, — her only one! She forced herself to recapitulate all the events of their disunited existence, and the result of her communings with herself was, that if she, perchance, had been more courageous and less timid, she might have made more impression on the hardened nature of her sole relative, and she blamed herself severely, and not Philip Egerton. Now, this was Mrs. Sanderson's characteristic, the casting of all blame on herself, and exonerating her brother. Perhaps, a more fearlessly energetic person might have succeeded better, but with the unrevealed secret which the departed had just divulged to Mr. Barclay, — a load on his soul, — it does not appear probable his sister could have effected any radical change in the character of a man who idolized even the fabulous reputation of great wealth, to the extent of abandoning kith and kin for its supposititious possession; and even with but a bare sufficiency for daily wants, assumed the semblance and bearing of a nabob, and was willing to incur the disgrace of even being universally considered an uncommon miser for Mammon's sake. While that ever carefully guarded secret remained undivulged, Mr.

Egerton was like a man in mailed armour clad, or the Neopolitan entangled in the fisher's net, the meshes constantly growing smaller and smaller as time waned. There could have been no release whatever from his self-imposed thraldom.

Death, even unaccompanied by troops of agonized relatives, mourning friends and sorrowing survivors, is always and ever a solemn messenger, performing his melancholy errand impressively. Neither Gerald nor Charles Sanderson loved their departed uncle. And wherefore should they? He had assuredly never given them any cause to do so, for love comes not at duty's call, but affection's thrall; yet they nevertheless felt solemnly and impressively that the grim tyrant had entered the old house and 'ta'en away its lord.' And as he rarely deals his blows singly, they trembled; for who might be the next victim? The darkened rooms, the whispering voices of the attendants on funereal obsequies, the silence and hushed footsteps of all around, combined to arouse sad reflections on the instability of human affairs, and to teach that 'this is no continuing city.'

On examination, a few indistinct lines were found, traced with a pencil, in which Mr. Egerton expressed his desire to be buried as privately as possible, and requesting that his sister, her sons and servants should alone follow him to his last resting-place; but if Mr. Barclay himself should feel disposed to pay his memory the respect of joining his relatives and seeing him *home*, he begged him to do so. Accordingly, every thing was ordered in the most unpretending manner; Mr. Meredith performing the ceremony devoutly and acceptably, and the last of the proud and lofty Philip Egerton was laid in the Copp's Hill Cemetery, and, side by side, he and his father slept. Mrs. Sanderson was unspeakably affected, as she stood on the hallowed spot containing all her kindred, and turning from it threw herself into Gerald's arms, and was borne fainting to her carriage by her two sons.

A week had elapsed when Mr. Barclay wrote a note to Mrs. Sanderson, and requested an interview with her and her children. This being accorded, he saw them, and then came the explanation of all the glaring incongruities in their deceased relative's conduct, the origin of the lights and the shadows. They were all sadly pained, as they listened to this strange revelation, and Charley, who had, times without mind, thought his uncle 'an old miser,' now reproached himself bitterly for this aspersion of his character, and, at the same moment, rejoiced he had never given any expression to his opinions, or allowed others to do so in his presence. Gerald, also considering himself to have erred in the same way, was equally penitent, and they all felt, mother and sons, that they never had appreciated Mr. Egerton until the causes of his apparent cold-heartedness were revealed to them. They remembered his failings only to bestow pity and commiseration upon them, and prayed that the sin of his all-absorbing pride might be pardoned, in view of the melancholy conflicts and sufferings it had engendered during his long life.

The brothers were in nowise disappointed respecting the loss of fortune ; they had never anticipated any inheritance from their uncle, other than the old house ; indeed, he had constantly told them that a few thousands to their mother would be all they would enjoy of his fortune. They had ever known that they must win their own bread, and had done so entirely independent of their relative, and they perceived and acknowledged the wisdom of his proceedings. Mrs. Sanderson, imagining that her brother had taken a decided dislike to her sons, however incomprehensible this might appear to her, supposed he would leave his immense fortune to some public establishment, charitable or literary, to found a name for himself. Then greatly was she gratified when she discovered that no such prejudice existed, and that the deceased had done full justice to the excellent qualities of her darlings.

Thus it appeared, that this disinterested family was more satisfied without a rich inheritance than many who, reaching the goal of all their aspirations, attain the height of what they believed to be the culminating point of human prosperity. There is one thing incontrovertible, — that nothing excites such a revolution in habits and feeling as the sudden accession of immense wealth, the recipients becoming changeable and unsettled, nothing satisfying, they launch forth into a sea of trouble and expense, rarely remembering the poor, and deserting all their old haunts for new ones. At least the Sandersons were not subjected to any temptations of this sort, and things took their wonted course. It was certainly surprising to behold how little Mr. Egerton was missed in his own household; how soon its members became accustomed to the vacant seat at the board where he had presided so long in solemn state; and how much his departure had increased the list of his sister's acquaintances. Persons, who had before never entered the doors, called and made kind offers of bearing her company in her solitude, and begged her to walk abroad and breathe the air, and thus recruit her strength, and elevate her depressed spirits. All this was pleasant enough; and possessing the charm of novelty, she gradually and imperceptibly revived. Her children were devoted to her, and, both having the means of adding luxuries and enjoyments to her existence, were truly a blessing to her.

Mr. Barclay's whole family were also an inappreciable comfort to her, paying her all sorts of delicate attentions. Mr. Egerton's insurance-office mates, missing him from his old arm-chair, clutched eagerly at the newspapers he had so pertinaciously retained during his life, and, having thoroughly discussed him in all his bearings, they repeated, what they had said five hundred times before, that he was a haughty, proud, and cold-hearted man, having never a friend in the wide world; but this time they were constrained to omit their favourite appellation of 'The old miser.'

CHAPTER XXXV.

'It is our nature's strong necessity,
And this the soul's unerring instincts tell;
Therefore, I say, let us love worthily,
Dear child, and then we cannot love too well.'
SOUTHEY.

MR. BARCLAY was passing through the hall, and just about to leave his house for the day, when he beheld Mr. Meredith sitting in his own little room apparently waiting his coming. He instantly entered and greeted him most cordially. As this gentleman was in the habit of coming at all hours, on errands of charity and other purposes, Mr. Barclay was not surprised to find him there thus early; but he was greatly astonished at the excited and agitated state of his usually calm and collected friend. Mr. Meredith seated himself, and after a long pause, in which he was apparently arranging his thoughts in order to frame a proper and set speech, he burst forth, and in uncontrollable emotion, requested Mr. Barclay to bestow upon him the hand of his daughter in marriage, declaring that his future happiness entirely depended on the answer he should receive.

'My dear Sir,' said Mr. Barclay 'need I say what entire and perfect satisfaction such an event as really possessing you for a member of my family, would give both myself and wife? I know nothing that could surpass the pleasure we both should feel in having the comfort and the honour of calling you our son; but it cannot be. I confess that I am amazed you have not seen that another has gained the affections of my child; to be sure, nothing has as yet been positively arranged, for I, in my selfishness, have not dared to think of parting with my daughter, and therefore have procrastinated the evil moment as much as possible. I well know the time must come, and shortly, yet every month seems to me a grateful respite.'

'I thank you, my dear Sir,' said Mr. Meredith, 'for your frankness, and for the flattering way in which you have announced to me this unexpected intelligence. It is, indeed, distressing to me, and will require all the stock of fortitude I possess to enable me to bear up against this sad blow to my future hopes of happiness.'

'I cannot avoid expressing my surprise,' said Mr. Barclay, 'that you have permitted yourself to nurse such hopes in the face of such an open and declared demonstration of affection as exists between Grace and our dear Charley Sanderson.'

'Grace,' cried Mr. Meredith, and hastily jumping out of his chair, he caught Mr. Barclay by the hand and exclaimed, 'I have not asked for Grace; you have another daughter, —Catherine, Catherine!'

'What!' cried Mr. Barclay; 'Kate! my Dolly! the child! This cannot be possible! I beg your pardon; but this is too absurd to be credited.'

'Absurd or not, my dear Sir, 'tis nevertheless true, most true.'

'But think, I entreat you, of the folly of taking such a volatile creature; such a romping, waltzing young thing to a parsonage; reflect for a moment upon the manifest impropriety of such a procedure.'

'I have looked upon this aspect of the case and every other,' said the lover, 'and I firmly believe that any man who can inspire Catherine Barclay with a profound attachment, may mould her character precisely as he pleases. The basis of that character is admirable. I am no blinded adorer of imaginary perfections; I think I see her exactly as she is; and you will excuse me when I say, that I really believe the position of a clergyman's wife in the faithful discharge of all the onerous duties incumbent upon it, is precisely the one for her. Your daughter is an enthusiastic creature, overflowing with energy and feeling. These qualities, once well directed into safe and proper channels, will produce the most felicitous results. Nothing of any importance was ever attained in this world, in my opinion, without enthusiasm. I know it is the fashion, in New England, to think that a man must be deficient in correct judgment who possesses this quality: my own observation goeth to the contrary entirely. Let it be tempered with discretion, and every thing good and great may be anticipated.'

'But,' said Mr. Barclay, 'you have undoubtedly heard her say many a time and oft, that nothing would induce her to marry a clergyman, and be obliged to visit all the old women in the parish.'

'Yes, many a time and oft, as you observe, but I am none the more discouraged for that. Let me try to win your daughter, I pray and conjure you, my dear friend, and she will do that very thing cheerfully.'

'But there certainly must be some latent cause for the security you almost appear to manifest on this occasion. Have you any reason to believe, that if I consent to part with my child, she will ever herself consent to leave me and her mother?'

'We are positively sure of nothing in this changing world; but if you will make me supremely happy by granting me your permission to urge my suit, I shall then be better able to answer you. You must, indeed, excuse my apparent boldness in my seeming certainty of your gracious assent; but you expressed yourself so flatteringly towards me when you thought me the suitor for Miss Gracy's hand, that I trust to your acknowledged benevolence for my excuse.'

Upon this, Mr. Barclay, laughing heartily at his own mistake, desired Mr. Meredith to go and try his fortune with the Dolly; 'and,' said he, 'you need be in no hurry, I will await your return here, and write some letters meanwhile.'

So he sat down to his desk to write, but did very little else than ruminate upon the extraordinary event which had just transpired. That the creature whom he had dandled on his knee, without perceiving that she had grown up to be a woman, had found a lover so entirely after his own heart, — how he hoped he might be after hers, — was indeed marvellous; and although he would gladly have retained her many years longer, yet still he could not help believing that Mr. Meredith was right in his estimate of her character, and the beneficial results which would accrue from the course of life she must necessarily lead with such a partner. Kate had always been a source of great anxiety to her father, the impulsiveness of her nature, so dangerous in its uncontrolled state, requiring the greatest possible judgment in the selection of a husband, and the perfect assurance that he always felt that there would be absolutely none at all evinced. Now, indeed, there was hope in its pleasantest coloured picture, and he prayed that Mr. Meredith might be successful. How long his musings continued, it is not well to relate; it might be asserted by critics, that the damsel yielded all too soon; but certain it was that the door of the little office was gently opened, and Mr. Meredith entered, leading the Dolly, who, throwing herself into her father's arms, hid her blushing cheeks on his shoulder.

Mr. Barclay was inexpressibly affected with joy and gratitude to God for his signal mercies, his prayers for the welfare of his child having thus been benignly answered. He sent immediately for her mother, who came and rejoiced with him, and warmly welcomed her new and unexpected son-in-law.

When a little composure had been restored to the actors in this scene, Mr. Barclay asked the Dolly, slily, how she, who had always vowed she would never marry a clergyman, had consented to change her mind. She replied most frankly, that she had ever been trying, by such assertions, to fortify her mind in her disappointment; that she no longer scrupled to avow she had loved Mr. Meredith a long while; and also, as she supposed, hopelessly. 'I have not looked as if I wore the willow,' said she, 'and resolved nobody should ever say I did; but if he had not chosen me I should have been an old maid, and you would have had the pleasure of my intellectual society for ever and a day. I hope you will acknowledge, my dear father, what an escape you have had; I should not have been the angel that Georgy is by any means.'

'I am convinced, my child,' said her mother, 'that you have chosen most admirably for your welfare here and hereafter.'

'Will it be the same for Mr. Meredith?' queried the young lady.'

'It is in your power to make it so,' replied her mother.

'I do nothing but ask questions, I know,' said Mr. Barclay, 'yet I must frankly declare myself very curious about this new chapter in my history, and wish to inquire how my son-in-law, that is to be, was so seemingly sure of his success?'

'He must answer, himself,' said the Dolly.

'I grounded my little faith, it was no more,' replied the gentleman, 'on the constant assurances mentioned by Miss Barclay,' and her rather decided demonstration of perfect indifference to me. If it had not been so positive, I should not have doubted; but this is sometimes a measure adopted by very young ladies as a mask for concealing deeper feelings, and on this hint I took comfort and spake. The result has proved I was not wrong in my conjectures, and nothing surpasses my gratitude for the gift of her affections, but my entire thankfulness to my Creator for vouchsafing me such a treasure.'

'The Dolly will have very important duties to perform,' said her father, 'and she must begin to think of them deeply and seriously.'

'I shall make no promises,' said the betrothed, 'lest I may

break them when I go to the parsonage, which will not be for a long time; I shall then let you all see what a shining light I shall be, or otherwise.'

'I can bide my time to see it show forth,' said her lover, 'which I truly hope will not be for a long time, for I have perfect faith in my future wife, and am thoroughly convinced she will be a pattern for all clergymen's spouses.'

'It's an excellent plan,' said the Dolly, 'to begin with a vast deal of faith and love in married life, so much of it gets frittered away on the roadside.'

'And pray where did you get all this matured experience?' said her mother.

'Not in your house, my own blessed mother,' replied the daughter, embracing her most tenderly.

'Well,' said Mr. Barclay, 'I must go immediately and impart this good news to Uncle Richard.'

'And he will not believe you, father, for he has told me over and over again, that nobody would ever take me for better or worse.'

So, Mr. Barclay went, and his brother was indeed delighted. 'Just the very best person in the wide world,' exclaimed he, 'to manage that young thing; she will never know a word of the matter, but she will be ruled gently, most judiciously; all her superabounding qualities pruned, she'll become a glorious creature. Mr. Meredith has chosen admirably, in my opinion, and she, even better. What a blessing to you, my dear brother John, to have such a son-in-law; but you deserve this and every good thing that can be showered on your excellent head. You are doing good from the time you open your eyes in the morning till you close them at night, and I must say I do like to see a few rewards for such excellence on earth.'

'But,' replied his brother, 'just look, Dick, how I am favoured, and many of my friends so much better than myself are pining in desolation; I am, indeed, most grateful.'

'You always, in your humility, underrate yourself, John.

Now if I were in your place, I should be as vain-glorious of my good deeds as a peacock; but then I never was the least like you or ever shall be.'

'You have excellent qualities, my beloved brother, but I will not say you might not be better, because you seem to desire to hide those you already possess. Now, for my sake, please let them be more visible.'

'Well, well,' said Mr. Richard, 'I'll think about it, if it will make you any happier;' and so they parted.

Miss Tidmarsh said Mr. Meredith was crazed, and Jane Redmond, in her fiercest tones, proclaimed him, far and wide, to be a fool. 'A pretty clergyman's wife Kate Barclay will make!' she screamed; 'why, the whole parish will be in fits before the first anniversary of their marriage. She'll affront every body, — a saucy thing that she is!'

'So much for ordaining such very young men over parishes; they always make such injudicious choices in their wives,' said Miss Serena.

'We're not much given to sin in the matter of juvenilities in New England,' replied Jane; 'a man hardly ever gets an office here of any kind, until he is gray-haired.'

'And past being either useful or ornamental,' said Miss Tidmarsh.

'That's the reason why all the youngsters run away from us,' said Jane. 'I remember nobody could persuade me I had seen the Governor of Maryland, when I had been presented to quite a handsome young fellow, who was accompanied by an old broken-down individual, and I, with my settled eastern notions, took the latter for the real presence. But to return to Kate — what possesses her to marry and doze away her days in a parsonage?'

'The first offer, probably,' replied Miss Tidmarsh.

'No such thing; it's the second, I know.'

'I don't believe a word of this,' snarled Miss Serena. 'You, who have no faith, Jane, in any one, always appear to give credence to whatever those hateful Barclays say.

You would never contradict the most improbable story, if it proceeded from that family.'

'I shall ever award them one precious quality, Serena. They are truly honest people, and may be believed, whatever else I may assert in their disparagement, and, moreover, they never mentioned any thing of the sort to me, as they are very honourable.'

'Miracles will never cease, Jane. Your praising the Barclays! On what sweet-scented grass have you walked lately?'

But just as these devoted friends were beginning to squabble, Mrs. Tidmarsh tottered into the room, green-bonneted, and announced that she had just completed a sonnet on Kate's engagement, which remarkably novel circumstance diverted her amiable daughter's wrath into its legitimate channel, and the poor old mother suffered for Jane's misdeeds.

CHAPTER XXXVI.

'Soft eyes look'd love to eyes that spake again,
And all went merry as a marriage bell.' — LORD BYRON.

AND there were to be two weddings at the Barclays! One is enough in all reason to fill a house with confusion and excitement, — but two!! Mrs. Barclay declared that she entrenched herself behind mountains of bride-cake and wedding favors; that marriage being an event the happy couples' fancy can never be repeated, should be celebrated with great solemnity and vast rejoicing; and so she governed herself accordingly, and gave orders for grand festivities, as on this eventful occasion the felicities were duplicated. No objections were made to these proceedings. Grace and Charley were both charmingly sympathetic and gay. The Dolly had always declared that when she was married there should be wondrous doings, and Mr. Meredith delighted in happy faces. Mr. Richard perfectly agreed with his sister, making only one reservation, that older people should do such things more quietly. To which Mrs. Barclay cheerfully assented.

Mrs. Ashley could never be sufficiently busied, so anxious was she that the plenishing of the two young creatures' wardrobes and households should be faultless, and to which she contributed most judiciously, saying, that, as in her opinion no one should marry a second time, every thing should be done to commemorate this important step in a woman's life.

'But,' said Gracy, 'will you never marry, dear Auntie, with your innumerable adorers? How can you manage? You'll be obliged to surrender at discretion some time or other.'

'Never, my Gracy, I shall never marry mortal man.'

'What an irrevocable decree! Now Auntie mine, I should have infinitely more faith in your assertion, if it were not so positively and solemnly asseverated, as I can't help thinking that you have been revolving the subject in your own mind, and must have encountered some pros and cons.'

'You're a saucy young chit, Miss Gracy, though you are to be so shortly a matron.'

'I know seven who stand ready to fall at your feet, and in fact, I never saw any one but my uncle Richard who did not allow you were a most fascinating creature. Charley thinks you quite adorable.'

'That is when he can snatch a moment from your attractions to bestow his thoughts upon any one, and as to Mr. Richard, he is intolerable; and if he were not your dear father's brother, I should not condescend to even speak to him. He's positively rude, and does not promise any improvement.'

'Uncle Richard does not mean all he says, dear Auntie, so do not trouble yourself about him a bit.'

'That I'm very far from doing, Gracy.'

'And have you heard, Auntie, that our Mr. Naseby, having knocked at all the doors in the city, has at last had one opened to him, and is positively betrothed to Miss Araminta Cora Barton? He called last evening to impart this felicitous bit of news to my mother, and begged she would honour him by visiting his wife on his marriage. It appears he was so extremely anxious to insure her presence, that he quite overlooked the old grudge against Georgy and I, and even condescended to entreat us to do the same, saying that as the lady, whom he pictured in glowing extravagant terms, was not precisely in our circle, he should esteem our notice an especial favour, so we graciously accorded our royal consent. Gerald told me that the first day Mr. Naseby dined there, he knocked down a centre-table covered with the most ill-assorted and expensive collection of porcelain, and Mrs. Barton, after he departed, declared she never again wished to set her two eyes upon him. But it appears her daughter thought otherwise, and has consented to make the swain of the many weeping willows happy.'

Mr. Barclay having been consulted as to his pleasure touching the bridal preparations, declared the women must manage them all their own way, and whatever they did he should like. He was, however, by no means so complaisant when Mr. Johnstone proposed that Charley and Gracy should live with him; then he fairly rebelled, and said that no child of his should accept a home from any one but himself. In the first place, he thought young people should always begin and blunder themselves into good housekeepers, — there was no other phrase to be used; and secondly, he had erected houses expressly that when his daughters married, he might install them in their own dwellings, and every time he looked out of his own windows he could behold their residences, the homes of those he best loved in the world. This he declared was to be the great solace of his old age, if God spared his life. So Mr. Johnstone's proposition was gratefully declined, Charley promising to see him every day, and Gracy as often as possible.

Mr. Johnstone was truly oriental in his magnificent proceedings. He vowed that Gracy should outshine all the brides present, and to come in silver and gold muslins and shawls and diamonds. The bride elect protested that she was too young to wear many of his gifts, but he would not hear her; he would not listen to any objections. He said he had no relatives in the wide world, that he had been beating about it without having found an anchorage for his affections, and now that this desideratum had been discovered, he should avail himself of it in its most enlarged acceptation, and would not allow any objections to be made. So he had his way, and most people thought it was quite a pleasant one, Gracy imagining all her great favour in Mr. Johnstone's eyes proceeded from a very beloved source.

In the dear, delightful library, brilliantly illuminated, the conservatory redolent of flowers, the birds, awakened by the glittering of lights, singing pæans of rejoicing, and surrounded by all they held most dear on earth, were these sisters united to the possessors of their affections. Mr. Meredith performed the ceremony for Charles Sanderson and Grace most impressively, and then his colleague joined the hands of the young pastor and Kate Barclay. Uncle Richard was jubilant upon this festive occasion; he declared that weddings being proverbially sad, this should be 'contrarywise.' Mrs. Sanderson wept notwithstanding the autocrat's imperial edict, but they were tears of joy she shed. Mrs. Ashley, more charming than ever, quite captivated the nabob, who was immoderately gay. Mr. and Mrs. Gordon and their sons added more than their usual quota to the general enjoyment. Gerald exerted himself to his utmost capacity; and Georgy, deeply and truly participating in the happiness of her sisters, cast aside all her own tribulations, and appeared the gayest of the gay. Nursey Bristow was too happy to be very demonstrative; and Peter and Dinah, in full dress, not being able to be noisy, and rather overawed by the assembled company, contented themselves with such an infinite variety of contortions and twitches, signifying delight, that they were almost frightful to behold, and caused Johnny Barclay nearly to expire with laughter. In fact, that young gentleman rather devoted the whole of his time to them until supper was announced, and then so vigorously addressed himself to the boy consumption of its superabounding delicacies, that a most profound somnolency overwhelming him, he was fain to take refuge in the arms of Morpheus on a sofa, where he said 'he slept like a top until the next morning.' The heir apparent having been entirely overlooked in the gaieties, he was left to his slumbers and lost half the evening thereby. The succeeding week there were receptions and collations, which the rich and the poor shared alike, and 'all went merry as a marriage bell.' At its expiration the young brides removed to their own dwellings, and took upon themselves the important state of budding housekeepers. Then came house-warmings and friendly dinners, in which Mrs. Ashley and the Nabob shone pre-eminent.

'I never saw,' said Miss Serena Tidmarsh, 'two brides look worse — did you, Jane?'

'I am constrained to differ from you, Serena; and declare they were most lovely. You know I always tell the truth.' And so she did, as far as her own individual opinions went, but she had no scruples whatever in repeating any scandal, however absurdly false it might be, emanating from others.

'And that old, ugly, green-eyed monster, the Nabob, how devoted he was to Mrs. Ashley, Jane. She'll have him, I've no doubt. What a sacrifice for such a pretty woman!'

'Now, don't you think you might be tempted, even you, Serena, by that little palace, and the muslin turbans of his retainers, to say nothing of rubies and emeralds?'

'My dear Serena,' said Mrs. Tidmarsh, 'please seal these packages.'

Miss Tidmarsh turned and looked contemptuously upon envelopes covered with sprawling cupids, hearts, and darts, and containing two epithalamiums which she had composed on what it was her pleasure to denominate, The Twin Marriages. Mrs. Tidmarsh stated that she did not exactly think these productions quite creditable to herself, inasmuch as sonnets being her forte, she could not be expected to succeed as well in other things. Miss Serena dutifully advised her mother not to make a fool of herself by sending them at all, but, as she had just escaped the infliction of Mrs. Tidmarsh's appearance, in the best green bonnet, at one of the wedding visits, she consented to append her seal to the missives.

It appeared that the venerable lady had thought it absolutely incumbent upon her to pay her respects to the brides, and was just sallying forth when the dirty little handmaiden, who served her, thought she had better advise Miss Serena of this important fact, which was accordingly done, and poor Mrs. Tidmarsh was constrained, by her daughter's violent resistance, to remain at home. To do her justice, she did not retaliate upon the little tale-bearer, as she considered the child had troubles enough without this addition to their number.

'Mrs. Charles Sanderson's dresses are magnificent,' said Miss Serena; 'snd what affectation and pretension in the Dolly to start with so much simplicity of attire — she who always declared that nothing should surpass the splendour of her wardrobe!'

'Her dresses are, nevertheless, very costly, but not so showy as her sister's. Did you examine them, Serena? I rather liked this in a clergyman's wife, and was inclined to give her due credit for good taste and proper discretion.'

'What do you suppose the Nabob gave to Charley, Jane?'

'Nothing, for the young man refused a splendid gift, Serena, and in money also; he said he could give his wife the luxuries she had enjoyed at home, from the proceeds of his business, and that he most gratefully declined any addition to his income. Now I call that miraculous, in this dollar-loving age.'

'And the estate, the old house, Jane, they say it will all sell immensely well.'

'That's true, but silly Mrs. Sanderson has not yet sold the property from respect to her brother's memory, though she has had great offers. They say the Nabob proposes putting up an immense pile of superb warehouses, in order to invest some of his lacks of rupees, and no doubt, wishes to pay double to favour the Sandersons.'

'So the Sandersons will be very rich, after all, Jane. What luck some people have!'

'Yes, they'll be like the old Manhattan burgher, who so

comically enough took to his bed, thinking to die of starvation, and awoke the next morning a very Crœsus, the corporation having run a street through his cabbage-garden. We see many such changes every day in America; the Sandersons' property has risen famously.'

'The Barclays are favoured indeed by the smiles of the fickle goddess.'

'You forget Georgy, Miss Serena.'

'I don't at all, but things die away here. I did my very best to keep that story alive, I'm sure; but now it seems almost forgotten. I sometimes think it was a myth got up for effect, and to make a splash, and that Georgy Barclay never was married to any one.'

'Her husband will turn up one of these days, I know, Serena; I believe in my heart her story, and so do you, if you would but confess it. I hope he'll prove a wretch, just to punish that family for appearing to be so much better than their neighbours.'

'They're a proud set, Jane.'

'Not at all proud,—just remember who visits them. I am sure, in all their recent festivities, they must have clothed as well as fed some of their guests. They care nothing for what is called fashion, and choose for themselves; it must be confessed education is every thing there. I don't like them and never shall; but I see these things with my two eyes, and seeing is believing.'

'I really think you praise the Barclays to teaze me, Jane.'

Mrs. Tidmarsh sat looking at these two disagreeable persons, and pondering in her own mind what manner of bond of union this could be which was so perpetually threatened with fractures; for the twain seemed ever on the eve of discord, and what Jane Redmond called a 'blow-up' was constantly so near, that the old lady wondered they did not explode altogether.

'Yes,' resumed Jane, 'the Barclays do choose for themselves. Most unfashionable people visit there, and very poor ones too, but then there's always something in them, some talents or great or good qualities, with very few exceptions; it may be safe to say, whoever you meet there is worth knowing.'

'I 'm sure there are exceptions, Jane, and I would not give them the entrée to my house.'

'But you are not a Barclay, Serena; you can't uphold any one; it's just as much as you can do to get along in society yourself. That family have the will and the way, and no silly and vulgar fears about being intimate with merit, however obscure it may be. The Barclays know their own position to the thoroughly respectable, and can afford to be gracious to those on whom fortune has frowned. Their old friends are every thing to them; they never cast them off, come what will, and their charities are unbounded to them. If there is any thing in this world I despise, it's the everlasting chatter I hear of position, and of this person's being in society and that one out. Mrs. Gordon, who has lived so long in Europe, declares the whole affair to lie in a nutshell, and thinks the people who are so tormented with fastidious scruples, should depart instantly and pitch their tents where they would not be contaminated with republicanism; and I thoroughly agree with her. If these extra exclusives can't be satisfied here, why e'en let them go, we can do without them; their cry ever is "vulgarity," little reck they that the world sets them down for unmitigated snobs — thanks to Mr. Thackeray for so accurately defining the class that there's no mistake.'

'Dear me, Jane, how very warm you get on this subject.'

'I detest pretension, Serena, and shall always set my face against it as long as I live, and shall have plenty of work on my hands, I'm quite sure. I must leave you now, as I've an engagement, and am going to pay a visit to Mrs. Gordon. I rather like her; she sees many things to improve here, but never rails against her own countrymen, though she has lived so long in Europe.'

CHAPTER XXXVII.

'Schoolboy's tears
Take up the glasses of my sight.'
SHAKSPEARE.

JOHNNY BARCLAY, whose head had been nearly turned by the extraordinary circumstance of two weddings in his family, and having exhausted all his rejoicings before the pair of events transpired, indited a letter, a few weeks after, to his friend, Joseph Staples, who had entreated him to impart to him a glowing account of the festivities; he having been retained at school during the vacation for divers misdemeanours. Johnny wrote:

'I promised you, my dear Joe, to send you an accurate description of all the wonderful doings at our house on the pair of weddings. Well, as the family was in such a dreadful mess, for some time before, with such preparations, I had a glorious chance of doing up forty little prohibited things, which I declare honestly I cared not much about; but then, you know, they were forbidden, and there laid the whole gist of the matter. Some things I did that were exceedingly pleasant. I've always had a grudge against Miss Tidmarsh, you know, the old maid I've told you about. Well, I unscrewed her knocker, and absconded with it, being sure she would cry over its loss forever, and never will she see it again, for 'tis buried. Now, ask no questions. She, the old thing, had a big story, about as heavy as the lost article, which she always finished by saying that the knocker was aristocratic, and belonged to her father. I hesitated between that and her cat, but decided for what

I thought she'd grieve for most. She's told many a tale of me to my mother, and I'm even with her now, thank the stars and a dark night.

'And Jane Redmond's another of my distinguished favourites, for the self-same reasons, and I soaped the iron railings of her steps, on the night of a grand ball to which she was going, and she covered her white kid gloves with the article, to which was added a little black paint, and then held up her dress, a white satin one!! Oh! how she stormed! But then she lives in a whirlwind. She never discovered the mischief. I've taken particular care to ascertain the fact, until she was told of her mishap, ever so many times, just as she was beginning to flourish forth in a quadrille; then out she flounced into the hall, and raged furiously all the way home, and after she got there too. Capital fun! wasn't it, my good fellow?

'Then, I've given two balls in the harness-room. It's not very large; that was the only difficulty. You know I play on the flute a bit, and we had an excellent supper. You see, our house has been so full of dress-makers and every thing else, that my doings have been totally disregarded. The weddings were charming, no doubt, and very merry, and I ate so much, and the last piece of Strasbourg pie did the business for me; for I felt creepy all over, and mortal sick, and fell asleep on one of the sofas, lost the serenades, and never waked up till the next morning, and was rather stiffish or so, but got over it, and began to feed again. That's the only way, my boy. I like my two new brothers very much, — Charley Sanderson's a roarer; but then the Dolly's husband is, you know, A PARSON, and I was dreadfully afraid of him. Only think of my sister, 'the Dolly,' marrying a preacher! Dear me! how it troubled me at first. What will she do? She'll be obliged to renounce dancing and laughing, I thought, but I dined with her yesterday, and my mind was much relieved. Will you believe? No, I am sure you won't; Mr. Meredith turns up quite a trump. He was as gay as possible, and the Dolly, Mrs. Meredith, and I, talked over our old theatricals and military, and he laughed heartily — only think of that, Sir! Well! then, after dinner, I ran all over the new house. It's beautiful, and chased my sister up stairs and down, and such a real frolic as we had, — just like old times. I'm quite reconciled to her choice; and then she seems so happy! quite as much so as Gracy; and Mr. Meredith begged me to come as often as possible, and I shall go.

'The vacation will soon be over, and, to tell you the truth, I shall be rather glad to get back to the old fogy, Sterling, after all, for it's a little bit dull here without "the Dolly." To be sure, she has not, since the water-butt dodge, had any thing to do with our sports and plays, but she was always such a resource in extremities, I miss her horridly, more and more every day. My mother has given me a splendid plum-cake, weighing ever so many pounds, frosted and gilded, and somebody has sent me, anonymously, in sixty-four wrappers, a ten dollar gold piece, and I've purchased six half bottles of champagne, and six wax lights, so we'll have a magnificent time the night of my arrival. The only difficulty is, that all the feast of reason and flow of soul must be abandoned for dumb show; but pantomime's my forte, and the rest must do as well as they can, for if old Sterling hears us, we shall certainly *catch it.*

'Ever yours, JOHNNY BARCLAY.'

'P. S. I shall smuggle the wine in my pockets. That's the reason why I bought small bottles. I should much rather had big ones, — they're grander; not that I care much for champagne, it always gives me the headache; but then, you know, it's a wedding feast. Yours, ever, J. B.'

It unfortunately happened for the fruition of the projected entertainment, that Joe Staples, being a sadly careless fellow, left his precious letter in his bed, having read it over every day before he arose, and the chamber-maid, a reading young lady, having perused it first herself, consigned it to the safe keeping of Mr. Sterling, it being of no possible use to her. When Johnny arrived, his trunks and boxes passed Mr. Sterling's customs; but his person was searched, and the accusing spirits were found. He was thunderstruck, and fancied that his friend had betrayed him, but farther developments showed the contrary. Still Johnny was very angry with Joe for his heedlessness, and reproached him bitterly, and the offender was very miserable. The magnificent plumcake was unpacked, exhibited to longing eyes, and confiscated for a whole month,—its restoration depending then upon the most admirable conduct in the interim. Here was a category, with a vengeance! The schoolboys were all furious, and poor Joe was assailed with an unaccountable quantity of abuse and vituperation, which he, not bearing meekly, sundry fights ensued, and sundry sequestrations followed, so that the plumcake became a terrible source of discord in this never paradisiacal seminary of learning. Johnny cared very little for the cake himself, for he had endured countless nightmares in consequence of over-eating the coverted article; but he regretted its temporary disappearance for his friends' sake, and vowed never to take another nice thing into that establishment again.

And Johnny had returned to his school in the full and perfect assurance that his favourite sister was happy. He loved Georgiana and Grace, but his playmate was the boy's heart's treasure. And Mrs. Meredith was just as happy as her young brother believed her to be. She and her sister, Mrs. Sanderson, compared notes in the arrangement of their respective houses and domestic details, and, although the clergyman's wife found that she would have much less time for her own purposes than Mrs. Sanderson, yet she repined not, and, furthermore, resolved to busy herself, as much as possible, that she might save her husband a portion of his hours for the theological works in which he was earnestly engaged. She had not communed with any one but her mother on her projects of usefulness, because, as she frankly avowed, she might yet falter and linger by the wayside; and Mrs. Barclay was astonished to discover what profound reflection and good resolutions her youthful daughter had taken with her into the abode of her husband; what a strong sense of her coming duties her child entertained, and what an ardent desire she felt to fulfil them. 'She had made no promises,' she said, 'but intended to surprise Mr. Meredith with her exertions, and be to him truly a helpmate. It appeared that her reverence and affection for Mr. Meredith had developed many remarkable qualities, which would have otherwise lain dormant; and her mother had great reason to congratulate herself on the choice which this young creature had made, since every day added to the perfecting of her character.

With Grace and Charley Mrs. Barclay's assurance of congeniality was unquestionable; but she had doubted if the impressible and excitable nature of Kate would, in the end, assimilate so happily with Mr. Meredith, and awaited, rather anxiously the result. These doubts she had expressed to her husband; but he, on the other hand, believed this union to be just the most felicitous event which could have possibly occurred to his child, and bade his wife be of good cheer, and asserted that all would be right. Mr. Barclay entertained the most exalted ideas of the excellent qualities of his new son, and hailed with delight the entrance of such an admirable person into his family. And succeeding observations induced Mrs. Barclay to believe he was correct in his views.

Mr. Meredith had married

> 'A creature not too bright or good
> For human nature's daily food;
> For transient sorrows, simple wiles,
> Praise, blame, love, kisses, tears and smiles.'

And he had married with a complete knowledge of all the imperfections, as well as the good qualities, of his wife.

He had made up his mind to guide her gently and discreetly; he knew she devotedly loved him, and that conviction amply sufficed to inspire him with a strong sense of security as to her future career. She was enthusiastic, impulsive, and warm-hearted; her whole happiness was centred in pleasing him, and she was, moreover, fascinatingly attractive, and with this state of things he considered himself blest in the possession of such a treasure. But he was wholly unprepared for the serious manner with which she entered upon the arduous duties of her station; he had imagined he should gradually introduce her to them as much by example as precept, but he discovered, to his amazement, that she fully comprehended their importance, and was prepared not only to fulfil them, but even to assist him greatly. When this conviction dawned upon his mind, and on further observation he perceived that her exertions were untiring, he was indeed delighted.

There had not been wanting, as usual, many kind advisers, who, when they discovered he was affianced to Kate Barclay, had ventured upon timely remonstrances respecting his choice, thinking that, even at the last moment, it was better to do something, than allow their young and beloved pastor to rush madly on his evil destiny. For although they all greatly respected her father and mother, they had ever considered the daughter to be a very flighty young girl, and knew she had always been an irreclaimable romp. Mr. Meredith received these remonstrances respectfully, but informed these anxious individuals that he considered himself the best judge of his own affairs, and especially in the matter of the choice of a partner for life; that he knew the young lady thoroughly, having been long intimate in Mr. Barclay's family, and finally assured them that he had ever entertained a strong prejudice in favour of irreclaimable romps, and had found that they generally made very captivating and excellent wives. So his meddlesome friends departed with many dismal forebodings touching their clergyman's prospects of happiness, and made sundry and divers predictions which were never destined to be fulfilled. Now these persons were certainly not ill-disposed; but if they had reflected, even for a moment, they would have perceived the folly of interfering when vows had been registered and faith pledged, and might also have reflected upon the great mistake they committed when they attempted to infuse doubts and fears into the mind of a man whom they loved. But Mr. Meredith's affection and trust in the 'irreclaimable romp' was not to be shaken by any interference of that kind, and he made his advisers feel the necessity of silence for the future, by entreating them never again to recur to the subject, and, as they knew him to be in nowise pecuniarily dependent upon them, and wished earnestly to retain him, they concluded to hold their peace.

CHAPTER XXXVIII.

'When I said I would die a bachelor, I did not think I should live till I were married.' SHAKSPEARE.

About this time, as the almanacs say, there occurred a most astounding event in Boston; nobody in the vast excitement it created, remembering to examine in what conjunction were the planets, so busy was the circle in which it happened in commenting and criticising. There was a marriage! which, in the words of the dear, delicious old Frenchwoman, Madame de Sevigné, 'was the most surprising, the most marvellous, the most miraculous, the most uncommon, the most bewildering, the most singular, the most incredible, and the most absorbing.'

Mr. Richard Barclay was married!!

And to whom?

It is to be hoped that, by this time, the reader is sufficiently interested in the bachelor's destiny, to wish that this important question may be answered. 'Guess, then,— four times is given to guess it in—six—a hundred.'

'Truly,' says the reader, 'it must be a very difficult thing to guess.' And so it proved, the gentleman in question, about whose affairs the public was so intensely interested, never having, within the memory of the oldest inhabitant, that ubiquitous personage, showed the minutest polite attention to any mortal woman, save Mrs. John Barclay, Mrs. Sanderson, Mrs. Gordon, and his nieces. Then who could 'the impossible she' be? Not the great Mademoiselle— all the fair sex are princesses in favoured America. Not

Mrs. Sanderson — she was altogether too tame for 'the bear.' Then the grandiose revelation must be made; for the newspapers had published the catastrophe, and they are always correct: 'On Thursday evening, by the Reverend Mr. Meredith, Richard Barclay, Esq. to Mrs. Fanny Ashley, widow of the late Samuel Ashley, Esq.'

Such a commotion as occurred in Miss Tidmarsh's parlour never was before known — no, never; this lady seemingly regarding this momentous event as a decidedly personal affront. She had abused Mr. Richard in all the set and choice terms of which she was an accomplished mistress, but then she might have been deluded into marrying him, had he positively asked her; and her rage was overboiling that he had failed to do so. 'To think of his taking that silly, flirting widow!' screamed the vexed damsel to her sympathizer, Jane Redmond — 'to think of his marrying, at last, his pet dislike! was ever any thing so ridiculous?' Suddenly Miss Serena remembered that Johnny Barclay, that terrible child! had informed her that she herself was his uncle's second abhorrence — might there not be a chance still? — but the bride was provokingly healthy, and certainly gave abundant promise of thus remaining.

Miss Serena, in the fever of her excitement, totally forgot her company manners. The tones of her dulcet voice, losing its diapason in its unwonted elevation, became frightfully screechy, and thereupon several neophytes in the lady's habits and ways became extremely amazed and astonished at this powerful change, Mrs. Gordon amongst others.

'But,' said Miss Redmond, 'you are perpetually bewailing Mr. Richard Barclay having taken unto himself Mrs. Ashley; now I think the condescension is all on the lady's side. How could she marry him? She must have forgotten the motto I placed on his brow years ago, "Bewar the Bar." Mr. Richard has absolutely nothing to recommend him; neither looks, manners nor money. Now Mrs. Ashley is certainly a pretty woman, prettily dressed, and all the world declares her to be pleasing in the extreme; nobody has more attention from both men and women. She might fifty times, to my certain knowledge, have married.'

'I don't believe a word of it,' exclaimed Miss Tidmarsh.

'Very well,' responded Miss Redmond, 'I shan't enter into discussions upon indisputable facts.'

Then such a chorus of exclamations as arose amidst the assemblage, in which the poor bride and bridegroom were sadly belaboured,— no softer word can be used. Mrs. Gordon was highly amused at this hubbub, it being precisely 'what she went for to hear.' She laughed immoderately, and when the group had exhausted themselves, and an interval of cessation occurred in this hail-storm of words, she said 'I am reminded by all the noise you make, ladies, of a little circumstance in my very early days. When I was a child I was extremely happy to be permitted to go into the stable occasionally, just to take a peep at a pair of snow-white horses which my father owned. One day our old coachman, black Joe, said to me "Look here, little Missy, here's a beautiful lot of white soap Missis has sent me, and I'm going to give the horses such a washing! for she has ordered me to harness up and bring home a live Countess, to stay with her." I opened my big eyes in stupefied amazement — a live Countess! This was news indeed! what would she be like? What would she resemble? — one ot the beautiful women dancing round the chariot in which stood the superb young man, in the great picture in our dining-room? I could think and dream of nothing else, and was in a fever of impatience until she arrived. She came, and, after dinner, I was permitted to gratify my intense curiosity, having waited motionless at the head of the hall stairs four hours without food. I entered with the fruit, and having taken my accustomed place on my father's knee, I watched her with an eaglet's eye. Oh! the dire disappointment! she was as unlike what "my fancy painted her" as she possibly could be, and it was long ere I recovered from my despair at finding a live Countess, ugly. . Intelligent and accomplished she certainly was. The conversation turned upon the acquisition of foreign languages, which she strongly recommended, as also did my mother, and they both thought French the most useful. Then they talked of particularly expressive words, and the lady pronounced hullabaloo to be one of the most emphatic in the English language. Now, permit me, ladies, to assert that you have decidedly reminded me of this big word by your noisy excitement this morning.' So saying, Mrs. Gordon arose and departed, and gained, by her rebuke, many spiteful expressions of dislike, but little cared she for them, as she had not proposed to make herself either pleasing or agreeable.

The whole thing resolved itself into a nut-shell. Mr. Richard had lost his heart to his fair enemy, even at the precise moment he was most perfectly sure as to its entire possession. The transition from the sublime to the ridiculous is effected in a moment. Then why should not the bachelor have committed his offence against the almighty public in the same period of time, though what that public had to do with the matter no one could tell?

It appeared that one bright morning, long after Georgiana Barclay's restoration to health, her uncle arose with a firm and solemn conviction that he should be made supremely happy, if Mrs. Ashley would condescend to smile upon him; and this being the first time, in his natural life, that the idea of happiness had ever suggested itself to his imagination, he felt rather inclined to take it into his heart of hearts and make much of it slowly, quietly. Accordingly, he did so, but how he contrived to bring round the fair widow to the same view of the engrossing subject remains to be discovered, as nobody ever knew, or ever will, — not even Miss Tidmarsh, who left no stone unturned in her praiseworthy efforts to enlighten the public, touching the how and the when of this particular passage in Mr. Richard Barclay's career,.so eventful in its consequences and so tardy in its fruition.

Mr. and Mrs. Barclay were as much astonished as their friends and neighbours, when the engagement between the pair they so dearly loved was announced to them, but wisely asked no questions. Mrs. Barclay warmly congratulated the happy man, and his brother embraced him affectionately, declaring himself extremely satisfied with this pleasant news. The daughters of the family were quite beside themselves with joy, for would not the aunt of their adoption be truly their own at last? Mrs. Meredith, entirely oblivious of her dignified position, whirled her uncle Richard round the library in a waltz after her old fashion, and then rushed up stairs to impart the joyful intelligence to Nursey Bristow, who begged her to remember she was a clergyman's wife.

Mr. Richard made one stipulation, and it was, that no one, out of the house should be informed of his affianced condition, he said he desired to be married as quietly as possible, and get off. Poor man! he well knew what a martyrdom would ensue if his secret were divulged.

Mrs. Barclay seemed to be the only person who had formed any conjecture touching the commencement of her brother's marvellous change of sentiments. She imagined that it had occurred a long time before, when he was left so much alone with the lady during Georgy's illness. And perchance she was right; there is high authority, no less than Miss Edgeworth, that propinquity works miracles in such cases. At any rate, Mr. Richard was married and off, and, after a month, returned, looking many shades happier than he had ever done before. The bride received her innumerable friends in her usual agreeable manner, that being hardly susceptible of improvement, and responded to some Tidmarsh-like insinuations, that she had consulted her own happiness in her choice, and should allow no remarks to be made, jestingly or otherwise, respecting it.

To Mrs. Barclay she declared, that, having become wearied of tables and chairs for company, — they were not then as gay and frisky as now, — she had selected an intelligent man; that she well knew his defects, — nobody better, — but they were, in her own opinion, counterbalanced by noble qualities, and she had no doubt they should get on admirably together. 'Added to all this, my dearest friend,' she exclaimed, 'am I not now your sister, and truly the beloved aunt of your darling children?' It was indeed, wonderful to behold with what a good grace Mr. Richard submitted to the infliction of dinners and routes and soirées; the balls were abandoned, and whether pleased or not, gave no indications of being otherwise. He received and welcomed all his hospitable wife's innumerable friends and visitors cordially, and performed this courtesy voluntarily; for she had provided for her 'bear,' she said, a den, and wonderful to relate, he refused to remain in it.

In fact, a pleasanter establishment could nowhere be found. This harmonious state of things vastly disappointed the preconceived opinions of the public, and Miss Serena Tidmarsh, in particular, she having predicted, far and wide, that nobody would desire to enter Mrs. Richard Barclay's doors a second time, her husband would make himself so disagreeable.

Mr. Richard entered his bride's home, as if he were a guest on probation, for he never gave an order, or changed the arrangement of a single thing in it: being perfectly satisfied with her management, he never interfered. His wife was deferential, and consulted him respecting her domestic details, festal and otherwise; but he entreated her not to open her mouth to him on those subjects, saying that he thought all those kind of things belonged exclusively to women, and he should never have married one who could not regulate them.

Where was then Mr. Richard Barclay's iron rule? Dissolved into thin air, like the baseless fabric of a vision, not a vestige remained, — 'the bear' was tamed. Mr. Barclay was vastly amused by this grand revolution in his rough brother's views, but sagely abstained from reminding him of his desperate threats of autocratic sway and power in married life. He was satisfied that the bachelor was happy, and had found a haven at last, and as he had heard many such high resolves and seen the same results, his motto had always been silence. It cannot, with truth, be asserted that every one was equally forbearing. Mr. Richard was hit right and left, and not very gently either; but he behaved with great discretion, and comported himself admirably, and consequently furnished the public additional food for astonishment and speculation.

And the truth was, that Mr. and Mrs. Richard Barclay were a very happy couple. They were certainly sufficiently acquainted with each other to comprehend what would be their relative positions when united, and having resolved to live together, were perfectly conscious that there must be a certain degree of forbearance exercised on both sides. This state of feeling often produces more lasting and happy results than exaggerated views of life and over-wrought pictures of ideal felicity, which must be dispelled by the realities of existence. Now, these are the common-sense, practical remarks on the subject to which we all fully subscribe in our common-sense moments, but if these are wise and lucid, we have or have had some which are not quite so denominated in the bond. It must be avowed that there is something extremely attractive in a really old-fashioned love-match; and we are very apt to turn from the rationalities and give our undivided attention, — despite all our conventionalisms and aphorisms, — to any remarkably silly pair of fledglings, who are precipitating themselves into matrimony without a single requisite for domestic happiness.

CHAPTER XXXIX.

'Truth crushed to earth shall rise again,
Eternal years of God are hers;
But error wounded writhes in pain,
And dies among her worshippers.'

BRYANT.

MR. BARCLAY was one morning favoured with a visit from Captain Eliathan Williams, a brave, kind-hearted, 'Down East' sailor, engaged in the merchant service. He had just then returned from Leghorn, and had formerly been employed by that gentleman, and having entertained a high regard for him he called to pay his respects. He entered Mr. Barclay's office, and after shaking him by the hand with an iron grip, and formally inquiring after every member of his family by name, he settled himself down in an arm-chair, and made very decided signals of spinning a pretty long sea-yarn by stowing away an enormous quid of tobacco in a corner of his capacious mouth, placing a broad-brimmed hat between his knees, in which figured conspicuously a bandanna handkerchief, large enough for a flag-staff, half a dozen invoices, six newspapers, and a dozen bills of lading. Having carefully arranged this most precious travelling casket, he combed up with his thick fingers each particular hair on his bullet-shaped head, so erect that the quills on 'the fretful porcupine' were nothing to them, and solemnly began his long story.

'You must know, Sir, that my Betsy Williams is a very good kind of woman in the main, when she has every thing right her own way, but is sometimes a little contrary when she is crossed, — most women-kind are just about the same thing, they tell me. Well, then, I never put her out much. They do say that the gray mare is the better horse at our house ; of that I make no dispute, but then she is, and ought so to be, commander on board her own craft. But I take mighty good care, I can tell you, that she has nothin to do with my barque, the Betsy and Mary, and so we get on pretty considerably straight, though I won't swear there isn't a squall ahead sometimes. She's not a very likely woman, my wife ; I didn't choose her for her outside, as Sam Kidder did his'n, and has never done repentin his bargain. Why, Judith Kidder's ugly behaviour has entirely spiled her good looks, and Betsy Williams holds her own — such as it is. But this is neither here nor there, as you'll allow, Sir.'

Now Mr. Barclay certainly coincided with the worthy captain, and had begun to think that this involved preamble would never come to a close ; but he well knew from dire experience that there was no use in stopping him, as that only made matters worse, and that in process of time he would get to the end of his rope, and then there was always something worth hearing, so he patiently submitted.

'Now, Betsy doesn't like to have the house riled a bit, — she's dreadful nice, and its just as much as I can do to find a place to spit in, and I have at last caught the trick of sending my shots right straight up the chimney. It cost me a lot of time to learn this, but it pays; for you see, she gets rampagious mad when I miss, and sets up such a sesserary it's perfectly ridiculous ! Well, as I was tellin you, I've been to Leghorn, and as I did pretty well, considering, I thought I'd make a trade for a straw flat for Betsy, which they do say is very handsome, and likewise a pin, — it's raither large for a pin, — and all made of little pieces of glassware dovetailed together, and is right curious, very peculiar, I can tell you. Well, the man I traded with charged me not to forget the subject, — I think he said it was three pigeons drinking out of a wash-bowl. And upon the whole, I guess I made a pretty good trade, for I swapped away some codfish, the real dun, for these things. I wish I could remember the name of the pin, — my memory's failin I do believe. As I didn't begin to make this grand trade till the barque was pretty considerably near ready, we sailed soon after. We'd ben out a few days and were spankin along at a famous rate,— she's a capital sailer, that Betsy and Mary, I can tell you,— when we saw a great light right ahead of us. It turned out to be a ship on fire. Oh! such a horrid sight my eyes never beheld! and the signal guns, they bellowed away, — and didn't we crowd all sail! At last we reached her. Most of the crew and passengers had jumped into the boats, and the minute they saw us were half crazed with joy. One youngster and a woman was standin on the deck. He seemed to be trying to coax her to go over the side with the rest, but she wouldn't budge an inch; it seems she was so frightened that she'd no wits left. Presently what did he do but take her right up in his arms and jump overboard with her. How he did this I couldn't tell, for he's a slim-made fellow; but there she was flounderin about in the salt brine in a jiffey. It served her right for her obstinacy. They soon got 'em into a boat, and the whole of 'em we took aboard and did all we could for 'em. Them women always make just such a fuss at sea! I never want one aboard the Betsy and Mary. When I was first mate in the Sally, the captain's wife took it into her head to go too, and such a real tarnation critter as she was! I swan if there wasn't a petticoat nailed to the mainmast the whole voyage, — tisn't lucky 'nother, I can tell you. Well, as I said afore, we got the whole squad on board, and did all we could for 'em. There was no clothes for the woman, so she wore my Sunday suit, which did very well. At first she was *raither* ashamed, — she hadn't heerd of Bloomerism, — but got used to them in the end. Well, the lad who saved her was a right good fellow, I can tell you, and I took to him mightily. At first he seemed very well; he sung for us beautifully, and drew all sorts of funny picturs of all our ship's company. Every body loved him on board. Whether or no he strained himself when he jumped overboard with the woman I can't tell, but he soon began to ail, and complained of a pain in his breast and side, and one day I found him faintin with his mouth full of blood; — he said he had broken a blood-vessel. I thought the woman was crazed; she wrung her hands and tore her hair, and called on fifty saints, and made such a to-do about this lad. She said he had destroyed himself in savin her, a total stranger; but he said no, that he had almost always enjoyed bad health, and was no worse then than common. A bad cough set in, and he was tied to his berth and seemed to get worse and worse every day, and the sicker he grew the better I loved the lad. Oh, he's a prince of a fellow, with such a big heart! Well, when we anchored, the first thing I did was to rig up smart, make all tight, see the owners, and then take the Leghorn flat and the mosicky pin, — now I've got it, — straight up to the house, and as I went along I thought how nice it would be to slick up that poor fellow I'd just left in his narrow berth, into the best chamber, white curtains and all. Well, I found Betsy, and she *was* glad to see me; she always is, and liked her pin very much and the flat also, but says she shall never be able to make up her mind how to have it cut; and, as the fashions won't let her wear it whole, she's dreadfully afraid that she'll never be able to put it on her head, but says she can keep it for a show. It's just so always, — poor little Mary had got the measles, and was put in the best chamber, — every body is that's sick in our house — and so there was no place for the poor lad; and I thought I'd just come and tell you the whole story, as you're always good at listening to me and helping all distressed people. I once asked this young man if he knew any one in America, and he answered, no one to whom he could apply for assistance. I can't bear the thoughts of his being sent to the hospital, good as it is. He don't look like a person who has ever done hard work; his hands are very soft. How I do wish Mary hadn't the measles; she's not very sick, but cant't be moved. I'm sure he's a gentleman. Now if we could get a good room, I'm perfectly willin to pay one half if you will the other. He's got *the* consumption.'

Mr. Barclay was as usual repaid for his patient listening, and assured the captain that he would engage to defray all expenses, and would immediately accompany him on board the barque and see his passenger. He then ordered a coach, and jumping in with the captain, they proceeded to Gerald's old quarters, and engaged a nice airy room, and gave directions for a good fire to be prepared. Then they hastened on board the barque. Mr. Barclay found an uncommonly handsome young man, with most prepossessing manners and refined address, lying exhausted and suffering in his berth, the cold winds of autumn blowing fiercely around him. The captain bustled about and informed him that every thing was ready, and that they desired he would try to rouse himself and get on shore. After many ineffectual efforts, they succeeded in having the invalid transported to the wharf, and from thence to the boarding-house, where the mistress of the house received them at the door in the kindest manner, and installed the sufferer in a warm and comfortable bed in a remarkably cheerful and sunny room. Mr. Barclay then sent for a medical man, who came and administered some alleviating potion, and the patient sank into a profound slumber. A good nurse was engaged, and he was left to her care. Mr. Barclay sent in the evening to inquire for the young stranger, and found that he had greatly rallied under the combined influence of warmth and comfort, and was much better.

The next morning he went to visit him. The good captain was already there, and the stranger was sitting up in bed propped with pillows. When Mr. Barclay entered, Captain Williams formally introduced his passenger to him as Mr. Julian Seaton, having forgotten in the hurry of the preceding day, to perform the ceremony. Mr. Barclay started when he heard the name, and when his own was pronounced the stranger fainted. After some time he revived, and entreated to be left alone with Mr. Barclay. He then said, 'God grant me strength to impart so you, Sir, the miserable tale of my wickedness. I can scarcely find words in which to express my own sense of my utter unworthiness; the only appeal I shall make to your mercy and forgiveness is, that I shall not for a long time cross your pathway. The sands in my glass of life are nearly run, and it is a miserable and dying sinner who now throws himself on your clemency for protection. I am Julian Seaton, the only son of your wife's cousin, Paul Seaton; and I am — oh God, that I should live to confess this to you! — your daughter's husband — the deceiver, the traitor who stole away the heart of your child under false pretences. Blame her not, I conjure you, — let the whole weight of your just displeasure fall upon me, wretch that I am.'

Mr. Barclay was, as may naturally be supposed, thunderstruck at this revelation; he administered a renovating cordial to his fainting relative, and after this had taken effect he renewed the conversation, and heard exactly the same narrative as far as his daughter was concerned, as she had already given to him of her acquaintance with her husband. A long and intensely interesting interview was this, in which the good merchant accorded a full pardon to the erring young man, and poured the balm of forgiveness into his penitent and humble spirit. On leaving Julian Seaton, he instantly repaired to his brother's and communicated the intelligence of his wonderful discovery. Mr. Richard was surprised — overjoyed. 'Oh, said he, 'my dear little niece's reputation for veracity, I have reason to know, though I never told you, John, had been implicated. There are people who have dared to doubt her word; thank God, they can do it no longer, — she is righted and we are saved — so long as there was a stain upon her honour, I was miserable. Now all is revealed, the truth of her story made manifest, and it is to no low and objectionable person that she is married, but to one of your own kith and kin, or your wife's, which is the same thing. To be sure, the father is a good-for-nothing rascal, but I have heard the most admirable account of the mother; the boy can't be very bad, I'm sure. What a relief! John, I feel as if an Atlas had been lifted up from my shoulders. What an incubus has been removed this blessed morning by this revelation! We must mark this day with a white stone in the calendar of our lives, and bless God for his mercies. I must go to home with you, John, and hear you tell your wife; she has behaved like an angel through all her tribulations, and I'm determined to see how she will bear this good and joyful news.'

Mr. Barclay was delighted with this proposition, for he was greatly overcome with the interview he had just passed through, and required the assistance of his brother in imparting it to his wife. He had found joy almost as overwhelming as sorrow. So, with light steps and lighter hearts these united brothers wended their way on their joyful errand, and, reaching the house, begged to see Mrs. Barclay alone. She came to them with an agitated and inquiring air, and demanded the cause of this interview so ceremoniously requested. She perceived, at once, that the intelligence her husband and brother were about to communicate was not of an afflicting nature.

'Catherine,' said Mr. Richard, 'you, who have borne, — as few women could have done — a great and absorbing calamity, and, under the infliction, have showed yourself to possess the greatest self-control and the most unequalled fortitude, and have, through the whole of your troubles, preserved your cheerfulness in an extraordinary manner; can you bear equally well their removal?'

'I assure you, I consider this one of the happiest moments of my life, when I am permitted, by my brother's kindness, to be the harbinger of great and good news, and entreat you to receive it calmly.'

'Is Georgy's husband discovered?' exclaimed Mrs. Barclay; 'this can be nothing else.'

'He is found, and is in Boston.'

'Who is he? What is he? For the love of heaven, tell me?'

'He is Julian Seaton, your own cousin's son.'

'God be praised!' she cried, and threw herself into her husband's arms.

On recovering from the first effects of her delightful surprise, Mrs. Barclay professed herself to be overflowing with gratitude for this great blessing vouchsafed to her, — the restoration of her child's honour. But she was in nowise inclined to pardon Julian. She had a rooted aversion to his father — arising from some passages in his life connected with hers — and imagined that no good whatever could proceed from such a source. It appeared that Paul Seaton had fruitlessly tried to win her favour, and had, on her constant refusals of his hand, vowed vengeance against her, plunged into all sorts of dissipation, and then laid all his misdoings at her door. He had declared openly, that if she had married him, he should have pursued a different course, and that he attributed his ruin entirely to her rejection of his suit. This often occurs where women are entirely blameless, and, certainly, Mrs. Barclay had no reproaches of conscience, for her cousin was, as Mr. Richard had averred, a great rascal from the beginning, and no woman on earth could have made him either better or worse. But he had chosen to make her the scapegoat for all his offences, and persisted in considering himself a most ill-used man, when, in fact, he was nothing more than a worthless profligate. Women often bear a vast deal of odium for offences quite as ill founded as this.

Mr. Barclay imparted to Mrs. Sanderson and Mrs. Meredith the great good fortune that had befallen them all.

They both declared, that, firmly believing in their sister's innocence, not a shadow of a doubt had ever for a moment rested upon their minds; but that, naturally, they were transported with delight to be able to proclaim the restoration of her husband, and that he was exactly the person they could have wished him to be. They could not be persuaded to look upon the romance he had enacted in the same light as their mother; they rather glossed it over, but they were young and romantic, and looked forward to long days of happiness for their sister and her newly-found husband.

This time Mrs. Meredith waltzed her father round the room, to her heart's content — for he was so overflowing with happiness that he never resisted. Mrs. Barclay, on breaking to her daughter the intelligence she had received on this eventful morning, was still palpitating under the excitement it had produced in her own feelings, but she effected her purpose judiciously. Georgy received the joyful news of the re-establishment of her honour and truth with intense delight and gratitude. She thanked her Creator for having vouchsafed this great and signal mercy to her, and wept tears of contrition on the bosom of the mother, who had been her solace and comfort through her tribulations. But she distinctly and positively refused to see Julian Seaton; she declared she had irrevocably made up her mind to this course; that her feelings were entirely changed towards him; and that an interview with him would but open anew the floodgates of her sorrows and his. She said, that this having been her fixed determination for a long time, it was unchangeable, and no efforts of others — not even those she most loved and worshipped in the world — would induce her to rescind this resolve. She said she had come to this state of mind from long and deeply solemn reflection, and was convinced that, for the welfare of both, it was best.

Mrs. Barclay imparted her daughter's determination to her

husband. He would have wished it otherwise, but was convinced that Georgy had good and sufficient reasons for her conduct, which she might, perchance, desire to conceal; of their rectitude he was firmly assured, and neither he nor his wife ever inquired their nature.

Gerald Sanderson went immediately to Julian Seaton, and proffered his services in his sick room as reader, attendant, or friend. Robert Redmond and Charley Sanderson did the same. Uncle Richard actually installed himself as major domo, and ordered away his brother and all of them, when they talked too much and fatigued the invalid. There was, however, one exception, and this was Mrs. Betsy Williams, who would not be commanded by any man living, she said; and came and went at her own bidding. The captain loved Julian like a child, and he carried little Mary when she had emerged from her Pandora's box — for chicken-pox had been added to the measles — to see his favourite, and Julian taking a fancy to her, she went to visit him daily. Mrs. Betsy overloaded him with what she called 'goodies' — and very excellent they were — such jellies and creams and custards as she made for him! they were only too good.

The medical man who attended him, seemed to be highly interested in his patient, and passed hours with him. His landlady was also ever indefatigable, so that the friendless and forlorn creature, who had landed on the American shore in complete destitution, found himself surrounded by friends, luxuries, and comforts. Julian Seaton received the fiat of his doom from the lips of Mr. Barclay, who, as gently as possible, imparted to him his daughter's decision. He listened with tearful eyes, and, groaning in spirit, declared that he had richly merited his punishment. He was convinced that Georgiana Barclay loathed him for his duplicity, his treachery, that her pure spirit could never mingle with his. 'And what good would accrue,' he exclaimed, 'from a meeting where hearts dissevered can never more be joined together? Your daughter, my revered friend, has ceased to love me, I should expire under averted glances; the eyes, once turned to mine and beaming with love and affection, now averted, would annihilate me. I could never survive the meeting. I am convinced she detests me.'

'She has pardoned you.'

'With that I must rest content. I have not long to bear my martyrdom; death, welcome death, will shortly release me from my sufferings, and I shall rejoin my sainted mother where sin and sorrow are no more. She loved me, and I had not forfeited her affection. As I can now sit up a portion of the day, I propose, my dearest benefactor, to write for you — with your consent — a little history of my life, which, as I finish, I will give to you. You will therein discover that I am the creature of circumstances, having been left without guidance or direction; and, forgetful of the monitions of the saint now in paradise, I fell, and great was my fall. It was a sad one. I carried with me even your daughter, accursed that I am. My death will restore her to liberty, all aspersions on her fair fame being removed by my re-appearance in your land. She will yet be spared for a long life of happiness, and for death, I pray, and ever shall. I watch my decaying strength with intense satisfaction, day by day, and ask not for another sun to rise over my devoted head.'

Mr. Barclay was deeply affected by this interview. This young creature becoming daily more dear to him, he sympathized with him, and endeavoured to console him under the afflictions which gathered around him. Julian Seaton desired to see a Catholic priest. Mr. Barclay sent one to him — from whose presence and ministrations he seemed to derive infinite peace and contentment — and was much calmer and more cheerful after every visit he received from his confessor. Indeed, the good man devoted himself to the sufferer, and remained with him in the watches of the night, when, nervous and feverish, he could obtain no repose, and only left him when he saw him surrounded by his friends. He also promised to be with him, when the night, which, coming to all, precedes 'the day-spring from on high,' emanating from heaven's wide portals.

Mr. Barclay received a letter from Julian Seaton, which will be read in the next chapter. It was brought by Captain Williams, who stated that he had just seen off that plaguey woman, whose good-for-nothing life had been saved at the expense of a fellow, who was worth a million such petticoats. 'She'd gone to Kentucky,' he said, 'for to find her sweetheart, who had written for her to come to America, and had sent her the money to pay her way along; and the worst harm he wished her, was that he himself might never set his two eyes upon her again.'

Mr. Barclay was quite astonished at this ebullition of temper on the part of his old friend; but it afterwards transpired that Mrs. Betsy Williams had actually got jealous of 'the Italian crittur,' and the poor captain had no peace in his life, and was naturally greatly relieved when the girl departed. She had taken an affecting farewell of her preserver, and had made him quite ill by the violence of her grief at parting.

CHAPTER XL.

> 'Oh Rome! my country! city of the soul!
> The orphans of the heart must turn to thee,
> Lone mother of dead empires! and control,
> In their shut breasts, their petty misery.'
>
> BYRON.

'To JOHN BARCLAY, ESQ.

'NOT daring, Sir, to address this letter to your angelic daughter, over whose young days it has been my melancholy lot to cast a mantle of sorrow and trouble, which not all the repentant agony I am now enduring will ever dispel, I venture, at your solicitation, to write you the history of my life, now that it is fast closing. I could not, for a moment, dream that you would take any interest in one so fallen as myself, were not the destiny of your child so fearfully mixed up with mine as to make my own insignificant course of importance to you. On the eve of standing before my great Judge, and in his awful presence, receiving the award of my punishment for my sins, I can confess nothing but the sacred truth; and that you shall learn without any fruitless attempt at extenuation or diminution.

'I do not think I was born to the heritage of dishonour, which has weighed down my spirit and bowed my head to my mother earth in shame and despair, for I have ever so felt my degradation, even in my wildest flights of imagination and misdeeds. This, and my present state of regenerated life, induces me to believe, that if I could have enjoyed the priceless blessing of a home, I might have been a widely different being from the one who now pours forth his whole soul in supplications for your mercy, and who asks but the boon of your forgiveness, and that of your afflicted child, to die in comparative peace.

'In order that you should thoroughly understand my history, I must naturally mingle with it a relation of my father's course of life, and that this development will cost me many a pang, need I say to you, whose whole existence has been one of such unblemished purity? Would to God that I could tell my sad and miserable tale without mentioning the name of the author of my being, but it cannot be, and, as I proceed, I feel that to no one but to you, and influenced by the sad circumstances which have produced the necessity of this missive, could I have found strength and resolution to unfold the pages of my own existence, which so fearfully involve my father's reputation.

'Of the antecedents of my parent's career in Boston I believe you to be well acquainted, having been his classmate in college-life. I have often heard him say, he, for some reason unknown to me, bore towards you and yours a deadly hatred, and although I have essayed, times out of mind, to get at its cause, I utterly failed. My general impression, from my knowledge of your character, is that he never forgave you for having been through life in advance of him, in every thing. I have often heard him, in his stormy gusts of passion, swear vengeance against you; but when I prayed him to reveal to me the cause of this deeply rooted hatred, he would never accede to my request, but, on the other hand, ill treated me, and commanded me never to touch upon a subject so revolting to him.

'On one occasion, and one only, I heard him mention a name, and that was in a fit of delirium, arising from a violent fever, under which he was labouring, after my sainted mother's death in Florence. Not paying much attention to it at the time, I did not remember the word, but now that my reminiscences are vividly aroused, and every circumstance appertaining to that period arises like a living picture before my sight, I think he declared he would be revenged on you for supplanting him in the favour of Catherine ——; the rest of the name I heard not.

'In Florence, the city of flowers, I saw the light, and basking in the bright sunshine of my mother's eyes I revelled in all the joys accompanying the childhood of an idolized first-born. The demonstrations of affection I received, were much more ardent than those which the well-tempered nature of your countrywomen bestow upon their offspring, however tender and absorbing may be their maternal feelings. Again, I believe, that my mother, who had lavished all the rich treasure of her impassioned soul on my father, on finding herself deceived and disappointed in him, centred her whole heart in me, — and such a heart! I thus became to her the spring-tide of her existence, the fount from which she drew her whole being.

'My first recollections of her, were those of a creature beaming with resplendent beauty, and full of poetry, religion, and love. My mother would have been considered uneducated in America, but the very language she spoke was music, and her passion for the poets of her own beauteous land was intense. Not a day passed that she did not repeat to me the verses of Tasso and Ariosto, and, in fact, I was taught to lisp in numbers, and exhibited to her friends as a prodigy of attainment. Family, my mother had none, — she was an unprotected orphan, with a small fortune, when my father made her acquaintance. Captivated by her beauty and native talent, he sought, and won the lovely creature, and, having married her, he tired of her almost immediately. She was treated with some degree of affection until after my birth, and then he resumed his old habits of gambling, and she saw little of him; for the time he passed in his own house was usually consumed in sleep. Sometimes, for days, and even weeks, he never left the hells he frequented, and only returned to look upon his young wife and child when a run of ill luck had come over him, or a bank was broken.

'At first, she was very miserable at his neglect, but her buoyant nature actually rebelled against sorrow, and then she had her boy, her worshipped child, over whom she would hang in an ecstasy of maternal tenderness. She would exclaim, " Every thing but thee can I renounce, my heart's treasure, my soul, my light of life, my jewel." She would wander about with me in the gardens and galleries, showing me all the wonders of the palaces of art with which Florence abounds, and teaching me the history of all the saints whom she worshipped. We regularly attended all the church festivals, and amidst their pomp and ceremonies she would thank God that he had allowed her to breathe her first breath of life in glorious Italy, the land of the poet and the painter. Sometimes there would a cloud pass over the spirit of her dream, and she would ask me in the most impassioned tones if I thought my father would ever have the cruelty to tear her away from this Eden, and force her to go to his own cold and ice-bound country. " I should die," she would exclaim, " in that frigid zone, my very heart would be frozen up ; he says there are no pictures, no gardens, no statues there. Alas! alas! what will become of your poor mother, with no friends, no neighbours, no theatres, no churches, and no English ! '

'At these times I comforted her as well as I could. Many of these things which I now relate respecting my earliest days my mother confided to me ; such as the first indications of my father's declining love for her, and his consequent neglect. " Ah," she would exclaim, " my beloved Julian, I should have laid me down in one of the churches, at the feet of the blessed Virgin and slept my last sleep, had I not possessed my adored child ; my life would have been a dreary waste, but for the blessing vouchsafed to me in my boy. At first, I thought my heart would break, and surely none ever will if mine did not, but I prayed to the Holy

Mother, and she, taking pity on my acute sufferings, raised up such a feeble creature as I am, and gave me my child. And then I soon began to perceive that the stream of love which had flowed so rapidly towards your father was centred in my innocent babe, and I cared no longer for his absences, at which I had been in the habit of weeping my soul out. I cared no longer for them! how terrible this sad truth appeared to me when it broke upon me!

'"I was then encompassed in clouds and darkness, a midnight in my soul, but soon a little ray of light illumed this dense gloom. It was, indeed, so small, so very small, but it increased and became the morning's dawn with all its dewy, balmy freshness. Ah! how I rejoiced in it. I was another creature; never had I been so happy before, not even when HE worshipped me in the earliest period of my acquaintance with him, — not even when he first poured forth his love for me." Well do I remember the time and the scene wherein these outpourings of my beautiful mother's feelings were made. We lived in the first floor of an old palace; all our rooms opening on to a large garden thickly planted with superb trees, and to which my mother had added myriads of flowers. The sitting-room of the family was so large, that in the evening when she taught me my lessons at the table, by the light of a bright lamp, it was mostly enveloped in shadow. The children here would be frightened out of their senses to live in such a place; but my mother was there, and I never had known fear. It was not in the house, however, that her revelations were made to me; she always preferred a stone seat in the garden, where, under the umbrageous protection of wide-spread trees, she repeated her simple history. It seemed to me that the walls of our dwelling produced some decidedly oppressive effect upon her spirits, so doated she upon the open air; for she never was half so communicative, or half so charming in-doors. Oh! those blessed days! How I pine to live them over. That garden of Armida, my gloriously beautiful mother, all gone! never to re-appear.

'I have mentioned my lessons, — these consisted of all she could teach, — my church practices, reading, writing, and music. A beautiful Italian hand was my mother's; and she played delightfully on the guitar, and accompanied herself with great skill and talent, having been thoroughly taught. These things she imparted to me in such a winning manner, that I knew not when, or how, I acquired them. It was a melancholy proof of the all-devouring and absorbing nature of my father's hateful pursuits, if any were wanting, that he, an American, should have permitted his only son, for aught he knew to the contrary, to be brought up in utter ignorance. But so it was. He would, when in a pleasant mood, take me upon his knee and caress me; but then these moods were rare, few, and far between, and his constant absences prevented his knowing hardly any thing about me. My father was in the habit of running down to Venice. He never invited my mother to accompany him, nor did she appear to wish to go, for she was satisfied to be left at home. She had a little circle of friends who sufficed for her amusement, as far as social life went; and certainly they had a vast deal more genial intercourse than I have ever seen in this country.

'These good people met together in the summer evenings in their different dwellings constantly; nothing was given in the way of refreshments, and consequently there were no tedious preparatory arrangements to mar their pleasure. The talk was of the next Church festival, the poets, some distinguished holy father's preaching, some remarkable artist who had but lately sprung up, the vagaries of the foreigners abiding in the place. I well remember the horror of my mother's circle at the appearance of a stage-coach set up by a stranger nobleman, driven by himself! — they could not be reconciled to such things; to which was added the enormity of putting his men and women servants inside. These little parties always finished with music, and many a concert have I heard in this country that was not half so good, — the soul, the enthusiasm was wanting.

'One day my father came rushing home, in most exuberant spirits, and kissing my mother, a thing he rarely did, threw into her lap a very large sum in rouleaus of gold, saying, "There, take this money, and go to Rome and enjoy the holy city to your heart's content. Stay as long as you like; I will go and see you when I have leisure. You know you have always desired this above all things on earth." And very true was this, for my mother had been lately pining to behold the Pope, and besides the Montinis, a family she dearly loved, were about to remove there. So all these things combined to make this delightful to her, and she fell on my father's neck, and thanked him in a flood of joyful tears.

'At last, came the happy day. I was then ten years of age, and crazed with delight at the prospect of beholding my mother's blessed haven, for so she called it. All prospered; the Montinis taking charge of us, engaged a vetturino; honest Babel, who permitted me the great favour of sitting by his side on the coach-box, told me all manner of pleasant tales besides. This man was a person who would have talked to himself had I not been perched upon the box with him; so he was very gracious indeed, and charmingly communicative. My father lifted me into the seat, embracing me the while, and having performed the same ceremony to my mother, he waived his hat in the air; Babel cracked his long whip with a terrible noise, and we were off. The journey was enchanting, our companions so kind and attentive to my mother and myself, — and Babel, I shall never forget him. We crossed the mountains happily with one most interesting event. I was awakened from a profound sleep by Babel, who exclaimed, "Up, up, boy, and see the robbers!" and surely there were before me three men, guarded by soldiers, who, in their picturesque costumes, velvet dresses, and plumed hats, with even a bouquet in the button-hole, were a sight indeed! They were tied to their horses, but seemed any thing but miserable. Our whole party congratulated themselves on having encountered them under such circumstances, and I thanked the vetturino heartily for having shown them to me.

'We came within sight of the "Eternal City." "Bellissima Roma!" my mother cried. Indeed she had even added out of her own purse another horse at the last post-house, that we might reach "the haven" by sunset. And such a sunset! Glorious ones you have in your own land, but nothing to ours. We all descended from the carriage at Babel's shout of "Roma! Roma!" and, kneeling, thanked God for his mercy in being allowed to behold St. Peter's. My mother afterwards cried, laughed, sang, and danced, in which variety of joyful exercises she was joined by her friends, and I am quite sure, had the whole party been seen by any Americans, they would have been considered fitting subjects for an insane establishment. As we entered the gates of Rome, and were stopped by the "customs," we saw a woman holding the head of a horse, while a man was engaged with the officers. This pair had passed us in our day's journey, and we had supposed they were out on a pleasure excursion of a few hours. Not a bit,—they had travelled from Paris with a one-horse stanhope without a top. Of course they were English, and my mother said she suppose it was some wager. We met them again at our hotel, and they said they were going to Naples, after remaining a week in Rome.

'After a good night's sleep my mother aroused me and said, "Awake, my Julian, awake, we are in Rome. And oh! how very happy I am, and I hope you are also. Now we will have a good breakfast, and depart for St. Peter's. The Montinis take a carriage, and you shall go with them, but I will approach that sacred building in no way but on foot." I, however, pleaded and begged so hard to accompany her that she, being unable to refuse me any thing, consented, and weary enough was I, when, having traversed all manner of dirty streets and narrow lanes, we emerged into the magnificent part of the blessed city, and passing the Castle of St. Angelo, found ourselves in front of the Church. My mother, kneeling, returned thanks on the pavement, and we walked up the grand entrance, and drawing aside the curtain which is before the side-door, we stood breathless with awe and amazement in Saint Peter's. I say we, for though too young for such a state of excitement, my mother's enthusiasm had been communicated to me in an uncommon degree, and never have I since experienced the same sensations. She said she would not go into the Vatican that day, Saint Peter's was all-sufficient; but the Montinis insisting, she was dragged there much against her will, as she seemed to think this proceeding almost disrespectful to the holy place. They, however, pleaded, and said she must see the Apollo. She did not go down on her knees to it, though I almost thought she would; for my own part, I had an earnest desire to pay the same compliment to a lion in the hall of the animals.

'My mother took an apartment in the Via Babuino, a sufficiently dark and gloomy street, but the Montinis liked it as being near their business, and so we resided together in great peace and harmony.

'Oh, Sir! will you ever pardon me for my wearisome prolixity? You have been too indulgent to me; and, as you have begged me to omit nothing which would throw light upon my career, I have borne this request in mind. I am fearful that I have imposed upon your kindness and patience. Neither do I write so very readily in English; it is just so in my conversation, for I am apt to halt terribly; and then when I drop my pen and reflect for a moment to whom I am writing, I am deeply impressed with your goodness and forbearance, and blush at my own hardihood.

'I shall forward to you this long epistle to-day, which will be followed by another to-morrow, and so on, until concluded; for I never tire of lingering amid the scenes of my lost innocence, and dread the moment when I must emerge from them, and enter upon a recital of my misery and my misdeeds. May the peace that passeth all earthly show, and the blessing of the orphan, rest upon your head.

'With great consideration and profound respect, I am your obliged and devoted JULIAN.'

CHAPTER XLI.

'Five years — like yon bright valley, sown
Alternately with weeds and flowers,
Had swiftly, if not gaily, flown,
And I still loved the rosy hours.'

N. P. Willis.

'Since you have been pleased to say, my best friend, that you liked not the formality of my style to you in my former letter, I will now address my benefactor, and resume the thread of my narrative.

'We lived, my mother and myself, with the dear Montinis, five short years. Oh! how rapidly they vanished; they were always and ever the same simple, kind-hearted people. I think nothing can surpass the naturalness of the Italians; there is no affectation in them, high and low are all alike, in that respect equally true to themselves.

'Our housekeeping in Florence had been always of the most unpretending character; our modest repasts consisting chiefly of vegetables and fruit, which an old woman prepared. At Rome, my mother, having literally nothing to do, wandered about the livelong day in the ruins, galleries, gardens and churches. We often sallied forth in the morning, taking our simple dinner with us, and returned only when the shadows of evening fell upon the Campagna, seldom or never failing to climb the Pincian Hill, to look out upon the glorious sun in his setting. During this time I took lessons in drawing, as I had a small natural talent at sketching, and practised my little art in these excursions. The evenings were devoted to music and books and society, for we soon had a pleasant circle around us; my mother's genial and social qualities always attracting pleasant people. They accused her of having some method even in her rambles, for she was always at home by eight in the evening, and delighted to see them.

'My father would "run up to Rome," as he said, for a few days, but soon tired of the city. He thought it dull, very dull, — he never took much notice of me, and I fancied my mother felt much relieved when he departed. The society of artists was never much to his taste; he liked the foreigners, and they were quieter in Rome than in Florence. The Montinis said, "They had the grace to pay the Eternal City that respect, if they did nothing else; there were no English stage-coaches there," — those vehicles were sad bugbears to our friends. We always went two or three times a week to Saint Peter's; then we repaired to the Vatican, and having remained in its "halls of living light" until we were frozen up in the winter, we then returned to the Church, and warmed ourselves in its perfect atmosphere. My dear simple mother really believed that the holiness of this tabernacle produced this genial temperature. The artists told me it was the thickness of its walls. They, however, never thought proper to enlighten her. While she was praying at all the shrines, I would sit, for hours, before the tomb of the last of the Stuarts. How very beautiful it was to me! less elaborate than others, I could the more easily take it into my heart's core, — the mournful caryatides! trailing their funeral torches on the ground, and patiently awaiting the opening of its closed portals when the last trump shall sound, possessed for me an indescribable charm. Often my mother had finished her orisons long ere I could be aroused from my day-dreams, before this shrine of beauty.

'This sort of life had no chastening or strengthening character in it for me; I required a bad habit of dreaming, with my eyes wide open; I am sure I was often as sound asleep as if they had been shut. I became thoughtful, abstracted, not unhappy, — no, never with *her*, — but a castle-builder, a visionary, just what Gerald Sanderson has so miraculously escaped. Perhaps if I had enjoyed the inestimable advantage of such counsel as he received and accepted, I might have been radically cured of my folly. It was not so to be, and I will not now repine. The decree of Providence has gone forth, and I humbly submit. Were my life spared, I should never be much more than I am now, and for one all-important reason I ask it not, — *she* will be free.

'One day when I had fallen into an absent fit before the tomb of Clement the Thirteenth, — Oh! the wonderful lions! — I was rudely awoke by a grand procession of horrid old men and women emerging from the mausoleum, carrying mops, pails, dusters, watering-pots, brooms, and brushes, and was thus painfully made aware of its being cleaning day in Saint Peter's. At first, I imagined this to be a frightful nightmare, but afterwards discovered there was a receptacle for all these utilities somewhere about the tomb; the waking lions seemed to glare upon them ferociously. My mother laughed heartily at this adventure.

'I read a vast many novels, and devoured all the works on chivalry I could procure, and began to aspire to do battle for some fair damsel; but, somehow, never found one. The Roman girls of my age were all locked up in convents and schools, and, though there were many beautiful English, I was unacquainted with them, and consequently could have no access to them. I have informed you that I lived in the Via Babuino. This street is almost entirely devoted to lodging-houses. My mother and I had great amusement in the winter in watching the arrivals and departures of the occupants, who did not remain long. At last, an American family took the apartments in the first story, directly opposite us, and we heard they were to remain many months. I had always a great thirst for any information respecting my father's birthplace, and, judge of my delight, when I heard they were from Boston. I resolved to become acquainted with them, if possible, and this was not difficult. I succeeded in arresting the attention of the ladies of the party by some slightly rendered service, and they invited me to visit them. My first appearance amongst them, — for there were two gentlemen also, — was not at all advantageous to me, for I was so excessively agitated I could hardly command my overwrought feelings. The second time I did better, and informed them of the cause of my apparent stupidity; they asked me many questions, and amongst others, the name of my father, which I answered. They kindly begged permission to visit my mother, but their request was politely refused; she said she could not speak English, and never wished to do so. I urged her to receive these ladies, but she was inexorable; so I made all the necessary apologies for her apparent deficiency in hospitality; and I should have gone to them oftener myself, but for the terrible fires they kept. I would leave our own windows open, while my mother, in a thin white dress, was looking out from them, and go across the street and find my American friends shivering and shaking with what they were pleased to call the intense cold, and crouching around the hearth. Now, I believe that, measured by a thermometer, you have more real cold in this country, in a month, than we have in a whole year in all Italy. They kindly invited me to dine; but such dinners as I then thought them, such loads of meat; I ventured to tell them they could not continue this practice if they remained for any time in our climate.

'There was also another custom, very disagreeable to me, the abundance of flowers. We think them unhealthy, and one day when the ladies offered me a bouquet for my mother I gratefully declined their proffer, at which they were astonished, and inquired the reason. I told them she would not allow them to remain in her room; we liked flowers in the open air, but not in our houses. They then remembered that their Italian maid had declared she was made ill by the great profusion of flowers and perfumes they had ever about them, and speculated upon the singularity of these things, attributing them to difference of climate. Finding myself always ill after their repasts, I was obliged after this to decline invitations, but went, occasionally in the evening, when they had a charming variety of persons. The conversation was delightful, — such a number of interesting topics were discussed.

'These lodgings were ill-furnished, and this gave rise to many amusing scenes. One evening the lady who always presided at the tea-table, — I could never be persuaded to drink any of the nauseous stuff, — confided to me a great misadventure. Just as she was preparing to make the "exhilarating beverage," I think they called it, Peter, their servant, informed her that the only tea-pot they possessed was broken. Here was a dilemma, indeed. The lady told him he must find one, and he departed, saying he would not return without one. So she whispered to me we must be as agreeable as we can to cover and hide our trouble, and you must play and sing. Accordingly I did, and in an hour and a half Peter returned with such a thing! The shops all shut, it was impossible to buy one, and he had scoured all Rome before he could even borrow one. Its arrival was a source of great joy and amusement to the assembled guests. Many times there were not spoons enough, so many visitors were there; and then she always begged the frequenters of the house patiently to await the serving of those who were more of strangers. Very merry times were these, and I enjoyed them immensely.

'My mother said to me, after a description I had given to her of one of my visits to the ladies, "Julian, if I thought those women would make you forget me for an instant, you should never enter their doors again." I threw myself into her arms, and told her I would never see them more. Upon this, she relented, and said, "I do not wish to deprive you of any pleasure on earth, but you are all I possess in this world, and the deprivation of one tithe of your affection would make me wretched." I was, however, not called upon to make this sacrifice, for soon they all departed after the Holy Week, and I lost my kind friends, and resolved to make no more acquaintances, as I perceived that this sort of thing pained my dear mother, who had become jealous of even my short absences. In the spring we resumed our pleasant gipsey course of life; the Montinis called my mother "the amiable vagabond," and declared she was not an Italian in that respect, though an excellent one in others. She answered that, having married an American, he had taught her to walk. "Travel, you mean," they laughingly replied, "for you walk miles and miles every day." I do not think, however, that the women are great pedestrians here, and rather fancy my father had copied the English, who excel in this respect; at any rate, the good effects of exercise were very visible. The Italian women are constantly in the open air, in courts and gardens, but no walkers. But this enchanting life was not to endure. My father came and asked us if we had any idea how long we had been in Rome. We answered, Five years. How short this time had seemed to us! He then informed us we were to return to Florence, and that I was to be placed under the care of an Englishman, in order, as he said, to learn something useful at last. "You are a dunce," he said; at which I cried my heart out, and then he called me a baby.

'And then came the sad, sad leave-taking of all our idols, the churches where we had prayed, the galleries we had almost lived in, the gardens, the ruins, the Vatican, and lastly, Saint Peter's. My mother and I sat on the Pincian Hill, and sorely wept; we dared not shed tears at home before my father, who regarded our sensibility as sheer nonsense, childish in the extreme. "Julian," he said, "you are an absurd, silly, spoiled boy, who must be taken in hand immediately, and taught something." "You were always a foolish creature," he exclaimed, turning to my afflicted mother, "and, instead of improving, grow worse and worse every year. I have borne with your nonsense long enough, and have left the boy dangling at your petticoat strings until he is half ruined, and nothing will ever be made of him now. So you must decide to part from him on our arrival at Florence. I shall be utterly ashamed to take such an ignoramus home with me to America, where they will expect to see something very different."

'Our doom was sealed, we embraced the dear Montinis repeatedly, and my mother whispered, "You never will again behold me, if my husband executes his threat, and separates me from my child. He virtually deserted me long, long years gone, and I adopted Julian in his stead. He now occupies the place in my breast, where his father once reigned supreme, and I shall never survive his departure." Sad words, and, alas! how prophetic! "I have endured," — she seemed actually choked by the intensity of her sensations, — but she proceeded, — "I have survived torture once, and shall never have sufficient strength to bear it a second time." And so we mournfully retraced our steps to Florence, and found ourselves once more in the same old palace, which my father had again hired, thinking to please my mother; but little recked she of this place or that, if I shared it not.

'May God be with you, my best friend, prays your devoted JULIAN.'

CHAPTER XLII.

> 'But Arno wins us to the fair white walls,
> Where the Etrurian Athens claims and keeps
> A softer feeling for her fairy halls.'
>
> BYRON.

'WE returned to Florence, as I stated in my last letter, my dearest benefactor and friend, and to the old palace, and our same old woman was there to greet and welcome my mother. In one week from our arrival my father commanded my mother to prepare me for my school. This command threw her into an agony of grief; she even fell on her knees at his feet, and prayed and conjured him, with many tears and supplications, not to take me from her. He answered loudly and imperatively, that the boy must go; he had been idling away his precious time years too long, to please her silly fancies, and had become a perfect milksop, living upon poetry and romances. He would make a man of him; he desired to see no girls in boy's attire — not he.

'"Ah Paul, my husband!" she responded, "you will kill me by so doing. I never shall survive this separation from my child; my heart-strings will break."

'"A truce with such nonsense," he cried; "the boy shall go."

'And forth I went, and my dear mother hung about my neck in a frantic state, and then fainted. This delayed my departure a little; but on her revival I was torn from her, and confided to the charge of the Englishman, who was waiting for me at the door in a carriage.

'When I entered the vehicle, I found three boys, about

my own age, all looking very sad and melancholy. I cried bitterly, and they, seeing that I did so, and that our master, Mr. Hibbert, took no notice whatever of my sorrow, they began also to weep; so we journeyed twenty miles this way and reached our destination. Those boys were ever and always my best friends during my stay in the school; we had sorrowed together; and if we had not, should probably have quarrelled and fought.

'The establishment was large and roomy, with fine trees and fine gardens, in which we worked. Mr. Hibbert was a good man, and his wife better — women always are. We were obliged to study very hard; but we had plenty of time allotted for air and exercise and bathing. We raised all our own vegetables ourselves; we cultivated flowers, in which Mrs. Hibbert greatly delighted; and we had music and dancing every week. The only fault I ever had to find, was the abundance of meat to be eaten. I was sent every Sunday to church, about five miles distant, with the other Catholics; Mr. Hibbert, being himself a Church of England clergyman, performed the service at home for the Protestants. I take great shame to myself that I was happy, but I must tell the whole truth. No boy's love is as strong and powerful as his mother's; and I have never ceased to repent that I enjoyed myself when she was pining out her life for me at home.

'My father gave her permission to see me once a month. Oh, what meetings were those! — blessed indeed, as under the trees we sat and communed together. She told me she did not see my father for weeks, and he was colder and more indifferent than ever, or so he seemed to her, now that I was no longer with her. She spoke of her solitariness, and I said, But do you no longer see your friends and neighbours, as in bye-past times? — and she would reply, "No, I no longer take any pleasure in their society." Oh! the thoughtlessness of young days; I paid not the attention I should have done to these confessions. But then I often reflect, in this very room, made so pleasant by your bounty, what could I have done? My father was obstinately bent upon separating us, and no efforts of mine would have swayed him. Will you not, my best friend, agree with me when next I see you? I feel, as I proceed in my journal, that every line brings me nearer to you. I have been wicked, I know, but now that you declare I am not so bad as you for years have thought me to be, I feel that I may love and respect you.

'One day I waited at the end of the avenue of olive-trees for my mother the livelong day. She came not. I was very miserable, and knew not what to think of her absence. Monday I received a short note from her, informing me that she was injured slightly by a fall, and should come to me shortly; but if a week or so elapsed, and I saw her not, I must not be alarmed. So my mind being satisfied, I only thought of her as having met with a slight accident.

'A fortnight elapsed, and still another, when I received a letter from Mrs. Montini, who wrote that she and her husband had arrived in Florence, and repaired immediately to my mother's house, and found her in a very sad state indeed. It appeared, she wrote, that her friend had declined almost from the first week of my departure, and had not rallied even for a day. She had seemed dead to every thing, no longer taking any interest in her former pursuits, and sitting all day, without moving, on the stone bench in the garden. Her appetite had entirely left her, and to this succeeded faintings; in one of these she had fallen and injured her head. She desired our old woman not to mention these things on any account to her husband, and accordingly she did not. But the Montinis having heard these things, went boldly to him, and told him they were convinced his wife was pining herself to death for the loss of her child. At this he was indignant, and declared it was nothing but pretence, by which his wife hoped to get their boy back again, and spoil him worse than ever. The Montinis told him plainly that he would repent of his conduct, for that they well knew how she idolized her son, and then they told him the words she had whispered in their ears on quitting Rome. My father said they might take her back to that city of her affections, if she wished to go; but as to his son, he had a right to do as he pleased with his own child, and would never consent to his leaving the school where he had placed him for four years. The course of studies he had marked out for him, he said, would be broken up, and the boy was ignorant enough, Heaven knew. He had been sufficiently weak in allowing him to remain so long under the guidance of his wife, and would do it no longer. He farther informed them that he intended to return home in a few years, and was not willing to carry with him an ignoramus who knew not his right hand from his left. So the Montinis departed, taking a tender and melancholy farewell of their miserable friend, thinking, as they wrote me, never to look upon her sweet face again, until they should meet her, as they hoped to do, in heaven.

'Immediately on the receipt of this letter, which I hastily scanned, I ran to Florence, even without my hat. I asked no leave of my master, for I knew he would forbid me to go. How I reached our house I know not, nor ever shall. I ran all the way, I think, and reaching the door, knocked violently. The old woman appeared. I burst into the hall, shrieking, Mother! mother! For the first time in my life, there was no response in those walls. The old woman looked at me mysteriously, and bursting into tears, said, "Your mother is in her grave, my poor child!"

'I heard no more, and knew no more for weeks; then youth conquered, and I arose from my bed of suffering, and my father, who had been rather kinder to me than ever before, said I must return to school; that change of air and scene would revive me entirely. So I departed and resumed again my studies. The old woman told me my mother had been found dead at sunset on the stone bench, with her head leaning against her favourite tree, and a miniature of myself in her hand. Thus she had died, broken-hearted — my sainted mother — for the loss of her child. She told the old woman, at several different periods, that she was convinced her husband proposed abandoning her, and taking with him her son, would return to his own land, never again to behold Italy, and that his placing me in that school was the preparatory step. So, she said, the sooner I die the better; I never can survive the execution of this plan. Tell my boy I worshipped him to the last, and beg him so to live that he may meet me above, in that blessed country where there are no separations.

'Two years before, she had given me her miniature, and, just as I went to school, she had one painted by a skilful artist, of myself. The two were placed, back to back, in a medallion set round with large pearls; she said, for the first time in our lives we looked not in each others faces. These miniatures, which have never left my bosom, I pray you, my best friend, to accept, as a slight testimonial of my eternal gratitude, when I shall go to my mother. On my return to Mr. Hibbert, I begged pardon for so unceremoniously leaving his house, — which, in consequence of the circumstances, he graciously granted.

'I devoted myself most particularly to the study of Rome, its history, its legislation, and its antiquities. I looked upon it as the city of my sainted and lamented mother's predilection, and thereby discovered how much more I might have enjoyed my visit had my knowledge been greater. Just in the ratio of what is taken into the Eternal City is that which is brought out; its very stones speak, — and oh! how I lamented my ignorance! and how had I wasted my precious hours there! But the wailing for lost time is useless, and so I resolved to work and make up for this misspent period of my life. I mingled not much with my schoolmates. They were, for the most part, English; they liked all manner of hardy sports and games, for which my tastes disinclined me.

31*

I thought their boxing barbarous, and they called my Tasso a "spoon." With the Italians I fraternized better; we read the sonnets of my favourite poet together, and built air-castles together, in which we placed Leonores. And we thought, should we ever find in the wide wide world such a beautiful creation! I always maintained that I had seen one, but was afraid to say the person was my mother, lest they should jeer me; and I could illy have borne any unceremonious mention of her blessed name.

'My sainted mother,—she came between me and all evil thoughts and aspirations; she was THEN my shield and my safeguard. Alas! that I should live to confess my back-slidings,—why did I not hold fast to my true faith in her, a model of purity and virtue? I have not been half as much punished as I deserved; instead of finding the kindest of friends, I have richly merited poverty, desertion and misery. When I look on the past, and remember my own transparent character, my abhorrence of deceit and duplicity, and sacred love of truth, my very heart bleeds with anguish. No penance is too great for me to suffer when I reflect upon her teachings, and how I have rewarded them—what base ingratitude to her memory. Why did I ever permit the beautiful picture of her excellence to disappear from my sight?—a vision of purity placed between myself and crime. Were it not for the comforting assurances of my priest and yourself, I should despair of forgiveness. A lapse from virtue in the neglected and ignorant is venial, but for one like myself, having received every advantage, it is monstrous. I shudder when I think of my wickedness, and earnestly pray for mercy.

'I know these digressions are all wrong, they will occupy too much of your precious time, my benefactor; but you yesterday reiterated the request that I should pour out my whole soul to you—and even so it is done. Pardon me, I pray, my egotism. You would hear the story of my life, and very little have I to tell but of myself, my own feelings and thoughts; so lonely and solitary became my existence when my mother went home to paradise. That you have become my staff and stay on earth is a blessing I do not merit, and I accept this assurance as an especial instance of God's kindly affectionate providence in my behalf, and bow myself down to Him in deep and abiding gratitude.

'The four years rapidly departed, and the term of my stay with Mr. Hibbert expiring, my father came punctually and took me away with him. I left my kind master sorrowfully; he had been always forbearingly indulgent to me, and we parted mutually grieved at the separation. Mrs. Hibbert, good creature, wept over me as if I had been her own child. She knew, with a mother's keen sensibility, all the trials to which youth is exposed, deprived of the influence of woman, and she foreshadowed my destiny, — and sad enough it was. We went to Leghorn almost immediately, and embarked on board a barque bound to Boston. After a tedious voyage, in which I was always sick — the sea and I deciding to disagree — we landed at the birthplace of my father. The snow was six feet deep, the wind east, and the humidity of the atmosphere penetrated into the very marrow of my Italian bones. I dared not venture out of our hotel after my first attempt, as on that occasion I measured my length on the snow and ice, and the stunning effect of the fall almost bewildered my poor brain. Afterwards, during my stay, I contented myself with looking out of the Tremont House windows on the delicate and fragile-looking young girls who seemed to be flying about as if it were a midsummer-night dream, instead of a Nova Zembla.

'My father seemed to know no one. We had a parlour and private table, and very dull it would have been for me, but for the sleighs, they made the city so gay; and the numerous parties out on pleasure excursions, tempted me to ask my father to indulge me in the same way. He forthwith gave his consent, and I returned to my hotel with my ears frost-bitten and my feet so much benumbed with the cold, that I thought I should never again recover the use of them. My father asked me if I felt satisfied with my frosty experience, and I replied affirmatively, and in addition said I never again desired to renew this misnamed amusement. At the expiration of a week we departed for New York, and fixed ourselves in a retired and small hotel, frequented by foreigners, just off Broadway, for the winter.

'And now, my dear friend, I will give you a breathing space. May good angels and the saints in heaven guard you. JULIAN.

'P. S. I forgot to inform you that the letter of the Montinis was confided to a particular hand, and that caused the unfortunate delay, — alas! what a sad and melancholy mischance for me — otherwise —— But I will not trouble you with my sorrowings for things beyond recall. Yours,

JULIAN.'

CHAPTER XLIII.

'As o'er the mountain's snowy height,
In bright Apollo's beams arrayed,
So flowed her golden tresses light,
And down her spotless vesture strayed.'
LORENZO DE MEDICIS.

'WE remained in New York one year. Ah! my dearest benefactor! I would that it had been erased from my life, for it was the precursor of my misfortunes. By why do I use such a mild term? — crimes should be the word. In that city I first began to abandon the external rites of my church; matins were altogether too early for my newly acquired habits of idleness; then I neglected confession, passing my time so recklessly, I cared not to avow it; so one bad thing followed another, and my downfall was terrible. I dared not look within myself, or on my mother's miniature which I ever carried next my heart; it should have been my ægis and safeguard, but it was not, and I became, in the end, afraid to look at it. I beheld a frown upon her lovely brow. Conscience makes such cowards of us all.

'One day, in our hotel a man, who had lately been quite friendly with my father, applied to him a sadly opprobrious epithet, and, although he was much older, and vastly stronger than myself, I was able, so violent was my indignation, to knock him down. Judge of my great astonishment, when my father actually reproached me for so doing; for he was living in profound retirement, and wished not his name, or that of any one who belonged to him, to appear before the public. I had reason, afterwards, to know that he had paid quite a large sum of money to hush up this adventure of mine.

'I liked not New York; there was too much noise and too little pleasure for me. I heard some music, and now and then went to the theatres with the foreigners in our hotel. At first, I had money in plenty; my father was never niggardly; what he had won he spent freely, but in a few months his luck had apparently changed, and he said fortune no longer smiled, and that he would shortly leave the city. He soon departed, taking me with him. We went to Philadelphia — I liked that place no better; for, if New York was too bustling and noisy, "the home of brotherly love" was altogether too quiet for my taste. But I have no right to criticise; for I knew no one in either place, and, as there is so little amusement in this country, compared with the enjoyment we derive from pictures, statues, and the fine arts generally abroad, if a stranger has no circle into which he can enter, he must dislike all the cities equally.

'We remained in Philadelphia a few months, and then came to Boston. My father took a furnished apartment, mean and comfortless, in an obscure part of the city, and was careful not to appear too much in public. Boston being so much smaller than New York, he was very much more careful of avoiding recognition, though I am sure it would have been impossible for even his own mother to have known him under the disguise of beard, moustache and imperial, he so resembled an Italian in every thing. At any rate, he seemed very much afraid of being known; he had commanded me, on my arrival in America, to call myself Julian Paul, and that was my name ever after.

'Once settled here, he told me he had supported me in idleness already too long, and I must forthwith begin to work. This I was very ready to do, and, having found a scholar here and there, I gave lessons in Italian, singing, and the guitar. Amongst these pupils were the two brothers

Sanderson; they were the only persons who were really kind to me; they treated me like a gentleman, and appreciated my acquisitions in other things beside my mere lessons; for this I was abundantly grateful. I fell into a habit of passing many hours with them at each lesson, and, in that way, they came to speak my own delicious tongue very well; for their music, you well know how it prospered. In our conversations, your family had always the largest part; Charley never tired of chaunting its praises, and Gerald indulged his brother in listening sometimes attentively, in which I joined until it became the whole dream of my life to behold the beautiful and enchanting sisters.

'And then I reached the hateful epoch in my existence. Whatever wrong things I had done before, they all vanish into thin air in comparison with my crime towards you and yours. When I reflect upon the goodness you have manifested to such an offender as myself, I am overwhelmed with gratitude, and, at the same time, astonished at your charity and benevolence toward me. When I remember that you, my dearest friend, have forgiven me, sinner that I am, I regard you as a superiour being; a man, of whom we may say, "Of such is the kingdom of heaven." But I well know you like not to hear your own praises, so I will proceed with my sad tale.

'The week preceding the ball I heard of nothing else; the sisters were actually going, and Charley Sanderson was beside himself with joy. He would dance with them alternately all the evening, and then it would be with Miss Georgy mostly, and so he ran on. Gerald inquiring if he could discern them apart, he was indignant, but this lasted not long; he was so thoroughly good-natured, and he never ceased urging his brother to accompany him likewise. Gerald refused, but Charley persevering in his entreaties, his brother at last, always jesting, declared he would accompany him to the ball, if Miss Barclay could be persuaded to bestow upon him the honour of her hand for the first quadrille. Thus encouraged in his desires, Charley, the night of the long anticipated party, sallied forth in full dress, with a bouquet of violets in his hand; Gerald and I following him.

'Where was then my good genius? where was then the memory of my sainted mother, that it interposed not between me and my desolation and ruin? But I deserved no such boon from Providence. Although I ever bore my mother's presentment next my heart, its potent charm was broken, destroyed; it was no longer my talisman against evil thoughts and evil doings. I followed my young friend, and was lost.

'Charley Sanderson left his brother standing at Mrs. Ashley's door; I crept lightly after him and heard the request he made, and answered, you well know how. He flew down stairs to inform Gerald of the result. I cared little for this, as I knew Gerald had no intention of going to the ball, as, from not frequenting society, he had not even a proper dress for the occasion. I will not attempt to describe my sensations when the dazzling vision of your daughter's supernatural beauty broke upon my bewildered and enraptured senses, and, for some moments, I stood wrapt in oblivion of all in the world beside.

'Suddenly the thought crossed my mind to personate Gerald Sanderson for the moment, — only for the moment, — I had no plan, no project, nothing beyond an insatiable and overpowering desire to speak to the celestial creature who stood before me, radiant in loveliness and beauty. I must speak or die on the spot; she must look upon me once, and that would suffice for a life. I did speak, and from that hour was a lost man. I closed not my eyes all that night; I railed madly against my adverse fortune that forbade me to enter the lists with her admirers; I envied the dear Charley, and despised Gerald for his indifference, and walked my room in a species of hallucination. Here was the true Leonore! I had sought her for aye, and now she was found. Ah! thought I, could my companions, at Mr. Hibbert's, see this divine creature, would they not exclaim with me, she is found! our visions are embodied! Then I began to ask myself why I might not win such a treasure, as well as Charley Sanderson. To be sure, there was no money, or family connections that I knew, but this was a country where every man could hope for distinction. Might I but win the guerdon of her smiles, and then every thing else would be easily won, — fame, fortune and prosperity must follow the first great boon; all else would be as naught. This was, indeed, love at first sight; my very heart and soul was filled with it; it pervaded instantaneously my whole system, and from that eventful night, there was nothing in the universe for me, but Georgiana Barclay.

'I loathed my occupations, and above all the lessons at the Sandersons. These I immediately renounced, being unable to listen to Charley's rhapsodies. It appeared to me he had no right or title to mention her peerless name, and my feelings were so ungovernable that I could no longer command myself. The brothers both kindly requested me to remain and teach them, as they appeared to enjoy great pleasure in my society, apart from the advantage they had gained. All this was gracious and polite, but I was obstinately bent upon leaving them, and I said I had not the time, having other things to do more desirable. So you, my best friend, must perceive how I began to sink deeper and deeper in my pit of perdition, when I, who had been taught by my mother to regard the truth as an eternally sacred obligation, thus violated it.

'I sought the object of my passion every where; I followed her to the school; I watched her returning; I scattered flowers in her path, and wrote sonnets to her eyes, her hair, her hands, her feet. There was no folly, conceivable or inconceivable, which I failed not to commit. I serenaded her at night, and, in fact, lived but in her presence during the day. These efforts, in process of time, were successful. She walked with me often; and, one day, I met my father. In the evening, he said to me, "Julian, who was that young girl with whom I saw you walking, this morning?" I liked not to answer, but he commanded me to do so. And when I told him, he said, "You love her, then? — that fair-haired creature!"

' "As my own soul, and better! I would peril my existence to save a hair of her beautiful head."

" 'Do you imagine she would marry you?"

" 'I know not; never having dared to ask her such a momentous question."

'."Do so, then, immediately."

' I fell at his feet in a paroxysm of joy and gratitude, and thanked him a thousand times.

' "Do so," he repeated, "and, she consenting, I will take upon myself to arrange every thing without a possibility of failure. Her haughty, proud mother shall repent in dust and ashes certain passages in her life!"

' I knew not, I asked not wherefore my father should so willingly consent to my union with Miss Barclay, but perceived that he did; and that sufficed nearly to craze my poor brain with excess of happiness.

' My father, however uncommunicative at other times, was not so then; he told me, that the preceding evening he had received a letter from Florence, bringing the glad intelligence of a fortune for me. A distant relative of my sainted mother had died, and bequeathed lands and money to her child, and it became absolutely necessary that we should depart immediately, as other heirs proposed disputing my rights. He furthermore added, that if I did not secure the object of my adoration before my departure, I should infallibly lose her. He said this could be effected by a civil marriage, which, when I returned rich and prosperous, would be solemnized by the rites of my own church, and the young lady's also. My father then informed me, that he had known my course lately, and had thoroughly approved of it from the first: that I must follow his injunctions in word and deed; and that my future prosperity, and even the power of supporting in suitable style the idol of my affections, depended upon my implicit obedience. "For," said he, "her father and mother will be so furiously angry when they learn her marriage, that they will infallibly disinherit her." And my idol, on learning that I must depart instantly, with many tears and sighs consented to become mine. Need I relate the prayers, supplications and entreaties, that this consent cost me, and the many letters I wrote, and the many times I saw her before my happiness was secured!

'She met me on the appointed day, at last; for oftentimes before, the day had been fixed, and she had not appeared, so many were the conflicts she endured before she could persuade herself to this act. We appeared before a magistrate, and were married. As Heaven is my witness, I — who am so near the awful moment of my appearance before the judgment-seat of my Creator — most solemnly swear, that so profound was my respect and love for the fair creature who had confided her destiny to me, I dared not even kiss her hand. We parted that morning, on leaving the house where the marriage was performed, at the door, and I have never seen this object of my idolatry since, and, God knows, never expect do so again. I will not repine; it is but an expiation of my offence. Bitterly have I been punished, and richly do I deserve my fate.

'We sailed the very next day. Our passage was a good one, and we reached Leghorn, and repaired immediately to Florence. There we were received by our lawyers, who were very civil, and had no doubt of our success. My first visit was to my mother's grave, where, casting myself beside her, I bewailed my wickedness and neglect of her admonitions, and prayed for her forgiveness and the welfare of the dear creature, holding the second place in my affections. For, madly as I adored your child, there was never a moment that this mother of mine reigned not in my heart. It seemed even that I loved better and better her memory; and so was it rightly ordered. My last idol has forsaken me, justly enough I concede; but, thank God for his great and enduring mercies, my blessed mother remains to me still!

'Alas, the law's delay! We remained a year awaiting the result of my suit, and at its expiration, were no farther advanced than when we arrived. Then I caught a violent cold, and was confined to my chamber six months — not being permitted by the medical man to cross the threshold of my door — and even after I was what they called convalescent, I was ordered to the baths of Lucca. They said my lungs were very much affected, and that the American climate had weakened them. This was a fact, for, during my residence here, I was never wholly free from catarrhal affections, and, at times, suffered from great pain in my chest. Thus was a second year consumed, and the third entered upon, and still our lawsuit dragged its slow length along. All this time I wrote innumerable letters to your daughter, never desisting, though I never received a single response. This affliction greatly added to my sufferings, and hindered my restoration to health. I was rendered nervous and irritable, and my mind ever dwelling upon her desertion of me, made me very ill, and I made no advances in strength. The dear Montinis, learning my grave illness, came to me and remained a month in Florence. Blessed communion had we on the happy days passed together in my mother's bellissima Roma. When they departed they would fain have taken me with them, but it was absolutely necessary I should remain in Florence. It was a sad parting that! I had a gloomy presentiment I should never see them more; I never shall. I have just now forwarded to them my farewell letter on earth. Tried friends were they to me and mine, and I would not leave this troublous world without giving them some testimony of my affection.

'Many a time and oft I determined to go to America in that third year; but my father said he had no means to send me properly — I being an invalid — and that if your daughter should abandon me as I deserved, no good result would accrue from my presence in a beggared state. And besides, he urged, "You are not in a condition to go; you require all manner of care personally, and if you depart before the lawsuit is settled, I will not undertake to answer for the consequences. Your sole chance for claiming the young lady lies in the full possession of your inheritance."

'My father had a servant who always took my letters to the post. I am now convinced that he carried them to his master, who burned them. Over this we will drop a veil. I wish not to dwell on my unfortunate parent's delinquencies. If your daughter's heart was changed to me, all the outpourings of my passionate and constant affection would have been as naught. At last, our lawsuit was decided in my favour, and I was a rich man. But poor, abjectly poor in spirit and affection, what was gold to me? Less than dross. I had cast my fortunes on the die of her love — that gone, all else was worthless. Why, alas! should I now fear the passage through the dark valley of death, who have made it o'er and o'er again the last three miserable years of a wretched existence! Nevertheless, I resolved to go to America, and I left Florence; but, as I imagined my father might throw obstacles in my way, if he became aware of my intentions, I departed secretly, taking with me very little money, and neglecting to supply myself with letters of credit in my haste and trepidation. On getting to sea, my health recruited, and with this change came hope and trust, and I was better than I had been for a long time. My mind was in such a chaotic state when I left Italy, that I made no more provision for my advent here than a child would have done; I thought of nothing but escaping. This may appear absurd in America, but the power of a parent over his child in Italy is very much greater than here.

From certain indications I had concluded that all means would be used to force me to remain. God knows if I were correct in my opinion. I can hardly bear to write, much less to think of this. I only know my father was powerful, and I was weak, and wish to explain no more.

'And now, my benefactor, my best friend, receive my most heartfelt and deeply-rooted expression of ardent thanks for all your goodness to me. I possess not words wherein to pour forth my gratitude. May the blessing of God and all the saints rest upon your head. Proffer to all the friends who have devoted themselves to me my reiterated thanks, and to one and all my sincere love.

'With profound respect, your devoted JULIAN.'

CHAPTER XLIV.

'I lov'd thee once, I'll love no more,
Thine be the grief as is the blame;
Thou art not what thou wast before,
What reason I should be the same?'

ANONYMOUS.

If any thing could have augmented Mr. Barclay's love for the object of his care and devotion, these letters would have effected it; but he felt this was impossible. The childlike simplicity, the affectionate nature, the delicacy and nobleness of character developed in them was truly captivating. The deep and heartfelt penitence manifested by Julian Seaton for his derelictions from the paths of virtue, commanded his sympathy and respect, and he wept over the touching and affecting recital of his short life with deep and abiding sorrow. Mr. Barclay appreciated to its fullest extent the delicate manner in which the young man had treated the relation in which he stood to himself, never adverting to his claim as kinsman to Mrs. Barclay, or son-in-law to himself; never touching upon Georgiana, except when unavoidable, and then so respectfully and deferentially.

After reading the missives twice, he took them to his brother, and he having perused them, declared that both Mrs. Barclay and her daughter would be stony-hearted wretches, if, after reading them, they should refuse to visit Julian Seaton. Mr. Richard also thought that Mr. Barclay should remind his wife of the relationship existing between herself and her cousin. 'When she sees,' said he, 'that Julian has been more sinned against than sinning, she will relent: I trust to her own noble spirit to recognise its fellow in that of her relative.' Accordingly, Mr. Barclay entreated his wife to read Julian's confessions, which she consented to do very readily at her husband's earnest request. Thus it appeared that Mr. Barclay had been wrong in believing her prejudices against the father would influence her feelings towards the son, and was much gratified by the facts.

Mrs. Barclay was inexpressibly affected, and felt that not a moment was to be lost; so she laid down the packet and went immediately to her cousin. Julian was overjoyed to receive her; their interview proved most satisfactory and interesting, and Mrs. Barclay from that day took her place at his bedside with his other friends, for his strength began to fail so rapidly that he could no longer sit up.

'Ah!' said Mr. Richard one day to his sister, 'I wish I had never known the dying creature; he has wound himself so completely around my heart that I cannot bear to think of our parting,' and as he pronounced these words, the big tears rolled down his cheeks. This was an unparalleled degree of emotion for a man who despised all demonstration. 'Ah!' he resumed, when he had conquered this ebullition of sensibility, of which he was greatly ashamed, 'this is the miscreant! caitiff! that I have so many a time and oft execrated. If I but learn a lesson of forbearance and charity from him, I shall have become myself a better man. The poor darling fellow! how I pity him!' And most true was it that the humility and strong religious faith of the suffering Julian Seaton had produced a remarkable effect upon Mr. Richard Barclay, and that the gentleness and patience of the dying youth had done more than any thing else in the world, to mollify the asperities of a man who prided himself upon their possession. The daily intercourse with such a being had shed its balmy influence over his spirit, and had a beneficial effect upon him. A nature must be callous indeed, that can remain in communion with such virtues as adorned the character of the invalid, to whom he was devoting hours every day of his life, and not receive a real and lasting advantage.

Mrs. Barclay had presented the packet of letters to her daughter, with a request that she would read it. She consented, and her mother did not again see her for a day; Georgiana requesting to be left alone, no one intruded upon her privacy. The next morning Georgiana begged to see her mother in her own room. Mrs. Barclay found her calm and composed, but looking as if she had greatly suffered. Georgy returned the letters, and addressing her said, 'I have been, my dear mother, endeavouring all night to gain power from on high to pass through the ordeal which awaits me in this interview. God in his mercy grant me strength to be able to impart to you my final resolution. You have educated me, my blessed mother, in a sacred regard for truth. How I have rewarded all your assiduous teachings and tender care, you alas! too well know. In one instance I forfeited my right to your confidence, and that first lapse from virtue has coloured my whole destiny, destroyed the happiness of my beloved family, and marred my father's irreproachably honourable name. That I have been bitterly, severely, and justly punished, is most true; for, from my first deviation from rectitude, I have never enjoyed one moment of serenity or peace; my life has been a dreary blank. Even the angelic goodness which I have felt in my inmost soul, in the forbearance exhibited by my adored father and yourself towards me, has increased my misery. I deserved it not, ungrateful child that I am!'

Mrs. Barclay was amazed at this outbreak in her usually so calm and collected daughter. She had flattered herself that time, with healing on its wings, had performed its wonted good work; but now, alas! she discovered that the heart was bleeding still.

'My child, my child!' interposed Mrs. Barclay, 'apply not, I conjure you, such terrible epithets to yourself, for my sake, for your father's, — cease, I pray you.'

'Mother,' resumed Georgiana, 'I will try to be composed, and endeavour to still the beatings of my overcharged heart while I reveal to you my fixed resolution. I will not see Julian Seaton; I have long, long ceased to love him; another has supplanted him in my affections. Neither am I sure that I can even dignify with the name of love the ungovernable fancy I experienced in my childish days, for my boy-lover; at any rate it is now, and has been for years, completely extinguished by his treachery. My presence in Julian Seaton's sick room will be of no avail; I can carry with me no consolation. He full well knows I have forgiven him, and with that assurance must rest contented. I had thought that the depths of my soul could never be again stirred, the calmness of my mind disturbed, and had schooled myself to bear the cross I had made for myself; but such, it appears, is not to be my destiny. The flood-gates of my pent-up feelings are once more destroyed, and the last night has been to me an excess of agony. I am disabused of the consolatory illusion that a certain degree of serenity had fallen upon me; and awake to find that intense suffering is henceforth to be my lot. I repeat, I cannot behold Julian Seaton; no good can possibly accrue to him or to me from the interview. I feel that I could never endure it. I may be mistaken, but I believe all the love I bore Julian is gone forever. When I make to you the confession, my mother, that I have placed my affections elsewhere, it is with no intention of ever doing more than making this revelation of the state of my feelings, which has, in truth, been now torn rudely from me by force of circumstances. I shall never marry; I have vowed a vow to devote the rest of my days to you and my father; it is the least thing I can do in return for your kindness to me. When I reflect that no reproach has ever passed your lips or his to your erring child; that no sign has ever been made by which I have had occasion even to infer that my sad misconduct was remembered, I am overwhelmed with gratitude for the kindness I have received at your hands. God knows how I have prayed for strength to bear the semblance of cheerfulness in your presence, and I am overjoyed to find that I have been successful.

'Now, my mother, I will confide to you the possessor of my true affections. You will probably not be surprised when I mention Gerald Sanderson. I know that he loves me. Of his ignorance of my interest in him I am just as perfectly convinced, and in that state he will ever remain. I shall never marry him. No woman, I think, could have remained insensible to such chivalrous devotion, and such affection so respectfully demonstrated. I know that he has been defending — I wish I could say — my fair fame for years. I know he adores me, but I have other duties more holy, more important, and I lay my affection for him, a holocaust on my parental altar. In no way can I better show my sincere and deep-felt penitence.'

Mrs. Barclay tenderly embraced her child. She entered into no argument then in the overwrought state of her daughter's feelings touching Gerald, but trusted to time. She knew that Julian's life-sands were fast ebbing away, and that Georgy would be emancipated, for in that light she was constrained to believe that her daughter would regard his departure. She had heard her solemnly declared that she would never recognise 'the deceiver;' would never live with him; that she forgave him; and more could not be demanded of her, and the mother knew that her child's decision was unalterable. Mrs. Barclay, when she looked upon the radiant creature before her, was amazed as the sternness of her nature developed itself, and the fixedness of her purpose was brought to light by adverse circumstances.

On repeating this conversation to her husband, he shared her astonishment, that one apparently so gentle should be so wondrous firm. 'Ah!' said he, 'I tremble for poor Gerald Sanderson;' in which feeling Mrs. Barclay thoroughly sympathized.

On Georgiana's decision being made known to Julian Seaton he submitted, and, declaring it to be but another penance inflicted upon him for his sins, never again resumed the subject. Mr. Richard was terribly incensed, and declared he would give his niece 'a bit of his mind,' but was dissuaded from his purpose by the entreaties of his amiable wife, who was always a peace-maker.

A few days closed the earthly career of Julian Seaton. To the last, he was overflowing with love and gratitude to his friends. After a violent fit of coughing, they raised him in his bed. He had just sufficient strength left to place his arm around Mr. Barclay's neck, and on his fostering bosom, breathing the names of Georgiana and his mother, he expired. The good Catholic priest had been with him the whole day, and just as the shades of evening gathered round, the youthful spirit departed, having been cheered to the last moment by religion and friendship. The funeral ceremonies were performed in the Catholic church, all Mr. Barclay's family attending, and all the friends who had solaced and comforted the sufferer during his illness.

In a short time Gerald Sanderson waited upon Mr. Barclay with Julian Seaton's will. It appeared that it had been executed a month before his decease, and that he had devised two thousand dollars a-piece to his Church, Mr. Richard Barclay, Gerald Sanderson and his brother, Robert Redmond, the Montinis and Captain Williams; the residue of his fortune being equally divided between his father and Mr. John Barclay. In a codicil appended to this document, he requested that his body might be sent to Florence and laid by the side of his mother's. Mr. Barclay, his brother, and Gerald Sanderson were appointed executors.

Mr. Barclay's first wish was to resign his portion altogether, but the delicacy of the arrangement disclosed itself. Julian had not even mentioned his daughter's name, had never claimed her as his wife, and in this, his dying testament, had preserved the same silence; still he had, in all human probability, wished her to inherit his patrimony, and being assured she would never accept it from himself, had adopted this plan of securing it to her. Mr. Barclay becoming convinced of this fact, from learning certain conversations that Julian had held with Gerald and Robert, determined to receive the property and settle it upon Georgiana.

When Julian's testamentary dispositions were mâde known to Mr. Richard Barclay, he declared his intention of proceeding to Italy with the remains of Julian Seaton, and placing them by the side of a mother whom he so idolized. 'For, besides,' said he, 'loving the poor fellow as if he were my own son, it is worth a man's while to make a pilgrimage to the tomb of a woman who had inspired such love and devotion in her child's bosom ; she must have been a rare creature indeed ! '

Mr. Barclay was much pleased with this plan, and immediately sought for Captain Williams, who was just then about to proceed to the Mediterranean in a barque of his own. The accommodations were excellent, all being new and fresh, and to these Mr. Barclay added every imaginable luxury for his brother and wife ; she being entirely willing to accompany her husband on his pious mission.

Captain Eliathan Williams, whose grief had been more audibly expressed at the funeral than that of any other person, was rejoiced to fulfil the last injunctions of his young friend. So every thing being arranged, Mr. Richard Barclay, with his wife, sailed for Leghorn, and as they stood on the deck of their good vessel, the shores of their native land receding from their sight, they beheld their affectionate friends greeting them with cheering signals. And these friends, as they wended their way back sadly to their homes, looked upon the events of the last few months as a tale that had been told, both pleasant and mournful. Pleasant, that they had possessed the will and the power to create an atmosphere of love and devotion around the departing days of their young friend; and melancholy, that they had just beheld his remains borne swiftly away by the pretty argosy then trimming its white canvas to the wind in their own beautiful harbour. They thought of Richard Barclay, and dwelt with intense satisfaction on his noble devotion to Julian Seaton, renouncing his new home, where, grumbler as he was, and ever would be, he confessed himself to enjoy pure and unalloyed happiness; and giving up all his newly acquired comforts to cross the Atlantic, in an inclement season, for love of the poor youth who had entwined himself around his warm heart. And yet when they mused upon all the endearing and excellent qualities, and the positive fascination of Julian Seaton, who had seemed to scatter 'love-powders' around him, they marvelled not at the sacrifice. They prayed that prosperous gales might waft the high-souled man to his destination, and in due time restore him and his charming wife to their own pleasant home.

Mr. Barclay returned home, sadly missing his brother, who, whatever his minor faults might be, was a daily blessing to him. It often happens that absence, like death, swallowing up all the little discrepancies of character, leaves nothing behind save its excellences, the defects being completely forgotten in the sad blank occasioned by the departure of a relative or friend, beloved despite his faults. The French proverb, that the absent are always in the wrong, is hardly a correct one.

That evening was a particularly gloomy one in Mr. Barclay's family. Georgy had hardly been visible for a month, and Mrs. Meredith, every time she looked upon uncle Richard's empty chair, felt her eyes suffused with tears. Mrs. Sanderson was ever pretexting some excuse to slip away from her family to minister to her suffering sister, so that the burthen of making things even apparently comfortable laid upon the husbands of the ladies, who were also quite unequal to the task. Mr. Barclay retired early, having lately passed many sleepless nights, and the little party was dispersed.

CHAPTER XLV.

'I could forgive the miserable hours
His falsehood, and his only, taught my heart;
But I cannot forgive that for his sake
My faith in good is shaken.'

L. E. L.

MR. BARCLAY'S family had resumed its usual routine of existence, chequered as it so lately had been; this was a great comfort to him. Several of its members had received pleasant letters from Mrs. Richard Barclay, full of renewed interest and intense satisfaction in her present visit to Italy, and very amusing recitals of their uncle's sayings and doings; but nothing from him, except a few hurried notes when he reached Florence, respecting his melancholy errand and other things. He had, however, long promised to write a ponderous letter.

Some time elapsed, but at last it came. Now an epistolary correspondence was Mr. Richard's horror; not that he disliked receiving agreeable missives, for who does? He loathed the trouble of answering them, but nobody was more anxious for the arrival of the mails than was he. On the much desired, thickly folded packet being opened in full conclave by Mrs. Barclay, she read:

'ROME, ——.

'I wrote you, my dear brother, from Florence. giving you a short account of our safe arrival there, and the laying in the tomb, by the side of his mother, of our beloved Julian. God bless his sweet memory, and may I ever preserve it as freshly in my heart as now. I could write many things on this subject, but you know I abhor what is usually called sentiment, and shall leave all that sort of things to my wife.

'So here we are in the "Eternal City," which the dear boy loved so well. I have seen the Montinis, and paid them their legacy; whether I get mine or not, will signify nothing to me. They are not rich, and two thousand dollars is a vast deal of money here. They received the sum with floods of tears. My wife is enchanted with them, and a great intimacy has sprung up between them.

'The sight-seeing here,—Oh! how heartily wearied I am of it!—it is as eternal as the city itself; and, as we have a large carriage, Fanny offers two places to the Montinis in it, and they accompany us every where, and are excellent guides, and then they usually return to dine and pass the evening with us. These people have told me many disgraceful anecdotes of that rascal, Paul Seaton, and I am now more rejoiced than ever that I refused to receive him in Florence, and insisted that all communications between us should pass through the hands of my lawyers,—'tis the only way to treat such cattle. Whatever humbug he may write to you, answer him never a word, he is wholly beneath the notice of a gentleman, and is universally despised wherever he is known, as a dishonoured gambler and miserable creature. I absolutely sicken when I think of his wickedness, deceit, and treachery to his own child, the dear angel now in heaven. How he came to possess such a son, Heaven only knows. The goodness of our lost one, I think, must have descended from his mother; Spurzheim always held to this doctrine in similar cases. At any rate, never had poor child a worse father.

'I believe the money is all safe, thanks to the probity of the Italian lawyers; for Paul Seaton has tried hard enough to grasp the whole, but quite unsuccessfully. Let us now drop his name forever; 'tis melancholy to think that the earth is cumbered with such wretches.

'Nothing can surpass my wife's overboiling enthusiasm touching Rome, save her indefatigable industry; she works hard all day, and talks all the evening with a host of virtuosos, literary people, and artists. I leave them all to her, — you know she likes to ask questions, — and confine my intercourse to some sensible John Bulls, — capital fellows! who agree with me thoroughly. Now, it must be confessed I am every day victimized, and so are they by their wives, and that's a great comfort to me; for Fanny almost drives me distracted with her confounded sight-seeing friends. We are taken by a squad of antiquaries and solemnly informed, one day, that such and such ruins bear such and such names, and all manner of learned authorities quoted to back these all-important assertions; the very next morning comes another cohort of seers, and, carrying us to the identical spots we visited but yesterday, tell us, most emphatically, that the preceding set were all wrong, and we must unlearn our lesson and spell out another. I wish you could but hear these two contending parties squabble in the evenings at Fanny's tea-table; it's glorious fun; they do every thing but come to blows; and what hinders them, I and my chosen friends, the English, can never tell. Somehow the natives of the white cliffs of Albion and we Americans do fraternize better together in foreign parts than other nations, so we get together in corners and enjoy the sport amazingly.

'You well know what my wife is. If she were to set up housekeeping in the desert of Arabia the Stony, she would have a crowd round her. I'm not in the least jealous of the antiquaries, they might be set up to frighten crows; and the artists and others are all well-behaved enough; so if this kind of thing amuses her, I'm content and never object. But what I do rebel against forcibly is, the being obliged to go sight-seeing, every hour in the daylight. Sometimes she very reluctantly lets me off, but she thinks that, as I was never here before, I must not miss a single columbarium; and down we go into such poky-holes and corners as I shall not attempt to describe, and I, for one of the party, come up again to the blessed light of the sun never a whit the wiser. Then we stand up to our knees in mud and filth, our teeth chattering with the cold, even in bellissima Roma, before magnificent buildings which once had superb flights of broad marble steps to their entrances; now all have disappeared. There we speculate upon their sunken condition, the why and the wherefore, and all sorts of theories are broached and disputed, of course. The only sensible remark I have heard made on this subject, came from a rollicking Irishman, who turning to me, probably from sympathy, asked what was the use of all this bother. 'Nothing so easy,' said he, 'as to answer, Every thing grows in this world — why shouldn't the earth?' I leave you to fancy what contemptuous looks he got from Fanny's friends for this profane speech. Nobody ever seems to be cold, but poor I, in these explorations of dungeons, under-ground churches, and ice-houses of palaces and galleries. I presume enthusiasm keeps these idolaters warm; for my part, if I had any, it would all ooze out of my frozen fingers. I try hard for a holiday, and now and then succeed, but Fanny is generally inexorable. We have a solemn looking man of all work who cooks our dinners amongst other things, and excellent they are; and, as my rule is not precisely what my saucy niece, the Dolly, — I humbly beg her pardon, Mrs. Meredith, — predicted it would be, IRON, I only beg and pray that I may return home in due season for our repasts. And this, to do Fanny justice, is generally accorded. I think I never, in my natural life, enjoyed a dinner as I do in Rome, — tell it not in Gath; worn and wearied, it is the very best thing I have in the twenty-four hours, — such beef and half-dried grapes! All this is shockingly heretical, I know, but you entreated me to write, and so here goes for the truth and nothing else. I would not allow Fanny to see this letter for worlds, as she begins to fancy I'm getting round famously to the true faith, and would not be at all gratified at its contents.

'We shall go from here to Naples, where another inevitable campaign of sight-seeing awaits me, — pity me, my brother; and then, presto! to Paris. Once there, I am on my own hunting-grounds and free as air, having lived there so long; and, as my wife has also enjoyed the signal advantage of sojourning in the capital where mortals can dispense with happiness, she will not tease me to death to go trooping about with her. A short stay will, I most devoutly hope, suffice for Fanny to effect the ordering of forty-four dresses, and to fill up the catalogue of her offerings at the shrines of her innumerable friends on the other side of the Atlantic; and then, thrice blessed news! we shall make our way out to America, where, thank Heaven! there is nothing to be seen.

'God bless you, my dear brother, and all your belongings. Fanny sends her best love; kiss your wife and daughters for their old uncle; and box Johnny's ears, — I dare say he merits punishment for some mischief or other.

'Yours faithfully, RICHARD BARCLAY.'

This characteristic epistle created a vast deal of amusement for the assembled listeners, as uncle Richard's fascinating grumbling always did. His perseveringly untiring efforts to make himself appear much worse than he was, were somehow never very successful. In his short notice of Julian they recognised their eccentric relative's weakness.

'I'm thoroughly convinced,' said Mrs. Meredith, 'that my dear uncle Dick is the most henpecked husband in all Christendom, and will finish by earning the title of "Goodman Richard."'

'But I thought,' said her father, 'you had predicted precisely the reverse, some time since.'

'I know I did,' she replied; 'but I'm not so ignorant now as I then was,' at the same time bestowing a rather sly look upon her husband.

'Aunt Fanny,' said Mrs. Charles Sanderson, 'perfectly understands her husband's character; certainly his wooing was of the most mysterious nature; nobody can deny that. When I think of uncle Richard as a Benedict, I fancy I'm dreaming, and yet how harmoniously he and his wife live together.'

'All nature's difference makes all nature's peace,' said Mrs. Barclay.

'My brother is an excellent fellow in the main,' said Mr. Barclay; and he looked around for Georgy, but she had disappeared.

The mention of Julian had produced such sad and varied emotions, that she was unable to bear the scrutiny of even her own family. There were moments when he appeared to her in the recesses of her memory, bearing the old guise of 'the first love,' 'the hallowed form,' and she became unable to controul her emotions; then the impassable barrier raised by his treachery and falsehood, her own desolation, the years of shame and suffering she had endured, assumed colossal proportions, and she seemed to sink completely under them. But worst of all, her trust in mankind had been shaken, that faith so infinitely dear to youth. It had been, she thought, her duty to cast all remembrance of her young lover from her, and this one word duty creates a wonder-working effect with our New England women. It is heard all too often, there is no doubt, and as often monstrously misapplied, and also falsely embodies a vast many things irrespective of the quality represented, making these women more respectable than loveable; but it has a great and beneficial effect upon their characters, when it is adoped as an important part of their natures, in the spirit and not the letter.

Georgiana had cast off the memory of Julian Seaton, and another had usurped his place in her heart; and so firmly was he rooted as never to be displaced. Yet would the shadow of the lost one even pass between the reality, and produce moments of acute agony; then would she retire from her own beloved circle, and pray for strength to bear the heavy burthen of her sorrow. These were sad and wearisome conflicts; they had been of rare recurrence before his death, — that melancholy event had renewed them. She was not always sure if she had been right in refusing to see him; but she had believed such an act would have been hypocritical in the extreme if she divulged not the change in her sentiments, and what might such a terrible revelation have produced? Even instant death, for aught she knew to the contrary. Her sincere forgiveness had been freely proffered and eagerly accepted, and Julian died ignorant that another had usurped his place in her bosom. She felt that this secret might remain undiscovered to her husband, so long as she absented herself, but once in his presence, it must be revealed. This young creature was blamed and criticised for not appearing at the deathbed of her husband, accused of insensibility, of hardness of heart by those who, unaware of the secret springs of feeling by which she was actuated, sat in judgment on her conduct. Even her own mother had seemed, at first, to wish she would make the effort, until, in pouring forth all the agony of her soul into her sympathizing bosom, her daughter had convinced her that she could not behold Julian Seaton without making the dreaded confession. And such was Mrs. Barclay's horror of duplicity that she felt obliged to concede that her child was right, for no one could foresee, she well knew, what the consequences might be of the disclosure.

From the moment of her husband's decease, Georgiana's mind had insensibly gained a reasonable degree of composure, which she was hardly willing to acknowledge even to herself, but there were various causes combining to produce this result, — her own strong will, all hateful mystery dispelled, her own fair fame re-established, the knowledge that her youthful choice had been neither low nor mean, and, more than all besides, Julian's ties of kindred with her mother. She could never forgive herself, or wish any one else to do so, the concealment she had practised towards her excellent parents; but she hoped to make a sufficient atonement to them in devoting her whole existence to their welfare. Mrs. Barclay had also abstained from seeing Julian Seaton. She dreaded the many questions he would inevitably ask of her; she had pardoned his treachery, but she no more desired an interview with him than did her daughter. She knew he was surrounded by affectionate friends and countless luxuries, and this satisfied her; but when she had once perused his letters, she relented, and watched over him tenderly.

When Mr. Barclay's daughters were married, he had settled on each fifty thousand dollars, and did the same for Georgiana. The interest of this money was paid quarterly, and, as she had few expenses, her charitable nature revelled in the power of alleviating distress and dispensing her wealth freely; and, as she had ever possessed the signal advantage of an admirable example in her mother in this way, her bounties were most judiciously bestowed. She was, in fact, a well drest 'Sister of Charity,' going about doing good in an unostentatious manner, secretly and wisely; she had been schooled in affliction, and had thereby acquired habits of self-controul; she had become thoroughly mistress of herself. To the world Georgiana was cheerful, and apparently happy.

In process of time, how soon or how late, need hardly be narrated, Gerald Sanderson preferred his suit, and poured forth his long-concealed love, his faith and devotion to the woman to whom he had vowed his life. Georgiana received this declaration, which she had so long foreseen awaited her, with great apparent calmness, thanked him sincerely for the expression of his affections, but firmly and decidedly rejected them. Beside himself with grief, he urged her to reconsider her refusal, to take pity on his desolation, and in such a noble and loyal manner as almost destroyed the composure which veiled the sacrifice she made. But it was made, and he was informed that they could never meet again, except as friends; that he must cherish no hopes or aspirations of any other nature; none must exist.

Gerald departed, in the perfect assurance that Georgiana felt completely indifferent towards him, and that no efforts of his could ever effect a change in her feelings. And she! — she flew to her own chamber, and, locking the door, threw herself on her bed and wept floods of bitter tears. The sacrifice was made, and he was gone, and forever. Lost to her, and by her own free-will, the man who had devoted himself to her cause in all the spirit of chivalry and love! Lost! lost!

It was but a short interval of the luxury of grief that this young creature permitted herself to indulge. Soon she arose, bathed her eyes in pure water, removing all traces of her tears, and, nerving herself to the appointed task of suffering in silence, she re-appeared in her own domestic circle, — the same Georgiana who was the centre of its attraction, the idol of her father, and the source of infinite happiness to her mother; and by dint of imparting felicity to those around her she became imbued with a portion of its pervading essence, even herself. One other trial awaited her in the dismissal of Mr. Robert Redmond; but this was as naught in comparison with the preceding one. She had but to impart to him the utter impossibility of succeeding in his pretensions to her favour, and her thanks for his good-will, — mere forms of speech and courtesy, leaving but slight traces behind of their passage. Verily woman's destiny is to suffer, and she must nerve herself nobly to the task, and remember,

> 'Man's a king, his throne is Duty,
> Since his work on earth began.'

CHAPTER XLVI.

> 'Think'st thou that this love can stand,
> Whilst thou still dost say me nay?
> Love unpaid does soon disband,
> Love binds love as hay binds hay.' MARVELL.

SHORTLY after the rejection of Mr. Robert Redmond's suit by Mrs. Georgiana Seaton, his father was seized with a violent attack of paralysis, occasioned by intense application and excessive hard work. This had been preceded by several faintings in court, which had greatly alarmed his son, and he had earnestly remonstrated with him on the mode of his life, and entreated him to give himself some relaxation; but he heeded not his child or his wife, who was also induced by Robert's urgent request to arouse herself sufficiently to do the same.

Mr. Redmond insisted that if he ceased working he should inevitably die, and that he would infinitely prefer to expire in his harness than pass his days in idleness. On one occasion during an illness, he was absolutely placed in bed by his medical attendant, and ordered to keep perfectly quiet; he was found several hours afterwards with twenty-four volumes of law books all arranged about his bed, and with pencil and paper taking notes. Robert saw full well that things must inevitably take their course; that his father being incorrigible, all the efforts he could make would be fruitless, and so it eventually proved.

Mr Redmond rallied after his illness, but being again attacked, was found one morning dead in his bed, with his twenty-four friends, the law books, surrounding him; in this case they proved his worst enemies. Mrs. Redmond received the intelligence of her husband's decease with great calmness; busied herself immensely for her with her mourning; was extremely particular touching the width of her crape and the quality of her bombazine, and altogether bore her widowhood discreetly. She sat with the newspapers in her hands, reading for hours their heralding forth of the great and good qualities of the deceased, and had a sort of dim consciousness that she must herself have been very blind to so many excellences.

A learned man was Mr. Redmond, a great chamber council advocate, and nothing else; he had neither been a good husband, father, nor friend; his life had been passed amid folios, to the extinction of all the good qualities he might have possessed when he began his prosperous career. Not one half hour in the twenty-four had he given to his family. God had raised up for it in the person of his son, Robert Redmond, a friend and judicious adviser, and this had been a signal mercy. Many evil consequences had ensued from the father's utter negligence of his duties, which even all the efforts of the son had not been able to avert. It had been a subject of perpetual astonishment to all Robert's friends how he had become the man he was under the circumstances. It sometimes however happens that children, by the very reason of perceiving the bad consequences of mismanagement, or none at all, as in this case, mark out for themselves a totally contrary course, and strictly follow it.

Jane was obstreperous, as she must ever be; but having finally exhausted the first grand ebullition of her grief, she resumed her usual routine of existence as if nothing had occurred; her sister showed much sensibility of a more endearing quality.

Robert Redmond, after judiciously arranging his father's affairs, — for Mr. Redmond, who had executed countless last wills and testaments for his clients, had never found a disposable moment to make one for himself, — then announced his intention of going to Europe immediately for a couple of years, and invited his mother and sisters to accompany him. Mrs. Redmond actually recoiled from her son's proposition with a species of horror; not that she disliked the idea of a change of scene, on the contrary rather desired it, but the exertion she must make to get herself in readiness! How was she ever to put in order her travelling trunks and boxes? This question she propounded to herself fifty times a day, and, at last, as a finishing resource, sent for Mrs. Barclay. That lady immediately flew to her assistance, well comprehending her inanimate friend's dilemma, and found Mrs. Redmond who had made up her mighty mind to go, with all her new and lugubrious wardrobe laid on the chairs, tables, bed and floor. She turned as Mrs. Barclay entered, and in most imploring accents demanded of her how she was ever to get all those things into all those trunks. Mrs. Barclay having cleared a way for herself, asked for Mrs. Redmond's maid, who appearing, declared her mistress had asked her the same question over and over again, and that she knew no more than the babe unborn how to answer her. Mrs. Barclay then assured the proprietor of this grand display of grief, that she must decide to leave at least one half behind, which she sorrowingly consented to do, and then all things being arranged, the packing was satisfactorily completed.

Mrs. Redmond and her family sailed, her valedictory speech being, 'that but for the immense exertions of my kind neighbour we should never have been able to depart.' Robert, being unable to trust himself with another interview with Georgiana, took an affectionate leave of the rest of the family.

They passed the winter in Paris, and Georgy had the extreme satisfaction to learn that her lover had replaced her image in his breast by admitting another of great beauty and attraction, he having met in that gay capital a young American girl from Baltimore, fallen suddenly and desperately in love with her, and married her, to the great delight of his mother and sisters.

No passion, however eternal it may promise to be, will ever survive the impossibility of a return; there may have been exceptions, but they are very rare and uncommon; there must be a ray of hope. Mrs. Robert Redmond had a young cousin, a small, pale, quiet, unpretending individual, who never raised his voice above a whisper, and was besides excessively shy and nervous, — he was travelling with her and her mother for his health. This gentleman, who rejoiced in the imposing patronymic of Dionysius Hornblower, a name which in nowise designated his feeble character, was nearly as helpless as a child. He possessed a good fortune, which he had neither spirit nor taste to spend, his whole time being in fact occupied with looking after his immense variety of ailments, imaginary and otherwise. He carried with him always a medicine chest, which was not however very cumbrous, he being a homœopathist; but as it took him a comfortable while to count the infinitesimal doses in the course of the day, and served to kill time, it was generally useful on that account.

Di Hornblower, as he was called for shortness, — some people added Miss, — rarely ventured forth until mid-day, and always returned in excellent season for his dinner, which he ate with an enormous appetite at five of the clock, all the while declaring stoutly he had none whatever. After a short nap he always awoke, and asked his aunt and cousin, — 'What shall I do with myself until twelve o'clock to-night?' They invariably replied, 'Go to the theatre;' but he answered that he did not understand the French language; so he found the theatre was a horrid bore. Then they would suggest the opera, to which he responded that he detested music; they urged that his medical man had ordered him to amuse himself, — a little opera, a little theatre, a few balls, being the prescription. Di was not to be persuaded, so they recommended some pleasant book, and he averred he could not read at night, his eyes being very weak. So this ceremony regularly occurring every evening, the aunt and cousin were just beginning to declare to each other that, of all the inflictions two poor lone women were ever saddled with, theirs was the most intolerable, when Robert Redmond came, saw, and conquered ; and his gentle sister Jane obligingly took the invalid off their hands, for she married him.

It may be positively asserted that Miss Jane Redmond married Mr. Dionysius Hornblower, for he being much younger than herself, and moreover awfully afraid of her, had apparently never dared to open his lips in her august presence, and would have as soon thought of facing a green dragon as expressing an opinion before her ; besides she was so very tall and he so short. It was true, nevertheless, that little Di had ventured to whisper to his aunt his aversion to Mr. Redmond's sister, 'the ferocious Miss Jane,' and Jane knew this, she having accidentally heard this confidential communication. Whether she incontinently resolved to take him upon the spot in pure opposition, is not positively recorded, but that she possessed herself forthwith of this jewel of high price in quick time, every body was assured by a grandiose ceremony in the way of a wedding, to which all the Americans in Paris were bidden. The bride was all dominant, as usual ; her dress was of white velvet, orange blossoms, and Chantilly lace, becoming in the extreme degree, and was vastly admired ; the breakfast was superb. Mrs. Dionysius Hornblower presided over this magnificent repast in great state ; her little spouse was present, but the guests being intensely occupied in the discussion of Parisian delicacies, were very unobservant of that unobtrusive individual, and only remembered afterwards that he left the table in the middle of the feast, on the plea of slight indisposition, and that the bride elect took no manner of notice of his disappearance.

Mr. and Mrs. Dionysius Hornblower left Paris that day for beautiful Italy, and all the family was vastly relieved of a certain and positive degree of oppression by her absence, and of a vast amount of dullness by that of the bridegroom.

Mary Redmond immediately expanded into a young lady, the absence of her tyrannical sister causing an entire revolution in her habits and feelings ; and the care of her helpless mother devolving upon her, she evinced great good sense and discretion in the discharge of this duty. Mrs. Redmond rejoiced in the change of affairs — and all the more, as she dared not give expression to her feelings — so she lavished upon her youngest daughter a good degree of tenderness. All efforts, agreeable or otherwise, being extremely repugnant to her habits, she made great exertions to prove to her child the value of her attentions, by making her most beautiful presents in jewelry and books, and actually sallied forth alone to purchase them ; and, on the first of these grand excursions, sadly alarmed her daughter by not returning until night. By constant practice she learned to walk a little, but never much admired the exercise ; still, there were so many things to be seen in the streets, that, her attention being diverted from herself, and her mind occupied, she certainly made more progress in pedestrianism than she had ever done before ; but, after all, hers was a snail's pace. She was much pleased with Mrs. Robert Redmond, and though she would have preferred Georgiana Seaton, still she was not insensible to the pretty face and pleasing manners of her new daughter — the more especially, as she proved to be quite a busy person, liking housekeeping very much, and promising to take all care off her hands; and this qualification Mrs. Redmond appreciated much more than all the accomplishments of the blooming bride.

Robert Redmond was extremely glad to perceive that his mother was beginning to use her feet — which heretofore had been of no more use to her than those of Mrs. Chin-Cho-Ling, or any other Chinese lady — and hoped she would continue this salutary habit on returning home. Mary Redmond was not particularly pleased with Parisian society, decidedly thinking it was no sphere for young American girls. Mrs. Robert Redmond had a few French acquaintances, and Mary accompanied her to a beautiful ball, with another family from New York, which consisted of a handsome mother and three good-looking daughters. The latter had ruled and reigned at home — giving entertainments, receiving visits, &c. What was their unbounded disappointment at finding themselves restricted, even before they went, in the arrangement of their dress, but on arriving, being obliged to be carefully seated by the side of their mother, and she invited to dance in preference to themselves! This was, indeed, a new phase of society for them, to which they submitted with very ill grace. The lady, who had still retained a fancy for her dancing days, accepted her invitations, which were quite numerous ; whereas Mary and her companions sat in speechless amazement. At last, they were invited once, and once only. The gentlemen, who figured with them, made no attempts at conversation during the quadrille, and, re-conducting them to their places, left them, and never returned.

After returning to their hotel, Mrs. Robert Redmond and the lady mamma spoke in high terms of the enjoyment they had received that evening; but the young girls solemnly vowed never to make another such sacrifice, and never did. Consequently, Mary Redmond ardently longed for a restoration to her native land and her rights, which she laughingly declared were usurped by Mrs. Robert. To be sure, she had not 'been out' in America, but was extremely well advised of the state of things there. Neither Mrs. Robert nor her friend abstained from enjoying themselves on account of the rebellion of the younger branches, but went wherever they obtained an entrance, insisting they were quite right so to do, it being their *last* chance ; as, on their return home, they would be obliged to have recourse to their disagreeable occupation of holding up the walls once more in matronly meditation, 'fancy free.'

CHAPTER XLVII.

'She says she had a gentleman who came thirty miles to her to hear the relation; and that she told it to a roomful of people at the time.'
WONDERFUL STORY OF ONE MRS. VEAL.

MR. BARCLAY had heard several rumours that his brother had been ill in Rome, but being quite sure that, if there were any danger, Mr. Richard's wife would have advised him of it, he did not mention them to his family. Some time elapsed when glad tidings came, in the shape of a letter from pleasant Aunt Fanny. It was addressed to Mrs. Barclay. She wrote:

'NAPLES, ——.

'We have been here, my dear sister, several weeks, and my time having been very much occupied with the sight-seeing at which my husband rails so heartily, must be my apology for not having written before this; your brother has none other than sheer laziness as his excuse.

'I am sorry to write that my husband was threatened with a fever in Rome, which he ascribes to being carried, or forced, into an underground church by his wife and her friends; but, I assure you on honour that, being tempted by a delicious day, he left his overcoat at home, and thereby contracted a cold, of which he wilfully took no note whatever, until he was obliged to take to his bed, where he remained two or three days. From this cold he recovered very quickly, not having allowed me to enjoy more than one adventure during his illness, which was very cruel; indeed it was this:

'On my arrival at Florence I engaged a Swiss maid, a travelling servant, she having been in Italy several years. I procured an excellent character of her for honesty and other good qualities from an American lady, whom she had served a long while, who, however, added that she was very bad-tempered. We have got on remarkably well together, notwithstanding. I kept house in Rome very pleasantly, and had an agreeable circle around me every evening, my tea being the attraction. Your brother enjoyed those little parties very much, whatever he may please to say to the contrary. One evening, as the company assembled, each person brought intelligence of a murder which had been committed on a jeweller, and, as he was robbed of money, the Romans present stoutly averred that no inhabitant of the Eternal City had perpetrated the deed. They said Romans murdered for jealousy and revenge, but never for money. This produced a discussion, and elicited many interesting stories of all sorts of horrid adventures. When our guests departed, your brother informed me he should have enjoyed the recitals extremely, but for a violent pain in his back and head; this sadly alarming me, I ordered a fire to be made in a chamber, which was at the end of a rather long and narrow corridor, and immediately commenced most vigorous operations with baths, frictions, &c., to which was added a tolerable dose of medicine. The patient grumbled awfully, but I was absolute, and as he really began to improve, he looked upon my proceedings more favourably in the end. Having finished, I ordered Antonio, the cook, to carry his bed and throw it on the floor by the side of my husband, and then left him, with many injunctions to call me, if his master awoke, which, it appears, he did not. It was naturally very late when I retired to my own chamber, and, being much fatigued from my unwonted exertions, I dismissed my maid, as soon as possible, and was shortly in a profound sleep.

'How long this had lasted I am unable to tell, but I awoke

finding myself sitting upright in bed, and staring, in great affright, at the reflection on the wall of the light from a lamp in the adjoining chamber. Now in this room slept my maid, and, as she was a person much given to vociferating and noisy demonstrations on the slightest possible and impossible occasions, I had a dim consciousness that Issaline was not in that room. This feeling became appalling certainty, when sundry stealthy movements, and opening of drawers and trunks were added. I think I never knew what perfect fright was before. I was convinced Issaline was murdered, and in her sleep, for in no other way could the deed have been perpetrated, except in her slumbers, for she would, otherwise, have aroused all Rome with her cries and shrieks.

'The examination of all the corners of the chamber was then made, and I imagined that a person crawled under the bed and dragged out some cumbrous article. If this should be poor Issaline's body!! My blood actually curdled in my veins, — my very hair stood on end with terror, — but I neither shrieked nor groaned; for I well knew how perfectly fruitless would be any effort of that sort, as my husband and Antonio's room was at so great a distance from me, and in my total silence seemed to lie my only security. And there I sat, — it seemed to me an age of torture. All the horrid stories to which I had lent such an attentive ear before I retired to rest, arose before me in a living, moving mass, and passed before my sight like the scenes in an overwrought tragedy on the stage, when the senses being held captive, all is fearful reality, and, palpitating and breathless, naught remained but the certainty of a violent death. At last, the investigation of Issaline's premises seemed to have come to a close, and the footsteps approached my own door. There was doubt and hesitation; the lock was gently, slowly turned. By this time big drops of perspiration were chasing each other rapidly down my cheeks and even arms, and the fearful and horrible click of that lock will live in my memory to my latest hour, — uttering no sound, I fainted dead away.

'From this heavy swoon I was aroused by the opening of my shutters, and a bright sun showed me Issaline. I started up confused, bewildered; my first impressions were that I had experienced a paralyzing nightmare. I sent her to inquire for my husband's state; she returned, reporting a favourable night, and then I said to her, "Did you go out of the house last night, after I retired? I hope not."

'"Oh! no, ma'am, assuredly not; I should never think of such a thing without asking your permission."

'"Then where did you sleep? certainly not in your own room."

'Upon this, out she rushed, and returned bearing aloft in the air a nightgown.

'"Here, ma'am!" screamed she, "this will answer why I did not sleep in that room. Look and see for yourself, how the wicked fleas treated me last night. I could not close my eyes for them, and at last took my bed and placed it on the table in the dining-room, and climbed up into it out of their way, — the abominable imps of darkness!"

'It was impossible to resist this account, backed as it was by the dress, covered, as she declared, with her own blood, — her own blood! I burst into a hearty laugh, which did me a world of good under the circumstances.

'"But," said I, "there was certainly some one in your chamber last night."

'"Oh, no, ma'am!" said she, "not in my room. Antonio's nephew, Domenico, got up in the night with a violent colic. My master has given him some money, and he has gone to the hospital."

'This did not at all satisfy me; I was, more and more, convinced that he had ransacked Issaline's drawers and boxes before he departed. She, however, persisted in thinking him innocent of this charge; "for was he not," she cried, "studying for the church?"

'I went to my husband, found him much better, and related to him my adventure. He evidently did not believe a word of it, but thought I had been excited before going to sleep, and had suffered from a horrid dream. At this, I was rather vexed, but thought I would await his restoration to entire health before I gave him a good scolding for his incredulousness.

'In about two hours I heard terrible shrieks, and flying into Issaline's room, from whence they had proceeded, found her in strong hysterics, wringing her hands and tearing her hair, and declaring she had been robbed of several Napoleons, and amongst them was one given her by her father, many years previous to her leaving home, which she had always preserved as a "lucky penny," and would not have lost for worlds. Indeed, there was no calamity which she did not predict for herself in consequence of her loss, and openly accused Antonio's nephew of the larceny. That worthy, boiling over with rage, declared that his relative was a candidate for the church; that he felt the honour of his family disgraced, and demanded of my husband instant satisfaction. Your brother referred him to me, saying that it was my maid who had committed the offence, — a sly way men always have of getting themselves out of trouble, — and I suppose on that occasion congratulated himself on the possession of a wife; at any rate, I had a hard task to keep the peace, the parties being so very pugnacious. Issaline insisted upon examining my trunks and bureaus, and discovered that a superb gold watch of mine had also disappeared. Things then began to confirm the suspicions I had expressed, and my dream seemed to have taken a tangible form. The watch was of remarkable workmanship and beauty, a present to me, and extremely valuable for the donor's sake, and was also very costly.

'As soon as your brother got out again, I accompanied him to an official's office, to make a statement of my loss, and the gentleman being in bed with a cold, we were invited into his chamber. Such a bed! I really think it was intended to accommodate his whole family, so immense was its size. He was lying in state, the sheets and pillow-cases trimmed with rich lace, the counterpane magnificent, two common wooden chairs and a table completing the furniture. I related my story, and he wrote to the governor of Rome, who ordered a number of the police to search Domenico's house, which was in a village ten miles from the city. Nothing was found. There was in this place one jeweller's shop, and that was searched also ineffectually, so my husband renounced all idea of ever regaining my watch.

'The evening before I left Rome I took Antonio aside, and told him I was convinced that his nephew had stolen my watch; that I knew him to be a very shrewd person, and depended upon him to find it; that a sufficient reward had already been offered, but that he should be additionally paid if the missing article were restored. As to his nephew being a person studying for the church, I did not believe a syllable of the story, for the work of my kitchen was no preparatory step to such an important situation. Antonio talked very loud, but I told him to keep still, and look out sharply after my watch.

'We left Rome the next day, and in six weeks from that time I received my precious watch safe and sound, a long and most grateful epistle from Antonio, and such a quantity of documents from the police officers as was certainly amazing—all respecting the recovery and restoration of my timepiece. Domenico had stolen it, and when he knew we had quitted Rome, he offered it for sale, and Antonio, watching and waiting, pounced upon his prey.

'I must, by way of explanation, just tell you how I came to have such a good view of Domenico's doings in Issaline's chamber. All the doors in our Roman lodgings were covered with green baize, and so shrunken that light and sounds were freely admitted, and they, moreover, were excessively capricious, sometimes remaining shut for a week and baffling all our united efforts to open them, and then no human force could close them. Fortunately for me, it was their shutting up time, and Issaline, when she left her chamber for her dinner-table dormitory, took the key of my door with her. Domenico had somehow, nobody could answer why, taken up his abode in our kitchen, as scullion, under the distinguished patronage of his uncle, and Issaline had found him, on the morning of my adventure, in my chamber, and threatened to broomstick him, she said, for the offence. It is probable he then stole the watch.

'I assure you I was triumphant when I saw my watch, unbelievers being scattered to the winds. I now wish, my dear sister, most solemnly to assert that I have not, even in one solitary instance, invited my husband to accompany me in any "sight-seeing" here, in consequence of his illness in Rome; and desire you will remember that he has never once failed to go with me on all my excursions. I embrace you all, and shall have the happiness to see you shortly.

'Yours in love and affection. FANNY.

'P. S. Your brother requests me to inform you all, with his best love, that this is no traveller's tale, but a veracious chronicle, and that he considers it to comprise all the pure elements of Italian life — fleas, fright and felony. F.'

The Barclays were made very happy just after the reception of Aunt Fanny's letter, by the advent of a tiny creature. Mrs. Sanderson had presented her husband with a son, whom it was instantly decided was to bear his grandfather's name of John Barclay. Charley Sanderson, every body had called him so, married or single, was beside himself with joy, and expected every one should congratulate him. Mrs. Barclay became intensely busy with caudle, and the grandpapa seemed almost as much enchanted as the parents. But Johnny felt himself half a foot taller when he commanded every body to call him uncle; and Nursey Bristow declared that such a child had never been seen in the world before. Georgy and Mrs. Meredith longed more earnestly than ever for dear Aunt Fanny's arrival, that she might pronounce her opinion on the wondrous charms of the little stranger. And Mr. and Mrs. Richard Barclay made their appearance once more amidst their affectionate friends; he in great spirits and high glee, she prettier and better dressed than ever. They had brought home for all their family and friends innumerable presents, and had all manner of interesting things to tell of the countries they had visited and the people they had seen, and were an immense addition to many other families besides that of their relatives.

Mr. Richard persisted in returning thanks for his restoration to a land in which there was nothing to be seen, and professed himself delighted to arise in the morning without a load of sights on his mind; but still he seemed to have not forgotten the most insignificant of the foreign shows. In France he had been disappointed, and thought all things changed, and not at all for the better; and it was observed that he certainly did not quote that country in the same enthusiastic manner as had been his custom before his departure. He declared his whole family had got their heads turned by a little baby, and yet he stole into Mrs. Sanderson's nursery very often himself, and looked the least bit in the world ashamed when he was found there. Altogether the Benedict conducted himself remarkably well, and a happier couple were rarely seen.

Miss Tidmarsh, who had roundly asserted that the evident improvement in his manners which had developed itself on his marriage, would never last, disliked immensely to hear any mention of Mr. and Mrs. Richard Barclay's well-being. This, however, she was doomed to hear and survive, if she could, for their house became once more, as it had always been, the resort of all the pleasant people in the city, and as they and their friends were always made welcome, nothing was more frequently remarked upon than its manifold attractions. Indeed, there were found persons bold enough to assert, even in Miss Serena's presence, that it was more agreeable than ever since Mrs. Ashley had married Mr. Richard Barclay. This being vastly more than that amiable YOUNG person could reasonably endure, she instantaneously quarrelled with 'the bears' friends, and, in fact, had so many little affairs of this kind on her hands, that her visiting list became sadly diminished in numbers. There was a rumour abroad, that many of her acquaintances — friends she had none — took this method of ridding themselves of Miss Serena Tidmarsh.

CHAPTER XLVIII.

'Although thou maun never be mine,
Although even hope is denied;
'Tis sweeter for thee despairing,
Than aught in the world beside.'

BURNS.

MR. BARCLAY having been successfully brought to the culminating point of his career, when, surrounded by his children and friends, in the possession of the undying affection of his cherished wife, in the full enjoyment of the good things of this world, and the perfect assurance of the discharge of his duties, he may be safely left with the conviction that his lines are cast in pleasant places. As belonging to the time-honoured race of Boston merchants, he has nobly sustained their acknowledged reputation for probity, uprightness and benevolence; he has ever been the orphan's friend; has encouraged the youth of his time, and solaced and consoled the widow. Adored by his family, loved and respected by his townsmen, he seems destined to pursue the peaceful tenour of his way, for the residue of his existence, in the moral sunshine which he has created around him to gild the evening of his days. Art and science having been fostered and cherished by his untiring and persevering efforts, he enjoys the perfect satisfaction of beholding the felicitous results of his own good works in the persons of those whom his own right hand has raised from poverty and depression, weariness and faint-heartedness to absolute prosperity, and they arise and bless him. Mr. Barclay's whole character may be then summed up in three words — A good citizen.

> 'How blest is he who crowns in scenes like these
> A youth of labour with an age of ease.'

Mrs. Barclay, from having cordially aided and assisted her noble husband in his admirable efforts, and deferring to him in the important events of her existence, has succeeded in producing these felicitous results, and has proved herself worthy the happiness of sharing her destiny with a truly good man.

Mr. Richard Barclay, subdued, and consequently improved by the gentler teachings and gentler influence of his amiable and pleasing wife, certainly promises not to relapse into his old misanthropic ways, and is in a fair way to renounce entirely his fault-finding and grumbling habits, which is considered by his friends as quite miraculous, and a vast improvement in that gentleman's character.

Mrs. Sanderson has sold the old house, and bitterly she deplored at the time the necessity of such a proceeding; but the estate becoming, by the increase of the population and growth of the city, so immensely valuable, she became a most wealthy widow instanter, and immediately received several proffers of marriage, containing the usual hypocritical protestations of affection with which fortune-hunters attack ladies of a certain age. But she was altogether too wise to be snared by such stratagems, and, never forgetting the husband of her young days, her beatified vision of perfectibility, she with studied dignity declined the false pretences of her quondam adorers, thereby bestowing upon them each 'a Roland for an Oliver.'

Gerald and Charley, refusing decidedly any participation in their mother's newly acquired wealth, begged her to purchase a handsome house near her friends, to open it, and receive them hospitably, and enjoy the good fortune which had so opportunely fallen upon her, and to their wishes she cheerfully acceded.

It was a long while before Peter and Dinah and Tiger the third could be at all reconciled to the small square of earth, to which they were consigned by this change in their domicil; indeed, these poor creatures were almost heart-broken. Dinah's lamentations and interrogatories as to the getting up of a washing-day in a nutshell, — how the linen was ever to be thoroughly dried, — how she was ever again to whiten a counterpane, — were marvellously affecting; and Peter found no space and verge for any thing. The good old times were evermore in their mouths, and the gas and kitchen ranges considered perfect abominations, — such thorough conservatives were they. Mrs. Sanderson was, at one time, quite alarmed, for Dinah's health and strength seemed absolutely declining; but, fortunately, there lived in the neighbourhood a Methodist clergyman of great renown amongst the coloured population; she happened to know him, and narrating to him the sad state of her servant's mind, he kindly lent himself to the dispelling and ejecting of these thick-coming fancies from Miss Dinah's brain, and the good creature was restored to her pristine state of equanimity. Mrs. Sanderson also deeply felt the deprivation of the old house and garden, and sorely wept when she beheld the beautiful flowers and venerable trees struck to the earth by the ruthless hands of the 'improvers.' Gerald managed to transplant one of her idols clandestinely, and place it in the corner of the patch she now called her own. This kind act was highly approved by his mother, who embraced and thanked him most gratefully; the tree having been one she had herself planted in her girlish days.

Gerald continues to live with his mother, to live and love on. It is generally believed that unrequited affection evanesces and decays, without sustenance. May not a suspicion of the real truth have dawned upon his hitherto benighted mind with regard to Georgiana? This is mere conjecture;

he has seen 'lovers around her sighing,' and the woman who still holds his affections in thrall, has waived them from her presence, and will none of them, — may he not have thereby conceived a suspicion that the heart of the beloved one is occupied? 'Man never is, but always to be blest.' Perchance, the young lover may enjoy as great a share of happiness under 'this pleasing delusion, this flattering unction,' as if he had really obtained the object of his idolatry, and gone forth to share with her the changes and the chances of this sublunary sphere. At least, what comes to him henceforth in the saddened guise of sorrow's garb will be endured alone, and this to many is a vast source of contentment. To deeply impressible hearts the sharing of troublous days and gloomy hours with loved ones gives no consolation whatever; they send forth the joys and pleasures of their lives for all to share, opening wide their portals when flooded with sunshine, but closing them fast and firm when dark clouds lower.

Fortune smiles on Gerald Sanderson in all beside. He is fast rising in his profession, and from principle has become deeply engrossed therein; he works, occupies himself, and rejects manfully all gloomy retrospection, but he has no pleasing hope for the future on earth. His dreams have vanished, his youth is gone; it is an old man who lives in the person of the young and handsome Gerald Sanderson; 'he has died many deaths in fearing one.' This he truly believes, and much more besides. But will not time, the assuager, disabuse him? Will he not be subject to its influence with his fellow-men? and time alone can tell. At any rate, there is hope though he rejects it, just so long as he firmly resists, and, looking his fortunes sternly in the face, upholds himself below, trusting to a higher Source above for consolation. — His mother! She is a guardian angel to him, in his sometimes fitful moods; 'tis she who brings him home from his fancied flights, which will even, though repelled and scorned, still assail him. Gerald regards these visionary dreams as the source of all his misfortunes, and manfully exerts himself to cast them off; he loathes them, consequently their recurrence becomes less and less frequent, and soon they will entirely disappear. Gerald's is an onward and upward path; the law an exacting mistress, rebelling against all romance and castle-building.

Charles Sanderson, — 'tis time to drop the Charley, now that he is a respectable head of a family, — is supremely happy; his lovely wife shares the felicity. The tiny bit baby is so wonderful in their eyes, that they assert, twenty times a day, 'there never was such a child ever before seen,' and no one openly contradicts them, though Miss Tidmarsh declares aside that all babies are hideous, and this one particularly so. Mr. Johnstone is enchanted with this novelty, and is only puzzled to know what to give the little creature. He is, however, constantly ordering silver cups and whistles, and other knicknacks; and he lives much more with the young mother than at home, — and takes lessons in nursery discipline.

Mr. Meredith devotes his life to good works, in which his wife, falsifying all the predictions launched forth at her marriage, nobly assists him, eliciting the admiration of her husband, and by far surpassing his fondest hopes and aspirations. Mrs. Meredith is charmingly gay as ever, her ebullitions only a little tempered by the discretion gathered from a source she so entirely respects, — her own most excellent husband; she never tires of well-doing. It thus appears that a judicious direction of her enthusiastic spirit into proper channels, has completed and perfected what, under other circumstances, might have proved a very unequal character, to say the least. Watched and guided, she gives a fair promise of becoming a most superiour woman; the performance of her parochial duties being really extraordinary. She always declares, in her usual frank manner, that it was the most blessedly fortunate period of her life, when Mr. Meredith turned his loving eyes to the thoughtless and inconsiderate Dolly. Mr. and Mrs. Barclay regard Mr. Meredith as the benefactor of their child, and fully appreciate the remarkable change he has effected in her character. Mr. Meredith declares, however, that the germs of all this excellence were lying hidden, requiring only to be brought forth through the affections, and that his wife is becoming every day more and more discreet and matronly; in which opinion his fastidious parish fully concur.

Robert Redmond has returned home, bringing with him his wife, who proves a most agreeable addition to the society of his native city; his young sister, very much improved by her travels; and his mother with such a wardrobe! and an incomparable lady's maid. Mrs. Redmond is now more helpless than ever, but she has no housekeeping. Mrs. Robert takes that incumbrance off her hands, if any it ever were, and the above mentioned French soubrette keeps her most artistically and critically arrayed in the last Parisian fashions; and by dint of keeping up an eternal chattering in her mistress's ears, has taught her a curious admixture of broken French; and she wades through interminable volumes of George Sand, Eugene Sue, and Alexander Dumas in their original tongue, no longer discussing the translations, and all this gained by her foreign tour.

Mrs. Dionysius Hornblower followed her family shortly after. There never was too much of the little Benedict before his marriage, and that event had apparently abstracted an integrant part of his outer man; for such a nonentity, morally and physically, had never before been exhibited. But he was a Southerner, and finding the snow wreaths taller than himself, and that many people thought his syntax required reforming, he, for the first time in his marital condition, 'spoke out,' and avowed his fixed determination to leave Boston. This was asserted, to be sure, with fear and trembling, but still the mighty words were uttered, and Jane feared the consequences to her frail partner if she remained; so she left and emigrated to Florida.

Johnny Barclay, now an aspirant for high-heel boots, says that, if Mr. Hornblower has found a wife, he thinks his own chance is not a bad one, and shall govern himself accordingly.

Mr. Gordon has just been elected to a high official station, which gratifies his wife immensely, and himself not a little. Mrs. Rosevelt still continues firm in the faith that sailor's wives are the happiest women in the world.

Captain Williams received from the Italian woman's husband a most grateful letter, and a present in money, which vastly reconciled Mrs. Betsy to *that person*, whom, by the bye, she has never seen, and never wishes to behold.

And Georgiana Seaton, — will she marry Gerald Sanderson? This is a question so often mooted in her circle that it is worn threadbare, and yet is of constant recurrence. The shade of the lost husband too frequently passes between the young and widowed creature and her lover, overwhelming her with sorrow, all the more heavily since she feels obliged to conceal it. It is, in fact, a mixed emotion; an undefined sentiment which prevents the entire expansion of Georgiana's love for Gerald. She acknowledges this love to herself and her mother, but at the same time protests she can never marry the object of her affection. She declares that a passion so pure and disinterested as his demands the possession of a virgin heart, — a first love; and that she cannot bestow, and she does not believe that her lover would rest satisfied with what she can offer in return for the wealth of affection which he would lavish upon her, however he might be persuaded to the contrary; but that time would certainly disabuse him of his illusions, and inevitable unhappiness would ensue.

We must all, she thinks, have in this world something to love and cherish. She has her parents, her family, and friends; her interests will in time all centre completely in these attractive objects, and Gerald Sanderson will find a partner to share his lot who can entirely respond to his ardent and enthusiastic nature; whereas with himself there would be an aching void in his breast, a rankling wound, hidden, at first, but ever ready to be probed to the quick at the slightest suspicion of a diminution of her affection. To this conclusion she has come at last, that marriage is not an all-important and essential portion of woman's happiness. There are other fields in which to seek it, and those should be tried in all cases where doubts and fears predominate. No shadow should ever fall upon the marriage vow.

But above all, she religiously believes that having deviated from the path of rectitude, having erred in her relations with her beloved parents, she is bound to make all possible expiation and devote her life to them. She has then decided irrevocably, she thinks, that she shall not unite her destiny with the man of her choice; and when a New England woman comes to a fixed determination *conscientiously*, there is little room for change. Upon other grounds, opinions and high resolves may be susceptible of variation, but a resolution based upon such all-dominant principles as conscience and duty combined, is sure to be considered as indestructible; and it may be then fairly concluded, that, clinging to her own happy home, the young creature, whose trials have engrossed a large portion of this simple Boston story, will forever remain the affectionately devoted daughter, Georgiana Seaton.

HENRY W. LONGFELLOW'S WRITINGS.

THE GOLDEN LEGEND. A Poem. Just Published. Price $1.00.

POETICAL WORKS. This edition contains the six Volumes mentioned below. In two volumes. 16mo. Boards. $2.00.

In separate Volumes, each 75 cents.

VOICES OF THE NIGHT.

BALLADS AND OTHER POEMS.

SPANISH STUDENT; A PLAY IN THREE ACTS.

BELFRY OF BRUGES, AND OTHER POEMS.

EVANGELINE; A TALE OF ACADIE.

THE SEASIDE AND THE FIRESIDE.

THE WAIF. A Collection of Poems. Edited by Longfellow.

THE ESTRAY. A Collection of Poems. Edited by Longfellow.

MR. LONGFELLOW'S PROSE WORKS.

HYPERION. A ROMANCE. Price $1.00.

OUTRE-MER. A PILGRIMAGE. Price $1.00.

KAVANAGH. A TALE. Price 75 cents.

Illustrated editions of EVANGELINE, POEMS, and HYPERION.

NATHANIEL HAWTHORNE'S WRITINGS.

TWICE-TOLD TALES. Two Volumes. Price $1.50.

THE SCARLET LETTER. Price 75 cents.

THE HOUSE OF THE SEVEN GABLES. Price $1.00.

THE SNOW IMAGE, AND OTHER TWICE-TOLD TALES. Price 75 cents.

THE BLITHEDALE ROMANCE. Price 75 cents.

TRUE STORIES FROM HISTORY AND BIOGRAPHY. With four fine Engravings. Price 75 cents.

A WONDER-BOOK FOR GIRLS AND BOYS. With seven fine Engravings. Price 75 cents.

TANGLEWOOD TALES. Another 'Wonder-Book.' With Engravings. Price 88 cents.

LIFE OF GEN. PIERCE. 1 vol. 16mo. Cloth. 50 cts.

JOHN G. WHITTIER'S WRITINGS.

OLD PORTRAITS AND MODERN SKETCHES. 75 cents.

MARGARET SMITH'S JOURNAL. Price 75 cents.

SONGS OF LABOR, AND OTHER POEMS. Boards. 50 cts.

THE CHAPEL OF THE HERMITS. Cloth. 50 cents.

JAMES RUSSELL LOWELL'S WRITINGS.

COMPLETE POETICAL WORKS. Revised, with Additions. In two volumes, 16mo. Cloth. Price $1.50.

SIR LAUNFAL. New Edition. Price 25 cents.

THE BIGLOW PAPERS. A New Edition. Price 63 cents.

EDWIN P. WHIPPLE'S WRITINGS.

ESSAYS AND REVIEWS. 2 Vols. Price $2.00.

LECTURES ON SUBJECTS CONNECTED WITH LITERATURE AND LIFE. Price 63 cents.

WASHINGTON AND THE REVOLUTION. Price 20 cts.

OLIVER WENDELL HOLMES'S WRITINGS.

POETICAL WORKS. With fine Portrait. Boards. $1.00.

ASTRÆA. Fancy paper. Price 25 cents.

GRACE GREENWOOD'S WRITINGS.

GREENWOOD LEAVES. 1st & 2d Series. $1.25 each.

POETICAL WORKS. With fine Portrait. Price 75 cents.

HISTORY OF MY PETS. With six fine Engravings. Scarlet cloth. Price 50 cents.

RECOLLECTIONS OF MY CHILDHOOD. With six fine Engravings. Scarlet cloth. Price 50 cents.

HAPS AND MISHAPS OF A TOUR IN EUROPE. (Just out.) Price $1.25.

GEORGE S. HILLARD'S WRITINGS.

SIX MONTHS IN ITALY. 2 vols. 16mo. Price $2.50.

DANGERS AND DUTIES OF THE MERCANTILE PROFESSION. Price 25 cents.

MRS. JUDSON'S WRITINGS.

ALDERBROOK. By FANNY FORESTER. 2 Vols. Price $1.75.

THE KATHAYAN SLAVE, AND OTHER PAPERS. 1 vol. Price 63 cents.

MY TWO SISTERS: A SKETCH FROM MEMORY. Price 50 cts.

HENRY GILES'S WRITINGS.

LECTURES, ESSAYS, AND MISCELLANEOUS WRITINGS. 2 Vols. Price $1.50.

DISCOURSES ON LIFE. Price 75 cents.

R. H. STODDARD'S WRITINGS.

POEMS. Cloth. Price 63 cents.

ADVENTURES IN FAIRY LAND. Just out. 75 cents.

WILLIAM MOTHERWELL'S WRITINGS.

POEMS, NARRATIVE AND LYRICAL. New Ed. $1.25.

POSTHUMOUS POEMS. Boards. Price 50 cents.

MINSTRELSY, ANC. AND MOD. 2 Vols. Boards. $1.50.

GOETHE'S WRITINGS.

WILHELM MEISTER. Translated by THOMAS CARLYLE. 2 Vols. Price $2.50.

GOETHE'S FAUST. Translated by HAYWARD. Price 75 cts.

MRS. CROSLAND'S WRITINGS.

LYDIA: A WOMAN'S BOOK. Cloth. 75 cents.

ENGLISH TALES AND SKETCHES. Cloth. $1.00.

CAPT. MAYNE REID'S JUVENILE BOOKS.

THE DESERT HOME, OR, THE ADVENTURES OF A LOST FAMILY IN THE WILDERNESS. With fine plates, $1.00.

THE BOY HUNTERS. With fine plates. Just published. Price 75 cents.

THE YOUNG VOYAGEURS, OR, THE BOY HUNTERS IN THE NORTH. With plates. Price 75 cents.

POETRY.

ALEXANDER SMITH'S POEMS. 1 vol. 16mo. Cloth. Price 50 cents.

CHARLES MACKAY'S POEMS. 1 Vol. Cloth. Price $1.00.

ROBERT BROWNING'S POETICAL WORKS. 2 Vols. $2.00.

HENRY ALFORD'S POEMS. Just out. Price $1.25.

RICHARD MONCKTON MILNES. POEMS OF MANY YEARS. Boards. Price 75 cents.

CHARLES SPRAGUE. POETICAL AND PROSE WRITINGS. With fine Portrait. Boards. Price 75 cents.

BAYARD TAYLOR. POEMS. Cloth. Price 63 cents.

JOHN G. SAXE. POEMS. With Portrait. Boards, 63 cents. Cloth, 75 cents.

HENRY T. TUCKERMAN. POEMS. Cloth. Price 75 cents.

BOWRING'S MATINS AND VESPERS. Price 50 cents.

GEORGE LUNT. LYRIC POEMS, &c. 1 vol. Cloth, 63 cents.

PHŒBE CAREY. POEMS AND PARODIES. 75 cents.

MEMORY AND HOPE. A BOOK OF POEMS, REFERRING TO CHILDHOOD. Cloth. Price $2.00.

THALATTA: A BOOK FOR THE SEA-SIDE. 1 vol. 16mo. Cloth. Price 75 cents.

PASSION-FLOWERS. 1 vol. 16mo. Price 75 cents.

MISCELLANEOUS.

MRS. MOWATT. AUTOBIOGRAPHY OF AN ACTRESS. 1 vol. 16mo. Cloth. $1.25.

OUR VILLAGE. By MARY RUSSELL MITFORD. Illustrated. 2 vols. 16mo. Cloth Price $2.50.

THE BARCLAYS OF BOSTON. By MRS. H. G. OTIS. 1 vol. 12mo. $1.25.

NOTES FROM LIFE. BY HENRY TAYLOR, author of 'Philip Van Artevelde.' 1 vol. 16mo. Cloth. Price 63 cents.

REJECTED ADDRESSES. By HORACE and JAMES SMITH. Boards, Price 50 cents. Cloth, 63 cents.

WARRENIANA. A Companion to the 'Rejected Addresses.' Price 63 cents.

WILLIAM WORDSWORTH'S BIOGRAPHY. By Dr. C. WORDSWORTH. 2 vols. Price $2.50.

ART OF PROLONGING LIFE. By HUFELAND. Edited by ERASMUS WILSON, F. R. S. 1 vol. 16mo. Price 75 cents.

JOSEPH T. BUCKINGHAM'S PERSONAL MEMOIRS AND RECOLLECTIONS OF EDITORIAL LIFE. With Portrait. 2 vols. 16mo. Price $1.50.

VILLAGE LIFE IN EGYPT. By the Author of 'Adventures in the Lybian Desert.' 2 vols. 16mo. Price $1.25.

PRIOR'S LIFE OF EDMUND BURKE. 2 vols. 16mo. Price $2.00.

PALISSY THE POTTER. By the Author of 'How to make Home Unhealthy.' 2 vols. 16mo. Price $1.50.

WILLIAM MOUNTFORD. THORPE: A QUIET ENGLISH TOWN, AND HUMAN LIFE THEREIN. 16mo. Price $1.00.

MRS. A. C. LOWELL. THOUGHTS ON THE EDUCATION OF GIRLS. Price 25 cents.

CHARLES SUMNER. ORATIONS AND SPEECHES. 2 Vols. Price $2.50.

HORACE MANN. A FEW THOUGHTS FOR A YOUNG MAN. Price 25 cents.

JOHN G. WHITTIER.

OLD PORTRAITS AND MODERN SKETCHES. Contents: John Bunyan, Thomas Ellwood, James Naylor, Andrew Marvell, John Roberts, Samuel Hopkins, Richard Baxter, William Leggett, Nathaniel P. Rogers, Robert Dinsmore. 1 vol. 16mo. 75 cents; gilt, $1.25.

"Whatever topic Whittier takes he handles with a master's hand. The portraits of these sturdy men are sketched with fidelity. Their faults are not hidden from view, but their sturdy virtues are clearly revealed to the eye. Go to the publishers, purchase and read these thrilling portraits of some of the noblest men the world has seen, sketched by one of the purest writers and truest men of our times." — REPUBLICAN.

LEAVES FROM MARGARET SMITH'S JOURNAL in the Province of Massachusetts Bay, 1678-9. 1 vol. 16mo. Paper, 50 cts.; cloth, 75 cts.

"The author has used his material skilfully, and in the exercise of that plastic faculty with which he is so highly gifted has wrought out a vivid portraiture of scenery, character, and manners in the old colonial age of Massachusetts. The style suits well to the character of a well-educated woman at that period, and the reader may imagine Margaret to be one of Whittier's ancestors, whose mental traits he has himself inherited. The book deserves praise as a work of art: it is instructive as well as entertaining; and if any lady at the head of a family should happen on some evening to read from its pages for the pleasure of her husband, she would probably find all the children who may be over seven years of age eagerly listening." — CHRISTIAN WATCHMAN.

SONGS OF LABOR, and other Poems. 1 vol. 16mo. 50 cents.

"One of the finest expressions of the muse of one of America's most eloquent poets." — LONDON ATHENÆUM.

REV. HENRY GILES.

LECTURES AND ESSAYS. Contents: Falstaff, Crabbe, Moral Philosophy of Byron's Life, Moral Spirit of Byron's Genius, Ebenezer Elliott, Oliver Goldsmith, Spirit of Irish History, Ireland and the Irish, the Worth of Liberty, True Manhood, The Pulpit, Patriotism, Economies, Music, The Young Musician, A Day in Springfield, Chatterton, Carlyle, Savage, and Dermody. 2 vols. 16mo. $1.50.

"Those persons who have listened to the greater part of the contents of these two volumes, in the various lecture-rooms throughout the country, will probably be even more anxious to read them than many who have only heard the name of the author. They will revive in the reader the delightful wit, the clear, mental attraction, and the high pleasure which they uniformly excited on their delivery." — EXAMINER.

CHRISTIAN THOUGHT ON LIFE. Contents: The Worth of Life, The Personality of Life, The Continuity of Life, The Struggle of Life, The Discipline of Life, Faith and Passion, Temper, The Guilt of Contempt, Evangelical Goodness, David, Spiritual Incongruities, Weariness of Life, Mysteries in Religion and in Life. 1 vol. 16mo. 75 cents.

"More glowing and thrilling productions were never committed to the press. The many friends and admirers of the gifted and popular lecturer will eagerly embrace the opportunity to obtain copies." — PHIL. GAZETTE.

EDWIN P. WHIPPLE.

ESSAYS AND REVIEWS. A new edition. 2 vols. 16mo. $2.

LECTURES ON LITERATURE AND LIFE. Contents: Authors in their Relations to life, Novels and Novelists, Charles Dickens, Wit and Humor, The Ludicrous Side of Life, Genius, Intellectual Health and Disease Third edition 1 vol. 16mo. 62 cents.

WASHINGTON AND THE PRINCIPLES OF THE REVOLUTION. 1 vol. 16mo. 25 cents.

"Mr. Whipple may now fairly be called the most popular essayist in this country; and he has substantial merits which go far to justify the favor with which his writings have been received." — N. A. REVIEW.

"Mr. Whipple is one of the few American types of the genuine literary man. He would have been at home in that glorious conclave of wits and scholars where Burke, Johnson, Goldsmith, Garrick, and others used to meet and discourse. He seems penetrated with their spirit, and to be gifted with that same intellectual nerve which distinguished them. Get his books, read them, and place them on the same shelf with your 'Boswell's Johnson,' and your 'Spectator'" — TRANSCRIPT

CHARLES SPRAGUE.

THE POETICAL AND PROSE WRITINGS. A new and enlarged edition, revised by the author. This copy of Mr. Sprague's works is the only complete one in the market, and is accompanied with a new Portrait, just engraved in the finest style of the art, by Andrews. 1 vol. 16mo. 75 cents. Gilt, $1.25.

"This is a volume to read by the family fireside — to carry into the country — to take up at any leisure moment; and delightfully will the time so bestowed pass away." — KNICKERBOCKER.

GRACE GREENWOOD.

GREENWOOD LEAVES. First and second Series. A Collection of Stories and Letters by Grace Greenwood. 2 vols. 12mo. $1.25 each. Gilt, $1.75.

"The name of Grace Greenwood has now become a household word in the popular literature of our country and our day. Of the intellectual woman we are not called to say much, as her writings speak for themselves, and they have spoken widely. They are eminently characteristic; they are strictly national; they are likewise decisively individual. All true individuality is hon estly social; and, also, in Miss Clarke's writings nothing is sectional, and nothing sectarian. She is one of the spiritual products of the soil, which has, of late, given evidence of spiritual fertility; and she promises not to be the least healthy, as she is not the least choice, among them." — HENRY GILES.

HISTORY OF MY PETS. With fine Illustrations by Billings 1 vol. 16mo. 50 cents.

RECOLLECTIONS OF MY CHILDHOOD. With Designs by Billings. 1 vol. 50 cents.

THE POETICAL WRITINGS OF GRACE GREENWOOD. With fine Portrait. 1 vol. 16mo. 75 cents.

"Grace Greenwood (the borrowed *plume* of Miss Sara J. Clarke) is well known to all readers of ladies' magazines as one of the most graceful story writers in this or any other country. As a poet, also, we are disposed, if but for a single effort, to place her in the very highest rank of American poets, both male and female. We allude to her 'Ariadne' — a poem as rich in passionate expression and classic grace as any thing to be found in all Griswold's collection of American poetry." — N. Y. MIRROR.

"The fair authoress of this work has already won so wide a reputation, that it is only necessary to announce the appearance of this volume to secure for it numerous readers. It contains some of her most graceful and beautiful pieces, is ornamented with an admirable engraving of the author, and is brought out in the beautiful style for which this publishing house in Boston is celebrated. We commend it to the lovers of the True and the Beautiful." — ALBANY STATE REG.

NATHANIEL HAWTHORNE.

THE SCARLET LETTER. A Romance. Sixth thousand. 1 vol. 16mo. 75 cents.

"In the deep tragedy of Hester Prynne's experiences we are borne through the pages as by an irresistible impulse — hardly stopping to notice the exquisite touches which are to be found in the midst of the most harrowing and distressing scenes. It is indeed a wonderful book; and we venture to predict that no one will put it down before he reaches the last page of it, unless it is forcibly taken out of his hands." — SALEM GAZETTE.

THE HOUSE OF THE SEVEN GABLES. Sixth thousand. 1 vol. 16mo. $ 1.

"Though we cannot do him justice, let us remember the name of Nathaniel Hawthorne, deserving a place second to none in that band of humorists whose beautiful depth of cheerful feeling is the very poetry of mirth. In ease, grace, delicate sharpness of satire, — in a felicity of touch which often surpasses the felicity of Addison, in a subtilty of insight which often reaches farther than the subtilty of Steele, — the humor of Hawthorne presents traits so fine as to be almost too excellent for popularity; as, to every one who has attempted their criticism, they are too refined for statement. The brilliant atoms flit, hover, and glance before our minds, but the remote sources of their ethereal light lie beyond our analysis, —

'And no speed of ours avails
To hunt upon their shining trails.'" — E. P. WHIPPLE.

TWICE-TOLD TALES. A new and revised edition, with fine Portrait. 2 vols. 16mo. $ 1.50.

"This book comes from the hand of a man of genius. Every thing about it has the freshness of morning and of May. A calm, thoughtful face seems to be looking at you from every page." — N. A. REVIEW.

TRUE STORIES FROM HISTORY AND BIOGRAPHY. With fine plates. 1 vol. 16mo. 75 cents.

A WONDER BOOK FOR BOYS AND GIRLS. With designs by Billings. 1 vol. 16mo. 75 cents.

JAMES RUSSELL LOWELL.

THE COMPLETE POETICAL WORKS. 2 vols. 16mo. Boards, $ 1.50; cloth, $ 1 75; cloth gilt, $ 2.50.

"We regard Lowell as one of the truest poets of our age — as true to the high and holy teaching of the spirit of poetry — true to mankind and his God. He is also the poet of the future, casting his great thoughts out into the coming unknown, in the unshaken faith that they will spring up, and bear fruit a hundred fold. His works, to be as widely read as they deserve, should be in every dwelling in the land." — PORTLAND TRANSCRIPT.

THE VISION OF SIR LAUNFAL. 1 vol. 16mo. 25 cents.

HORACE MANN.

A FEW THOUGHTS FOR A YOUNG MAN WHEN ENTERING UPON LIFE. A Lecture. Although this little work has been published but a short time, many thousand copies have been sold. 1 vol. 16mo. Cloth, 25 cents.

"For plainness of speech, for strength of expression, and decision in stating what the writer believes to be the truth, this lecture may be matched against any thing that ever came from the press." — CHRISTIAN EXAMINER.

GOETHE'S WORKS.

THE FAUST. Translated by Hayward. A new edition. 1 vol. 16mo. 75 cents.

WILHELM MEISTER'S APPRENTICESHIP AND TRAVELS Translated by Carlyle. A new edition, revised. In 2 vols. 16mo. $2.50.

JOHN G. SAXE.

HUMOROUS AND SATIRICAL POEMS. 1 vol. 16mo. 50 cents.

"Mr. Saxe has struck upon a vein, for which few of our dealers in verse have exhibited an aptitude. He gives us the comical phase of things, preserving always a serene good humor. He writes with vigor, ease, and a sort of *bonhomie*, which at once places him and his reader on good and friendly terms. There is a pungency full of sparkle and point in his stanzas."—BOSTON TRANSCRIPT.

GEORGE S. HILLARD.

THE DANGERS AND DUTIES OF THE MERCANTILE PROFESSION. 1 vol. 16mo. 25 cents.

"We have twice read this admirable address, and feel that we cannot too warmly commend it to all our readers. It is written in a noble spirit, and in that style of simple elegance which attests not alone the rare scholarship, but the refined taste, of the author."—NATIONAL ERA.

PHILIP JAMES BAILEY.

THE ANGEL WORLD, and other Poems. By the author of "Festus." 1 vol. 16mo. 50 cents.

"The principal poem is full of beauties, and seems to us, on a hasty perusal, to be far above 'Festus,' in point of moral eminence at least. The commencement is worthy of the subject; and the description of a 'Young and Shining Angel,' who steps into the throng of bright immortals, seems to us to embody all that is holy and beautiful in poesy.

'In his air
Sat kingly sweetness, kind and calm command,
Yet with long suffering blended; for the soil
Of dust was on his garb and sandalled sole—
Dust on the locks of fertile gold which flowed
From his fair forehead, rippling down his neck—
Bedropt, defiled with cold and cave-like dew.
One hand a staff of virent emerald held
As 'twere a sapling of the tree of life;
And one smoothed in his breast a radiant dove,
Fluttering its wings in lightnings, thousand hued,—
The sole companion of his pilgrimage.
Silent he stood and gazed.'

"The shorter poems seem to us quite worthy of the author's distinguished celebrity. Somebody said of Bailey—we think it was Elliott, the Corn-Law poet—that there was matter enough in the author of 'Festus' to set up fifty poets; and Alfred Tennyson wrote not long ago that he could scarcely trust himself to say how much he admired Bailey's poems, for fear of falling into extravagance. We have no doubt that the judgment of these two great authorities will be fully indorsed by the readers of 'The Angel World' throughout our country."—BOSTON TRANSCRIPT

GEORGE COMBE.

THE CONSTITUTION OF MAN, considered in Relation to External Objects. By George Combe. 1 vol. 12mo. 75 cents.

"Of the merits of this work it is almost needless to speak, as its extensive adoption, as a general reading book in families and class book in schools, has made its reputation every where familiar. There are few books extant, the universal introduction of which would be productive of more benefit." — NAT. INTEL.

ALFRED TENNYSON.

COMPLETE POETICAL WORKS. Illustrated with a fine portrait of the author. 2 vols. 16mo. $1.50. Cloth, $1.75; gilt, $2.50.

"There are few living poets who can be compared with Tennyson in those peculiar, distinctive qualities which raise the true poet to that quick apprehension of spiritual beauty which furnishes him with perpetual inspiration, and to the glad world an overflowing song." — EDINBURGH REVIEW.

"Of the living poets of England — we include not the few choice spirits of Scotland — Tennyson at this time occupies the highest rank, and he is destined to a wide and high regard." — DR. GRISWOLD.

THE PRINCESS: A Medley. 1 vol. 16mo. 50 cents. Gilt, $1.

"If we were to express the feeling of satisfaction with which we have just read every word of this beautiful, charming, and profound little book, we should be thought extravagant. Nor does it stand in need of any enthusiastic commendation to secure for it a very large circle of readers; for, of all living poets, hardly any has a wider or more desirable reputation in this country than Tennyson. The mere announcement of a new poem from his pen will send thousands on an immediate pilgrimage to their respective bookstores." — N. Y. TRIBUNE.

IN MEMORIAM. 1 vol. 16mo. Cloth, 75 cents.

"The most exquisite creation by any man of genius during the last forty years." — EDINBURGH REVIEW.

WILLIAM MOTHERWELL.

THE POETICAL WORKS. With a Memoir by James M'Conechy, Esq. A new edition, enlarged. 1 vol. 16mo. 75 cents. Cloth, 88 cents; gilt, $1 25.

"Motherwell was a poet of the right cast — a man of fire and inspiration. When we read his verses we feel that the writer is not mocking us with an affectation of what he describes, but that he has surrendered himself, heart and soul, to the passion that carries us along with him." — LITERARY WORLD.

POSTHUMOUS POEMS. 1 vol. 16mo. 50 cents.

MINSTRELSY, ANCIENT AND MODERN. Edited by Motherwell. With an Historical Introduction and Notes. 2 vols. 16mo. $1.50. Cloth, $1.75; gilt, $2.50.

"In fact, it is a book which takes after the heart of almost any body who has one; and with its rich Scotch brogue, and its high-strung Scotch feeling, it must be a hard heart that will not be touched now and then with it." — CHRONOTYPE.

"Most of the ballads he has selected are beautiful specimens of that natural poetry which springs directly from the heart and imagination in words and images fresh and bright from Nature's own mint. The interest of the reader is enhanced by feeling that he is reading poems which were sung, centuries ago, in the palace halls, and by the cottage hearths of a whole nation, and which formed the literature of thousands on thousands of minds who had no other. Every thing in them betokens youth of feeling. The minstrels seem to have looked upon nature as if it had just come from the Creator's hand, and as if they were the first to exercise upon it the plastic powers of imagination and passion." — COURIER.

RICHARD MONCKTON MILNES.

POEMS OF MANY YEARS. 1 vol. 16mo. 75 cents; cloth, 88 cents; gilt, $1.25.

"The author, who is or was a member of Parliament, has, for the last ten years, divided with Tennyson the admiration and affection of 'Young England.' His style is eminently pure, and something in the Wordsworthian strain. 'The Lay of the Humble' is one of the most touching things in the language. We never saw a thoughtful child that could read it without shedding tears; and many a childlike man has wept over its simple pathos and beauty. Milnes is too sincere and sensitive not to please the million. His poems are full of beauties." — POST.

HORACE AND JAMES SMITH.

REJECTED ADDRESSES; or the New Theatrum Poetarum. From the last London edition, carefully revised, with an original preface and notes by the authors. 1 vol. 16mo. 50 cents.

"In selecting one of the raciest and wittiest works of the age for republication, Ticknor & Co. have certainly evinced as much judgment as the whole appearance of the work betrays good taste and the perfection of the art of printing." — TIMES.

WARRENIANA. 1 vol. 16mo. 63 cents.

BARRY CORNWALL.

ENGLISH SONGS, and other Small Poems. A new and enlarged edition. 1 vol. 16mo. 88 cents.

"Barry Cornwall (B. W. Proctor) is a name that should be on every book shelf which at all pretends to contain the works of modern English poets. In his own domain he is almost unexcelled." — TIMES.

"The songs of Barry Cornwall are too widely known, too justly prized, to be reviewed casually now. In contemplating them, criticism gives place to admiration, whose speech is silence. We had intended only to introduce a few selections from this glorious volume — selections difficult to make, because so many of these songs are already household words to us all. To quote 'King Death,' 'The Sea,' 'The Hunter's Song,' &c., would be superfluous." — TRIBUNE.

EPES SARGENT.

SONGS OF THE SEA, with other Poems. 1 vol. 16mo. 50 cents; gilt, 75 cents.

"Mr. Sargent has an admirable faculty of description; his pictures are true and living, and never exaggerated. The most striking feature of his verse is action; every thing moves with him. His diction, too, is uncommonly good. His 'Life on the Ocean Wave' is perfect; when we read it, we feel the fresh breeze rushing against our cheeks, and the blood starting in our veins, as the ship triumphs over the waves." — N. Y. TRIBUNE.

HENRY THEODORE TUCKERMAN.

POEMS. 1 vol. 16mo. 75 cents.

"One of the purest writers in America."—LONDON LEADER.

FANNY FORESTER.

ALDERBROOK. A Collection of Fanny Forester's Village Sketches, Poems, &c. With a fine mezzotinto portrait of the author, engraved by Sartain. Ninth edition. Enlarged. 2 vols. 12mo. $1.75; gilt, $2.50; extra gilt, $3.00. The same in 1 vol., $1.62; gilt, $2.25; extra gilt, $2.75.

"This is one of those charming books which well deserve a place in every family library, and which has already won a place in thousands of hearts. The sketches comprised in these beautiful volumes are so full of grace and tenderness, so pure in their style, and so elevated in their tone, that none can read them without delight and profit. We hazard little in saying that the touching story of 'Grace Linden,' which properly leads the collection, is scarcely surpassed in beauty by any thing in the works of Maria Edgeworth or Mary Russell Mitford. There are a great many other sketches in the volumes that deserve special praise, but we will not deal in particulars when all are so admirable."—So. LIT GAZETTE.

THE SOLITARY OF JUAN FERNANDEZ, or the Real Robinson Crusoe. By the Author of Picciola. Translated from the French by Anne T. Wilbur. 1 vol. 16mo. 50 cents.

MEMORY AND HOPE. A beautiful volume, referring to childhood. 1 vol. 8vo. $2.00.

LIGHTS AND SHADOWS OF DOMESTIC LIFE, and other Stories. By the authors of "Rose and her Lamb," "Two New Scholars," &c., &c. Contents: Lights and Shadows of Domestic Life; The Secret of Happiness; Laura Seymour; The Intimate Friends; Shadows and Realities; Sketches of Character, or Who is Free? 1 vol. 16mo. 62 cents

CHARLES SUMNER.

ORATIONS AND SPEECHES. "Another time perhaps shall come, worthier than ours, in which, hatreds being subdued, Truth shall triumph. With me desire this, O reader, and farewell!"—LEIBNITZ. 2 vols. 16mo. $2.50.

"We have Mr. Sumner's printed discourses before us, and can testify from personal knowledge to their singular merits. They are pregnant with thoughts of profound and universal interest. They are not productions to be laid aside with the occasion that called them forth, but to be preserved for our future instruction and delight. They derive this quality, in a great measure, from those characteristics of the author's mind—his earnestness, the union of moral fearlessness and intellectual caution in the statement of his opinions, and his reverence for original principles in comparison with popular custom or fashionable belief."—NEW YORK TRIBUNE.

"The oration of Mr. Sumner, for taste, eloquence, and scholarship, as well as for fearless intrepidity, has been rarely equalled in modern harangue." — CHAMBERS'S EDINBURGH JOURNAL.

"Such men as Victor Hugo, Richard Cobden, and Charles Sumner have much to do with the future of their respective countries." — LONDON HERALD OF PEACE.

THOMAS DE QUINCEY.

THE WRITINGS OF THE ENGLISH OPIUM EATER. Volumes already published: —

I. THE CONFESSIONS OF AN ENGLISH OPIUM EATER, and THE SUSPIRIA DE PROFUNDIS.

II. THE BIOGRAPHICAL ESSAYS.

III. THE MISCELLANEOUS ESSAYS.

IV. THE CÆSARS.

V. LIFE AND MANNERS.

VI. & VII. LITERARY REMINISCENCES.

Each 75 cents.

"Who that knows any thing of recent literature does not appreciate De Quincey as a man that stands alone and unapproachable in his sphere, a sphere that is, in itself, a magician's island, filled with strange and beautiful visions, and beaten all around by the waves of a deep, shadowy, and lonely ocean of power, that sound forever against the shore, in a strong, sweet, and melancholy music? The wild and the simple, the marvellous and the familiar, the nearest impulses with most remote associations, fresh spontaneity with elegant and various learning are mingled in the matter of De Quincey's writings as the mind of no living man could mingle them, and the spirit of them finds expression in a style of such weird-like pathos, of such manly, yet mournful eloquence, as comes from the depth of a genius in which the fountains of the heart have been terribly opened, in which *thought* has been purgatory on the margin of despair, escaped, and to which authorship has been at once penance, consolation, and confession." — HENRY GILES.

DR. GREENWOOD.

SERMONS OF CONSOLATION. By Rev. F. W. P. Greenwood, D. D., Minister of King's Chapel, Boston. Third edition. 1 vol. 12mo. $1; gilt, $1.50.

"We should be glad to know that this treasury of wisdom and holy thought was in the homes of all the people, without distinction of name or sect. It belongs to the universal brotherhood of the afflicted." — CHRISTIAN REGISTER.

"This is one of the best volumes of sermons for family reading we ever read; and its rapid passage to a third edition shows how soon it has taken hold of the public mind. Dr. Greenwood's character had a sweetness, sanctity, and gentleness which especially fitted him to carry light and consolation into the house of mourning. His sermons breathe the very spirit of peace and holiness. The style is exquisite. The volume cannot be read without having its tone of serious thought and devout aspiration insinuated into the most worldly mind, by 'a process of smoothness and delight.'" — GRAHAM'S MAGAZINE.

MEMOIRS OF WILLIAM WORDSWORTH, Poet Laureate, D. C. L. By Christopher Wordsworth, D. D. Edited by Henry Reed. 2 vols. 16mo. Cloth, $2.50

"It is natural that the admirers of Wordsworth should have looked with high-raised expectations for his promised memoirs, the volumes of which are now before us. And we believe that all their anticipations will be fully realized. It is a delightful work, giving us a key to the poet's true character, and making us acquainted, as it were, with his inner self. It is filled with references to his poems, for his works were his life. 'His poems are no visionary dreams, but practical realities. His poetry had its heart in his life, and his life found a voice in his poetry.'" — ALBANY REGISTER.

MRS. PUTNAM.

RECEIPT BOOK, and Young Housekeeper's Assistant. New and enlarged edition. 1 vol. 16mo. Price 50 cents.

"No family will long be without this capital book, the members of which have a just and proper estimate of what constitutes good cooking." — NEW YORK MIRROR.

"The author says in the preface that 'it is the result of twenty years' experience in housekeeping. The receipts which it contains were in a great part originally written down for her own convenience; others, from time to time, have been added, with the hope that they might be of service to her daughters.' All the receipts have been tried; there are a good number of them, and each one must be a valuable assistant to housekeepers. There is no better book in print for family use." — BOSTON DAILY ADVERTISER.

"Being somewhat of an amateur in gastronomical matters, we have caused various experiments to be tried after Mrs. Putnam's directions. They convinced us that the lady writes from experience, and not from theory. She is, moreover, economical, and therefore a valuable directress for families." — NEWARK DAILY ADVERTISER.

THE BOSTON BOOK. Being Specimens of Metropolitan Literature. Illustrated by a fine steel engraving, designed by Billings. Among the authors are George S. Hillard, Edward Everett, Nathaniel Hawthorne, N. P. Willis, Jacob Bigelow, R. C. Winthrop, R. W. Emerson, Henry W. Longfellow, John Pierpont, Charles Sumner, J. T. Buckingham, Wm. Croswell, N. L. Frothingham, Daniel Webster, Rufus Choate, J. G. Whittier, O. W. Holmes, Ephraim Peabody, Charles Sprague, Daniel Sharp, Wm. H. Prescott, H. T. Tuckerman, R. H. Dana, Jared Sparks, George Putnam, Andrews Norton, George Lunt, &c., &c. 1 vol. 12mo. Price $1.25.

"This volume cannot be surpassed by a *London Book*, certainly not approached by the collected writings of any other British city." — MARY RUSSELL MITFORD.

ANGEL VOICES; or Words of Counsel for Overcoming the World. After the Mode of Richter's "Best Hours." Third edition, revised and enlarged. Price 38 cents, cloth; gilt, 50 cents; extra gilt, 62 cents.

"This is a neat little volume of pious remembrances, published in a very tasteful style. It contains a variety of selections, both in poetry and prose, calculated to exercise a softening and comforting influence upon the human heart in the enjoyments of life and in the solemnities of death. A little bouquet for the bosom of a dying Christian." — N. Y. MIRROR.

MEMOIR OF REV. JOSEPH BUCKMINSTER, D. D., and of his Son, Rev. Joseph Stevens Buckminster. By Eliza Buckminster Lee. Second edition. 1 vol. 16mo. $1.25.

"One of the most touching books we ever read. As an example of biography its superior does not exist." — SPECTATOR

HEROINES OF THE MISSIONARY ENTERPRISE, or Sketches of Prominent Female Missionaries. By Daniel C. Eddy. Contents: Harriet Newell; Ann H. Judson; Esther Butler; Elizabeth Hervey; Harriet B. Stewart; Sarah L. Smith; Eleanor Macomber; Sarah D. Comstock; Henrietta Shuck; Sarah B. Judson; Annie P. James; Mary E. Van Lennep; Emily C. Judson. 1 vol. 16mo. Price 75 cents; gilt, $1.25.

"This is one of the most interesting volumes about missionaries that we have seen for several years. Here is a galaxy of heroines, more glorious than the knights of the Round Table." — ATLAS.

"Full of interest and instruction. The memoirs are generally brief, but very comprehensive, and present some of the most touching yet ennobling and inspiring instances of female devotion and virtue to be found on record." — SALEM REGISTER.

A BOOK OF HYMNS for Public and Private Devotion. Fourth edition. By Rev. Samuel Longfellow and Rev. Samuel Johnson. Price 62 cents.

CHAPEL LITURGY. Book of Common Prayer, according to the Use of King's Chapel. New and beautiful edition, in octavo. $2.50.

JUVENILE BOOKS.

JACOB ABBOTT.

JONAS'S STORIES. Related to Rollo and Lucy. With engravings. 18mo. 38 cents.

JONAS A JUDGE, or Law among the Boys. With engravings. 18mo. 38 cents.

JONAS ON A FARM IN SUMMER. With engravings. 18mo. 38 cents.

JONAS ON A FARM IN WINTER. With engravings. 18mo. 38 cents.

JACK HALLIARD. Voyages and Adventures in the Arctic Ocean. With engravings. 16mo. 38 cents.

LAMBERT LILLY'S HISTORY OF THE NEW ENGLAND STATES. With numerous engravings. 18mo. 38 cents.

LAMBERT LILLY'S HISTORY OF THE MIDDLE STATES. With numerous engravings. 18mo. 38 cents.

LAMBERT LILLY'S HISTORY OF THE SOUTHERN STATES, Virginia, North and South Carolina, and Georgia. With numerous engravings. 18mo 38 cents.

LAMBERT LILLY'S HISTORY OF THE WESTERN STATES. With numerous engravings. 18mo. 38 cents.

LAMBERT LILLY'S STORY OF THE AMERICAN REVOLUTION. With numerous engravings. 18mo. 38 cents.

MARY HOWITT'S BIRDS AND FLOWERS, and other Country Things. With engravings. 12mo. 50 cents.

OLYMPIC GAMES. A Gift for the Holidays. By the author of "Poetry for Home and School," &c. 16mo. 50 cents.

PARLEY'S SHORT STORIES FOR LONG NIGHTS. With eight colored engravings. 16mo. 50 cents; uncolored engravings, 40 cents.

PARLEY'S SMALL PICTURE BOOKS, with colored frontispieces. Printed covers. Eight kinds, assorted. $9 per gross.

SCHOOL BOOKS.

BUMSTEAD'S SECOND READING BOOK IN THE PRIMARY SCHOOL. 18mo. 17 cents.

BUMSTEAD'S THIRD READING BOOK IN THE PRIMARY SCHOOL. 18mo. 17 cents.

EDWARD'S FIRST LESSONS IN GEOMETRY. By the author of "Theory of Teaching," "Poetry for Home and School," &c. 25 cents.

GOOD'S BOOK OF NATURE. Abridged from the original work. With questions for the use of schools and illustrations from original designs. 16mo. Half morocco, 45 cents.

MURDOCH AND RUSSELL'S ORTHOPHONY; or the Cultivation of the Voice in Elocution. New and improved edition. 1 vol. 12mo. Half morocco, embossed, 75 cents.

PALMER'S MORAL INSTRUCTOR. Part I. 18mo. 10 cents.

PALMER'S MORAL INSTRUCTOR. Part II. 12mo. Half morocco, 25 cents.

PALMER'S MORAL INSTRUCTOR. Part III. 12mo. Half morocco, 25 cents.

PALMER'S MORAL INSTRUCTOR. Part IV. 12mo. Sheep, 50 cents.

RUSSELL'S (WILLIAM) LESSONS AT HOME IN SPELLING AND READING. Two Parts in one. Square 16mo. 16 cents.

www.ingramcontent.com/pod-product-compliance
Lightning Source LLC
LaVergne TN
LVHW021139110826
845150LV00005B/1068